TELLING MAYA

TELLING MAYA

a novel by
Brenda Guiled

www.tellingmaya.com

Kimae Books first edition, 2004
copyright © 2003 by Brenda Guiled

All rights reserved. Except for brief quotations in reviews, no part of this publication may be reproduced, stored in a retrieval system or transmitted, in any form or by any means, without the prior written consent of the publisher or a licence from The Canadian Copyright Licensing Agency (Access Copyright). For an Access Copyright licence, visit www.accesscopyright.ca or call toll free to 1-800-893-5777.

This is a work of fiction. Any resemblance to actual events or persons, with the exception of public and historical ones, is entirely coincidental.

National Library of Canada Cataloguing in Publication Data

Guiled, Brenda, 1951-
Telling Maya : a novel / by Brenda Guiled.

ISBN 0-9733558-0-8

I. Title.
PS8563.U52T44 2003   C813'.6   C2003-911195-4

cover by Julie McIntyre

Printed in Canada

For information and to purchase:
www.tellingmaya.com

When the student is ready,
a teacher appears.

*For my teachers
and my children.*

TELLING MAYA

 Larry had company in his office, a guest, an old lady occupying one of the two chairs facing his desk. Her white hair formed a halo around deeply wrinkled, tawny skin and sharp, slate-colored eyes. She wore a navy coat and shift with hose and shoes to match. No purse, jewelry, or watch, nothing extra—an ungilded lily who had been a great beauty and was still to those who appreciate the work of ninety-seven years.
 She took a small manila envelope from her coat pocket, extracted a color snapshot, and handed it to Larry. He looked coolly at the close-up photograph of a toddler with dark hair, rosy caramel skin, and dancing brown eyes flecked with blue-green-gold.
 "This girl can show her face, hair, and beauty to the world," the old woman said, her voice strong despite its tremolo of age. Her accent was slight, a mix from long ago and far away. "This grown-up girl cannot." She handed Larry a photo of a woman shrouded in black Muslim wraps with only her eyes visible. They were similar in shape and color to the baby's. "What difference is their need for freedom? For a woman's right to choose for herself?"

Larry's eyes flicked from photo to photo—mother and daughter, he wondered idly, or the same girl grown up?—then he handed them back.

"Mrs. Solari," he said, his voice warm, one of his best features, "I would love to send a reporter—an entire news team—to make a headline story of unveiled women voting in a suburb of Mashad, but ...." He sighed deeply, hoping to find just the right words.

She nodded her head gently as if agreeing, while giving him a quick once-over in assessment. Before her sat a balding man in good trim for his fifty-two years, comfortable in sage-colored slacks and sweater of complementary hues. She saw evidence yet of the keen freckle-faced boy he'd been, but she guessed that something was off. His deep-set blue eyes sat in dusky circles of resident fatigue.

He sat behind a desk piled with a maelstrom of notes, reports, books, newspapers, videos, audiotapes, CDs, and more, in contrast to an otherwise well-organized and tasteful office. He was struggling with more than forbearance of her importuning, more than overwork at this tumultuous time.

He breathed in, again catching her subtle scent, a hint of something oddly green as a meadow, fresh as a child. He couldn't tell her the truth, the directive he'd gotten to ignore all but the dominant, most pressing issues in the Middle East. He chafed at this, not the logic of the edict, but being told at all—damned new meddling boss. Obviously, if something explosive happened regarding women's rights and women wronged, he'd give it priority, but this didn't sound like anything crucial in the bigger picture, however obliged he felt toward this compelling woman.

Larry continued, "I'm sorry, I can't do it. I agree absolutely that women in repressive regimes must win the right to dress as they please. It's an important first step to achieving other, more vital rights. I applaud your initiative at this time, when larger changes may provide a context for smaller ones and vice versa."

She leaned forward to see if his weary eyes and vaguely sallow skin were a trick of lighting. He guessed she was going to press her case again. He quickly said, "I personally would like to be there, to be a Muslim woman, to cast my vote with head proudly bared, to be routed and punished for it, but that's not my lot in life. I'm stuck in this chair, and believe me, we're stretched—oh boy, are we stretched covering the big, big stories—recognizing, of course, that women achieving their full rights is a big, big cause."

There, she thought, *he said it himself, a throw-away word of more importance than perhaps he even knew:* 'stuck'. She glanced at the fluorescent light boxes overhead. She considered the dull February sky beyond the rain-streaked view from his twenty-first story perch of neighboring office towers. It wasn't a trick of lighting. He was off track—his health, his work, perhaps more.

He continued, "That a woman of your age is involved and taking such risks at this time—at any time—is wonderful and inspiring, but ... well, I haven't the resources. Our team in Iran is beyond overworked, as you can imagine. I'm very glad you alerted us, however. I'll make sure our people in Tehran are tuned in. If your protest takes an unexpected twist or leap, we'll be there in flash."

He discreetly checked his watch. Eight minutes. With luck, he'd have her out in the ten he'd promised her. He rose to skirt his desk and see her out. *Ouch*—he flinched slightly from a dull pain in his left leg. He continued, "I'm very sorry to disappoint you. Other news services may feel differently, and any number of women's channels, programs, etcetera ... well, you know all these possibilities, I'm sure. I wish you luck with them and with your undertaking. On a personal note, I'm delighted—no, more than that—I'm honored to have met you. Mae tells me that you've been friends for ninety years. Amazing. How lucky."

She stayed seated, looking up at him standing tall beside her. She smiled and nodded, more as if sizing him up than accepting his rejection. "Mr. Singer," she said, "I've come to talk with you."

"And I'm grateful. It's been a pleasure, and I'll keep an ear to the rail about your undertaking."

She didn't budge; her eyes didn't move from his. "No, I've come to talk with you about the news. The big news." He sat down on the chair beside her, partly because standing had reacquainted him with his deep tiredness, and partly because somehow she commanded it. What did she have? The power of a mother times ten?

She continued. "About what you're trying to do."

He smiled. "Get back to work, I'm sorry to say. My time is ridiculously tight."

"I know. That's why I wonder about this." She circled her hand to indicate his spacious, bright office. A bank of six televisions, their screens now blank, hung from the ceiling over the entry door opposite his desk. A large, tidy workstation rounded one corner. Books sat straight and ordered on shelves. He kept cabinet doors and drawers neatly shut. Discreet impressionist paintings filled spare wall space.

She pointed to his rat's nest desk. "Compared to this."

He laughed. "Yeah, it's a mess. This isn't the news falling in on me, it's just that we're making big changes—major restructuring, redefining how we deliver the news, integrating a lot of new technology and services ...."

"I know," she interjected firmly, stopping him short. From the same manila envelope that held her photographs, she took a plain sheet of paper folded in half. "This might interest you."

He took her paper reluctantly and started to open it.

"No, read it later please. What matters now is what's missing." Carefully, word by word, she said, "It's in the peripherals. It's in the context that defines the core. That's your strength. The center isn't holding."

Oh boy, you're so right, he thought.

She leaned forward and said conspiratorially, "Rosebud."

Goosebumps ran up his arms. How did she know? He hadn't told anyone in decades that "Citizen Kane" by Orson Welles propelled him into the news business and still fuelled his dream of writing the great book that every journalist thinks he's got in him. With a surprised smile, he said, "Exactly."

"I worked with Orson," she said, standing to go. She moved slowly, but fluidly. "He was ... attentive."

"You serious? I mean, the man himself?" Larry rose to his feet with her. He contained a grunt as he again felt the pressure in his left leg.

Her eyes swept him from thigh to feet. "There," she said, pointing to his left shin. "Asymmetries can be serious. Your coloring is off too. Are you getting help?"

Larry blinked hard. *My God,* he thought, *she sees everything. Who is this Maya Solari woman?* "No," he mumbled.

She reached into her coat pocket and, with an elegant twist of her wrist, opened her palm to proffer a small, unbleached cotton sachet on a thin, necklace-length thong. "This might get you started in the right direction."

As he took her gift, she said, "Herbs. From Mount Olympus. They're a tonic, not a cure. And a piece of Mount Parnassos at Delphi, where I was born."

He felt a pea-size rock inside, then sniffed the sachet. Ah, that scent, that lovely scent. "Thank you," he said warmly. "It smells ... mm-m, healthy."

She flashed a smile, a split-second unforgettable zap. "Then you know what to do."

"I do?" he blurted like a boy, his heart and mind racing. He really was sick, and it was making him far too emotional.

"Yes." She bowed slightly with body and eyes, a delicate eastern gesture. "The ten minutes you kindly found for me are up. Bless you, Larry Singer." She turned for the door.

"No, wait! I'd like to talk more, if you have another five, ten ...."

She shrugged apologetically. "I'm sorry." She fixed her eyes on his and measured her words to make sure he got every one. "I, like you, have very little time."

Larry's breathing tightened. Had she guessed that, old as she was, she might outlive him? He'd told no one but his partner about his diagnosis—certainly not Mae—and then only in round-about terms, unable to say "cancer" aloud. It was just a little lump under his shin, self-contained. It wasn't the deadly gut/bone/brain kind. He was determined to make it disappear by strength of mind and healthy habits, no medical meddling or heroics. Such cases existed, and there was every reason he could be one of them.

Maya was at the doorway now. He stood rooted, watching her go as if the clock had stopped. He would remember her exit, frame by frame. She held up a soft fist as if still clutching the sachet, or was she gesturing solidarity for her cause?

"Thank you," he said, meaning it fully.

With the grace of a Tai Chi master, she circled her hand open to reveal her open palm. He felt as if her blessing had slid off her hand to his heart. With a trace of a smile—an ancient imp—she vanished behind the closing slit of the door.

Larry stared at the blank door, thinking, "God help me, I'm desperate for angels." He looped the sachet around his neck, then tried to imitate her fist-to-twisting-wrist motion, the exquisiteness of her simple gesture. He smiled. It wasn't easy.

He tried repeatedly with one hand, then the other, while watching from his window to the street far below. His office oversaw the Baltimore harbor, with an impressive view of its single World Trade Center tower, rising 30-stories high, and the *U.S.S. Constellation*, the U.S. Navy's last all-sail ship, anchored beyond it. He might see Maya leave the building or he might not, so small were the swarms of tiny cars and tinier people from such height. No matter. He needed to think, and the view calmed him.

His high perch had thrilled him when he first moved into the News Director's office in the Media 8 tower, headquarters of the ever-expanding conglomerate fondly and otherwise known as "The Octopus." Its eight giant tentacles employed newspapers, books, radio, TV, film, video, digital disks, and the Internet to deliver every form of information and entertainment available and in development. After six years, he'd worked too many long days with his back to the real world and his mind on every place else to appreciate, literally, his vantage point. This was the first time he'd given it more than a glance in many months.

Within minutes, Maya Solari emerged onto the plaza, her white head uncovered in the rain, her old legs taking her slowly to a waiting dark gray sedan—a Fiat, Larry guessed, not many in the city. *Gone,* he thought. *Just one of millions down there, and I feel unbelievably ... what? Like I need her. Miss her. I've got to see her again.* The car pulled away and merged with the endless wheeled stream. "Go safely, Maya. Godspeed," he said quietly.

He returned to his desk and the demands stacked high on it. *Of course, I know what to do,* he thought, cursing the shambles of his work and health. He snorted and muttered, "I don't have a freakin' clue."

Larry sat down heavily and took a weary whiff of his new sachet. Her voice echoed in his head, "... what's missing ... in the peripherals ... Rosebud."

From his top desk drawer, he took a lined notebook, the kind he'd used since junior high school. On the cover, he'd scrawled "Telling News #72", the name of the tell-all novel he was going to publish about his years in the news game.

He flipped through his notes to a new page. "Maya Solari, Feb. 06," he wrote atop it. Then what? She'd knocked the words right out of him. He was totally compromised—he'd have sent a reporter in an instant if he had any real say—and she'd just made that crystal clear. He'd told her to get lost, essentially, because his new boss was more keen on invitations to the White House than taking any news-breaking initiatives in key trouble spots.

But if coverage whipped up more trouble, then who was sure to suffer the most for it? Children, women, the old, the frail. Having your head covered or uncovered in such circumstances would be trivial. Who was he to stir up news from women voting without headscarves? If anything significant happened, he'd hear about it. He'd send Fran Roma, his ace and favorite reporter, to Iran to do the follow-up.

For now, he had to shake down why Maya had shaken him up so much. He hadn't felt so touched by a single encounter since ... what? Meeting Mother Theresa? The Dalai Lama? Nelson Mandela? No, she outdid them, so clearly did she see him, so uncannily did she read him.

He closed his notebook. He didn't need to write a word to describe her, so etched in his mind was every moment they'd shared. He couldn't grasp the thoughts and feelings she'd roused in him, let alone put them into neat rows of nouns and verbs on a clean page.

The phone rang, jarring him back to the war zone of his desk. To his assistant, he said, "Thanks, Nora. Yeah, tell him I'll call back in ten. Hold my calls till then."

Larry opened the piece of paper Maya had given him. In small, tidy handwriting, he read:

1. News embedded in ecol/econ/psych/demographic context
2. By subscriber-shareholder
3. Integrated ethical advertisers/shareholder perks
4. Web delivery, self-printing, alt. paper stock

He skipped over the words, unable to focus or connect them. He sighed, thinking, *Ah Maya, I'm sure it's brilliant, but it's all too much.*

He tucked the paper into his notebook and put it into his desk drawer. He lay his head down on a small stack of reports on his desk and succumbed to giant waves of overpowering sleep.

Too soon, the phone jangled him awake, then rang every few minutes after. Between incoming calls he made more. He checked his e-mails and sent quick replies. He sifted through his paper midden. At the top of each hour, he tracked six different news reports on his television screens. He made notes, dictated letters, and called in reporters, assistants, and associates. Hours passed. His big view window became a mirror as the sky turned from gray to black.

Larry's old cousin Mae made her way carefully from kitchen through dining room to living room. Her beige mop of a dog waggled about her spindly legs, which rose from black rubber boots to rose-colored tights. She followed a winding path through stacks of files, binders, and boxes covering the worn oak floor of her worn old house.

Maya, in her usual navy shoes and hose, followed Mae and mutt past folders bearing names writ large in black felt marker in an old school-marm's hand: Mater Matua, Isis, Ashtar, Persephone, Teleia, Cerredwen, Holl— hundreds of goddesses and mythical women from around the world. More such highrises of paper rose from the dining table and chairs, obviously long unused for meals.

Each old lady carried a saucer and cup of steaming tea. Mae's rattled in a shaky hand. Her wizened fingers ended in rose-painted nails, matching a circle of rhodonite beads about her scrawny neck. She wore a purple cowl-neck sweater and skinny black sheath skirt.

Mae's paper industry burdened the living room as well, except for the scruffy old chair she took and a narrow spot on the sofa, which Maya claimed.

The dog flopped contentedly at Mae's feet. "Good lad, Byron," she said through once-lush lips that had collapsed to a wrinkled portal over ill-fitting dentures. An unbrushed black wig sat awry on her head, leaving wisps of white hair flying from blue-veined temples. A delicate old ear held a small hearing aid.

She had been gorgeous in her youth, with broad cheekbones and quick eyes, as the small black-and-white studio photo atop the nearby upright piano showed. She had signed it in her generous hand, "Best Love, Mae". Next to it sat larger color shot of Larry, with microphone in hand, broadcasting live from a city in mayhem behind him.

Mae said to Maya, "Thank goodness Larry said no. But what if he'd said yes? How would you have talked him out of it?"

Maya shrugged. "I'd have digressed to ... oh, I don't know. Something handy. What we need is usually under our noses, if we're paying attention."

"Hm," Mae said, taking a sip of tea. "Like the photographs of Luna and Pavla, right under Larry's nose. Did he ask anything about them?"

"Of course not."

"Dear fellow, he'll kick himself one day. He tends to get distracted by the obvious, the nature of his business and all."

"He's not well," Maya said.

"Really?" Mae's eyes widened.

"His blood's off, he's fighting something. It could be serious. We didn't have time to discuss it, although I'm sure he'd like to have. For this and other reasons, I'm sure he wants to see me again."

Mae smiled. "Good. That means he'll be around soon to pump me for information about you. I'll mete it out judiciously, keeping him keen but not overwhelmed. I'll pump him in turn about his health."

"Tell him that I'll see him next time I come this way. In a few weeks, I hope. In the meantime, I gave him an idea that might help him, if he pursues it ... understands it."

"Wonderful. Anything I can help with or encourage?"

"No, not really. He needs to puzzle a bit, and I need to talk to you about something else. You see, as I looked at the pile of papers and confusion on Larry's desk and sensed his confusion at this pivotal time, I realized that I must do something I've been thinking about since ... oh, Hiroshima, really. The mess on Larry's desk perfectly symbolizes the far greater, ever-growing, uncontrollable mess everywhere. He needs a new paradigm by which to restructure his work and his world, as do countless others. I'm increasingly convinced that we have the requisite critical mass of people ready for the truth, if we dare tell them." She leaned forward and said, with quiet urgency, "I've decided that it's time to tell my tale. To publish my biography."

Mae's eyes darkened with fear. "No," she whispered, her head now trembling with her hands.

Maya nodded calmly. "Yes. We've never been more needed—overtly, directly needed after millennia behind the scenes. The time is right to be brave and bold."

"Oh Maya, at what price? Your line ... Luna ... you could be sentencing her to death."

"Babies die all the time. Are killed. I've decided, with thanks to Larry for inadvertently making it clear, that we must test our faith and take this chance. At this critical juncture in history, I believe that our best covert work is done, and we must surface or disappear."

Mae struggled for breath. "I understand, but I ... I can't ...." She lost her voice to sobs.

"I'm not asking you to write it, heavens no. You're doing more than enough, dear Mae, far more. You have contacts, however, who could work from our notes. I'd like you to narrow the list for me, then we'll discuss it when I return. I'll take it from there, unless you reconsider and want to be active in the writing."

Mae took a deep calming sip of tea and forced a smile. Her voice wavered, "The singular Maya. Identical to the rest, yet none like you. I will do all I can to forward the written, published celebration of your life."

"Thank you," Maya said. "My foibles and failings too. The complete Maya."

At nine o'clock that evening, Maya went to bed in the small room Mae kept for her at the back of the house. She shut the curtains to a moonlit view onto the large, high-fenced yard with fruit trees and overgrown remnants of Mae's once-active vegetable, herb, and Japanese gardening. All was silent now in this brambled paradise for squirrels and songbirds. She would rise at four a.m. to begin her long flight to Mashad.

Mae played quietly on her upright piano, with Byron curled at her feet. Her dentures sat beside Larry's photo and her former loveliness. As she warbled an antique tune, a rap sounded at her front door.

Byron leapt up with a yap. She continued her bass arpeggio, while rewarding him with a right-hand pat on the head. "Good boy, you sing too." Her left hand repeated the bass run an octave higher. Byron shushed, his tail thumping the floor furiously, eyes expectantly on his lady love.

Rat-tat-tat—a second summons. Byron stood up and growled. He snapped at a spider dropping from the ceiling past black-lacquered shelves. They held dozens of brass ornaments blanketed with dust, threaded with spiderwebs. Candleholders dripped with thick layers of wept wax, dusty for years now too.

By the third knock, Byron yowled, then pulled at the top of a rubber boot. She stopped playing and cocked an ear. "Must be the door," she said. "What would I do without you?"

As she rose to reach for her dentures, Byron pulled at her skirt, knocking her off balance. She saved herself with a quick plunk back onto the bench. She put her teeth into her mouth as she shuffled to the front door, with Byron bouncing around her wobbly legs.

"Larry!" she said delightedly, opening the door wide to welcome him.

"Mae, my beautiful Mae," he replied, wrapping her in a big hug.

"I guessed you'd be by soon. Here, give me your coat."

Larry shed his all-weather jacket and hung it on a nearby hook. Mae continued, "Maya said it went well."

"She did? I turned her down."

"I know. Don't worry, she understands and was pleased to meet you?"

"I'm sorry, really sorry. I was hoping she'd be here."

"She is, dear, but she's gone to bed, and I can't disturb her. She has a short night, then some very long days. She leaves before dawn."

"Oh no," Larry groaned. "I worked too late. I couldn't get away sooner."

"Come in anyway, if my company will do. Would you like tea?"

"No, thank you. It would be nice just to sit and talk a bit, if you have the time."

Mae set Larry on her sofa in the spot Maya had taken. Byron danced at Larry's knees and nosed about for an ear-scratch.

Mae sat in her ragged old chair and looked intently at Larry. "Maya's right. You look tired, not as pink as you should be."

Larry winced. "She didn't miss a thing did she? I'm overworked, that's all."

"Have you seen a doctor?"

"I have, and I'm eating my veggies, I promise. How 'bout you?"

"Veggies *and* vitamins, thank you. Now Maya tells me that your desk is worse than this." Mae cackled and waved a hand over her paper maze. "That's not like you."

"Far worse. It's a disaster zone. The big boss has hired a nephew to haul us into some integrated-media warp zone, and he's wreaking havoc."

"Nepotism," Mae said. "Nephew-ism, literally. The bane of all ages, if you know your history."

"This Randy bane is a top-down guy, all surface and trends and glitz, doesn't have a clue how things work from the inside out. Luckily, he's on salary but doesn't have any production budget—ever, if I can help it."

"Well, I hope he's the worst of your problems. Maya's concerned that you're losing your drive or focus. She senses that something's ...." Mae looked worriedly at Larry. Byron looked equally worriedly at her. "Wrong," she finished. Byron put his head on his paws, resigned to the verdict.

Larry quickly shook his head. "No, no, I just have to organize the mess in the middle out to my tidy edges, just like Maya said. It's a nuts and bolts thing, plus a little psychological warfare with the boss's pet." He lightly rubbed up one arm to a tight shoulder muscle, which he squeezed to unknot.

"Maya said she'll see you soon, when she's back this way."

Larry brightened. "Great. Give me some warning, and I'll clear the deck for her—the desk, the dance floor, I'll meet her wherever and whenever she wants."

"Oh no, Larry, we can't plan this. I never know when she's coming, and I can't contact her. I see her when I see her, and so will you."

"Really? I thought you were close friends."

"We are, but she comes to me. That's been our arrangement since we met, which is why we stay friends."

He teased, "What, is she a fugitive, on the lam?"

Mae chuckled and shook her head. "She's many things and nothing you'd ever guess."

"So why the mystery? Who is this Maya woman?"

Mae thought for a moment, then asked, "Do you remember when you and I first met?"

Larry nodded. "Twenty ... let's see, twenty-three years ago at that horrible funeral—they're all horrible, with all due respect for your husband."

"Second husband."

"Mother dragged me, what a trial. I didn't understand her enthusiasm for funerals—in fact, I still don't—as she faced her own. I was miserable, imagining her dead in a few months, which she was."

"You were indeed miserable. As happy to meet this old cousin as a hornet at a rained-out picnic. Don't ask me why, but I thought you were worth getting to know."

Larry laughed. "I'm glad you persisted."

"Maya was there."

Larry's eyebrows shot up.

"I was surprised that she knew Irwin had died—I hadn't told her, hadn't seen her for months—and I was immensely grateful that she came. I introduced you to her."

"Oh no, how awful, I don't remember. Pearls before swine—two pearls."

Mae chortled. "She brought a small bouquet of fresh herbs."

"You know, I do remember that," Larry said, pulling out his sachet from under his sweater. "Not that she brought it but the bouquet itself. She gave me this today." He sniffed it. "Something about her was so familiar, so .... What else? There was something else about that bouquet."

"A small black doll."

"Yes! That was so strange. I mean the herbs to start with, not your usual bunch of glads and mums, then the little Moses in the bulrushes. What was that all about?"

Mae smiled. "We met on a ship from France to home, I in second class with my parents, after a purchasing trip for my mother's dressmaking business—we'd seen all the latest fashions in Paris—and Maya in what we called steerage. I was five. She was seven. Do you want to hear this story?"

"Of course!"

"We were on very separate decks, locked one from the other, but early in the voyage we met during a lifeboat drill. She had a black doll in her arms, over which we made instant friends. She gave me her beautiful baby when we parted, with the idea that we might sneak through this door and that to meet again.

"Mama thought the doll was lovely, and Daddy was glad I'd made a new friend, from which deck he didn't know, unaware of the intrigues required if we were to continue our friendship. They let me take the doll to dinner that evening all fancied up in satin ribbons. A senior officer—not the captain, he kept to first class—shared our table, and the minute he saw my baby, he whisked her from my arms and out of the room.

"I tried to follow, ready to raise a great protest, but Mother and Father kept me pinned in my seat with very stern looks. We were the only Jews above steerage—that's another story—and they were afraid of any scene.

"'No blacks on board,' the officer whispered when he returned." Mae imitated his trollish hiss. "When Daddy asked what he'd done with the doll, he indicated throwing it overboard, then he wiped his hands together ...." Mae made two swipes of her own hands. "... and that was that. My parents were horrified, but what could they do? I was too stunned at first to cry and far too upset to eat.

"Mama took me to our cabin, promising repeatedly to replace the doll when we landed. I ate the rest of my meals there, and when I ventured on deck, my parents kept me from confronting that wicked officer, for I'd have kicked him in the shins or worse.

"I didn't see Maya again until we debarked. Mama and Daddy made me wait for her and explain what happened and apologize—oh how I apologized!—and get an address to send her a new doll.

"She wouldn't give me an address, and her mother wouldn't take any money. We told them where we lived—this very house, which Father was building for us then—and she promised to visit me when she could. Her mother gave me a pocketful of herbs, the same as those." Mae pointed to Larry's sachet. "I don't know where Maya and her mother went from there, but they visited some months later, and she continues to drop by to this day."

Larry blinked, taking a moment to sort his swirling thoughts, then asked, "I understand the little black doll now, but why for the funeral?"

"My first husband was my great love, as you know, and a great musician. I was his muse, he said, and his compositions were our offspring, our love forever. Oh, it sounds impossible after so many years, but ...." Tears filled her old eyes. "... I'll never get over him." She smiled softly. "Davide. Even his name is music."

She pulled herself up and continued, "My second husband was a great mistake. That he lied and cheated to win my affections I could forgive, for at least that places some value on my heart. He thought I was rich, however, and after we entered holy wedlock, he gambled away my savings and modest inheritance, excepting this house. He feigned worldliness when a show was required, but he really was a horrid bigot, the sort who threw black dolls overboard. He had no love of culture or the arts. He had the ears of an insect, the tastes of a toad."

Larry winced. "Why didn't you leave him? Divorce him?"

"I feared I'd have to forfeit the house, which I could not do. For Maya. To his credit, he behaved himself in front of my friends when sober and had the good sense to disappear when drunk. He was a sloppy sot but never violent. At his funeral, Maya knew that I was free again, one of the only people there who knew that I was rejoicing, not grieving."

"My God, what a story. And I saw it all and missed everything." Larry snorted. "Maybe I'm in the wrong business."

Mae smiled. "It's a little late, and you're a little too successful to say that. Times of re-examination are good, dear, as long as you have your health, and that means good habits, good attitude ...."

Larry grinned disarmingly. "I'm fine, Mae, don't worry. I'm a Singer."

"Like your grandfather, now there was a Singer." She chortled. "And a rascal too, from the day I met him."

"Tell me," Larry said quietly.

"Oh, I mustn't bore you with another ancient story."

"Bore away, please," Larry said, as happy as a boy with another bedtime tale.

"Well, if you insist." Mae paused. "I was four years old that summer. We had traveled for days, long hot days to get to Uncle Jacob's farm. Big cousin Samuel, your grandfather—he was eight or nine—took me straight into a field. There were cow pies everywhere, and I fussed about the smell. Sammy kicked off his shoes, stepped in one, and dared me to do the same. I quickly learned that cow pies squish wonderfully up between your toes, especially new warm ones."

Larry laughed. "Our dainty little Mae?"

"Oh yes. We hopped from patty to patty looking for the biggest, steamiest ones, having a gay old time. Sammy led me to even better ones behind a fence, which he failed to mention was part of the bull's pen. Apparently, his father had been talking of selling the bull, and to Sammy, no bull in sight meant no bull anywhere.

"Suddenly—he must have come from behind a hay rick—Mr. Bull appeared, snorting mad at our fun in his business, and he charged. I scrambled to the fence—some good that would have done—but your grandpa Samuel, for reasons of bravado or madness, stood defiantly in a huge plop, and when the bull was unbearably close, he opened his mouth and started singing '*O sole mio!* La la la la la!' as loudly as he could."

Larry gasped, "Oh no!"

"The poor bull lurched to a stop, his eyes wide until the whites were showing, and at the last second, he snorted off the other way."

Larry grinned. "Whew!"

"Now Larry, I can't match Maya's insight and advice, but ...." Mae paused, looking intently at him. "... when the bull's charging and you're ankle-deep in steaming bull pies, never forget you're a Singer."

Larry burst with laughter. "Mae, you are a treasure!" He rose to kiss her on the forehead. "Now, alas, I've got to go. Thank you so much."

At the door, he said, "And thank you especially for sending Maya my way. Rip Van Winkle here seems to be waking up."

"Good. You'll see her again soon, God willing. She has a daughter and granddaughter you should meet too. And a baby great-granddaughter Luna. They're all remarkable."

"I bet. One at a time though, if you don't mind. Good night."

A Muslim woman stood at the Lufthansa check-in counter at JFK Airport in New York. She was covered from head to foot in a brown silk *hijaab* and *jalbaab*, or headscarf and baggy coat. An expensive canvas carry-on bag sat by her sensible brown shoes.

"Are you checking that?" the clerk asked sharply, pointing to the canvas bag. "Any other luggage?"

The Muslim woman shook her head. With elegant hands, she deftly produced her ticket and passport. The third finger on each hand bore antique gold rings—a married woman whatever the continent. The clerk expertly scanned the ticket: Mrs. Reza Vazani, Business Class, Tehran via Frankfurt, leaving in three hours. She flipped open the Iranian passport.

She quickly scrutinized the photo and the hooded woman before her, a tawny skinned, dark-haired beauty without embellishment. Her eyes matched those in Maya's snapshot. First name 'Jila' the little book said, age thirty-eight, although she looked a few birthdays short. The clerk narrowed her eyes and glanced again from face to hands, then closed the passport and returned it. Manicures, pedicures, all kinds of cures keep the wealthy polished and young.

"Returning home?" the clerk asked as she waited for the computer to spit out a boarding pass.

Mrs. Vazani didn't reply. What could she say? That she was flying to Tehran to keep her grandmother from being flogged for supporting women in Mashad who dared to bare their heads as they voted for a progressive woman candidate who had no hope whatever of winning, whether her supporters were veiled or not, so why not have the courage of their convictions and act as they wish to live? The old woman was doubtless handled roughly during arrest and when transferred to a prison in Tehran. She was likely too fragile to survive more than a few lashes. Did her punishers know the risks they were taking? Could any would-be rescuers, mere women particularly, thwart fundamentalist authority and law? How? By infiltration? Bribes? Diversion and brute force to breach the prison? Or would it take a miracle?

The clerk asked, "Would you like a window or aisle seat?

The woman, distracted by her concerns, didn't answer immediately. The clerk guessed she didn't speak English, hence pulled out an aircraft seating plan to point out the seats available. She raised her voice to insist, "Window or aisle?" The woman quickly chose an aisle seat as close to the front of the plane as possible.

The silver-haired man behind her saw and smiled faintly to himself. He stood back, giving her slightly more space than usual in such a queue. He wore a butter-soft leather jacket, Guccis, and a Rolex, all tastefully understated. He appeared to be in admirably good health and fitness for a man in his mid-forties, with youthful Mediterranean features. By lineage and looks, he could doubtless be passionate, but his aura was detached and cool. He kept his honey brown, fox-like eyes patiently focused on nothing.

After the Muslim woman was processed and turned to leave, she brushed close to him. She noticed that the zipper pull on his jacket was a small gold crucifix. Reverent or irreverent? An odd mix. He smelled lightly of musk. Their eyes met but his didn't flicker with a moment's recognition or even curiosity. *Good,* she thought. *Or maybe too good.* She would have to be cautious. But then, when was she not?

In the pre-flight lounge, she easily tracked his silver-bright head above the Arab weekly she was reading. She went to a washroom and watched how he reacted. He did nothing that had any bearing on her movements, not even a look or a split-second catching of eyes.

Upon boarding, he took the window seat in her row. The seat between them stayed empty. After he stashed his jacket and leather shoulder bag in the overhead bin, he offered in mime to stash her bag too. She shook her head, dropping her eyes. She tucked her bag under the seat in front of her. With coat on and scarf shrouding her face, she buckled into her seat.

During take-off, he slipped on reading glasses and flipped through Italian on-board magazines. When they were at cruising altitude, he removed his glasses, tuned his headphones to the in-flight classical music channel, and napped. She hid behind a romance novel in Farsi, the paperback cover too love-struck and lightweight to invite conversation. She soon grew tired and nodded off.

Mealtime came and went. The woman and her seatmate ate silently. Both declined to watch the movie. He got up to use the lavatory only once, saying nothing as she made way for him.

After many hours, a deep male voice cut through their separate reveries. "This is Captain De Reuter," he announced in German. "We will be landing at the Frankfurt terminal in about forty minutes. We are a little ahead of schedule ...." He gave the weather, time, etcetera.

The seatbelt sign lit up and bonged. The Muslim woman ignored it and made quickly for the nearest vacant lavatory while a steward repeated the captain's message in English and French.

In the cubicle, she pulled a tiny state-of-the-art satellite phone from a pocket within the folds of her clothing. She punched a pre-programmed button. In American-accented English, she said into it, "Mother, we're landing at Frankfurt in forty minutes. The man seated next to me has been close by since I checked in. Italian, I think. He hasn't given me any reason to be suspicious—he hasn't said a word to me at all, not even to excuse himself to step past me—but I'm ... I don't know, probably paranoid. Hard not to be in an *hijaab*. I think I'd better bale at Frankfurt."

She listened and smiled. "Yes, I hear her. 'Mom, Mom, Mom.' Tell Luna Mom-Mom loves her." A loud announcement insisted that all passengers return to their seats immediately. "I've got to go. If you can't get anything lined up, don't worry. I'll stick to this plan and make it work. I'm probably overreacting. I'll call you the second everything's clear."

When she returned from the lavatory, her seatmate wore his jacket again and had set his luggage in the seat between them. He flashed her an intimate look and slight smile, then smoothly averted his eyes back to his magazine. Her heart rate quickened as she settled, clicked on her seatbelt, and also feigned interest in her reading.

Soon, February drizzle and the dull gray of Frankfurt airport buildings whizzed by the aircraft window. She said to the silver-haired man, "Nice weather for ducks."

He chuckled. "Ah, you speak English," he said in Italian-accented English, with a British twist. "Rather well."

She smiled. "I try." She quickly hid again in her novel.

The plane docked at the Frankfurt terminal, and a catwalk clunked onto the plane. The instant the steward opened the aircraft door, the silver-haired man slipped what felt like a fingertip to the Muslim woman's ribs through the unprotected side of her bullet-proof vest. "Cyanide," he said. "Disguised as an allergy shot."

He rose, forcing her to rise with him and step into the aisle, holding her near. He whispered to her, "I will use it, believe me, if you say a word or try anything."

A nearby attendant caught Pavla's drawn face and asked with concern, "Oh dear, are you ... ?"

"She is fine," the silver-haired man said authoritatively. "A little unsteady on her feet, that is all. She has asked me to help her. Please, no fuss."

Arm in arm, luggage over shoulders, they exited slowly along the walkway to the terminal. The woman leaned into him and slowed her pace, playing up her apparent illness.

"Good," he said. "An ambulance is waiting and an armed escort. There is no escape."

As passengers hurried past them, he said softly, "You are a beautiful woman, Pavla Blanca. I was prepared for this, but so close, your charisma is most ...."

"Spare me."

"What? My flattery? Or the certainty that I must kill you if you try to bolt? I would rather not, you know. My superiors want you eliminated, but I have got them half-convinced that you are worth more alive than dead. Half-convinced. The other half is up to you. I am Dr. Dino Trigliani."

She glanced at him with surprise. He continued, "Yes, you know my work. I have positioned myself both to forward our shared interests and to buy you time. A lifetime, if we are careful."

They were the last passengers to reach the wide view of the terminal lounge. Those ahead rushed to pick up their luggage or make connecting flights. Three airport security guards stood together watching the crowd disappear. One of them, a large goonish man, said something urgent to his two co-workers and pointed toward the baggage claim area. They hurried to investigate.

Only the two stragglers and the aircraft's crew remained to clear the area. A flight attendant caught up to them and again offered assistance. Trigliani waved her away, and she returned to the plane.

In the nearest boarding lounge, a young man in overalls squeegied the windows of an emergency exit door. He flashed his pinky finger as he worked.

The remaining guard strode toward Trigliani and his clinging woman, smiling smugly. Beneath his cap, his brushcut had three shaved stripes angling up from each ear. When he was ten paces away, she gooseheaded her fingers to make a close, lightning-fast strike to Trigliani's groin. As he buckled, she kneed the poison from his hand, then struck a pressure point on his neck to send him crumpling to the floor.

The security goon rushed in. She charged him, to his surprise, slipping to the floor, her long garb riding up enough for her to down him from the knees with a scissor kick. His arm, then his head, cracked as he fell. He tried to get up, then rolled back with a sick moan from the pain of a broken arm and possible concussion.

She ran to the janitor, and he led her quickly through the exit door, down a flight of stairs, and out to a waiting airport service car on the tarmac. She dove into the back seat with the man, and the car sped from the terminal.

In Italian, she said, "Bless you."

The driver said, "Bless Alma. We have a private jet lined up. One of Reza's friends. It's always available for you."

She said, "Wonderful. It's such a gamble. Public airlines offer anonymity and heightened security these days but obviously not enough."

They drove in silence until they pulled up to a small waiting jet, its engines roaring. She said, "Thank you. Most profoundly, thank you."

She rushed from the car up the stairs into the jet. Within half a minute, the sleek craft taxied toward the runway to await clearance for takeoff.

She was soon in the air, safe as the sole passenger in a luxury quasi-living room, with a discreet attendant.

Pavla slipped into the small, well-appointed lavatory and again used her phone. "Mother, it worked perfectly. I'm on one of Prince Hamid's jets. Thank you. I'll get to Tehran with a few extra hours, which I can definitely use.

"I was right to be suspicious. The white-haired man is Dr. Dino Trigliani." She spelled his last name. "His research is tangential to mine. He was counting on me cooperating because of it. Had I recognized him, of course I'd have bailed when I first saw him at JFK.

"Very clever attempt—a cyanide injection if I didn't play along. At a lucky moment, I disarmed and dropped him. Got his assistant too, and Mother, I don't think anyone saw, it's amazing.

"They have some explaining to do, which is perfect. They'll cover for themselves and me too. Reza will smooth things over from his end, so I expect I'm off scot-free, thanks to the help you so quickly lined up for me."

She listened for a moment, then said, "Everything you can get on him, yes. He wants me alive for research purposes, which makes him less a risk than others intent only on our destruction. No, don't worry. I'm fine, not a scratch. Yes, I will. *Khodah hafez*."

Under a black starless sky, Prince Hamid's jet circled the twinkling sprawl of teeming Tehran. Pavla landed as Mrs. Reza Vazani, with a note in hand from her husband permitting her to travel unescorted. She cleared airport customs without delay and was met by a wealthy gentleman who greeted her as his wife Jila. He took her to a luxury sedan waiting outside the nearby entryway. They slipped into the back seat, with a darkened privacy shield between them and the chauffeur who whisked them into the night.

Reza said in Farsi, "You're too late, I'm sorry. They advanced the punishment. They flogged her this morning."

Pavla groaned. "Oh no. Is she ... ?"

"Alive? Yes. She's in the prison hospital."

Pavla closed her eyes in pain. "How many lashes?"

"The full dozen, but we're more concerned about her face and neck."

"What?"

"Of course, how could you know? She was attacked in Mashad by a madman, a zealot. He used a blade of some sort to slash her from forehead to here." He drew his finger from eyebrow to the base of his neck. "I'm sorry. It's a long cut. She lost a lot of blood. It happened behind the scenes, nothing recorded or reported. The police watched and waited. When several women were bleeding, they made arrests using clubs and fists."

Pavla winced, fighting tears. "So barbaric. Sometimes it seems hopeless."

"Only insiders know, of course. The international press has been told lies and more lies."

Pavla nodded. "I've heard reports and guessed some whitewashing, although I'd hoped .... Where are the others?"

"In prison in our holiest city, being tortured, some raped, I'm sure, and promised death if they don't renounce their evil ways and do penance for life. The good news is that their candidate got more votes than expected, though not nearly enough to win, of course. Since she had not yet arrived to vote when the crackdown came, she is free as yet, although under close surveillance. Her family is under great pressure to straighten her out."

Pavla sank back in the seat and moaned, "So much pain, so little gained."

"Your grandmother would disagree, I think. Jila saw her this afternoon, when making charity rounds. She told her that you're coming—don't worry, no one overheard—and your grandmother rallied instantly, despite worrying about the dangers you face."

"With the worst behind me, I hope, and my luck holding as it did in Frankfurt, with great thanks to Hamid, you, and others. How difficult will it be to get her out of the hospital and the country?"

"Jila's already arranged to bring her to our house." Reza shook his head in mock annoyance. "My dear wife, always bringing trouble home and making it vanish. The hospital, the prison—they love her."

"As do we all. She's an angel."

He chuckled. "A contrary one. Jila will fetch your grandmother tomorrow, if she's well enough. Hamid's jet will come in handy again."

"Thank goodness. I am most grateful to all of you," Pavla said.

For long seconds, they watched the lights of Tehran blur by through the car's darkened windows. Finally, he said, "Your grandmother hasn't given up. When Jila left her, her eyes were bright. She believes that some important seeds have been sown."

Pavla touched his arm. "Thank you, Reza. On that, I'll say my prayers and try to sleep tonight. The hours will be long, much longer for her."

Morning. An overcast sky softened Tehran's hard edges and muffled its incessant traffic. An unmarked white van drove through a large wrought-iron gate to a modest mansion. The high fence skirted close to the house, each high wall of which had a heavy, bolted door and no windows. Prying eyes could not see the light and greenery of the spacious courtyard within this exemplary estate, where women played out their hidden lives.

The driver snugged the van up close to a side entrance, and the real Jila Vazani emerged from its back doors. She matched Pavla in size, with all other differences covered by a black *chador*. Two female attendants, swathed in black also, carefully lifted and carried a gurney bearing Maya Solari's blanketed body. She rested on her side to spare the lash wounds on her back.

A teenage girl opened the house door for them, keeping discreetly behind it lest any Peeping Tom see her tight jeans, bright T-shirt, and copper-streaked hair. Jila thanked her daughter as they hastened inside. She led the attendants to a guest room brightened with a spray of fresh flowers, appearing double their cheeriness in the dressing mirror behind them.

Jila and the attendants transferred the old woman to the bed, setting her back gently against a lambskin throw over many soft pillows. They spread a light afghan over her faded blue hospital gown and remarkably fit old arms.

Her hair, still dirty from dried blood and inadequate sponging, matted about her face. She had been sliced from above the left eyebrow to chin, then caught again on the neck, luckily missing the windpipe and jugular. The jagged, raw gash had been treated with a yellow-brown snake of iodine. Her eye puffed with deep purple bruising.

When she was fully settled, Pavla appeared wearing a plain brown *abayah* and shoulder-length hair flowing free. She gently kissed Maya on her uninjured cheek, lingering to savor the old woman's warmth and sweet scent underlying the smells of prison and crude care.

Pavla pulled a chair close and took a soft old hand. Maya drew strength from this, closing her eyes to feel it fully. Pavla studied her face and said quietly, "It's not stitched or even bandaged."

Maya rasped, her breathing labored, "It's better this way, air to heal it. I also thought they might lighten the lashes."

"Did they?"

Maya shook her head. "No matter." She shut her eyes. After several shallow breaths, she opened them and said, "At Mashad, I wasn't quick enough. Intervention came too late. It's a sign, Pavla." She paused. "I must go home."

A shiver ran up Pavla's back. "To Delphi?" she whispered.

Maya nodded slightly.

Pavla's eyes filled with tears. She said quickly, "I'll take you."

"No. You must get back to Luna and to safety as soon as you can. You could see me as far as Athens, then your mother ...." Maya struggled for breath.

Pavla whispered, "Yes, we'll arrange everything."

"Thank you, dear. Now I have to tell you .... Listen carefully." She paused. "I want my story told. Published. I've asked Mae ...."

"What?" Pavla gasped.

Maya summoned her strength to say firmly, "It's time. You know all the reasons, the state of the world. We must have courage. Faith."

Pavla caressed the wrinkle skin and blue veins on Maya's hand as she calmed her swirling thoughts and racing pulse. Finally, she said, "I can write it during my sabbatical year. I can start next month."

Maya shook her head. "No. Your own work ... Luna ... they're too important. I've begun arrangements. Your mother knows. It will take a year or two, not too much more, I hope."

Pavla sighed deeply and said, "We might even be safer this way."

Maya nodded, whispering, "Yes, but you and your mother will judge that after I'm gone. Publish or not: my wish, your choice." After long seconds of studying her granddaughter with deep appreciation, she reached up to run her fingers slowly down Pavla's cheek. "You are so beautiful."

Pavla replied softly, "As are you, my mirror to come. And Luna—your was, our to be. I have a new photo of her."

From a pocket in her dress, Pavla pulled a snapshot of an eight-month old girl, the same beautiful child Maya had shown Larry. She sat amid ferns growing from limestone rocks of an old quarry. "From Pipestone, last week," Pavla said.

Maya smiled. She took the photo, held it to her worn old breast, and surrendered to fevered sleep.

Mae sat at the dining table, her bird-boned frame tiny among the ever-growing stacks of files. She worked without her wig, her hair a ragged, self-trimmed mist of white strands too thin to hold a bobby pin. She wore a worn chenille housecoat and matching old slippers.

Byron lay at her feet, his tail thumping occasionally. Three scholarly books sat open in front of her, one propped on the other. Her teeth and hearing aid sat beside them. Pink-nailed fingertips pushed black felt pen in bold loops on foolscap, then switched to red pen to underline key phrases. She tucked her notes into a file folder marked "Tiamat".

Her old rotary-dial telephone rang loudly, startling Byron to his feet and full yap. Mae said, "I hear it too, good boy. You sit." He plunked his wiggling bottom down and watched Mae fiddle her dentures into her mouth by the third ring. She picked up her hearing aid, which squealed horribly in her hands. Byron howled. She tried stuffing it into her ear anyway, but the squeal repelled her. "Darn thing!" she cursed, shaking and twiddling with it until it was quiet. By the tenth ring, she got her hearing aid in place and answered the phone with a sing-songy, "Hello?"

"Mae. This is Alma Solari, Maya's daughter."

"Yes, dear. How nice to hear from you."

"And I you. It's been too long. My news, alas, is not nice. Mae, Mother is injured and dying."

Mae swayed and held the table top for balance. "What happened?"

"She was slashed at Mashad, flogged in Tehran."

"Oh no," Mae moaned deeply. "I clipped a tiny report that said dissidents were released unharmed."

"Lies, but just as well, since she wants to return to Delphi. There's little time, and it will be dangerous—impossible had there been any publicity, so the lack of reports is good at this point. I'm on my way to meet Mother in Athens, and we'll go from there."

"I know her wishes, dear. I can put Nikos on the next flight there, if arriving tomorrow isn't too late."

"No, that would be wonderful. Can you spare him on such short notice?"

"Of course. I have neighbors who check in on me, and he's due for a week or two off anyway."

"Good. When he arrives, have him go directly to the embassy district." Alma gave instructions, which Mae wrote down. "Have you prepared him at all for this?"

"No, I've told him nothing, and he never pries, that's why he's been my driver and helper for so long. He's met your mother and drives her occasionally. I'll fill him in, as much as he needs to know. You'll find he's very trustworthy, very discreet. You'll be in good hands."

"Thank you, Mae—sweet words at this time. If this all works out, if Mother makes the cave of her birth, the results could be spectacular."

"Let's hope. I'll be watching the news, collecting every co-incidence I can." She said 'co-incidence' as two words.

"Bless you."

"And dear ...." Mae's voice trailed off.

"Yes?"

"Tell your mother for me ...." She searched painfully for words. "Oh, you needn't tell her anything. She knows."

After Mae hung up the phone, she navigated unsteadily to her piano. Byron tagged close by. She sat down and held trembling pink talons over the keyboard to play, but brought only her index right finger down on middle C. Her head slumped. "Oh Maya."

Nikos Platithou landed in Athens on a red-eye special direct from Baltimore International Airport. He set his watch to the time announced on the plane's P.A. system: six minutes to noon, February 10th.

His eyes were large and long-lashed in a bassethound face. He was big-boned and loose-limbed, at home with his frame and fifty years. Like many Mediterranean men, he grew more handsome with age.

He had shaved quickly in the airplane lavatory, missing a tiny patch or two. His dark gray slacks and light gray shirt were rumpled; he carried a gray all-weather jacket over his shoulder. Through customs and baggage pick-up, he wiped cobwebs of jetlag from his face.

He rented a mid-range car with tinted windows and drove from the congested airport to the more congested streets of Athens. The sun shone hazily through brown smog but was still too bright for him, even with sunglasses.

He squinted and blinked his way to the embassy district of central Athens, where he glided up to a whitewashed gatehouse and announced himself,

"Nikos from Mae," into a likely looking box. The gate swung open without hired help or host in sight, and he pulled up to the huge whitewashed, blue-trimmed, flower-decked home. At the front door, he was ushered in before he could knock.

Nikos emerged mid-afternoon with Maya on his arm. Her white hair was bright again, and she wore a clean navy dress, hose, and shoes. Her wound had turned rusty red, the iodine to dirty yellow. The accompanying bruise had faded to light purplish green. With immense difficulty, she hobbled to his car.

Maya folded stiff bones into the back seat, moaning involuntarily when her savaged back hit the lambskin and pillows Nikos had prepared for her. She stretched out as best she could. Nikos put another lambskin on the floor beside her, then covered her with a light blanket. She said in Greek, "Thank you, dear. I'm fine."

A woman of middle height and middle years got into the front passenger seat. She stayed covered in a black coat, headscarf, and sunglasses until they were running fast and safe on highways beyond the big city.

Just past the quarry where the Parthenon sprang from Athena-inspired brows, she removed her excess wraps and shades. Alma Solari's likeness to her mother was uncanny; Pavla was doubtless her girl. She had a symmetrical face, *café-au-lait* complexion, and dark hair half-salted white. Her great beauty was now fading but notable still. She settled into a quiet journey toward sacred Parnassos, through sunset into dark night.

In grainy blackness, they zipped past the ruins of sacred Delphi and its several hotels, which had few lights burning in the off-season. Chryson, by comparison, was a sparkling town first glimpsed through black trees from the snaking mountain road. Alma sank from view and Nikos entered Chryson in darkness, apparently alone.

Chryson is a Greek town in the best way. It has whitewashed buildings that shine in the hot sun and glow in the moonlight. It has crooked, cobbled streets that wind up hillsides, where even weeds grow picture perfect.

It is an everyday village filled with lively families going about their everyday business. It has squat widows dressed in black criss-crossing the streets to shop, attend church, visit grandchildren, and have rumored affairs. It has tavernas filled with smoke and men whose best hours are spent producing the haze and playing *tavli*.

Chryson is also a lucky, famous village with Mount Parnassos just miles to the east. Parnassos: mountain of the gods; home of the great Oracle of Delphi; guardian of the Omphalos, Navel of the Universe.

Summer is crazy with tourists, all hands dedicated to serving their endless appetites. Winter gives the area back to the locals, the hardy few thousand who know that the true place is as much about the gods' gray storms as the easy gold of high-sun days.

Come February, the earth had begun to percolate again, but all was quiet yet. At Apollo's Taverna in Chryson, the owner—Spiro, a stout man of about sixty years, with beautiful teeth and teasing eyes—stood behind the bar pouring glasses of ouzo. In front of it, a young waiter filled a small bowl with calamata olives to serve with the drinks.

A handful of local musicians tuned up on a small stage. A straggle of customers sat at this table and that. Spiro stayed open year-round but made his living in summer. Winter hours were almost a charity to keep the town alive, a place for all to meet and gossip. He ran a cluttered establishment crowded with pots and pans, local pottery, braided garlic bundles, stuffed gamebirds, and liquor advertising. Local artists had brightened one wall with a mural of Apollo's Delphi. Good cooking, good music, and good dancing times permeated the place, giving it breath and life.

Spiro crooked his index finger for the waiter to come close, then whispered, "I have a surprise tonight for your aunties. Nikos is coming."

Cheekily, the young man replied, "So? He's not interested in our aunties."

"Yes, he is. It's been three years. He's ready now."

"No, he isn't. He wants a woman like his wife was, blond and cool and American. Our aunties are dark and passionate and ...." He made plump curves with his hands. "Fat."

"Exactly what he needs—no hot-house flowers. A Chryson woman ripe for babies, he needs those too. You tell all the ladies that it's their lucky night but don't say why. It's a secret. I have not told Elena yet."

The waiter laughed, for telling Spiro's wife was as good as telling the town. "Do I give all the single ladies free drinks to prepare them for their white knight?"

"Good idea, as soon as he arrives. Lots of retsina, bouzhouki ... we will dance and sing until he drops, then marry him off while he sleeps."

Nikos drove directly to a side street, then onto a winding lane. He turned off the engine and glided into a small parking spot at the back of a large house, pulling close to a nondescript doorway. He opened his car door quietly and got out, as did Alma, who shadowed him. He unlocked his apartment door, and they slipped in quickly. He saw no prying eyes in nearby windows, whether dark or lit through curtains and blinds.

Inside the tiny Spartan kitchen, Nikos turned on a radio to hide any hushed conversation. Roller blinds were closed and would stay that way.

He returned to the car and covered Maya with the lambskin from the rear floor, to disguise her as a stack of such merchandise. With great care, he picked her up, including the lambskin she rested on, and carried her to the double bed that filled the bedroom nook. Alma settled her in.

Nikos fetched their luggage, this time closing the trunk and doors without concern for spies. Sure enough, a curious face, then another, peeked through cracks in window coverings. He had to head to Spiro's taverna soon before word reached Elena and she came to flush him out.

"May I make tea?" Alma asked.

In his tiny kitchen, Nikos half-filled a steel pot with water and set it on a hot plate to boil. He got two white china cups and saucers out of a cupboard. Alma gave him a sachet of herbs for tea, the same as Maya had given Larry, minus the loop and thong. In hushed Greek, he said, "Mm, it smells good."

"Herbs from Olympus. Mom used to gather them as a girl with her mother. Friends supply us now. Will you have some?"

"No, thank you. Maybe tomorrow. I will be back by mid-morning, if that is okay. I have my cell phone. You may call at any time."

"How will you explain if you have to rush back here?"

"I have business, *ne*? Do not worry, I cover everything."

Alma smiled warmly. "Thank you."

Nikos carefully locked the door behind himself. He hastened to tell his tenants in the adjoining house that their landlord had arrived and would be coming and going for the next two weeks. On foot, he wound down cobblestone streets to Apollo's Taverna, where he was greeted by an uproar of hugs and cheers, the band blasting and banging its welcome. Elena brought forth dish after dish of treats from the kitchen, a celebrated cook whose hips carried ample proof of her life's great pleasure.

Eligible ladies sitting with family and friends eyed Nikos, but he was too shy to return flirtatious glances. He drank, laughed, sang, and danced heartily with his brother and old chums.

By midnight, he struggled up the back stairs to his brother's home above the taverna. Pleading exhaustion, he fell asleep on the sofa the second he lay down. Spiro removed his shoes, and Elena covered him with a blanket and snugged it under his chin.

Breakfast the next morning was a long, lively affair. She presided over a generous table of eggs, meats, fruits, and fresh-baked buns. A parade of grand-nieces and -nephews popped in to greet their favorite great-uncle. Nikos came prepared. He pressed an American ten-dollar bill into each big and small departing hand. Eyes lit up and heads nodded when he told them to put it in the bank. Stores would be exchanging them for candy by noon.

Nikos told Elena in detail about his import-export business, especially the lambskin samples he got in Athens, which came from Thessaloniki. He would drive north soon to talk to suppliers there, and to visit friends, of course. For this day and next, however, he would sleep off his jetlag. It would be nice if no one disturbed him at his apartment while he adjusted to home. Elena agreed to guard his privacy, to his relief.

By mid-morning, Nikos walked back to his little suite, gritty-eyed but buoyant. As he stepped over cobbled streets, he flicked his worry beads—ovals of sunlit amber on a worn string—silently praying "please" with each one that everything go as his ladies planned.

He tiptoed in and sighed with relief. Alma was fine. Maya was hanging on. She had no interest in food and little in liquid, even of her precious tea. Nikos left them again to make his rounds of family and friends, happily embraced on the street and in their homes.

The second night, Nikos ate a late supper at Spiro's taverna, then drove to visit an old classmate, the night guard at the Delphi Museum. They reminisced, sharing several beers in a room of frozen warriors, statues turned to phantoms by night and history's march. They laughed at the simplicity of such employment: a sophisticated alarm system allowed his friend a good night's sleep; several drinks guaranteed it.

Nikos returned to his suite an hour before midnight. He made a cup of strong coffee to stay alert and to while some time. Two late nights and long days were taking their toll. Alma stayed in the bedroom with Maya until the streets were empty and nearby windows dark. At 11:40 p.m., Nikos gently carried the old woman to his car, again as if she were an armload of lambskins. He clicked her car door shut and waited, watching to make sure no one was watching in turn. Their luck held. He and Alma simultaneously slipped into their front seats, and two doors closed as one.

Under a cloudless, moonless sky, bright with the spilled Milky Way, Nikos drove again to Delphi. They zipped past the museum where Nikos's friend was certain to be sleeping. They drove a minute farther and pulled into the parking lot closest to the Omphalos. It was empty, profoundly so.

Maya struggled from the car without help, then took an arm each from Nikos and Alma. They headed for the Navel Stone, over ground well trammeled by hordes of fair-season pilgrims. With each slow step, clouds of their breath puffed in the sharp night air. Finally, the conical rock, a silhouetted half-egg shape on a rectangular plinth, rose before them to almost Maya's height. She touched the ice-cold stone, then sat on a corner of the concrete base to gather her strength.

Nikos left mother and daughter and returned to his car. Within minutes, Alma joined him, and they drove back to his suite.

Alone in the dark, the old lady headed toward the Oracles' caves at the base of Parnassos. Starlight tracked her ghost-white hair. The rest of her blended into craggy black rocks over which her feet felt their way with great difficulty.

Nikos and Alma waited in his kitchen, listening to classical music drifting quietly from the radio, neither speaking. Outside, all was calm. Silent.

Then it came. A single lightning strike near Parnassos filled the valley with a surreal split-second of blue-white light. A prodigious thunderbolt rattled glass, jolted homes, and rustled trees down to the sea. Everyone in Chryson woke, if not from the burst and blast, then from others shaking them up, panicked about what had happened and why.

The heavens, in contrast, returned to a deeper silence than before. Flickering pinpoints of starlight continued their slow dance through the vast void of space. No more lightning struck from clear skies, no more cracks of Zeus's thunder shook the night. Chryson was left to restless sleep until dawn.

Nikos hurried to his brother's house. He argued that the thunderbolt had to be a natural phenomenon, not an angry god or a stray missile strike. Let the police investigate, he insisted. All others should stay inside rather than run out willy-nilly, to do what? Elena's telephone grapevine soon spread his sensible advice.

A police officer drove to Delphi and talked to the night guard at the museum. He reported that the lightning had struck so close to him that it blinded his closed eyes awake. The thunder shook his heart out of beat, making him struggle to breathe. After he caught his wind, he dared to search outside a few paces beyond the entrance. He saw nothing. He smelled ozone from the huge electric zap. The police shone his flashlight toward the mountain, saw nothing untoward through the blackness, and left further investigation for the morning shift.

At first light, the night guard walked with pounding pulse to where the lightning had struck. It had shattered a piece off Parnassos, leaving a dark scar near the entrance to the Oracles' caves. At his feet, the shape of an old woman had been burnt into the rock, leaving a dark shadow as the atomic blasts had done to people at Hiroshima and Nagasaki.

The guard raced to Chryson's bakery, the first-open shop, to tell what he'd found. Word spread to the next and the next shops as they opened, until the town was afire with his news.

Nikos woke from a few hours of sleep on Spiro's sofa and rose to serve coffee and olive oil-soaked eggs at his brother's crowded taverna. He deflected the wildest speculations with quiet comments that sent laughter rippling through the town. So a thunderbolt made a human shape on the ground? If a man had a birthmark on his backside the shape of a jetplane, would that make him an airport? Should he radio for clearance to sit down?

That afternoon, Nikos excused himself from the chatter to drive to Thessaloniki, ostensibly alone, ostensibly on business. He spun along a single-lane highway that wound around mountain flanks, encountering few other vehicles. The remoteness of the area and the stasis of winter were reassuring in a bleak way. Alma soon dared to sit up in the front passenger seat with her hair and face uncovered.

Half an hour out of Chryson, a silver Mercedes approached at high speed. Its two sunglassed men saw Nikos's passenger. Instantly, the car lurched with a pump of the brakes, then screeched around a curve. "Stop!" Alma shouted. Nikos pulled onto the narrow shoulder overlooking a steep, brambled embankment.

The Mercedes made a fast U-turn at the next widening of the road and quickly caught up with Nikos's car, in which he was now travelling alone. The men dogged him and thumped into his bumper, forcing him to pull over.

Both men emerged from the Mercedes. The driver, a trim client of Armani and Gucci, had white hair. His big swarthy companion sported a brushcut shorn in three stripes rising from his ears. He wore a neck brace and the left sleeve of his jacket hung empty, his arm within held by a sling. He approached Nikos's door, waving a small gun with a big silencer in his right hand for Nikos to get out.

Nikos complied quickly. The driver rounded Nikos's car and peered into the front passenger seat. Empty.

"Where is she?" the driver demanded in English with an Italian-British accent.

Nikos shook his head. "*Then meelow Angleeka.*"

Impatiently, the driver asked in crude Greek, "*Poo eenai yeenayka?*" His big partner peered through the dark-tinted window of the rear driver-side door.

Nikos looked puzzled.

The goon repeated in English, "The woman, you idiot."

Nikos asked, "*Tee yeenayka?*"

"Pavla, Jila, you tell me." The big man opened the rear door, kicked it wide open with his foot, and PTHWUK! fired a shot into a dark leather satchel on the floor.

His partner flinched in surprise and hissed furiously, "We take her alive!"

The goon muttered, "Yeah, yeah," as he pulled the satchel out of the car, opened it, and scattered Nikos's neatly packed clothing and business papers onto the ground.

Nikos shook his head fearfully and said in Greek, "No woman, I have no woman. My wife, she is dead three years and two months, God keep her."

The driver walked to the rear of the car and banged the trunk. "Open it!"

Nikos did so, revealing nothing but two lambskins and a pillow. The men pawed through, then looked at each other.

Nikos said slowly in Greek, not wanting to repeat it, "There was a woman ... in the car ... that just passed me." He showed the fast speed with his hands. "Zoom. Similar car. You saw it, *ne*?"

They leapt into their vehicle and tore off, tires spitting out shoulder gravel and squealing onto asphalt.

Nikos picked up his clothing and papers scattered on the ground. He stuffed them into his satchel and threw them into the trunk. Now what? He looked over the nearby embankment, steep and scrubby with dark evergreens. He walked a few paces down the road, thought better of it, and got into his car. Should he drive back to look for Alma? Should he wait? For how long?

For ten minutes, he continually checked his watch and the rear-view mirror. Finally, she clambered up the hillside, disheveled and muddied, dragging her overnight case by its shoulder strap. She tucked into the back seat of the car and gasped, "Drive. Please." Nikos did.

"What happened?" she asked.

He told her briefly. She closed her eyes when he said they were looking for a Pavla or Jila. She closed them harder when he told of the shot. After he finished, she said, "You handled it perfectly. I'm beyond grateful and deeply sorry to have endangered you this way."

Nikos shook his head. "They are fools."

Alma smiled. "And you—Mae was right—are very good and very smart. I should have known they'd hear within hours of Mother's death and be on their way. Grief has distracted me, and I honestly thought we'd have this day clear. I'll hide until we make Litochoron. If we encounter them again and they force you to stop, we're in terrible trouble."

"Do not worry, I will get you there," Nikos said. They spoke no more as he drove with jaw clenched and his eyes achingly alert to every vehicle on the road—all, fortunately, for naught.

At twilight, Litochoron shone in the distance as if the Pleiades had been dropped onto the hem of Mount Olympus's green-black gown. Up close, Litochoron was another postcard-perfect Greek village climbing the hillside of a great peak. The car bumped over cobblestone streets to an unassuming house at the back of town. Alma said, "Nikos, how can I thank you?"

Nikos shrugged. "Stay alive."

She laughed. "I will. I could get some tea for you here and leave it with Mae, if you'd like."

His eyes crinkled sweetly. "*Efharistó*. I pray for you."

The door of the house opened for Alma. She hurried to it, turning back to lightly blow him a kiss as she vanished within.

Nikos wheeled freely on his way. He soon sat in Thessaloniki eating olives and drinking ouzo at the house of an old chum, his wife, and several others. "Look at this olive, this perfect olive," his friend said in Greek, holding one up. "I have an endless supply for you. They will love them in America."

Nikos shrugged. "Perhaps. You know I deal in quality, not volume. My clients pay top dollar for the very best. These are good."

"Good? They are magnificent! You take my olives to America, you sell them for me."

Nikos grinned. "America, America—the answer to all your dreams, the place you love to hate. I will try but no promises."

Larry's receptionist, a motherly looking woman, sat at the end of a broad hallway lined with busy offices, conference rooms, post-production, and viewing areas. The brass plate on her L-shaped desk read "NORA." She kept a tidy work area and zone of calm around herself and Larry.

Nora looked up and saw the problem coming. Randy Tellman's tall frame loped toward her holding a large video camera on his shoulder, filming as he approached. His polished suit was more business school than camera jockey, his every move more geek than gainly. He pointed his 'weapon' at light fixtures, snooped into open office doors, scanned posted notices, and zoomed in on minor building details. Employees caught in his sweep laughed in surprise at the camera and rolled their eyes in disbelief as he continued on.

Nora quickly buzzed Larry, who was catnapping on his desk. He kept his head down as he pushed the speaker phone button. "Larry," she whispered urgently, "Randy's coming, he's videoing."

Larry jerked upright. "He's what?"

His door swung open without a knock and in came Tellman's recording eye, prying into Larry's domain. "What the hell are you doing, Randy?" Larry demanded

"Trying it," the tall man said, continuing to tape. "And that's Randolph J. Tellman the Third to you." He laughed. "All the hot new shows are using handheld shots, gives them an immediate look, a real happening feel. Looks good on the 'Net too. I want it." He shifted the camera off his shoulder, causing a stack of papers on the desk to hit the floor. Larry groaned. Without acknowledging the spill, Tellman put the camera down on the nearest chair. "New faces, lots of them, young, and hot. The latest techniques. Topics never touched before, like what's news to the next gen', the major growing market. It's all coming together, just watch."

Larry rubbed a hand over his weary face and sighed, then said emphatically, "This is the news, Randy. This is serious business." Stabbing the air, he continued, "Not social commentary, not satire, not documentaries. News. We do handheld when necessary, when nothing else is available, and occasionally by choice, for effect. It's powerful, like jalapeño peppers. Not a main ingredient."

"It's done in all the hot new shit, man, and I love it."

Larry closed his eyes to gather himself. Leaning forward, looking intently at Tellman, he said, "The edict from on high is to integrate and to be more compelling, and to me that means to be real and deep and holistic, not just showing off kids with new toys and clothes. We need clear operating principles, not just a grab bag of cheap tricks."

"So the operating principle is handheld in the field, and we're out roaming everywhere, on top of what's new even before it's new, know what I mean?" Larry rolled his eyes. "We got pizzazz, and we don't miss a thing."

"Tell you what." Larry pointed to Randy's camera. "You show that exact footage to Uncle Al, then get back to me and tell me what he thinks. And tell him that this big pile on my desk is all your ideas too, a new one every minute, a dime a dozen. I've never seen more computer games, junk videos, and limp excuses for content in my life. And all this paper, all these website printouts? Spare me, damn it, you're killing me."

Randy laughed. "No way, man. I'm polishing you up, making you look better than ever." He lifted the camera and pointed it at Larry as he backed out the door. "And I'm going to make you look better yet, just you watch."

Nora discreetly closed the door on Larry, blessedly alone again. He collapsed behind his desk and held his despairing head in both hands. *Video'd in the middle of this mess,* he thought. *This incompetence. It looks like hell—I look like hell. I've got to stop him; I've got to get back to my neat, smooth world, but how?*

He pulled the sachet Maya gave him out from under his shirt and sniffed it. "Peripherals," he heard her say. "... what's missing." Where was she anyway? Freed from Mashad but not rushing to his door. To Mae's door.

I need to talk with you, damn it Maya! I need some definitions, some help. I mean, do high school dreams count, my stupid naïve "Citizen Kane" dream? Some cutting-edge, cut-to-the-quick, wake-'em-up story. Hah. I thought I'd chase firetrucks for a few years, see it all from higher and higher up, and voila! boy genius tells it like it is. Makes some kind of new sense out of the chaos. He stared angrily at his overburdened desktop. *"This miserable mess in the middle. Except there's no sense, no pattern, just more and more mess. It really is going to do me in.*

He lifted his leg to rub his calf through light wool slacks. He rolled up his pants to feel the lump by his shin bone and winced from the dull pain. *Damn you! Just go away, you hear? You and Randy both, you rotten, infiltrating little lumps. Stop, stop, STOP!* His shoulders slumped. A long sob shuddered out of him.

He abruptly let go of his leg and forced himself to sit up. His thoughts spun on. *Oh, you jerk. Self-pity's the worst. You've got choices. So what if I'm tired? Pay attention to it, it's telling you something. You're not the only one tired of this bullshit. You're in the driver's seat ... well, you used to be. You've got a front row seat, at least, so use it.*

We're all fed up with the bullies and bastards and basketcases, so what do we do? We do more, faster, bigger, pile on the shock-schlock until the whole world's in a titillated, addicted tizzy. Except the smart ones, they're turning it off. It's too much, and it's not enough—like it ever really was. Did I really think that what I've been saying and doing and putting together was the end all and be all, as good as it gets? Good God, no.

So what do they want, all those 'theys' who buy the ads, pay my salary? He took a breath. *No, to hell with them. What do I want?—for my purposes, for my dream, for my telling? I want to know what happened before it happened, how the setup made it possible. Inevitable. Context, yeah, I want more context, damn it.*

Larry quickly pulled open his desk drawer and found Maya's piece of paper. Point number one: News embedded in ecol/econ/psych/demographic context.

That's exactly it. The peripherals that ... that define the center. Maya, I've got it! And what are we doing? Focusing ever narrower, looking ever more superficially, cutting out more and more of the context, going for good guy, bad guy bang-bang stuff, all the sexy without the setup, without the whole big structure and context. My God, Maya, you're brilliant! So big, so obvious, so missing.

Larry leapt for the phone and hit the 'Nora' button. Excitedly, he said, "Get me Fran in Manila. Wake her up, I don't care. I've got to talk to her."

◆ ◆ ◆

"Oh man, Larry," Fran groaned into her cell phone as she leaned over to click on the bedside lamp. Her hair was tousled, and in the blast of light, she scrunched her eyes, working every age line of her forty years. Naked, she had generous breasts and a solid build. In good light, she could be handsome if not pretty, with an edgy, compelling energy.

Her Manila hotel room was small and upscale enough to be anywhere. The bedside clock radio said 1:03 a.m. A round table held her closed laptop computer, a dormant beehive ringed by spiral-bound notebooks, printed papers, and over-flowing ashtrays. Two water glasses smudged with fingerprints, lip-prints, and dregs of red wine sat on the mantel of a fake fireplace. An empty wine bottle lay dead on the carpet.

A man's smooth brown hand slid under Fran's arm, groping for a breast. "Stop it. It's my boss," she said. The man, a thirty-something, well-made Filipino, reluctantly withdrew and pouted behind Fran. She continued into the phone, "It's one in the bloody morning, and my report's almost done. I'm not going anywhere right now, doing anything, seeing anyone, I don't care what just blew up, broke or fell from the sky."

"Fran, I'm sorry, but I've got to talk. It's important."

She ran a hand through her hair. "You alright?"

"No. I'm painted into a corner here, and I can't wait for the paint to dry to get out. Randy just outdid himself, he's driving me nuts. If he ever wangles a production budget out of his Sugar Uncle, we're dead. He's running full tilt on empty. It's all reactive, copy-cat stuff. I keep telling him that faster, harder, younger, glitzier—they're not good enough. I want different, I want a different operating principle, and I know what it is now, I've got it figured. It's sort of retro', but with all our new technology and integration, it's hot too, it's where we've got to go."

"So slow down a bit, at least until I get into overdrive with you."

"Listen, I met someone and she got me thinking, I mean really thinking, about what's wrong, what's missing in the big picture, and it's so obvious. The answer's in the peripherals, the structure and context that define every story. We've got to get back to that, we've got to focus hard on the peripherals."

Fran laughed. "Focus on the peripherals—isn't that an oxymoron?"

Larry chuckled. "Maybe, but I'm good at it. The old lady's absolutely right."

"What old lady?"

"I'll tell you when you're back, maybe introduce you to her. Right now, we've got to talk about what she said. And wrote. She's brilliant."

"Larry, Larry, what you smokin'?"

Larry laughed again. "Herbs." He felt the pebble in the sachet. "With a little stone. Fran, I'm dead sober, and I want you to try this. We've got to stop going for the central, core, obvious stuff—chasing firetrucks. We can pick that up from any number of other sources, cheap and dirty. Hit the edges, look farther into context than you've ever looked before. Go blind. Go exploring."

"Uh-uh, Larry. Twenty years into snooping, this old news-hound ain't stumbling around blind anywhere."

"No, not blind, I don't mean that. I mean looking deeper into the ecological, economic, psychological, and demographic contexts. These are the things that define the mess in the middle, you know what I mean?"

"So the immediate peripheral *and* mess in this middle—are you listening?—is that I'm buck naked in Snoozeville with a touch of wine lag."

"Aw jeez, I'm sorry. The bind here's getting worse, and if I don't come up with something, the rent-a-nephew's going do us all in."

"So let's get practical. How's this going to work? Connect it to the firetruck I'm chasing here."

"Okay, I'll wing it. Sex tourism in the Far East. You go to Bangkok, Jakarta, Manila, wherever the fire's still out of control. You go to villages where the girls come from, you talk to the local pimps and fly-in johns, you do the up-date. That's all obvious, central. You do it better than anyone else, but it's still just the mess in the middle. I want you to tie it to land use, have you done that? That's the ecological context. You've done the economics, I know, that's a given, except the 'eco' of economics and ecologics means 'home', right? and these girls are from homes, so link them, link the ecology and economy of their homes. Tie it to demographics, the number of young people there, and their place on the land, in their villages, as extras to sacrifice to the cities and the big bad world. Then there's the psychology ...."

Fran said, "Yeah okay, I'm getting it. I've touched on some of this but not the eco-freako stuff, that's separate."

"But it isn't. It's about which people fit where, and that's ground level—and I mean *ground* level—stuff. Rich people from one land—one *land*—coming to screw people from another *land*. You see, it sounds like a peripheral, but it's the bottom line."

Fran sighed. "Oh boy. No, I haven't talked to any ecologists and farmers, for God's sake, and who knows what they'd say. I guess that's reason enough to cover them, since I doubt anyone else has even thought to do it. Psychologists, demographers ... yeah, that makes sense, but listen, I'm just about wrapped up, and it's not a bad report—no worse than usual."

"Your usual is great, and you know it. Now I want you to do the unusual, so we can show these bastards where the news is going, what the future looks like—and it's not the Randy-dandy shit he's pelting me with. I want you to hit the peripherals, go to the edges like you've never done before, and file me the best bit of context reporting done since ... since Rosebud hit the screen."

"What?"

"'Citizen Kane', remember? The whole thing was about what was missing, and when that little piece of the puzzle showed up at the end—a little peripheral but core detail—everything made sense."

Fran's date snuggled against her backside. She muffled the phone's speaker with one hand and pushed the guy away with the other. "C'mon, back off!" He pulled away and ran his hand up her outer thigh. She held it there.

"Huh?" Larry puzzled.

"Company, Larry. I've got company, and he's a pest. You too, sweetheart, but I love you. I'll do some more interviews tomorrow. Ecologists, shrinks, number-spinners, demographers, farmers out standing in their fields. Rosebud growers, cutters, sniffers, sellers ...."

Larry laughed. "Great. It's going to work, trust me. Thanks, hey? Bye."

Fran clicked off the phone and turned to her bed partner. He sulked, eyes dark, and said, "You call me a pest."

"Well, you are when you come on like that when I'm talking with the boss. Now listen, the bossman says I need the whole bed right to the edges."

He moved in to kiss and fondle her. She pulled away. "No, I'm serious. You've got to go. I've got to get some sleep, I've got to ...."

"C'mon, babe-e-e." His eyes smoldered.

"No, I thought I was done, but I've got a pile more work to do and a kid to get home to in a couple of days, you understand? I'm out of time and right out of the mood now too."

"I got a mood too, babee-e, you understand?" His face hardened; the fingers of his free hand itched to curl into fists.

"No, don't," she said, matching his hard eyes. "Don't even think it." Then she dropped her voice to say, "What you've got to think about now is that pretty girl at the samosa stand, the one you called 'sister'."

He grinned. "I didn't wanna make you jealous." He shook his fanned fingers. "She's hot, lemme tell you." He pulled on his dress slacks, then white shirt.

As he tucked in ends and buckled his belt, Fran said, "So I'm your new sister. Don't make her jealous."

"Hah!" he snorted, shoving his feet into sandals. Standing before an entryway mirror, he finger-combed his hair.

"I'm sorry," Fran said softly.

Without a reply, he left, slamming the door.

"Peripherals," she muttered as she twisted the deadbolt shut. Thunk. "Definitely not my strength."

The next night, Fran worked until late on her sex trade story in the editing room of a Manila TV production facility. She spliced in new video footage and sound bites gathered that day in an effort to broaden the story as Larry had requested. "Damn," she muttered periodically. It wasn't working. Some of the new stuff was great, especially an unexpectedly brilliant analysis by a local ecology professor, but she'd have to redo the story to make it fit.

Larry's point exactly, she thought wryly. It's a different and better report within that context. What to do? Spend another week shaping up this new spin or fudge it as best she could? She looked up to a row of clocks on the wall above the editing console, set to local time in London, Athens, Delhi, Hong Kong, Los Angeles, and New York. It was 3:16 p.m. on the eastern U.S. seaboard. There was no question what she'd do. She reached for the in-room phone, punched in a long string of numbers, then drummed her fingers impatiently as she waited to connect.

Finally, her face lit into a wide smile. "Hey darlin', happy birthday, my beautiful girl. Happy Feb' twelve, thirteen years wonderful."

"Hi Mom," Dhyan [Thee-an] said flatly into her cordless phone. Her build was as solid as Fran's but twenty-seven years more tender. A new blue T-shirt bumped over developing breasts, bearing a small gold mandala of Kanji symbols and a Japanese monk circled by "DHYANA BUDDHIST RETREAT."

She sat on the side of her unmade bed, a pink and white frilly jumble in her pink, white, and fuzzy all-American, little-girl bedroom. Stuffed critters galore, shoulder to shoulder on every flat surface, kept her company. Family photos in cartoon character frames lined the dresser top. Dhyan picked up a snapshot of herself at age six in Mickey Mouse ears at Disneyland, giggling on Fran's lap.

"You sound down, sweetheart. I'm sorry. Did you get my present?"

"Yeah."

"So? Does it fit? Is it okay?"

"Yeah, it's definitely me."

"Is that a strike or a ball? The shirt's the real thing, sweetheart, right from the top monkey at the Dhyana monastery. Well, commercial wing, charity division."

Dhyan said nothing.

"So, this call's supposed to cheer us up, bridge the gap, get that long distance feeling. What can I do from here?"

"Nothin'. Where's 'here'?"

"Still Manila. I e-mailed you yesterday. You didn't get it?"

"Didn't check."

"Oh."

"It's not my birthday over there anyhow. It's like over, done."

"Yeah, but here doesn't count. It's the twelfth there, where my heart is. You were born right about now, you know that? Man, I was there and screamin'. Toughest, absolutely best day of my life."

Dhyan managed a wry half-smile.

"Dhyan?"

"Yeah."

"I'm here two more days, then I'm home as fast as jets fly. We'll celebrate then, okay? Big party, sleepover, night out, whatever you want. How are today's plans going?"

"They're not. Dad and Cindy are taking me to a stupid movie."

"What happened to the party?"

"Cindy-rella wanted a stupid dress-up thing, no boys, and get this: she said she'd hire us a clown—oh wow! I said no fucking way."

"You didn't?"

"Uh-huh."

"Oh boy."

"I mean, dress-ups and a clown! I'm not a little girl!" Dhyan swept everything off the top of her dresser with a quick slide of her forearm. "I don't need this shit." It landed with a clatter.

"What's that?" Fran asked.

"Nothing." A framed wedding photo of her dad and Cindy landed face up. It had doubled as a Christmas card with "Season's Greetings" floating over their heads. Her dad wore a tuxedo, an amiable-looking executive, pudgy in his satin cumberbund. Cindy was a plump, painted Christmas angel perfect for atop the decorator tree in the background. Dhyan cracked the picture glass under the heel of her sneaker.

"You okay?"

"Yeah, I'm fine. How are you?"

"Tired, honey. Wishing I was home. It kills me not to be there with you. I've got to make some changes, big changes." Blips on the line punctured her last words. She checked call display on her phone. "Damn, I've got to answer it. It's Larry. I'm really sorry, sweetheart. I love you, my gorgeous girl, you hear? I love you, and we'll have a happy birthday together next week, okay?"

"Sure. Bye." Dhyan clicked off the phone. She still held the photo of herself and her mom at Disneyland. Fighting tears, she took it from the frame and methodically tore it into tiny pieces.

Larry sat back in his office chair, his dark-circled eyes rising like Kilroy over the battleground of his desk. He talked via speakerphone. "Looks like you're it, Fran. What've you heard from there?"

"About what?"

"The crash. Real mess, rough terrain, I know, but you're closest ...."

"What crash? I've been nose to the grindstone, eyes on the big wide edges."

"West Orient jet down on Mount Sicapoo, just north of you. Get on a rescue flight if you can, rent something otherwise."

Fran groaned, "Oh shit."

"Sorry, Fran. I'm glad it's you though, because I want this covered the way we discussed—context, context, context. 'Understanding', Fran, what stands under it. The whole equation, from the math to the aftermath. The big salami wouldn't know a big-picture, bottom-line peripheral if it bit him, but to hell with him."

Fran laughed. "I'm not sure I would either. What's the little wiener want?"

"Bunch of cheap new cub reporters flying around like buckshot, doing handheld shots till we're all puking. We've got to show them. Go light on the bloody stuff, the obvious crap. Get the ground level story from flight central to the crash zone, look for the ecologic, economic, and psychological factors that everyone else steps over and misses but define the heart of it. And when you check right to the edges in the last scene, don't toss out and burn any old sleds called Rosebud thinking they don't matter. Damn, I wish I could be there. This is exciting."

"In principle, Larry, it's thrilling. In fact, dear heart, it sucks. Not this approach or that, but I told Dhyan I'd be home in a few days."

"So give it two weeks, okay? I want you back by month end."

Fran sighed deeply, her eyes blank.

Larry said, "Listen, I'm sorry. I don't plan the news."

"Well, someone should, damn it. Let's get some control at a causal level, what's all this react, react stuff?"

Larry laughed. "So let's show some causal understanding, at least, and blow every other report out of the water. Don't worry about filing right off.

We'll tap other sources for the quick and dirties. I'm really glad you're there. You're the best."

♦ ♦ ♦

"Dhya-a-an! Birthday dinner!" Cindy sang out in perfect pitch, the large lady decreeing the opera begin. She, Ralph, and their two boys, aged four and six, seated themselves at the dining table laden with Disney character balloons, favors, and complete plastic table setting down to napkin rings. They wore their Sunday best: slacks, dress shirts, and ties for the boys; purple satin and lace dress for Mama.

Dhyan emerged from her trashed hide-out where she'd cleared a few more surfaces and tore up a few more photos. Her navel winked from between a tiny black skirt and tight red sweater. She wore stylish boots, wild lacquered hair with red streaks, and Gothic face. Ralph's eyes popped at her curves, costume, and ghoulish makeup.

Cindy blurted, "Oh my goo'ness!" a là Shirley Temple. "Now don't you just wish you'd had that dress-up party with your friends? We could have had so much fun modeling all kinds of clothes and looks and Mardi Gras get-ups."

"God help us all," Ralph muttered under his breath.

Cindy produced a platter of Ralph's barbecued hamburgers, Dhyan's favorite and done to perfection. "Pass," Dhyan said, flopping herself into a chair.

"Pardon?" Cindy asked.

"No more dead cows, thank you. I'm giving them up for Lent and forever after that."

Ralph sighed. "Oh c'mon. You going all trendy on me? Can I barbecue you an egg?"

Dhyan rolled her eyes.

"I wish you'd told me," Ralph said. "I could've made soy burgers, you know."

"Little dead soys, yeah, I like those." Dhyan flashed a fake grin at Cindy as she spread mustard and ketchup on buns for her boys.

"Dead soys!" the six-year-old burst out laughing. "Beans," he explained to his little brother, then made farting sounds. "Dead beans. Ptht, ptht, ptht."

"Ee-uu, stinky!" the little one shrieked, holding his nose.

"Sh-h-h!" Cindy demanded with sharp looks and stiffened posture. The silliness stopped, and she kept it in strict check throughout a tense meal.

After, she cleared the table, turned down the lights, and brought in Dhyan's ice-cream cake. A ring of thirteen candles lit the way for Minnie

Mouse's pink-trimmed, all-icing sports car. Cindy led singing, "Happy Birthday to You," her voice a lovely liquid stream through otherwise bumpy terrain.

Ralph took a couple of photos, then Cindy arranged a shot with Ralph and the boys behind Dhyan blowing out her candles. Dhyan let them burn shorter and shorter while holding her half-brothers back from puffing at them. When Ralph and Cindy were nearly as riled as the boys, she limply blew at the blaze. Six candles snuffed.

The older boy teased, "Dhyan's got boyfriends, lots of kissy boyfriends!"

She quickly licked her thumb and forefinger and killed one flame, then another, to the boys' amazement. Ralph said, "Don't, Dhyan."

Dhyan licked her fingers again and reached to nip more. Cindy lightly smacked her hand away. "Dhyan, behave yourself—it's your birthday."

Dhyan got up. "Excuse me, I feel sick. I'm going to lie down in my room."

Cindy shrugged exaggeratedly at Ralph, who made a big puzzled face in return. The youngest son aped them so vigorously that he toppled off his chair. Both boys exploded in uncontrollable laughter and repeated the performance, complete with 'drunken' falling. Cindy tried to stop them. Ralph watched, stunned and shaking his head.

The noise and confusion in the dining room allowed Dhyan to walk out the front door and down the street.

Dhyan's exit tripped the outdoor motion-sensor lights, which lit the large, upscale Cape Cod house, a recent replica in classic good taste. Its clipped yard and double garage blended with the neighbors' matching notions of perfect living. No one noticed her.

Through chilly darkness, she doglegged down several tree-lined suburban streets to another gabled New England house, a variation on the same theme. All drapes were pulled, every light on. She knocked on the door and waited. No one answered. She bing-bonged the doorbell and waited longer.

She looked around. Next door, she could make out a dark old gingerbread place, with a sagging verandah set in mid-winter brambles. "Oo-ho-o," she shivered, hugging herself to keep warm. "Witchy." She held her finger hard on the doorbell. "C'mon, c'mon, I'm freezing."

An older teenage girl opened the door, letting loose the rich smell of pot and a battle of stereos from every room. She squinted through wide black pupils at Dhyan. "Hi. What's the password?"

"It's my birthday."

"You're kidding?"

Dhyan shook her head.

"So you need a party. Alright!" The young woman pulled Dhyan in by the arm, kicked the door shut with her foot, and quickly locked it. The party blasted hot and hazy before them, wasted kids in every room.

"What's your name?"

"Dhyan."

"Bree-ann?"

"Whatever."

"So listen, Bree-ann, only one rule: keep it down so the cops don't kill us before the old guys get home."

"When's that?"

"Next week. We've been going for like, three days. Enjoy."

Next door, Mae worked at her dining table, looking old beyond age. The party pulsed beyond her windows while she scribed in blessed silence *sans* hearing aid. She hummed the occasional snatch of something resembling song. Her handwritten notes found their way into the "Mashyoi" file.

When the telephone rang, she went through the usual ritual of fitting in her teeth and hearing aid while Byron bounced and barked. She was quick this time, only six rings to "Hello-o?"

"Mrs. Singer-Jones, Nikos Platithou here," he said loudly. "In Thessaloniki."

"Yes dear, I can hear you. How did it go?"

"As planned, I think. I left Alma safe. And Mrs. Solari ... I am sorry to tell you that your old friend is gone, apparently the way the good Lord intended."

"Bless you, Nikos. So difficult for you—all of you. Poor Maya. What time, exact time, did she die?"

"1:07 a.m., February 12th, Greek time. She was so brave, an angel. Alma too, she is a nice lady so much like her mother it is ... amazing. We had a small incident leaving Chryson, but we made it safe to Litochoron."

"Good. How are you doing?"

"Fine. I am always fine. And you?"

"I miss you, of course, but the young people next door keep checking to see if I'm okay. They think I'll phone the police or emergency if I run out of groceries." She chuckled. "You can relax now, dear, and have a holiday. I'll see you in ten days."

"I work here too, *ne*? I have olives to ship and feta, worry beads, perhaps even Olympus tea if I can find a supplier. Mrs. Solari's last drink."

"Oh no, Nikos, it's too rare. Don't waste your time."

"Oh." He paused. "Okay. I will call you again before I fly home."

"Thank you, dear. Thank you for everything. And good-bye."

By midnight, Dhyan had no desire to know who she was or where. Perched on a stool at a bar, that was certain. Shoeless, with bare legs and tiny skirt riding high up her thighs, yes. Too warm in her short sweater but no change of tops available, and even if there were, too hazy to do it.

She took another toke of weed and spun further into oblivion. Who handed it to her wasn't discernable through unfocused eyes. Dhyan reached slowly, giggling at her own seemingly detached hand, for a frosty bottle of beer put near her by a thoughtful person who had only drank half of it. She poured some into her mouth, over her thirsty, grateful tongue, and down her gullet. Some down her sweater too, but who cared?

Across the room, far from Dhyan's sphere and thoughts, another tarted up young woman turned a cold eye on a taut young man, his muscled frame and crotch bulging for her, and said, "Goodnight, asshole."

He reached sloppily for her. "You can't go. You're mine, you hear me."

"So watch this, jerk." She waved tauntingly, then dared turn on her heel and leave. She walked out of the room. She walked out of the house. She walked down the street into the night.

He tried to stumble on drunken feet after her, but bumped hard into the first doorframe. He raged blindly, "Don't turn on a fucking Ferrari, you fucking whore, unless you're up for the fucking ride!"

Someone laughed. "Fucking Ferrari in your dreams." Someone else said, "You're not even a fucking Jeep."

"Fucking dinky toy," a sweet-voiced young woman added, cracking up everyone close and sober enough to hear.

He walked to the bar, took the bottle from Dhyan's hand, and said, "Quit drinking my beer, you slut." She didn't respond. He finished it, then said, "I'm talkin' to you, slut. You listen to me."

She turned to him with blank eyes, nobody home.

He noticed a dartboard hung on a nearby wall and started angrily pulling the darts out of it. "Play with me," he demanded of Dhyan.

She looked up and saw the dartboard for the first time in hours. She giggled. "Where'd that come from?"

"I said, play fucking darts with me." Holding half a dozen darts, he walked across the room to where his date had left him. He threw a dart out the door she took, a hard, whizzing effort. It lodged in a wall of the next room. He threw the next dart at the laughter behind him. It glanced off a tiffany lampshade. He quickly made three more furious, lucky misses at furnishings and walls, then with the last dart, lined up Dhyan and let it fly at her.

It zinged true and stuck deep into her thigh. She barely flinched, didn't look down. Someone noticed her lack of reaction and laughed, "Look at that! A cartoon, man." Others looked and snickered. No one helped.

A thick gob of bright blood oozed up and slowly drooled down her thigh. "Hey Bree-ann!" she heard the girl who answered the door say. "Wake up. Look at your leg."

Dhyan looked down. "Wow," she mouthed. She touched the thick liquid, tasted it. "Blood," she whispered. Gradually, her rubbery hand fumbled the dart out of her skin, out of her leg, and dropped it to the floor. Dark red drops splatted beside it. She reached for the beer bottle and tipped it up to her mouth. Empty. Damn.

She reached further for another, unopened bottle. With concerted effort, she twisted the cap off it and sloshed a drink into and over herself. Mm-m. That was good.

The dart-thrower tripped into a side table, then vomited on a mess of snacks and dope dregs. "What the fuck you doin', man?" a big guy said. "You're outta here." An even bigger fellow hoisted and bounced him from the house. He stumbled down the street as nameless and faceless as he'd entered.

Dhyan crawled behind the bar and slept there until mid-morning. She woke up cold and stiff, her mouth disgusting, and her head aching off the Richter Scale.

She found a bathroom. Sitting on the toilet, she held her head in her hands, elbows on her thighs. "Holy shit!" she said, seeing a track of dried blood and the swollen source of it. "What's that?"

She got up and flushed the toilet, startling herself when she saw the girl in the huge over-sink mirror. Her makeup had slid down her face, more ghoulish now than Gothic. She wiped smudged mascara from sad cheeks onto grubby fingers. Holding her wild hair back, she searched in a drawer for an elastic or clip. A scrunchy surfaced, gaudy with sequins. Sure, why not?

She rummaged further for a clean facecloth but gave up and grabbed a dried one hanging from a hook by the sink. She splashed cold water at her face, then wet the cloth and put it over her throbbing thigh, water coursing down to her bare feet.

She gulped cool draughts straight from the tap. "Ah-h," she sighed. "Water. I love you." She laughed wryly. "At least I love something."

Next, the cloth scrubbed away the painted lady and found the kid underneath. She chose the newest toothbrush of half a dozen at hand, loaded up toothpaste, then hesitated. She ran her tongue around her teeth, grimaced a "yuk," and brushed hard.

Baggy jeans and sweatshirt hung on hooks on the bathroom door. They fit over her skimpy outfit and then some—instant little girl lost in them. A make-up drawer yielded some burgundy lipstick, twisted onto pouting lips as she made her haughtiest *Glamour* face.

She found life in the house by following the sounds of a boiling electric kettle and the clink of spoons stirring sugar and more sugar into stiff instant coffee. In the trashed, filthy kitchen, half a dozen kids sat nursing hangovers around a table, wincing at every sound, loud breathing included. "Hey, here comes the dartboard," croaked a ragged young man.

"Bree-ann, the human bull's eye," her hostess added.

"Is that what this red thing is?" Dhyan asked, circling her fingers over sore thigh.

They laughed uproariously, holding their fragile heads. She joined them— for two more days.

On the elm-lined street in front of Mae's old home, a light blue sedan pulled up and crunched onto the gravel driveway. By daylight, the house's gingerbread trim, broad veranda, and entangled rose trellises spoke of former wealth and house-proud care. Its paint was peeling now and details falling away. The house could be restored with much elbow grease; another decade of neglect would finish it.

The driver, a big-haired blond woman in sunglasses and beige pantsuit, got out. She carried a canvas tote. On Mae's sloping porch, she listened through the front door to the faint singing, more like wailing, coming from within. She smiled fondly, then rapped a serpent-shaped brass knocker.

In the living room, Byron barked at Mae, her black wig askew on her head and teeth atop the piano. Black rubber boots worked the pedals. Her sweater and hose were chartreuse today; her turquoise skirt matched stone beads. She continued to play and sing. Byron growled and pulled at her boots, forcing her to stop and listen. The rapper sounded again, louder this time.

"Ah, I see—or rather, hear. Good lad, Byron."

Mae's teeth found her mouth as she shuffled to the door. "Alma?" she said, peering at the blond woman in sunglasses who smiled broadly. Mae clapped her hands. "Oh, I'm so pleased! Come in quick."

Alma slipped in, removed her shades and wig, and shook out her hair. "Hello, dear Mae. I've got some D.C. business—always—so stopped by on route to thank you, and to leave a small gift for Nikos. He was brilliant. We had a close call, far too close, and he saved me with ease."

"He said there was an incident. I'm sorry. He's a good man. I've been counting on him for years now, since Irwin died. I knew you'd be safe with him."

"He left me at Litochoron. I got here with no trouble, no eyes upon me, thank goodness. It's been harrowing nonetheless."

"Of course, poor dear. Would you like coffee? Tea?"

"Tea, yes. Perhaps some of this." Alma pulled a small wooden box from her large purse. She slid the top of it open to reveal a neat row of cotton sachets, rich with the smell of her mother's tea. "This is for you. I have another box for you to give to Nikos."

Mae took the box and inhaled deeply. "The scent of Maya," she said softly, blinking back tears. "Maya forever."

"My last cup with was her. We could have this one with her too, if you wouldn't mind viewing one of her old films with me."

"What a lovely idea. They're all in the basement, as you know. Fetch as many as you like while I fix the tea. The projector, screen, everything's there."

Mae headed for her cluttered kitchen. Alma disappeared down a stairwell off the living room. The musty, dusty smell of the house grew thicker with each downward step.

A bare 100-watt lightbulb threw garish shadows on floor-to-ceiling shelves heaped with the trappings of Mae's long years of teaching drama, music, and visual arts. Old props, painting equipment, music stands, and books filled every nook and leaned one against another. Masks peered through empty eyes; drums had sat mute for decades; hand-carved models of canoes and paddles lay beached long after gliding through an early television show. Slow mildew and quick spiders worked this dark world.

An old film projector, like a small dinosaur, sat atop an antique white ice box about four feet tall. A metal tube leaned nearby, containing a rolled-up projector screen.

Alma opened the rusty latch on the cabinet's top door to reveal a dozen round galvanized canisters of film. She wiped the dust from a few rims—dust inside the ice box even—to reveal their titles written in Mae's bold hand. She chose two, "Maha Prajapati" and "Mary", considered them for a moment, then put "Mary" back.

While Alma made two trips carrying the projector, screen, and film to the living room, Mae prepared tea in her cramped kitchen. Her notes covered an alcove table and the top of a rounded 1950s fridge. Every other horizontal surface was covered with cooking implements, books, and stacks of dishes all matted with greasy dust from long disuse.

She had been an active hostess throughout her prime years, throwing great dinner parties for every artistic connection she could make from near and far. Her parents did the same from their house down the street, until her mother died suddenly of unshakable influenza, and her father's heart gave out shortly after. Mae sold their home to pay off Irwin's gambling debts on the condition that he repent and reform. His promise lasted half a year.

From being orphaned—that's how she felt despite her advanced age—to retiring from teaching, then widowed a decade later, she gradually stopped making brilliant parties for people who meant to invite her in return but seldom did. Old friends died; old neighbors left; newcomers moved in, too busy even for tea. As her research deepened to envelop her, she ate from the bags, cans, and boxes littering the narrow countertops and from the fresh produce bin in the fridge. Maya had been her only at-home mealtime guest in twenty years, and she ate as Mae did.

Nikos squired Mae about several times a week, to shop and to visit her beloved university library. She refused to get a computer and onto the Internet, sticking to her love of old, primary sources and her trust in handwritten copies. Larry dropped by every few months, and lately he'd taken to calling her every week or two. Because she was getting so old, she guessed, although she still felt more like the solid woman she'd been than the lightweight crone reflected by mirrors. She took him to restaurants two or three times a year but had never cooked for him. He'd had no taste of her former culinary prowess and sparkling social life.

Larry stayed in her thoughts as the water rumbled to a boil in the stovetop kettle. He didn't know about Maya yet. Poor Larry, he'd be upset. She put two Olympus teabags into her old Brown Betty pot and poured the boiling water onto them, releasing the delicate scent of far-away climes and a world of memories. She must let Larry know. In person, of course. Soon.

Mae set up the cups and saucers that she and Maya had last used together. As she fumbled gingersnaps from a bag and tucked two onto each saucer, Alma popped her head into the kitchen and said, "I've found everything we need, I think."

"Good. Clear a spot on the sofa for yourself, will you? I'll be with you in a minute."

In the living room, Alma moved a handful of current newspapers from sofa to floor and settled herself. The topmost newspaper, she noted, was folded to an inside page and had a small rectangle clipped from it.

In the kitchen, Mae poured the golden tea with pleasure and trembling hands. It snaked into the cups, which then rattled in their saucers as she walked to the living room. Lord Byron danced round her legs. Alma watched alertly, ready to rush to Mae's aid, but a noisy cup arrived safely to her hands, cookies neatly sogging up the sloshed tea.

"Mm-m," Alma said. "I haven't been so relaxed in days."

Mae sat down in her old chair. The mop-dog snuggled at her feet. Alma continued, "I brought up just one film, so I won't interrupt you for long."

"We can watch as many as you like, for as long as you like, dear. It will be wonderful to see your mother so young and lively."

"I miss her...," Alma sighed deeply, "inordinately." Her eyes brightened with tears. "Life played her very different cards than it has me, and I mean that only in an assessing, not complaining way. She took part in and fashioned so many pivotal moments while I ... I seem to be less connected, less able to act as she did and effect change. Without her, I feel rudderless, not ready yet to take the lead as she did."

Mae shook her head. "Oh Alma, you know her doubts, her grave concerns that she wasn't doing enough even as she worked with Churchill, Ghandi, Mr. Bell ...."

"Einstein, Wallenburg, Bethune, Kennedy ...."

"Such a list, so many dreamers and doers. Such disappointments too, when madness and war overwhelmed the world, and she cried for every hurting soul and her inability to make, she thought, the slightest difference. She always felt that she could do more and better, despite knowing that she planted endless seeds and nurtured a few to full fruition, none more important than you, Pavla, and Luna—her greatest successes and legacy."

"That's true, but ...."

"But she never gave up, that's the only 'but'."

Alma struggled to smile. "Oh Mae, you're so right. Thank you." She took a sip of healing tea. "I can't tell you how much I need this."

Mae watched her lovingly for a moment, then said quietly, "I miss her terribly too."

Alma nodded. Long seconds later, she asked, "How is your work going?"

"Very well, dear. I've covered most of the groundwork, which frees me at last to work on deductions and connections. Frees me to honor your mother's request and ...." Mae's voice quavered. "... look for a biographer."

Alma said steadily, "Yes, it worries me too. We talked at length and agreed that the assignment of a biographer should take a natural course, unfolding without being forced. We'll keep it actively in mind, that is, but won't choose until the best candidate comes to light him or herself. Now that Mother's wish is spoken, the right time and writer will appear."

Mae closed her eyes and sighed deeply. "Wise to the end, and beyond."

"Freeing you to work without interruption. So tell me, what deductions and connections are you making?"

Mae named several goddesses and ancient women identified differently in different locations and times that she was increasingly certain were one and the same. Alma knew the thrust of her research, so they spoke quickly and cryptically. Mae finished her tea and gave Byron her last half cookie.

She concluded that within five years she would have the lineage whittled down to three-hundred core names, under which all others could be arranged.

"What an undertaking," Alma said appreciatively, rising to close Mae's heavy red drapes by their clunky pull. "All this work, here and in your amazing head."

"The trick," Mae said, "is to get it out, so I don't take a stitch of it with me."

"But we all take treasures with us when we go. It can't be helped."

"Only resisted," Mae said as her bony old hands expertly threaded Maya's 1922 film into the projector sitting on the piano bench. "The effort keeps us upright—and progressing, if we're lucky."

"How intact is the film?" Alma asked, stooping to plug in the projector.

Mae squinted closely at a section of the celluloid. "It's excellent. Time has been far kinder to it than to me. Your mother's clever chemistry and cool, dry storage, it all adds up. There." She flicked on the projector's light bulb, which threw a flood of soft light onto the droopy old screen.

Alma said, "I'm so glad Pavla has her grandmother's bent for science and technology. I've neglected them, and I wonder at this late date if that's been my biggest failing …." Her voice trailed off as she rattled the drapes shut, sealing out the day completely. "… in terms of measurable outcomes."

"What? Because you've devoted your life to artistic rather than scientific explorations? Science saves lives, dear—and old films and kings' ransoms—but the arts will save humanity, mark my words."

Alma laughed. "Mae, you're the best tonic ever. Thank you."

Mae wound the film feed manually until the screen showed a fuzzy bull's eye, which she focused. Maya's talkie was a forerunner to Dr. Lee De Forest's sound-on-film system, which he first showed publicly in 1923. Mae flicked a switch and sprockets whirred.

A brilliant sitar solo underscored by gentle symphonic waves rose with the title "Maha Prajapati", then ebbed and flowed throughout the film.

MAHA PRAJAPATI wears a sari and sits crying under an ancient tree in a garden. She's played by Maya Solari as a radiant teenager, identical to a younger Pavla.

MAHA MAYA appears, largely pregnant, beside the weeping girl and draws her into an embrace, which fails to comfort. She's played by Maya's mother Sunoqua, indistinguishable from a younger Alma.

MAHA PRAJAPATI
Must it be this way, Mother?

MAHA MAYA
(nodding her head)
We have the baby boy, without trace or trouble.

MAHA PRAJAPATI
But we can get another newborn orphan, another time. Do you have to die in childbirth now?

MAHA MAYA
You're crying as if I really will. Yes, I must go. Lao-Tse and Confucius need me. Better to raise the boy thinking his mother dead than knowing she abandoned him. My work ends here, and yours begins.

MAHA PRAJAPATI
(whispers)
I'll be so alone, so lonely ....

MAHA MAYA
You'll have little Siddhartha to love, and you'll be queen. You'll be busy and fulfilled, believe me. And you know, of course, that it takes such traumas, such loss and gain of great love, to engender the next of us. This perhaps will be yours.

MAHA PRAJAPATI
It's so unfair. You begot me through a tumble, literally, into the greatest of love. Must I be abandoned and my heart break to trigger the miracle?

MAHA MAYA
(forefinger to Prajapati's lips)
Never compare. You will fall in love with Siddhartha, more than you can guess. How fate determines your motherhood is beyond your

MAHA MAYA (continued)
control, but within your acceptance. You must
live and love with that.

We are one, but not the same. The important
thing is that we continue and that our work
reaches understanding ears.

CUT TO:

KING SHUDDHODANA, a gray-haired monarch standing in the garden. He wears loose silk robes and carries a newborn baby in his arms. He cries over the flower-laden byre of Maha Maya, no longer pregnant, lying in suspended animation, expertly feigning death.

SHUDDHODANA
(to the baby)
She was too old to bear you, too delicate to survive. My prayers for a son are answered, at the
price of my queen. What a bittersweet blessing.

Shuddhodana gently touches Maha Maya's cheek.

SHUDDHODANA (continuing)
Where have the years gone? Twenty years line
your face, yet to my eyes you are as beautiful as
the day we met.

FADE TO:

An elephant carrying Maha Maya as a young woman, played by Maya Solari. Young King Shuddhodana and a small royal entourage crowd near its feet.

SHUDDHODANA (voice over)
Listen, my son, my pride, my heir: she appeared
before me on an elephant, a vision of perfect
beauty. I halted the elephant to better see its
lovely burden, which startled the beast, and it
tossed her at my feet.

The young Maha Maya lies crumpled on the ground.

SHUDDHODANA (voice over)
She nearly died. I saved her and wed her with my eyes the minute hers opened to mine. We had a child—alas a girl—as quickly as a child can come. Then for nearly twenty years of sweetest love and devotion, nothing, no more children, neither girl nor boy.

CUT TO:

The king, standing next to Maya's byre, speaking to the baby.

SHUDDHODANA (continuing)
I had to have an heir, so bless her, at this late date, she and the gods graced me with you, the boy of my dreams. Siddhartha—'every wish fulfilled'. Except I overlooked wishing that your mother live too and look, there she lies beyond us forever. I am so sorry ...

(turns to hide his tears)
... so sorry.

CUT TO:

In the palace nursery, Prajapati hums a lullaby to baby Siddhartha in her arms.

MAHA PRAJAPATI
Mother was right, I adore you. You fill my heart with love. I'll raise you to be the wisest, best prince ever, the buddha of all buddhas. The wise men have come and proclaimed this; I'll make sure it comes true.

King Shuddhodana enters the room and happily scoops the child from her arms.

SHUDDHODANA
Lucky Siddhartha. You have Prajapati, the best of mothers, so much like her own.

SHUDDHODANA (continued)
(musses Prajapati's hair)
And I have a daughter for queen.

MAHA PRAJAPATI
(hesitantly)
Father, I have ... this is difficult to tell you. I have news. Remember how Mother's trauma of falling from the elephant and the joy of meeting you led quickly to my conception and birth?

The king smiles with the memory.

MAHA PRAJAPATI (continuing)
For me, the trauma of losing Mother and the joy of loving Siddhartha has gotten me with child, I'm sure.

SHUDDHODANA
What? With whom? The gossips will say it was I who ... oh, wicked thought.

MAHA PRAJAPATI
They treat me already as if I were Mother reincarnate, your younger wife returned. They're so forgetful and confused, they say that Mother fell from the elephant and got pregnant with Siddhartha. They can make a miracle of this birth too, if they care to, except I'll have a girl, I promise, and their tongues won't wag at all.

SHUDDHODANA
So who have you been with? Do you wish to marry him?

MAHA PRAJAPATI
(shaking her head)
No one. And no. I am Siddhartha's mother first, not another's wife. I do not wish ever to marry. I will raise him to be a great man, good and wise.

SHUDDHODANA
And no begging buddha, not my son. He'll be a
prince and warrior ...

MAHA PRAJAPATI
He'll make you proud, Father. Your name will be
remembered among the stars.

SHUDDHODANA
If this pregnancy doesn't bring us shame.

MAHA PRAJAPATI
(smiles, shakes her head)
I'll have a daughter like me, a girl like Mother.
Have we ever shamed you in any way?

SHUDDHODANA
No. Never.

MAHA PRAJAPATI
Then trust me. Us. We never will.

SHUDDHODANA
(lovingly)
You are so like your mother—a mystery I can see
and touch, but never fathom. Siddhartha will
have a little sister, and that will be a blessing.

Maha Prajapati studies the king for a long moment, smiling warmly.

MAHA PRAJAPATI
Thank you, Father. You are a great king ... in
every way.

She takes Siddhartha back to her arms.

MAHA PRAJAPATI
(to Siddhartha)
Remember that. Our father is the king who keeps
us safe and well, so we might live to fulfill what
is written in the heavens.

♦ ♦ ♦

Alma leapt to the projector to stop the film before the end of it flip-flapped free. Mae rewound it while Alma opened the drapes. Dust poofed and danced in the day's light. Alma said. "I needed to see Mother so young, and Grandmother Sunoqua too, younger than I am now. The longer view, the larger context settles my heart somehow."

Mae nodded, her eyes brimming with tears.

"Oh Mae, this has upset you. I'm so sorry."

Mae smiled. "In the best way. Davide was Shuddhodana, and that's his music. Composed, conducted, and played on sitar." She sighed. "Such genius. We met making that film, it could have been yesterday. He was a friend of your grandmother's, nearly twice my age. Now I'm over twice his when he died—we only had ten years together—but this silly old heart is still seventeen, still in love at first sight. First song."

Alma said, "Such little time you had together, yet how lucky you remain, enchanted forever. What a gift he gave you."

"Those were happy days for all of us, making the films and sound tracks. Exhausting too—loads of equipment and working night after night until dawn when space and equipment were available—but so fulfilling, so necessary and worthwhile. I was wardrobe mistress, make-up artist, prop assistant, and general go-fer. It's all in my basement still, except the elephant."

Alma laughed. "We should remake these films, shouldn't we? Pavla has a sabbatical year coming up. After this trip, I'm going to mind Luna while her mother winds up her research. Then we'll have time for a little retelling. We can advanced the stories to when the youngest daughters were Luna's age—what an exciting prospect, building on Mother's work while finding our balance again without her."

Mae said, "I'll help you any way I can. And your room here is always clean and ready."

"I may take you up on that. Mother always felt especially safe here, and your research makes this a treasured haven."

"I hope Pavla knows she's welcome too. With Luna."

"I'm sure she does, but ... it's not quite suitable for a baby at present."

Mae laughed. "It's impossible for a baby now, but I'll get Nikos to help me tidy up when he returns. He'll be delighted. He's been nagging me—gently, of course—for years."

"If you wish, but realistically, I suspect your work is far too important to disturb. I'm sure you know where every paper is, and if you spend time moving it around, you'll lose valuable working time."

"Yes, but life takes precedence over papers. All these notes about your past mean nothing if your future isn't secure."

"True, but please don't do this for me. For us. I'm happy surrounded by your industry—inspired by it. The only question—and this is difficult—is what will become of your house and this great legacy after you're gone? I'm sure you've got it all arranged."

"A young cousin is my soul heir. That's him." She pointed to the photo of Larry on the piano top. "Larry Singer, director of television news at Media 8."

"And you're Singer-Jones. I've never put them together but of course Mother knew."

"She finally met him the day before she flew to Mashad. She'd asked to see him, oh ... about six years ago when he took the director's chair, but he hasn't been ready until recently. He's a dear boy but very driven, unmindful of details and peripherals that don't serve him directly. He's starting to pay more attention now that, I'm sorry to say, he's hit a bit of a rough patch: overwork, mid-life considerations, some illness or condition he's keeping to himself. Your mother caught it right away, the minute she saw him, though she had no time to discuss the particulars. You'll see it too, I'm sure, when you meet him."

Alma smiled. "How did they get on?"

"She thought he might want to see her again. The truth is, she bowled him over."

"I bet. Mother's magic. I'll do my best to, at least, bowl him under."

"I'll arrange it when you're next in town, if you'd like. His partner is in theater, you might want to meet him too. Director, actor—he's at the Old Vaudeville Theater. It's called the OVT now, all fixed up and beautiful again."

"Lovely! We might be of some use to each other, particularly if he's caught rumors of my theater work. I've got something in mind that requires a venue."

"I'll have them both lined up for you whenever it suits you. Your room is always ready, that's a given. In perpetuity, I hope, when Larry's clued into the importance of this place as a refuge for you and your family."

"Well, we have it now, and for that, we're grateful. What of your papers, dare I ask?"

"If I drop dead tomorrow—and I have no such plans I assure you; my grandfather lived to be one-hundred-and-four, and I expect to live at least that long—Larry will follow the instructions of my will and send them to Sinclair's, then ... well, you know the route."

Alma nodded with a smile. "Back to Henry." She sipped the last of her cold tea and said, "Now a few key details then, alas, I must fly. Mother died at exactly 1:07 a.m., local time, February 12th."

"Yes, Nikos told me."

"It was spectacular, so much shattered rock, so many coincidentals, I'm sure." She pointed to Mae's newspaper with the small rectangle cut out. "Is that what you've been clipping?"

"Yes, and I'm going to get Larry checking global sources for me. He won't know why, but it will come together quickly for him as the evidence mounts and I fill him in."

"Good. Thank you, dear Mae, for everything. I knew I had to see you. I knew you'd bolster me, and you've done it beyond my best hopes."

At the door, Alma wrapped her arms warmly around tiny Mae, who absorbed the hug as if it were spring sunshine. Alma then donned her wig and dark glasses, and the big-haired blond vanished.

In the Philippines, a small helicopter headed for a clearing on the green flank of Mount Sicapoo. It landed in a no-man's land of scattered airliner wreckage and scorched earth surrounded by lush sub-tropical jungle.

Fran ducked from the chopper, its thundering wind swirling up dust and tearing at her hair and khaki work clothing. Two men, local officials in dark olive uniforms, followed her. The helicopter lifted off immediately. The men waved for Fran to come with them to the center of the crash zone. She shook her head and indicated with a wide arch of her hand that she was going to the periphery.

As she headed out, the departing helicopter's roar faded into gentler sounds of wind and birds. One of the men shouted to her in Tagalog-accented English, "The best wreckage is over here. And look ...." He pulled a rapidly growing vine from a scrap of debris. "The jungle grows fast. Just two days, we have this. In two weeks, you won't find anything. The edges are hopeless already."

Fran ignored him and walked through tangled greenery toward the rainforest. She flipped open a spiral-bound notebook and drew a rough sketch of the site with an X to mark where she started her search.

She fought her way through over-growth and under-, looking for scattered pieces of airplane and personal belongings among foliage and stems. She picked up a woman's dress shoe, tiny and immaculate, then put it back and noted its location.

She found a wallet-sized flip booklet of family photographs that included an old black-and-white portrait of a young Asian couple who, in recent color photos, had become the wrinkled patriarch and matriarch presiding over a grandchild's wedding. Tears were inevitable; she didn't fight them. She carefully returned the family to its leafy perch and marked their resting place on her sketch. This might be her story if nothing better showed up. In any case, she'd alert her escorts to whatever she found, so they could document and remove it.

Flies covered a small object. She waved her foot over it, and the insects swarmed up to reveal a decomposing hand with liquefying thumb and fingers. She started to retch but held it down. She drew a tiny stick-hand on her drawing and hurried on.

When she was nearly finished her loop, sweating and drained, the hair rose on her arms and neck. She stopped and looked around. She listened. Nothing. The men in the distance continued quietly collecting debris near the wreckage. She took another step, then stopped again, weirdly spooked. She shouted to one of the men, "Hey Sami, what eats people out here?"

He shouted back, "Only cannibals! Don't worry."

"What about snakes?"

"Talk nice to them!" He and his partner laughed. The other man muttered, "Stupid Yankees, do what they please, think later."

She backed away a few steps. What was giving her goosebumps? Where was it? There, that bush, that bramble of dark leaves. Gingerly, she returned to it and pulled it aside. A set of eyes bore into her—six-year-old eyes, an Asian-Caucasian girl huddled in an airplane blanket, staring inscrutably at her.

"My God! Oh my God," Fran gasped. "What are you doing here? Who are you?" She crouched to look at the girl, reaching cautiously out to her.

The girl was as beautiful as a doll. She didn't move. She didn't blink.

"Do you live here? How did you get here? Of course, you don't speak English."

"Yes, I do," the girl said with an American accent.

Fran's eyes widened as she whispered, "You're from the plane."

The girl barely nodded.

"You've been here two whole days?"

Another nod.

"You never cried? You never called for anyone?"

"They're all dead."

"Oh dear God. Oh sweetheart, we have to look after you. We have to get you water and food and ...." She pulled an edge of the blanket away from the girl. "Are you hurt? Is that why you didn't move?"

The girl shook her head.

Fran removed the blanket to reveal the girl entirely intact, not a mark on her. Her pretty dress was scarcely dirty or awry. She asked, "May I carry you out?"

The girl nodded. Fran picked her up gently and gave her a kiss on the temple as the girl snuggled into her arms. Crying, Fran said, "Oh sweet baby, sweet precious girl. You are so brave. You are so wonderful."

Fran walked toward the closest of the two men. He looked up at her in disbelief, then whistled and waved to the other one. He looked over with equal astonishment, then rushed to join Fran and the girl. She said, "Radio the helicopter. We have a survivor."

When the police arrived at the front door of the party house, Dhyan slipped out the back door into a rainy, black night. She skirted the covered pool, climbed the back fence, and cut through a few neighbors' yards on the shortest route home. Dogs barked, but they were on decks and tethered. She disappeared past them like a shadow.

At her dad and Cindy's house, the motion-sensor lights caught her in their glare. She looked like a bedraggled puppy, eyes glittery black with dilated pupils. She hit the doorbell and waited. She rang it again, then sloppily pounded on the door.

While she was still thumping, her dad flipped on the entryway lights and opened the door to her. "Oh thank God!" Ralph exclaimed, then turned to yell, "Cindy-love, it's Dhyan!" To Dhyan, he said, "Where in heck have you been? Look at you. You're a mess."

She pushed passed him into the house. "Nice to see you too."

He closed the door and looked into her eyes. "Are you alright? Are you... ? Oh no. You're stoned. On what, Dhyan?"

"Lawn clippings." Dhyan giggled uncontrollably at her joke.

Ralph shook her shoulders to sober her. "Who did this to you?"

Cindy appeared, her braless breasts heaving under a filmy negligée. "Sweet Jesus, my prayers have been answered." Looking skyward, she said, "Thank you, God, thank you."

Ralph persisted, "C'mon, 'fess us. Who's been corrupting my little girl?"

Dhyan walked toward her bedroom, flaunting her tiny skirt and sweater. "Cin-Cin-Cindy bought them. You figure." Through the open doorway, she saw that her room had been restored to childish order. "Oh Christ," she moaned as she went in and kicked the door shut.

Ralph shouted after her, "We'll talk in the morning, little miss!"

Cindy said, "Call the police, Ralph, so they know she's home." She rolled her eyes upward again. "Oh, the power of prayer. That's what got her back, the Lord's sweet mercy and the power of my prayers. Hallelujah."

Ralph put his arm around her shoulder. "Yeah, and pass the whisky, sweetheart. I'm a wreck."

Fran insisted that the girl from the plane crash be taken to the nearest village hospital, to spare her the trauma of a longer flight into chaotic Manila until her emotional condition was assessed. Within a large thatched-roof building, the girl sat propped in a cot, a picture of perfect health. She shared the large open room with a dozen other female patients, young and old, lying low and quiet from various maladies and mishaps.

Fran sat on the edge of the bed holding one of the girl's hands. She kept her other one tightly clenched. Fran reached to cover the little fist with her big hand and said softly, "It's okay now, Angela. You're warm and safe, and everything's going to be as okay as we can make it. Come on, let's hold both hands."

Angela snatched her fist away and put it under the covers. She held her dark eyes fast on Fran's face as Fran wrapped her two hands around the girl's free one and said, "Well, you know what's best. That's how you survived. That, and a miracle. You know what happens next, don't you?"

The girl nodded.

"After you're back to the States and you're all settled at your aunt and uncle's house, could I phone you maybe? See how you're doing?"

The girl nodded again.

"I'll do that. Now I have to leave, okay? I'm going to see my own girl, the one who just turned thirteen. Your aunt's here now, and there are lots of other good people here to look after you too. In a couple of days, you'll be together with your cousins in Portland, yay!"

Fran kissed her on the forehead, whispering, "Goodbye, sweet Angela," then softly left the room. She hurried past the small, clean nursing station and several nurse-nuns in white wimples over dark smocks. At the exit doors, she brushed past the local doctor making his rounds, her head down to hide her crying eyes.

While broadcasting her final report on the crash, Fran fought to hold down a sea of untapped tears. Her throat ached and words scattered. She had nothing to say about any of it, except that it was over. One-hundred-and-forty-three lives had vanished, Angela's former life was finished and her own was too, in ways. She couldn't begin to articulate what had shifted and what it might mean. The news was about going from here, heading through shock and grief into new territory with only hope and tender hearts for guides. She signed off with the request that the news-hungry world give Angela—this little angel—the privacy she needed to live out her sweetest dreams.

Fran spent the night on the balcony of her hotel room, sitting on a deck chair, tears gushing beyond her control. Neon lights flashed garish colors over her face. Traffic whooshed, roared, and occasionally wailed in her ears. She smoked steadily, stubbing the butts in a potted palm beside her.

She asked herself repeatedly, what had come over her from the moment she found Angela? Why such shellshocked pain and grief now that Angela was safe and heading for a whole new life?

Fran knew well the feeling of being done with an interview or a story she'd been chasing. That instinct had made her one of the best in the business because she could cut to the quick, then cut and run, as politely as required, as soon as she got what she needed.

Something huge was done and had slammed shut in her when ... exactly when? Sitting with Angela in the hospital, holding her hands, her determined little fist. With astonishing certainty, Fran knew she was finished with her entire reporting career and—this is what threw her—life as she knew it.

No more longing for more time with Dhyan without missing a beat at work; no more promises to fix things up on the home front somehow, some day. The impossibility of what she'd been trying to do for years—to broadcast what's happening in this crazy world, as if that might nudge it toward increased awareness and understanding if not enlightenment and justice— came instantly clear. She was the same old Fran, same old instincts and bad habits, but she was different too, changed from the inside out. Irrevocably.

Touched by a miracle?—gak. She hated clichés as much as touchy-feely New Age cant, yet here she was, dogpaddling through a storm of tears, suffering a long black night of the soul.

Grief overwhelmed her, but for what? Not the plane crash victims, not Angela's fate, not all the years of all the tragedies she'd covered. Not the pattern of her own life, none of her own losses, certainly not the choices she'd made and the price she'd paid for them. It was the end, that was all. Time to hang up, walk away, then what? Aside from being Mom-in-town for Dhyan, she was utterly devoid of reasons and plans. It hurt, and it felt good, like a tough scrub. *Tabula raza*—the slate wiped wonderfully, frighteningly clean.

Or maybe this was burnout, a breakdown. She'd known her parents' inabilities to cope only too well, but this wasn't anything like the turns they took. She felt too solid about this catharsis, too sure that something positive lay at the heart of it. The problem was, what, and how to begin? And then what?

She was going to quit—no, she had quit; it was over—the only work she'd known, was really passionate about, and did exceptionally well. How would she break it to Larry? Make a living? Even if she could afford to play full-time Suzie Homemaker to Dhyan, it would be too little, too late. She could ... what, slice tomatoes in a neighborhood deli? That had a certain appeal. Nothing else came to mind. Running on empty. *Tabula raza*. Light another cigarette.

By dawn, the palm's soil was heaped with butts, and Fran's head ached as if a bolt had been driven through it. She scooped the cigarette dregs into a garbage basket, then gulped back a liter of bottled water along with three aspirins. After standing full face in a cool shower until she started to shiver, she packed her bags in record time.

In the back seat of a taxi deking through traffic, Fran dialed a long string of numbers into her cell phone and waited. Nothing. She dialed again. Squeals this time, then, "I'm sorry, we're unable to complete your call ...." On her third try, she seethed at the phone, "C'mon, don't do this to me!"

The driver jumped. "Do what?" He glanced back and chortled. "That thing drive you crazy, huh?" Eyes front again, he added, "I just drive you zig zag."

Fran laughed, then cringed from a stab of headache pain. Finally, she connected. "Ralph, thank goodness. I'm on the moon here, fighting to get back. I'm taking the next flight home, standby, whatever I can get. Tell Dhyan, okay?" She listened, her eyes widening, jaw dropping. "She what? For two days! Oh God ...." Fran dropped her voice, "Just grass? Lawn clippings—oh, that's very funny. Why the hell didn't you call me?"

Her temple veins bulged and throbbed. "Oh sure, sure! You didn't even think to call me, did you? I can't believe it. I'm on my way home now, you hear, and I'm staying home. Tell her she's going to have her mom in town for as long as it takes ...."

"What do you mean, what about my high-flying job? I'm quitting, I'm done forever, you just watch. I'll be home sometime tomorrow, and I'm heading straight for Dhyan, you tell her that, please. Bye."

As the cabby unloaded Fran's bags at the airport, he said, "Everything okay, Miss?"

"It's going to be," she said, fishing for every non-US coin she could find in her purse to make a large handful for a tip. His eyes widened. "Thanks for the zig zag," she said. "Now I'm gone for good—as good as I can make it. *Pa-alam na po. Pa-alam* Manila."

Randy Tellman had again invaded Larry's domain without warning or knocking. He ushered in two young companions pushing a dolly stacked with two cardboard boxes. The woman had three pierced-navel rings showing between tight top and low-rise jeans and more than a dozen rings in her eyebrows and ears. Her platinum brush cut sprouted a few long blue tendrils that curled down her snake-tattooed neck. The man smelled of cigarette smoke in his paint-spattered sweatshirt and jeans, oversize runners, tiny sunglasses, and purple tufted hair. A small silver coin sat in the middle of his chin, an eye-catching rivet.

Larry jumped to his feet, as much from annoyed surprise as to greet them. Randy said, "Permit me to introduce my graduate students. Well, graduating this year, with some help from me." He rapped the top box. "And your blessings."

The young woman extended her hand to Larry. "Hey," she said. He shook without a word.

"Oka-a-y," the young man said, flopping in the chair where Maya had sat. He looked around the office and nodded. "Yep. Been here, seen that." He grinned at Larry.

"What in hell is going on?" Larry quietly asked Randy.

"Hey, no budget, low budget don't stop this boy. I've been getting real about the way I want things done around here. I'm bringing you the plan, the execution, team reps, and ta da! one sweet final product." Randy opened the folded flaps of the top box and took out a DVD labeled "Rewind: One Life." He handed it to Larry.

"What is it?"

"Half-hour show."

"Twenty-two minutes," the woman said.

Randy continued, "An experiment, a prototype, the wave of the future, and we're on it. I hit the university and recruited a film prof and his little elves ...." The young woman snickered. "... who took my idea and ran with it. Half-a-dozen did the assignment—own scouting, own angles, all lone-wolf in the field, all handheld, except for stock footage. A day self-teching to edit, add sound, and voila! it's done. Low cost, no cost to us—university paid—and look, instant profile. The kids get credit, and I get what I want. Young, with-it reporters who don't need a crew. We're bringing you everything that went into it: rough footage, class and field notes, some hot new journalism texts, and Internet downloads thrown in, why not?"

"What's it about?" Larry asked, eyes narrowed suspiciously.

"You. Your life. It's brilliant."

"You made a show of my life?" Larry said, eyes wide now.

"Listen, we can whip these babies off two, three a week and beat 'Biography' all to hell. We'll scoop their audience and get the happening crowd too, it's like right now, you know? I did like you said, you're the original spark. I took the footage from here—remember I video'd you last week?—and showed ...." Randy pointed upward with his thumb to indicate the penthouse boss. "He got talking about you, how you've broken ground in this business and how I gotta learn from you, take it further, which gave me this great idea. It's perfect, an honor, a service I'm doing you, man. I mean, I show you what I mean by showing *you*, right? We covered you from day one as director here back through senior reporter, cub reporter, highschool, prom date, grade one, we even got a scoop on your dad—your real dad—and did your adoption ...."

Larry blinked. "You got what? My God, did it ever occur to you that this is immoral and unscrupulous, if not utterly illegal and indictable?"

"Uh-uh. All public information, public records. People talked freely, nothing we needed permission for, no deep dark searches."

The young woman said, "Nothing current either, like where you live, how you live, that could be too, you know ...."

Larry demanded, "Too invasive maybe? Too none-of-your-goddamned business?"

Randy said, "Hey, lighten up. It's a practice run at a great idea, it's not public or anything, and it's a nice little gift for you, a keepsake."

The young woman said, "Yeah, it's like, a major compliment. We think you're awesome and have done great things. We're trying to build something from it, go beyond, know what I mean?"

The young man added, "I love your ol' dude dad, still crazy about your mom, his virgin bride." He savored the last two words. "He's way cool."

Larry shouted, "That old dude's a jerk and a bum, he disappeared when I was a baby, for God's sake! Abel Singer's my dad, my only dad, you arrogant prying schmucks."

Randy stepped back and crossed his index fingers in mock fear, saying, "Whoa, man. You got issues, big time. I mean, if you can't accept your past and the way things are and how they're coming on, well, I'm sorry, but ...."

"Who's seen this?" Larry growled. "Other than the class?"

"You mean upstairs? No, big Al hasn't seen anything yet. Hah! 'You ain't seen nothing yet.' Whose line?" Randy looked at his companions, who shrugged. "Al Jolson, you 'Jeopardy' losers. First words in the first big talkie. Larry, you're going to love it, I know, and we're going to take this technique and fly with it. This is the hottest thing since ...." He turned to his acolytes. "Hey, since what?"

"You, man," she said. "It's been so fun."

The young man said, "It's half-way from music videos, you know, and that's where we come from, my generation, how we expect things to move when we're at the switch. Ch-ch-ch ...." He mimed pushing the buttons of a remote control, his head bobbing like a boxer's.

Larry asked, "How many copies?"

"This is it. I mean, there's all the footage and stuff, that's in the boxes, but this is the one and precious only DVD. Nothing left on any computers, no other disks. Hey, I got some scruples, you know? We show you, you love it, we show upstairs, he loves it, we go with the concept. Everything's in here, trust me, every bit and piece, that's why it takes a couple of boxes."

Larry steamed. "God, you've outdone yourself this time. I can't believe that you've ...."

Randy cut in. "No, I can't believe you're taking it like this. You haven't even seen it, you don't even know what you're up against. Why are you so resistant? Change is coming with or without you, so here's the best damned thing that's happening anywhere—I mean, you're looking at the future right here—and this whole piece is all about you, but you're fighting it like crazy Canute trying to stop the tide, and it's not fair, you just can't ...."

Larry held up his hand. "You stop right there. Crazy Canute was showing his assembled idiots that you can't stop the tide, but you're not interested in getting the story right, are you? You're just into the bullshit and razzle-dazzle and playing games, when people out there are living hard lives and dying harder—dying so hard you can't imagine it—and you're trying to tell me that anything in these boxes matters? Give me a break. And I mean—are you listening?—give me a break, as in leave, right now."

Randy squared himself up. The young man's and woman's shoulders slumped.

Larry said. "I'm sorry for you kids, I'm really sorry, but you've been part of something I consider unscrupulous and unprofessional, and you'd better start learning that right now if you want careers in the business. I won't hold it against you, I won't look at the class list, I won't remember you, okay? You're off scot-free. Now class dismissed, finished, out!"

"Whoa, surprise ending," the young man mumbled, heading for the door. "Sorr-ee."

Randy followed out Larry's door, saying, "Yeah, sorry for you, dude. By the time you get it, it'll be too late." To his companions, heading past

Nora's workstation, he said, "C'mon, I'll give you A-pluses and ice cream sundaes for taking this shit."

As Larry reached to close his door, Nora said hesitantly, "Mr. Singer? I'm really sorry to bother you, but this just arrived, and it's marked 'Urgent'." She picked up a large padded envelope and held it out for Larry. The waybill was addressed in black felt pen, his name underlined in red. Larry didn't need to look at the return address to know who'd couriered to him.

Larry took the envelope and returned to his riled cocoon, his former sanctuary. Randy was hard to believe. Did that really happen? A dolly bearing two new boxes said yes. How was Larry going to tell Uncle Al about this final straw without telling what this wart on his butt did? Then Al would want to see the tape, and be damned, that was unthinkable.

Larry dropped into his chair behind the rubble pile that once was his desk and opened the envelope from Mae. He pulled out a video cassette marked "Gerry McMann." He knew the story, a recent little item about a fisherman surviving a freak storm. A file folder accompanied the video, labeled "Coincidentals". A small Post-It note stuck on it said, "Call me soon, dear. Or just drop by. Best love." He smiled as he stuck the note on his phone, a sweet request in the midst of turmoil.

The file contained a dozen or so photocopied pages of newspaper articles Mae had clipped, noting their source and date. Larry quickly scanned them. All were about people surviving disasters in some way or other. Lucky them, he thought, they beat the reaper, but he wasn't calm enough to read their stories now. He put the material back and rubbed his pained head, longing for sleep. He couldn't remember ever having felt so spent.

With all the energy he could muster, he got up to play the DVD on his computer. He wearily started "Rewind: One Life" and fell into the nearest chair to watch.

It opened with Larry's office, all loopy and gut-churning, as expected, with chaotic music. That mess quickly cut to Uncle Al's huge office, bouncing in the same handheld quake. As the big chubby guy in rolled-up shirtsleeves pressed weights on a Universal gym, he talked about Larry being a role model for up-and-coming talent like young Randall Tellman the Third, who should study his life to see how he did it. Randy's voice-over said that's just what he "did, di-did, di-did," iterated countless annoying times.

The footage backtracked to clips—from a blessedly steady camera, but jumpy soundtrack—of Larry as director, producer, senior correspondent, pack reporter, and young stringer. Time reeled back via more handheld shots and stuttering samples of oldie songs to photos of him in highschool yearbooks. Time and sound then froze for long seconds on a grainy photo of Larry and his prom date, the dark-haired dazzler Lyndie Ann.

Fast-forward thirty-five years, and there she was, so blond he didn't recognize her, as tarted-up as a has-been starlet. She talked about how incredibly smart Larry was, and even though he was different from the other guys, she respected that. Wanted to help him and hoped she had. "Call me when you see this, hey Lar?" she said with a final wave using her baby finger, her little cue for when a handsome teacher they both liked walked by.

He closed his eyes and groaned, "Oh God."

His younger sister and brother had their say next—and just their say, all done as voice-overs—talking about the last time they saw Larry, at a family gathering in Iowa last summer. The accompanying images were flashes and whirls of wheat fields interspersed with home-video shots of the family barbecue, mostly little kids being rambunctious and bratty. "Big half-brother ... no, three-quarters technically," his brother said. "Great guy. Quiet, hard-working, got me through school."

His sister chuckled. "Remember the time he set up 'War of the Worlds', that old Orson Welles radio play, and got us totally convinced it was real? Scared the hell out of us. Sheesh. We've never been the same since. Great guy though, totally focused, totally into something or ... well, totally gone, on to something else. Always new-related though. Always."

Larry fast-forwarded through his receding past, from highschool to kindergarten in a blur. He whizzed by his parents' graves and stopped on a wedding photo of his mom and dad, Bea and Abel Singer.

Abel had died in a construction accident just months after Larry and Lyndie waltzed off to the prom. "The perfect couple," the old guy had whispered loud enough for the neighbors to hear. Perfectly odd if he'd known the truth, but he didn't, and it didn't matter now. The 'old guy' was fifty-four then, two years older than Larry was now. Mae's talk of Singers being long-lived couldn't be measured by his dad/uncle. His grandfather Samuel lived for ninety-plus years, but his last decades were a long backtrack into complete senility. Larry never knew him when there was much to know.

The story rushed on to the final star of the show, his birth father, Abel's older brother Solomon. That was Larry's main interest in this whole sorry exercise and for one reason only: medical. The old bastard would be pushing eighty now, and Larry needed to see what his own physical-mental fate might be if he could outwit this damned lump on his leg.

Sol Singer was a wreck, a bald geezer who'd chased trouble until it got the best of him. He was coherent, however, and canny enough to call himself a "freelance bottle collector" operating out of a New York dive for indigents. Experienced bottle emptier too, no doubt. His grimy fingers held a worn old photo of himself as a handsome groom with his beautiful *shikseh* bride, Beatrice Winters: "My virgin bride." He relished the words. "Mother of my boy, my only kid. And let me tell you, she did a great job raising him after I'd hadda ... well, do a little hard work, um ... outta town."

Larry groaned, "Oh, you scum. Hard time in the slammer, you filthy lying bigamist. Two wives, one kid here, couple of stepkids there, no goddamn conscience."

The tape ended with Sol and his buddies sitting in a smoky, filthy communal TV room watching Media 8 news. A recent report played in the background as Sol said, "That's my boy, my boy's boss of that show."

A toothless crony muttered, "You say that every damned time."

"Larry," Sol said. "His name is Larry."

Despite crappy camera-work, obnoxious soundtrack, and lousy editing, Larry knew that the story and his old man were dynamite, that Randy had nailed something. After several minutes of sitting stunned, feeling his pulse thumping from chest to tumid brain, Larry let the tears roll. It was all so stupidly sad with nothing in it for him, not personally, and definitely not as a way to tell any kind of news.

He got up and hit the eject button. Why not destroy it right now? *Just do it. C'mon, grind it under your heel, smash it to smithereens with a sledgehammer. Kill it. Kill Randy, that presumptuous, overbearing, unbelievable son-of-a- ....*

Larry couldn't though. That was his life in there, big chunks sliced up like chopped liver. He'd just tuck this misery into his "Telling News" notebook and file it forever. He'd destroy everything else in the boxes. What really mattered was, what was he going to do with Randy Tellman? Finding Larry's real father had put Randy in a once-singular category: Larry now hated two people's guts more than he'd have thought possible just one hour before.

Randy had to be diverted. There had to be a suitable exile for him in the fringes of Media 8's vast realm, some warp zone of its cyberspace, where he could rile up virtual hornets' nests to his heart's content. He had a rare talent for it, to be sure. Larry would figure out something when he calmed down, got some productive energy back, and could think straight. For now, Fran's continuing reports on Angela and the crash aftermath would show the world the power of the bigger story, none of this half-baked, back-assed, jitterbug stuff that assaulted the senses and went nowhere.

Fran knocked on Dhyan's bedroom door. No reply. She knocked again, then opened it a crack to the tinny sound of music playing too loudly through earbuds. Dhyan sprawled tummy down on her bed reading a comic book, immune to the blaring noise. Her room was still fluffy and pink, top to bottom. She wore baggy shirt and pants, her feet bare.

"Dhyan?" Fran said.

"Hi Mom." Dhyan didn't move.

"May I come in?"

Dhyan shrugged.

Fran walked to where she could see Dhyan's profile, then crouched down to face her. Dhyan pretended to continue reading, making a show of turning a page. Fran waited.

Finally, Dhyan removed an earbud and turned to say, "I've had my butt chewed out like, totally. There's nothin' left for you."

Fran laughed heartily. "God, you're funny. I love you."

Dhyan struggled to contain a laugh but couldn't.

"The Fran Estates is holding a room for you, major redecorating required. Full-time mom in service, all the lousy cooking you can eat."

"Are you really home for a while?"

"Try me."

At nine the next morning, Fran headed toward Larry's office, comfortable in jeans and no makeup, definitely not working clothes. From open doors along the hallway, colleagues of every sort and level said enthusiastically, "Hey Fran, way to go!" "Hot stuff!" "Award time, baby! We're looking good!" She waved and said thanks, not slowing a beat.

Nora watched, eyes wide to Fran's approach. "You're back so soon! I'll buzz Mr. Singer."

"Anyone else in there?"

Nora shook her head.

Fran said, "Then I'll surprise him."

Nora crooked her index finger for Fran to lean close and whispered, "He's a little tired, a little, oh ... worse for wear."

Fran said in a normal voice, "Yeah, the world's a mess, and all this shakedown, shakeup crap here, poor guy. I'm beat too."

Nora watched anxiously as Fran tapped on Larry's door, then stepped into his office.

Larry's drooping head bounced up in shock. "Fran! What the hell are you doing here?"

"Checking in, checking out. Got a minute?"

"You're not due back for a week. I mean, I'm glad to see you, but ...."

"Mind if I sit?"

"Please. Mind if I stand? Run around? Scream?"

Fran laughed and took a chair. "Yeah, kind of sudden, but something happened."

"What?"

"Angela."

"Oh man, talk about payoffs. Check the edges and miracles happen. The whole world's keen for the followup."

"Uh-uh. She's flying back to the States, moving in with relatives, starting life over, and I've already said that. A pox on any jerk who sticks a mike in her face."

"But we're doing the whole big picture, everything that happened before it happened, right? Who's getting that?"

"Not me."

"I can see that, unless you're chasing some hot lead here."

She shook her head. "No. I'm done. I'm home for my kid."

Larry blinked. "So it's not Angela, it's Dhyan."

"Both."

"What's happening with Dhyan? Is she okay?"

"Yeah, between spells of hell's apoppin'. A little AWOL, a little pot, a lot of sass. Our nanny took off and got married last year, right? Left my poor kid to unmitigated, unmediated Cindy every day. I'd be running and toking too, but don't tell her I said that."

"So get a new nanny. Ask me for a raise to cover it."

"No, and no. Juanita ... well, she knew Dhyan from a baby, and Cindy put up with her because she came with the package, but a new nanny? I wouldn't wish either Cindy or Dhyan on anyone."

"So what's happening with the crash story?"

Fran shrugged. "Nothing. We got the scoop, the sky-high ratings. Her aunt's going to keep it exclusive to us I'm pretty sure. Nothing in writing, but she agrees: no more interviews till Angela's ready, then she's ours first, maybe do a six month or one year update."

Larry held up his hand. "Okay, okay, you're dropping the hottest story around, and I don't mean Angela, but all the peripherals, I can't believe it." His voice was tight, volume rising. "I mean, I give you a new directive and everything starts cooking, then with no warning, just like that, you ...." He snapped his fingers and sputtered for words.

Fran winced, steeling herself for the dressing down. Larry stopped himself and let out a noisy breath. "Oh hell, forget it, I'll deal with it." He closed his eyes briefly to calm himself, then drilled them back on Fran, saying, "The problem right here, right now is you. What're we going to do with you?"

"Yelling and screaming might be a good idea. We'd both feel better."

Larry laughed. "No, I've got other tortures in mind. Well, I don't, but I'll think of something. What do you mean by you're 'done'? As in, you want something closer to home, to Dhyan? Maybe back to the District?"

Fran shook her head. "Uh-uh. Not a chance."

"How 'bout ... oh, I don't know, a producer's job in the tower?"

"Oh God no, I go nuts when I'm caged, and the bureaucracy would kill me."

"So listen, this is a long shot and shooting from the hip, but how'd you like to share this chair with me? Do all the fun parts while I kill Randy."

Fran laughed. "That would be the fun part."

"So we do it together. C'mon, half time each, you pick your hours, I'll take the rest. It'd be exciting, the two of us working like mad squirrels on the peripherals."

"And achieve my life's goal that quickly? Forget it."

Larry sat back. "Okay. For now. What *is* your life's goal workwise? Describe the perfect job."

Fran sighed, "I've been doing it, I've done it. I know when to cut out, Lar, that's my strength, and this is it. Holding Angela, coming home for Dhyan, a whole lot's over and done with, and I haven't a clue what's next. Right now, I just want to ... oh, I dunno, slice tomatoes at Joe's Deli. No tomatoes to take home to slice for tomorrow. No tomatoes falling from the sky, blowing up in my face, keeping me awake at night."

"No tomatoes here, I'm sorry. Damn, I can't lose you, Fran. The best I can do is buy you a little time while you ...."

"I don't want a little time. I want a lot, like the rest of my life."

"Hey, hot news flash, Fran. This life thing arrives one day at a time, that's all any of us gets, so let's start there. I think I've got something ...." Larry found the manila envelope from Mae under fresh drifts of memos and mail. He handed it to Fran. "Just arrived. I skimmed it, that's all. You figure it out. Stretch it to a month, I don't care how skimpy your report is or if you come up with anything at all. I'll give you a month at home—at home, not at the office—and full pay."

Fran looked inside the flap of the envelope. "You serious?"

"Desperate's the word."

Fran took a deep breath. "I don't know. I mean, it could be more of the same, and I really don't ...."

"Ple-e-ease, Fran. It's only more of whatever you make of it."

"Well, as a transition, I guess, but don't think you're getting the old me back with this."

Larry laughed. "Which would involve changing your mind, right? Has that ever been possible?"

Fran shook her head and smiled. "I don't know what you just finessed on me, but I'll do it. I'm still your slave."

"Heir to the throne, sweetheart, but don't let hidden agendas frighten you."

The phone rang. Larry said, "Call me if you want, when you want. Anytime, darlin'." He picked up the receiver and hit the 'Nora' button.

Fran got up to go. At the door, she mouthed, "Goodbye," then breezed by Nora with a small wave.

Larry said into the phone, "Yeah?"

Nora said quietly to Larry, "Dr. Symonds. Line three."

"Thanks." Larry pushed another button and said, "Dr. Symonds, hello."

Symonds said, "I've got a cancellation for you. We can start full treatment on Tuesday, eight a.m. Scans in the morning, radiation and chemotherapy right after. You know the odds."

"I do, but I just can't reconcile it. First, you smash my immune system to hell, then without the very thing that's going to save me, somehow I get better. It didn't do my mother any good."

"Things have changed. We stimulate bone marrow production now, along with ...."

"Yeah, yeah, I know, but it's still marginal."

"The odds are good with treatment."

"And the glass is half full too. I know the stats, right down to the decimal points. Besides, this thing's been stewing for years, right? I don't see the wild rush when I've got work things to tie up—string up if I ...."

"Next opening for sure is in six weeks, unless you want to pay the big bucks and jump the queue. Or do the emergency route if you take a sudden turn for the worst."

Larry thought for long seconds, his mouth dry, his jaw clenching and unclenching.

Symonds pressed, "Well? Tuesday at eight?"

Light sweat sheened Larry's brow. "Let it go, pencil me in for the next opening. Thanks for your trouble. Bye." He hung up the phone and looked out his window. The sky was clear, view sharp and bright. On the street below, he watched miniscule pedestrians by the dozens, but could see no white-haired angels among them. He fought tears as he said under his breath, "Where are you when I need you, damn it?"

Larry rapped Mae's brass snake doorknocker, gleaming in a wan winter sun. Byron barked and the sound of rubber-booted feet shuffled within.

"Larry!" she said happily, opening the door to him. She smiled broadly, her teeth in place, her black wig almost.

"Look at you," he said appreciatively. "You're picture perfect, as always." She sported a green-and-orange tartan kilt and bright orange scarf that sagged about her scrawny neck and shoulders, weighted by a Cairngorm quartz brooch. She'd painted her nails orange and smudged matching lipstick over wrinkled lips.

The little Lord pawed up Larry's thighs as he wrapped his arms around Mae. She pulled back with a shy blush and dancing eyes. "Oh you, you're a fertilizer salesman, worse than your grandpa. Come in and find a spot. I've got tea ready."

She and Byron went to the kitchen. Larry squeezed onto the sofa. When Mae reappeared with rattling teacups of Olympus tea, she said to Larry, "Move those papers, dear. I'm going to sit beside you, it's nicer that way."

Larry smelled the tea and instantly brightened. "Mm-m. Maya's herbs, am I right?" He brightened more. "Is she here?"

Mae shook her head somberly and sighed, "Oh Larry."

"What? What happened?"

Mae took her time. "You heard that dissidents were released unharmed?"

Larry nodded.

Mae took several small breaths, struggling to continue. "In Mashad, a zealot slashed Maya." Mae ran her forefinger down her face and neck. "She lost a lot of blood, then they shipped her to Tehran to be flogged—twelve lashes. She died four days ago at Delphi."

"Good lord, why didn't you tell me?"

"I *am* telling you, Larry. It's terrible news, too terrible to tell you by telephone."

"I meant earlier, when she was in trouble. I'd have sent a reporter, help, whatever it took."

"No. Publicity would have made things worse. Impossible, really. She wasn't a story when you saw her, and she isn't one now."

"What do you mean? It's the type of story ... I mean, I could have ...."

"No, you couldn't have anything. She used the protest as a pretext to see you, and she knew you'd say no. She was counting on it, in fact. The important thing is to remember what she talked about: peripheral details, what's missing, getting the story that's right under your nose."

"But the story in this case is her protest, her arrest and suffering, her death. It's got to be reported. I've got to find out what happened."

"It's not a story at all, and you're missing the point entirely. If you want to find out what happened, you have to start looking around you."

"Exactly. We did just that with the West Orient crash and found Angela. It's a miracle. I'm taking Maya's every word to heart."

"Good. So look around you, dear. Literally, look around you."

He knit his brow, confused for a moment. "Here?"

"Yes."

"What do you see?"

"Research. Years and tons of research."

"On what?"

"Goddesses. Myths. Legends."

"To what end?"

"How they connect, interrelate, I think."

"That's the length and breadth of it but not half the story. Maya's in here, in every file." Larry looked around anew as Mae continued, "She's also in the one I started for you of co-incidences. That's why I sent it to you."

Thoroughly puzzled, Larry said, "I didn't see any mention of her."

"Not directly, but she's in there. And here. You see, you're going to be in charge of all this one day, and it's time I clued you into it. I can't just tell you though and have you fully understand its import. I've got to introduce you properly, and that will take time. Meeting Maya was the first step and a successful one, I think. Have you made any sense of the file? Does it interest you?"

"The truth is, I just skimmed it and ... well, I hope you don't mind, but I passed it on."

Mae narrowed her eyes with concern.

"To the reporter who found Angela. Fran Roma. She showed up in my office out of the blue, back from Manila a lot sooner than I expected, and giving it to her solved a big problem. I couldn't believe it, she was quitting on me, so I gave her a month to work on it. At home. A sort of private assignment to keep her on."

"Quitting on you? Why?"

"I'm still not sure. She said that when she found Angela, something fundamental changed ...."

Mae smiled. "Of course. She's perfect then. A month is a good start. Keep me apprised, won't you? And no reports, please, on Maya's death or survivals coincident to it without letting me know beforehand. I must be very strict about that. It could be dangerous."

"In what way?"

"In ways I hope we never find out." Mae wasn't about to elaborate.

"No problem. It's pretty oddball, you've got to admit—I mean, first that she'll come up with anything to say about it, then ... well, how to report it? It's not exactly mainstream news."

"Did you tell Miss Roma about me?"

"No. Should I?"

"Only if she asks, when she asks. For now, let her root around and figure out a bit on her own. We'll meet soon, when it's time." Mae finished her tea. Byron turned and flopped the other way at her feet. "Now enough of this. You still look tired, your color's still off. What the problem?"

Larry sighed, "Work, Mae. Work brought me Solomon today, I saw the old coot." Mae's eyebrows shot up. "Not live. On my computer, from a DVD made by the idiot who's turning my office upside down. He dug up him up a few days ago, don't ask why."

"Oh my." Mae's voice dropped. "How is Sol?"

"Terrible. But alive ... and lucid and still telling lies. He's a bum, a bottle-collecting bum in New York City, and he'll probably live to be a hundred, I should be so lucky."

"Sh-h, of course, you will. Don't talk like that. You're a Singer. That bum broke your grandmother's heart, and he lives to be old. Poor Abel picked up the pieces, only to have your mother break his mother's heart again by shutting her out, then he died young before he could mend the rift. Where's the justice?"

"There were fifteen years for mending if Dad had wanted to."

"These things take time. Look at your mother—it took her twenty-five years to turn up at a few Singer gatherings."

"Yeah, funerals. Stacking the seats at her own maybe, I don't know. God, this is dreary and way too late to matter. It amazes me that after all these years I can still be shocked by such old news."

"Why should it amaze you? You're alive. You care. I'd worry if you weren't shocked. The past isn't that far gone, dear, and it's full of surprises, full of things we knew but never looked in the face. Look around you, like I said. That's particularly true here. And I don't mean to get off the topic of your concerns but to provide some perspective."

"Well, I mean to get off the topic, even though I brought it up. Perspective is everything, thank you. Enough of me. How are you? Are you managing okay without Nikos? Can I ... ?"

"No, you needn't do a thing. The girl across the street is a saint, and the teenagers next door have been helpful, although the police had to route out some troublemakers, I'm told, just before the parents got home from a holiday. I didn't hear a thing. They brought me a big basket of fruit yesterday. I'll give you some to take home; I can't eat half of it."

"You sure? That would be nice."

Mae's eyes softened as they drifted to long ago. "The basket reminds me of the time Aunt Devorah—Sammie's mother, your great-grandmother—

caught us warring in apple trees, pitching them at each other when we were supposed to ... well no, that's not quite the beginning. It was the basket's fault, you see. Oh, it's a silly old tale."

"So tell silly old me," Larry urged and soon relaxed into another of Mae's many stories from a vanished world.

Fran lived in a refurbished rowhouse on a semi-commercial street. The brick had been cleaned, balconies shored up, and trim painted clever colorwheel hues. Ambitious owners filled flower pots and boxes with cheery spring blooms. Others, like Fran, planted plastic geraniums that faded and grew dusty from season to season.

Shops, dry-cleaners, and a corner gas station kept the street hopping. Mae's old house, just blocks away, dated from the same era. Ralph and Cindy's designer home, one neighborhood over, came from recent infilling of post-World War Two sprawl.

Fran's home office overlooked the street from the second floor, a converted bedroom from the era of wainscoting and dormer windows. The walls held a hodge-podge of photographs she'd taken of household doorways from around the world, from igloos to treehouses, rowhouses to yurts.

A paper tornado had hit the room, with her computer, monitor, printer, and scanner sitting at the eye of the storm. A crude lilypad ashtray, pottery by little Dhyan, overflowed with butts. A black-rimmed wall clock hanging on a closet door semaphored a few minutes to noon on a gray winter day.

Fran schlepped into the room dressed in old sweats, her hair disheveled. She headed for the cassette player atop a small TV tucked on a corner shelf and plugged in the video Larry had given her. She lit a cigarette, then sat back in a swivel chair to watch.

"The 6 P.M. News" begins with signature MUSIC and an 'exploding' Canadian Broadcasting Corporation logo, followed by the date: Friday, February 12th.

An ANCHORMAN sits in a large studio behind a large desk. ZOOM IN to his face and shoulders.

                ANCHORMAN
    Good evening. The dollar slips then rebounds,
    Middle East tensions continue, and yesterday's

ANCHORMAN (continued)
savage storm off the Atlantic coast appears to
have claimed the lives of five fishermen. We go
first to Foggy Cove in Nova Scotia.

CUT TO:

A black and fierce night. The Foggy Cove lighthouse beam sweeps through wet, wild winds and huge waves battering the rocky shore.

ANCHORMAN (voice over)
This was Foggy Cove at the peak of the storm
about seven p.m. last night, recorded by the
lighthouse keeper. Radio contact with the *Black
Swan*, an eighteen-meter groundfish trawler from
this outport village, was lost soon after the storm
hit, and the last received message is grim.

FISHERMAN (voice over)
(crackling transmission)
Jeez, boy, she's a whirlpool, thousand feet
across, sucking us down like the devil, she is.

ANCHORMAN (voice over)
Transmission ended there with no further contact.
Night and the storm's ferocity delayed the Coast
Guard's search until dawn this morning. No
traces of the vessel have been found. Reporter
Cole Preston visited Foggy Cove earlier today.

CUT TO:

COLE PRESTON, a black man in a yellow sou'wester hat and rain slicks, standing on the road winding through Foggy Cove. His features are scarcely visible through the rain-smattered camera lens as he points out ghosts of houses scattered over the small, rocky bay. He fights the wind, which tears his voice away.

CUT TO:

Preston standing warm and dry inside a quaint kitchen. He's a well-dressed city fellow in the crowd of homespun LOCAL CITIZENS. He looks young, but speaks authoritatively.

PRESTON
The citizens of Foggy Cove number fourteen families in fourteen snug homes such as this. Over the years, they've come to know the fury of the sea and the price it exacts. No family has been spared. Today, five families wait in hope and dread for news about their fathers, grandfathers, brothers, uncles, and cousins.

(putting the mike to an old man)
You've sailed in hundreds of storms. Did you ever see a whirlpool?

OLD MAN
No, Sir, I didn't. There's tales aplenty, but them that sees them only sees them once.

PRESTON
So you're saying you don't hold much hope.

OLD MAN
My boy's out there. God is too. I wouldn't presume to outguess Him.

CUT TO:

Outside of the Environment Canada Meteorological building in unrelenting rain, Cole Preston stands under a large umbrella, wearing a trenchcoat.

PRESTON
Experts are divided about the likelihood of a giant whirlpool sucking a boat into it, although they don't rule it out.

CUT TO:

Preston inside the building holding a mike to a WEATHERMAN who points to the satellite image of the storm on a computer monitor.

WEATHERMAN
They were at the eye, right here. The physics of giant whirlpools at sea are unclear, although

WEATHERMAN (continued)
fishermen's tales abound with stories of being
sucked into the abyss. If it's true—and I
wouldn't dismiss it—the vessel would be drawn
into it and immediately destroyed.

PRESTON
No hope for survivors.

WEATHERMAN
Well, at this point the whirlpool is one fisherman's report, his interpretation of dire conditions.
Let's hope he mistook a deep trough associated
with a rogue wave for something worse.

PRESTON
Seas are too rough yet for air and sea craft to
search the waters where the *Black Swan* lost
radio contact. What's the forecast for tomorrow?

WEATHERMAN
Much the same, I'm afraid.

CUT TO:

"The 6 P.M.News" with signature MUSIC and CBC logo, Saturday, February 13th. ZOOM IN to the anchorman at his desk.

ANCHORMAN
Stormy seas off Nova Scotia still hamper the
search for the five fishermen whose boat
disappeared yesterday.

CUT TO:

Cole Preston is at Foggy Cove, where the weather is clear enough for him to report outside. The wind whips at his uncovered head and trenchcoat. A small group of residents surrounds him.

MATRONLY WOMAN
(wiping away tears)
Bless our lads, they're in a better place. We'll see
them by-and-by.

YOUNGER WOMAN
I'm not giving up. I'm looking for a miracle, and since the Lord's taken so many of our men over the years, I'm expecting one's due.

TEENAGE BOY
Overdue.

CUT TO:

"The 6 P.M.News" with signature MUSIC and CBC logo, Sunday, February 14th. ZOOM IN to the anchorman at his desk.

ANCHORMAN
The Coast Guard has called off all search vessels and helicopters looking for the five missing fishermen off the coast of Nova Scotia. They are all presumed lost and dead, victims of a vicious storm and possible freak whirlpool on February 11th. The outport is in mourning, with memorial services scheduled for Sunday.

On Monday, following the 10 p.m. news final, we'll carry a documentary report on this disaster in the context of the collapse of the Maritime fishery and the hardship of life without this mainstay industry.

CUT TO:

"The 6 P.M.News" with signature MUSIC and CBC logo, Monday, February 15th.

CUT TO:

Cole Preston standing on cold, clear, desolate shore of Nova Scotia.

PRESTON
Here, exactly here is where Gerry McMann washed up on shore late this afternoon, one-hundred-and-ten miles from where The *Black Swan* went down.

> PRESTON (continued)
> He walked two frozen miles to the nearest home and to safety. His clothing turned to ice in temperatures of minus ten degrees Celsius, thirty below with wind-chill factored in.
>
> He was taken immediately to the regional hospital, where his core temperature registered below that normally considered possible for an adult to survive. Gerry McMann is a walking miracle.

Preston holds up a photograph of Gerry McMann grinning beside the *Black Swan*, docked under bright summer skies. ZOOM IN to McMann's out-of-focus face.

> PRESTON (voice over)
> McMann is in acute care at present, with only immediate family allowed to see him. Word is that he's fully aware and *compos mentis*. His family has declined interviews at this point.
>
> More on this amazing story as it unfolds. Cole Preston, CBC News, Dreadnaught Beach, Nova Scotia.

    Fran sat back and drew hard on her cigarette. She looked at her watch, which showed international times on an extra outer band. She checked the calendar and muttered, "Down on the eleventh, last transmission ... hm, a little after ...." She quickly calculated. "One a.m. on the twelfth, Greek time. Washed up two days later. Who-o-o, too much for me." She stubbed out her cigarette.
    She headed downstairs to her small kitchen to get coffee from a thermos carafe. She prided herself on buying little on her countless foreign assignments, but bits of a hundred countries had found their way home with her anyway. Cooking utensils, gadgets and gewgaws fought for space, standing, hanging, stuck with magnets, or crammed into corners beside unlikely partners from half a world away. She could cube eggs, curl butter, tap sugar maples, kebab with dozens of ornamented sticks, *onegiri* rice, dry teabags on a little line, mortar and pestle many different ways, cook strange things

from a polyglot of books.... The possibilities were mindboggling, far ahead of her poorly stocked cupboards, which showed her neglect when she got sugarcubes to drop into her big pottery mug. Fast food boxes reigned in the fridge, although a fresh jug of milk kept three oranges company. Home life was improving.

She sat on a stool at a sidebar overlooking the sunroom, which doubled as the main and seldom-used dining area. It held a glass-topped bamboo-wicker table, four chairs, and several large silk plants. *They have to go,* she thought, then said, "Hey, fake plants, your real cousins are coming back." She got up to shake thick dust off a few leaves. "Disgusting."

Restless, with coffee cup in hand, she threw open the sunroom doors and stepped out. She surveyed her fenced backyard, a long, narrow rectangle of overgrown lawn and garden beds. At the far end, honeysuckle brambles covered a small shed.

She wandered through the remains of last year's pathetic attempts at growing beans, basil, and other neglected crops. A few brave crocuses emerged through mats of rotted leaves. She crouched to pay her respects to these tender volunteers.

She caught a faint smell in the air, cocked her nose, and traced it to the dark interior of the shed. Midst the rakes, old plant pots, and cobwebs, she saw the small red glow of the burning cigarette that Dhyan and a girlfriend were sharing. Fran shrieked, "What the hell are you doing?"

"Is this a trick question?" Dhyan asked.

Her girlfriend giggled and started choking.

"Put it out!"

Dhyan defiantly held the cigarette.

"Now! And why aren't you in school?" Fran's voice rose an octave.

Dhyan leisurely dropped the cigarette and killed it with a twist of her foot.

"Well?"

"Well what?"

"School, dear. Today is a school day. You are a school age child. Do you get my drift?"

"It's a half day. Besides I'm burned out. I'm taking a month off. And I'm like, practicing here, so we can smoke together. I mean, we're doing everything together this month, right?"

Fran laughed as she ran a hand through ragged hair. "God help me, you've got a tongue to die for. Good try, sweetheart, but like they say, no-o-o cigar. I quit smoking."

Dhyan pushed by Fran, leading her friend out of the shed. "Hah. Since when?"

"Since now. Since you've wanted me to quit for years."

Dhyan kicked a clod of dirt as she and her friend walked to the house. Fran followed, yanking up tall, rusty weeds on the way. As Dhyan disappeared into the sunroom, she shouted back to Fran, "I'll see it when I believe it."

Fran faced the revolving door into an expensive downtown highrise, took a deep breath, and pushed into the building. She worked to keep her calm and focus as she glided by elevator up to the 17th floor, then over plush carpeting to a high-end office suite marked "Roma and Schultz, Industrial Management Consultants, Personnel Division." A young receptionist, enveloped in a cloud of flowery perfume, worked alone behind a long, wide counter. Her absorption on the telephone was complete.

Fran stood belly-to-the-bar without gaining any proof of existence from this assemblage of teenage magazine dance club wear. Fran tapped her fingers without effect. Several times over, the girl repeated the simplest of directions to the underground parking entrance. "Two bimbos, God help me," Fran muttered.

Eventually, she hung up, looked vacuously pleasant at the apparently just-arrived client, and said, "Good morning, Roma and Schultz."

"I'm here to see Ralph."

"Is he expecting you?" she cooed.

Fran quoted from an old Monty Python skit: "One never expects the Spanish Inquisition."

"Pardon?" came back coquettishly.

Fran clenched her jaw. "Please tell Mr. Roma that Fran is here."

"Oh, you must be his ex. Wow!"

Fran's new fan buzzed Ralph. Fran took several long, forbearing breaths while waiting for him to appear from his office next to the receptionist's barricade.

His face belied no surprise, no particular emotion at all. His expensive suit and tie rode up over a substantial tummy. As he escorted Fran back to his office door, his Girl Friday watched with the interest of a soap opera buff. She only got the opening credits, however, as Ralph held the door for Fran and bade her enter with a sweet, "Come in, dear."

His office furnishings were Spartan, but the decor was lush with great splashes of artwork on the walls, several large well-tended orchid plants in bloom, and a pair of boxing gloves hanging beside his psychology degree.

As Ralph closed the door, Fran said, "Dear?" then cooed, "You must be my ex. Wow!"

"So she's not Einstein. I wish you didn't hold that against people."

"Ah, but what you hold against cupcakes like her is just fine."

"I married the cream of cupcakes, dear, and we're happier than ever."

"No seven-year itch? Or was that just a one-off with me?"

Ralph pointed to the boxing gloves. "Do you want those now or should we continue bare-fisted?"

"You think those gloves are hilarious, don't you?"

"University boxing champ, B.M.O.C."

"Come on, Dhyan knows they're a divorce gift, love that Schultz guy."

"You come on. Psychology degree, boxing gloves—they're funny together."

"Too funny. In front of our princess, you know, we're so civilized, we work everything out like we're dividing up the pastry cart—oh no, you take the cream puff, I'll take the éclair—but she knows what's going down, and she's swinging back."

"Oh, I get it. You have Dhyan for a month, can't straighten her out in three days, so march in to tell Ralph what a mess he's made ...."

"That's not true! God, I hate your martyr routine. It's my fault too, maybe mine more than yours, but what does it matter? We're here now, so let's deal with it."

"Maybe your fault more than mine? That's not how the old song goes."

"So here's a new verse." Fran's voice softened. "You've been great with her. And you've done a lot to make my life such as it is possible."

"Whoa! Can we back up a little? I'm the one who screwed up ...."

"And around, but I'm the one who needed freedom and jumped at the chance to get it. The divorce was hell, but I had my work, my ambitions, and the great big world to fill in the hole. You had Cindy, Dhyan had Juanita, and as long as she was well looked-after and I saw her between assignments, I thought I was winning."

"And you weren't?"

"Oh yeah, I won everything I wanted and more."

"And ... ?"

"And nothing. I'm not here for true confessions. I'm here to talk about solutions."

"Such as what? Get another nanny? Cindy and I have discussed this thoroughly, and first off, she's determined to be a full-time mother, and second off, we don't want another woman in the house. Juanita's irreplaceable."

"And how. Actually I was thinking ... maybe prep school in the fall."

"Prep school?" Ralph whistled between his teeth. "Then we're both rid of her. Great plan."

"Oh listen, please. She's run away once now, and there's more to come, believe me. She needs discipline. She needs authority figures she respects, and at this point that doesn't appear to be you or me or any other adults in her life."

"So let's ship her off, send the problem to someone else, that's the great Fran way."

"No wonder she treats me the way she does. I mean, your attitude is so-o-o bad."

"Sorry. I should just shut up around you, except for, 'Yes dear,' 'No dear.' It's certainly been best for Dhyan so far."

Fran looked at him darkly for a moment, then shook her head. "No, this isn't working." As she headed for the door, she said, "I haven't mentioned prep school to Dhyan yet, and I won't until we're some kind of together on this, okay?"

"Whatever you say."

"Dear," Fran said as she closed the door behind herself.

"Dear," Ralph muttered to himself.

That afternoon, Larry attended a trade gathering in the governor's mansion. He stood in the corner of an opulent ballroom in a sea of dark-suited delegates. Most were male and white, with a few Asians and blacks. A handful of Alaskan aboriginals in red and black button blankets brightened the affair and kept Larry awake with their drumming. When they finished, a soporific string quartet filled any holes left in the soundscape. The plastic wine glass Larry held was drained, as were his sleep-desperate, half-open eyes.

A tall East Indian fellow dressed in a stylish dark ochre suit with light ochre silk shirt and mustard tie approached him and said, "Larry! You still hate parties or just pretending?"

"Perfecting my act. Hey, it's good to see you, Sandhu. How are you?"

Sandhu grinned, his teeth broad rows of creamy white. "Too busy to tell. Must be what I wanted or I wouldn't have left the Octopus's garden."

"We'll take you back in a minute. You might be interested. Big changes afoot. Big battles with big dorks too, but I'm going to win."

"Sounds good, but switching back would be a trick. Remember what Churchill said when changing political parties? It's easy to rat. The real challenge is re-ratting."

"Well, the door's open. We can't match perks and fringes, but listen, we can give you more work and responsibility than you ever dreamed of, with a modest raise in pay and no real authority whatever."

Sandhu laughed. "How can I resist?"

"You're looking good, keeping fit. How's yoga with your uncle?"

"Not. He had a stroke a few months ago, then a bit of surgery nearly finished him off last week. In fact, it did. It's a miracle he survived."

"What happened?"

"He was in for impacted wisdom teeth. General anesthesia, routine stuff."

Friday, February 11th

In the operating theater, heart and brainwave monitors go flat. A large wall clock says 6:07 p.m. A doctor, anesthetist, nurse, and technician work feverishly for long minutes at the head end of a draped body.

"Forget it," the tech says. "We're done." She flips off several switches.

To everyone and no one, the surgeon says, "Sorry. Bloody, goddamned sorry!" He snaps off his gloves and goes directly to tell the patient's family in a nearby waiting area.

The eyes of a middle-aged daughter, son, two teenagers, and Sandhu are keenly on him. "Your father, grandfather ...."

"Yes."

The surgeon closes his eyes, takes a deep breath. "I'm sorry. His heart couldn't take it." His voice drops. "He died about ten minutes ago. We did everything we could, but ...."

Sandhu is strong; the others are devastated.

Inside the operating room, the elderly male patient moans and comes to, eyes clear and bright.

Larry asked Sandhu, "What day did it happen?"

"Last Friday."

"Really? I've got Fran on an oddball file, bunch of survivals about that time."

"Hey, she was brilliant with little Angela, electric stuff. How is she?"

"Working things out, like the rest of us. Why don't you ask her yourself? Give her a call, she's in town for a month. Tell her about your uncle too, if you don't mind. It fits the file."

"Yeah, I'd love to see her. I've got a couple days free before my pin moves on the map."

◆ ◆ ◆

From: "Sandhu Singh" <ssingh@ans.com>
To: "Fran" <fran@elink.net>
Date: Fri, February 18 12:43:03 -05:00
Subject: lunch pronto
Hey Fran, saw Larry yesterday. Miss you guys. Any chance for lunch today, twelve at the Rollups near you? May have something for your file. Sandhu.

◆ ◆ ◆

At ten to noon, Sandhu wheeled his turbaned Uncle Sid into a new California Rollups restaurant, bright with sunbursts, cactuses, and tomato-everything decor. At noon, the hostess showed them to their table. Sandhu locked the brakes on the wheelchair, then sat to his uncle's left. A server brought three menus.

At five past noon, the server poured three glasses of water. At 12:10, Sandhu checked his watch. His uncle sat impassively.

Fran flew in at 12:15, carrying the messy file folder marked 'Coincidentals'. "Sorry," she puffed. "It's one big red-light district out there."

Sandhu rose to give her a warm hug. "No problem. We still have forty-five minutes." He discreetly positioned Fran to Sid's left and said, "Uncle Sid, I'd like you to meet Fran. Fran, my dear Uncle Siddhartan."

Sid offered his left hand, which Fran squeezed gently and said, "Delighted."

Sandhu offered Fran his chair. She sat with the file folder on her lap. As he slipped into the remaining chair, he leaned close to whisper, "He's had a stroke. Can't see anything on his right side."

A server quickly appeared. Sandhu said, pointing to his uncle, "Soup and bun here, and today's special for me."

Fran gathered up the menus and handed them to the server. "Tuna Tango, thanks."

Sandhu nodded toward her file. "So what's the story?"

"Larry's pocketful of miracles. Take a look."

Sandhu flipped through copies of newsclippings and wire pieces, summarizing as he read, "Girl survives major fire in Lima, no burns. Swiss man survives fall off 500-metre cliff, walks away. Chinese woman found on mudslide that buries her family. Shipwrecked fisherman washes up on shore, all other hands lost. Your miracle kid, famous little Angela. Dozens here. Uncle Sid too, I guess. Did Larry tell you?"

Fran shook her head.

Sandhu quickly recounted his uncle's operating room recovery.

"Hm-m," Fran said, "Check the dates."

"February 11, February 11th, February 12th ...."

"All about the same time, give or take some time zones."

"Oo-o freaky."

"Naw. I keep thinking of Pope John the Twenty-third's dying words: 'Every day is a good day to be born. Every day is a good day to die.' You can slice that down to the second. People are abornin' and adyin' and defying the odds all the time. And with so many billions of us, for Pete's sake, coincidence is inevitable."

"Larry agrees? Or is he looking for a job at the *Enquirer*?"

"Now that is freaky." Fran pointed to the label. "It's marked 'Coincidentals', so I'm taking it from there."

"Taking it where?"

Fran shrugged, "Who knows? I just started."

"Touchy to report, I'd think."

"Yeah, and if I can't think of an angle, then that's how it goes. The newsroom floor is littered with false leads, pointless hunches, half-baked stuff that doesn't make it."

"And some of the best stories around."

The server brought Sid's soup. Sandhu offered the spoon to Sid's clenched left hand. He pushed Sandhu's hand away and slowly extended his fist to Fran, opening it to reveal a dark, rough stone about robin's-egg size.

Fran said, "Ah, a rock. Schist maybe? I'm no geologist."

Sid slowly closed and withdrew his hand.

Sandhu said, "He's been clutching it since the operation. Can't explain it, of course, because of the stroke."

"When did he have the stroke?"

"Last November. Apparently unrelated to what went wrong. I wonder though—both heart, blood, circulation related."

Sid beseeched Fran with earnest eyes. She said softly to him, "Thank you for showing me. I'll make a note of it."

Sid's eyes brightened with tears. He shakily tucked the rock into a leather pouch hanging from his neck then, with difficulty, began eating his soup. He grunted his approval.

Sandhu said to his uncle, "Glad you like it." To Fran, he said, "Uncle Sid's a wonder a hundred times over, my hero since I was a kid."

Sid beamed a lopsided smile.

The server delivered wicker baskets with rollups in big nests of sprouts and ruffled greens.

Sandhu asked Fran, "So what else is new?"

"Nothing, except I'm this far from quitting." She made a narrow space between thumb and forefinger. His eyes widened. She continued, "So Larry gave me a month to play with this and hang out with my kid."

"What's wrong?"

Fran shrugged. "With work? Nothing. I found Angela, and that was it for the news-chasing game, like that." She snapped her fingers. "Nothing wrong with Dhyan either, if I can get a grip on all her wild energy."

Sandhu laughed. "Mom's girl, hey? She must be, what ... ten, eleven now?"

"Thirteen."

"No kidding. We're getting old, Fran."

"At warp speed. How 'bout you? You know, I still can't believe you left us and for mere money, prestige, security—such a crass move, Sandhu. They treating you right?"

He shrugged. "Right enough. I'm off to Beijing tomorrow to check out the big dam, the growing Gobi, coal fires, organ transplants, refrigerators in every home. You know the beat."

Fran sighed deeply. "Oh yeah." She took a bite of sandwich. "Good tuna. Probably driftnet caught—not that they use them any more, right?—by highly subsidized boats begging for government bailouts. Fish wars, fish crisis, aquaculture ... God, there's no escape. Guilty with every delicious bite."

"You think too much. The show's the thing. The show and tell."

Fran smiled. "The show and no tell sometimes."

The clock on the closet door in Fran's home office said 2:47 p.m. Fran sat nose to her computer screen, its word-processing program blank. She fiddled with an unlit cigarette. She wrote a short sentence, then backspaced it out. She started typing again, then stopped, highlighted, and deleted the whole thing. She flipped impatiently through the 'Coincidentals' file.

Finally, she dialed the phone. "Hi, Lar, got a minute?"

Larry answered using the speaker phone. "Yeah, hi Fran, got some sanity? Our favorite trendoid just left. I thought not having a budget would keep him down, but he's finding ways to produce crap for nothing. He used a university class to do a miserable little piece, and now he's pissed off because I won't let him show anyone their lousy effort. I told him if he stages a penthouse demo' behind my back ... well, we're getting down to the shoot-out at OK Corral. It's him or me, I tell you."

"So come join my salsa team. I do the tomatoes, you do the peppers, we share the onions. And tears."

"No way. You take half my chair, and we gang up ...."

"Over your dead body."

Larry was silent.

"Like never, pal. Hey, I saw Sandhu for lunch today, he brought his Uncle Sid."

"Lucky you. Fits the file, doesn't he?"

"By timing, perfectly, but he's had a stroke, right? Who knows what's behind those big speechless eyes. I'm calling because Sandhu got me thinking. He asked a question I couldn't answer, the very first one I should have asked: why'd you start this file?"

"I didn't. Just between you and me, an old cousin sent it to me. I'm kind of interested though, whether anything reportable comes of it or not."

"You really think there's something going on, something connecting all these survivals?"

"I don't know, but somehow all those suckers made it, fooled the big one."

"True, but ... hey, I didn't know you were interested in this kind of stuff. You going all fringy on us, Lar?"

"Listen, as president of the newly formed Immortals Club ...."

Fran laughed. "And this is the membership list, I get it. As mere scribe to your undying greatness, the eternal Larry, what d'ya want?"

"I want you, hot from Angela, to apply the peripherals thing to her buddies in the file. Forget the obvious stuff in the middle, keep checking the edges."

Fran snorted. "Outer limits you mean. I really just see it as the bell curve of luck. With enough people in the world, you're bound to find some on the lucky and unlucky extremes. And things happen in bunches, that's how random numbers work. It's a statistical thing."

"So take that angle and run with it."

"I might. Otherwise I'm just an old cow chewing her cud. Nothing's hit the first stomach yet, and it'll be out the back end before I've figured a damned thing."

Larry laughed. "Then we'll run through the plops together. Did you know that they squish wonderfully between your toes when they're fresh and warm? The old cousin who gave me the file told me that. So how are things in your corner?"

"No corners, it's the Roma circus. I fight with Dhyan. I fight with Ralph. I fight with myself. You want a round?"

Larry chuckled. "With you, anytime."

Fran's voice softened. "I'm really glad to be home, bruises and all. And glad this goofy file makes it possible. Thanks, Lar."

Dhyan appeared in the doorway, unseen and unheard, just home from school. She watched her mom's back as Fran said goodbye and returned to staring at the monitor and toying with the unlit cigarette.

Dhyan shouted, "What the hell are you doing?"

Fran jumped and spun around. "Au-u-gh! Not smoking. It isn't lit."

"It's still cheating."

"No, the patch is cheating. This is just a soother, a distraction."

"Can I have one? I won't light it."

Fran broke the cigarette and threw it in the waste basket. "No. How was your day?"

"Bo-o-o-r-ring."

"You got homework?"

"A bit, but it's Friday, alright? Don't start nagging ...."

"So let's go out. Let's do something."

"Like what?"

"Pizza and ice cream? That new Disney movie?"

"Mom! I'm not a little girl."

"Porn flick? Escargot?"

"Oh gawd, you're so weird!"

"What would you like to do?"

"Really like to do?"

"Yeah."

"Nothing you'd do anyway."

"You sure?"

Dhyan shrugged, "Yeah. Well, prob'ly."

"So what is it? A rock concert with your friends? Cruising the mall? Shooting pool? Blue hair? Nose rings? Give me a clue."

Dhyan muttered shyly, eyes watching a fidgeting sneaker, "I want to see Angela."

Fran tapped the file. "This one?"

Dhyan nodded.

Fran asked softly, "Why?"

"I read some of your file, okay? Don't blow, okay? I'm just like, bored and it's interesting."

"No problem. Read it all. Or maybe you have."

"Just mostly the Angela stuff."

"What's the fascination?"

"I don't know. Must be hard losing your whole family like that, then sitting in the jungle for two whole days."

"Yeah, hard even to imagine. She was awesome. I should call her, shouldn't I? I promised I would."

Dhyan said almost inaudibly, "I already did."

"Really? Oh boy."

"Now you're pissed, I knew it. I never shoulda ...."

"No, it's okay. What did she say?"

"She said ... she said she'd like to see you—me too. We could go visit."

"And you said we would?"

Dhyan shrugged. "Maybe."

"Darling, this is my month home."

"See! I knew it was stupid, I knew I never shoulda said anything! You and your stupid job! You go when you want, stay when you want, send me to Dad and 'Cindy-rella'—God, gag me—then you drag me home! I don't hafta ...!"

"Wait, wait! You think of this as home?"

"I don't have a home! And I don't need one, and I don't need you or your stupid job or stupid Angela or anybody. I'm just like, so ... so fed up, but I'll deal with it, alright? So butt out!"

Dhyan turned on her heel and ran out of the house, leaving the front door open. Fran followed quickly, shouting, "Dhyan, don't do this! Dhyan!"

Half a block down the street, Fran saw Dhyan disappear through a pedestrian shortcut to the next block. Winded and fighting tears, Fran stopped. "Damn!"

Fran went directly to the phone in her living room and hit the "Ralph—work" button. "Ralph, Dhyan just blew up and took off, and I don't know where she's gone. What's her pattern? Where do I start looking?"

Ralph groaned, "Oh no." He stood up from his desk and started pacing. "Check her friends, go to the mall .... What happened?"

"She wants to go to Oregon, I didn't jump to it, and boom! she hits the street."

"Oregon?"

"She wants to see Angela, the girl I rescued."

"So why don't you take her, have a holiday with your kid?"

"And forget school I suppose? Solid Cs don't win any instant trips in my book. Besides it's my job, and I'm not up to a weekend jaunt to Portland. I'm home for a month ...."

"Home alone."

"Damn you! Are you going to help or just kick me every chance you get?"

"Sorry, sorry. Let's start with her friends, we've got a list of them at home. I'll get Cindy calling."

"Great. I'm going to drive around, check the malls. I've got my cell. Call the second you know anything."

Dhyan stormed her way through shortcuts, neighborhood parks, and school grounds. On a side street, a motorcycle roared up, then slowed beside her.

The small, good-looking young man on it, in full leathers, said, "Hey kid, where's the fire?"

Dhyan walked quickly, ignoring him.

He kept pace, taunting, "You're a J.C. Junior Hi-i-i-gh brat, right?"

Dhyan kept her head down. "Fuck off."

"J.C.'s my turf. I'm Brad, man, everyone knows Brad. I sell there, right?"

"You sell being left alone? I'll take a bi-i-g order."

"Hey, a smart-ass. I like smart-asses. Name your price, Dhyan."

She stopped and looked at him. "How'd you know my name?"

"I know what's goin' down. Tiffany—she's my sister, right?—she says you bought from a real loser last time. Whole school knows it."

"That's crap. I've never bought a thing. Tiffany's your sister?" Dhyan snorted. "That's too funny."

"Say that twice. I dare ya."

"She's like, cool and you're ...."

"Like what?" Brad gunned his motor. "You better say off the charts. Come with me, I'll show you cool."

"You got a hope."

"I'll take you home where me and Tiff hang out. No parents there to screw you around, know what I mean?"

"Oh man, do I ever. Is she there now?"

"Yeah, waitin' for me. The old dudes, they might be in, but they don't give a shit. It's just like, a few blocks away."

Dhyan thought for a moment, then shook her head. "Forget it. I got a friend waiting."

"What's your problem? Afraid of a little ride? Afraid of little Tiff?"

"Oh, pul-ease."

"So show me."

Dhyan studied him, didn't move, didn't speak.

"C'mon. I'll take you to your friend's after, in like, an hour."

She shrugged, said "Sure" and hopped on. They roared off.

Fran cruised in her small beater car—her major environmental statement—which she hadn't cleaned out for years or emptied the ashtray in months. "It's been an hour and a half, Ralph, and I'm coming up empty," she said into her cell phone. "She's not with any friends, not hanging anywhere usual. I'm calling the police."

"They won't do anything this early on. Give it a few more hours, until after midnight."

"I'll go crazy by dark. God, by then I'll ...."

"Welcome to my world. So sorry you missed last time, hey?"

"I still can't believe you didn't call me. And I can't believe you can be so cruel now. Will you ever get enough licks in?"

A long, uncomfortable silence ensued. Finally, Ralph said, "Yeah, we gotta keep it together. I learned from last time that she's pretty safety-conscious, not stupid about taking risks. And her friends are the key, friends of friends. She's got quite a network."

"A thirteen-year-old running off to a party house and zoning out for two days isn't risk-taking?"

"Of course, but she's smart—like you, Fran, she's got a good sixth sense. Likes trouble, but dodges the worst."

"Thanks, I think."

"Trust me, she's somewhere with friends, acquaintances. She's in the neighborhood."

"Let's hope. I'll keep cruising, call you in five or ten."

On a kitchen calendar of bank-issue sunset photos, Fran crossed off day one of Dhyan missing with a heavy black X. After two big Xs on the calendar, dark circles puffed under Fran's sleep-deprived eyes. Three midnight-to-dawn thrashings added another X to February and ten years to her face. Tears fell as easily as she breathed.

During the long days, she drank endless coffee and smoked in her weedy garden while waiting by the phone. She kept the cordless in hand at home and the cell as she walked and drove the streets looking for her girl, even venturing once as far as the kiddie prostitute stroll. "Ring, damn you!" she cursed and invoked when the innocuous receivers mocked her with agonizing stretches of silence.

Ralph telephoned often, and Dhyan's friends called occasionally, jangling her nerves with high hopes, then plunging her into deep disappointment and frustration when it was just a check-up, no-news call. Cheery telemarketers didn't know that behind Fran's brusque "How dare you!" was a breaking heart.

After five big Xs covered the third week of February, only coffee and cigarettes kept Fran upright. Food had no appeal. A casserole from Cindy went untasted in the fridge. "She's a sweet woman," Fran said to Ralph when he delivered it, then bit her tongue to keep from adding that she was sweet like saccharine, no nutritional value. But then, he was getting so fat that she was just his oversize cupcake, right? Fran winced; she was wicked in her distress and hated herself and the situation all the more for it. Ralph smiled faintly at her compliment, his face muscles exhausted from days of clenching his jaw and fighting tears.

Day six, afternoon six brought a police car cruising up to park in front of Fran's townhouse. Her heart leapt. Maybe they got her! Please, please, please.

But no. A burly officer unfolded himself from the car and walked somberly to her door, carrying a business-size envelope. "Oh God," Fran thought, "Dhyan's dead." She opened the door before he could buzz.

"Ms. Roma, ma'am." She steeled herself. He took long, unbearable seconds before saying slowly, "We need your signature to put up 'missing person' posters. Starting day after tomorrow."

Fran felt a little giddy from relief. "You mean she's ... she's still, you know .... Just a sec', I'll get a pen."

"Got one here, ma'am." He took a cheap ballpoint from a breast pocket, then took the permit for from the envelope.

"I guess this means you still don't have anything—no leads, clues, nothing?" She signed the permit against the door frame.

He didn't answer until she handed it back. "Kids usually show up after a few days."

"Yeah, but my girl hasn't."

"So we go this route. Sometimes posters help."

"Oh man, I hope so," Fran said, her heart pounding on her sleeve.

"If the kid wants to be found."

Slam her in the gut, why not? How could she guess if Dhyan wanted to be found? She could be huddled in some God-awful place, stoned and hurting from a lineup of johns, desperately wishing to get to a phone, to be able to run to one if she could run. This long arm of the law, this big guy who'd probably picked up his share of runaway corpses, was as comforting as a fencepost. As the cop tucked the signed permit into his pocket, he said, "Brought it to save you a trip. Kinda irregular."

Fran softened a little. "Thanks. I appreciate it."

"Is she smart?"

"As a whip."

"Good. She'll be fine—or I haven't seen it all. Afternoon, ma'am."

As his words sank in, Fran thought, "Some fencepost, the best kind: considerate, experienced, solid as a rock. Marry me," she wished, watching him drive off. "God, I need someone like you."

On the afternoon of the seventh day, another police car pulled up in front of Fran's place, this time with a policeman driving, a female officer in the front passenger seat, and ... and ... Dhyan riding in the back! The female officer opened the car door for Dhyan, who stepped out wearing the same clothing she'd run away in. The officer escorted her toward Fran, who stood grinning and crying at her front door.

"Oh baby," she sang out, ready to envelop Dhyan in welcoming arms.

The officer held Fran back. "Please don't. Her request."

"Where did you find her?"

"A few blocks away. Small time drug house, biker boyfriend."

Fran's eyes widened, mouth dropped. She whispered, "Biker boyfriend?"

Dhyan slipped into the house and went directly upstairs to her bedroom.

The officer said, "I'm with undercover drugs. We found a small grow op and some street kids. She seems to be fine—clean, coherent. No hard stuff, and we don't suspect attempted recruitment into prostitution at this point, no unwilling confinement, nothing like that."

In shock, Fran muttered, "A week with a biker boyfriend?"

"She had no possessions with her that we could ascertain, beyond what she's wearing. We'll be following up and contacting you as necessary. Here's my card; call anytime."

Fran took the card. "Thank you. Thank you so much."

"Welcome, ma'am."

Fran closed the door and slowly slumped against it, unable to move or think of what to do next.

The pendulum of a nearby cuckoo clock tick-ticked noisily. Just as a parrot popped out and squawked five times, the doorbell rang. Fran jumped and quickly tried to wipe some reality back into her face.

She opened the door to Nora, Larry's assistant, who took in Fran's appearance and said, "Oh dear, I shouldn't have ... I'm so sorry to disturb you."

Fran collected her wits. "No, it's okay. It's been a rough week, but things are ... well, they're looking up."

"I debated about stopping by and surprising you like this, but I'm just so worried."

"You heard about Dhyan? I haven't talked with Larry unless Ralph ...."

"Oh no, I haven't heard. What happened? Is she alright?"

"She's home now. She's ... yeah, she's going to be okay."

"Oh dear, I'm so sorry." Nora stepped back and turned to go. "I really shouldn't have stopped by. I'll call you or you call me when things are ...."

"No, wait. You're here, it must be important."

"It'll keep."

"No, please tell me or I'll worry."

"It's just Mr. Singer. He's a little ... oh, having a little health trouble, but we'll talk later. And please, please don't tell him that I came by."

"Larry's sick? I've been so distracted, so out of it, I ...."

"Don't fuss, don't worry." Nora put her forefinger to her lips. "And mum's the word. We'll talk soon. You look after yourself and your girl. Good luck."

"Thanks. Bye."

Fran walked slowly, heavily to Dhyan's bedroom. She tapped on the door, then peeked in without waiting for an answer. Inside was a poster-lined, clothing-strewn teenager's room—nothing childish in sight, except the shabby stuffed rabbit in Dhyan's arms. Fran walked in and sat on the end of the bed. A minute passed. Two. They looked everywhere but at each other's eyes. Finally, Fran dared ask softly, "Who is this guy to you, Dhyan?"

"Nobody."

"He can't be nobody. You spent a week with him."

Dhyan didn't answer.

"What kind of tests do we have to get done? Pregnancy? STDs?"

"Nothin', man! Get outta my face, alright?"

"I'm serious, sweetheart. Things like this don't just go away."

"There's nothing to test! Nothing like you're thinking."

"Really? God, I hope that's true. I mean, should I drop it or ask you right out if you're a virgin?"

"That is so crude and so rude. Why don't you believe me for once? You're so out of it, so off in your little fantasies."

"So tell me what happened. A week with a biker sets alarms ringing."

"And his sister Tiffany."

"Who's studying for the convent, right?"

Dhyan rolled her eyes, groaned. "Can we just drop it? Tiffany's totally cool, and Brad's like, a loser alright? I'm okay, just like I left here. Why can't you trust me?"

Slowly, Fran said, "Trust. That's what it comes down to, doesn't it?" Dhyan ran the bunny's ear down her cheek as she'd done when small to comfort herself. Fran resisted the powerful urge to hug her, to ease both of their too-big, bruised hearts.

After a long pause, she said, "Where do we go from here? I mean, separate from the cops and legal thing, whatever they might want from you."

"No way. I'm not talking to them or to you or to anyone."

"You might not have a choice. A counselor though, that's an option. Separate from me and your dad, totally confidential."

"No counselors! Nothing, nobody, you hear? It's like, nothing, and it's over."

Fran reluctantly agreed, "I guess so." More long moments passed, then Fran said, "Maybe I'm stupid to ask, but ... oh hell, if we're going to start where we left off, why not? What about Oregon? Angela? Still want to see her?"

Dhyan shrugged.

"Will you go if I book it?"

"You don't want to go."

"Not without you."

"Really?"

"You bet. What's Grampa's first rule?"

"Always call a bluff—but he's crazy."

Fran smiled. "So?"

Fran rang the front doorbell of a middle-class home in a Portland suburb. Cherry trees burst with blossoms throughout the neighborhood. She and Dhyan waited briefly. A plump African-American woman in stretch slacks and striped T-shirt opened the door and welcomed them in, her voice soft and kind.

In the living room, Angela sat on a cushion by a low coffee table playing Chinese checkers with her Korean-born uncle and ten-year-old cousin, a girl who was an attractive mix of her parents' coloring and features.

The uncle stood up to shake Fran's hand. "Welcome. You were a name in our household even before you found Angela." He shook Dhyan's hand. "Now you're famous here too."

Dhyan smiled shyly.

Fran grinned her thanks and looked to Angela, saying, "Hello Sunshine. Boy, it's good to see you."

Angela nodded, her eyes stuck on Dhyan.

Fran said, "Angela, this is Dhyan."

Dhyan's eyes twinkled as she said awkwardly, "Hi."

The aunt said to Dhyan, "And this is Joanne. We've got another girl sleeping—she's three—and our boy's over at a friend's place. He's twelve."

Fran asked Angela, "What are your other cousins' names?"
Angela lisped through missing front teeth, "Sarah and Alex."

In a Portland hotel room, Fran sat in an easy chair flipping through the TV guide. Dhyan bounced on the nearest of two double beds. "Please, Mom, please, please. Can I stay, please? She's so cute and fun."

"No, sweetheart, I've got to get back and talk to Larry about his health, find out what he's hiding from me."

"So you can go. Mrs. C. said I could stay, just another week, okay, okay? They're really nice, and you don't like, have to be here."

"Are you dismissing your old mom? Luckily, they are pretty nice. No motorbikes."

"Mom!"

"And I guess we could get more schoolwork sent out."

"Please, please, please."

"What is it about Angela?"

"I don't know, she's like a little sister, like ... sort of a puppy friend, you know. She's mad at Joanne and her stupid counselor too, so I can talk to her."

"What's she mad about?"

"Joanne's mean to her and her counselor's meaner."

"Really? In what ways?"

"Joanne's jealous and snitches all the time. And the counselor makes Angela tell her things, forces her to talk about her dreams, then gets all weird about it. She's a bitch, Mom, you should talk with her."

"Wow, I think I have to, if she'll see me tomorrow before I go. Maybe I can get something for the file from her. Angela certainly hasn't opened up to me. Not that we've had much chance."

"So can I stay, huh, huh? Just say yes."

"Well ... I'll talk with the Chos and make sure they've got enough of your favorite Monkey Chow."

"Yes!"

The counselor's office overflowed with colorful, comfortable furnishings, big pillows, and bright Rorschach-type paintings. Thank-you cards, small gifts, and testimonials filled every surface. Two black-framed certificates hung austerely on a side wall.

A middle-aged woman in a Swiss-inspired blouse and dirndl skirt leapt up from her desk to greet Fran. The former flower child had grown matronly in figure, with long windswept straggles of pinned-up gray hair. She darted her hand out to shake, her mouth tense. Her voice, however, was butterscotch. "Come in, please. I'm Serena Allen-Sanchez."

"Fran Roma. Thank you for fitting me in."

"You're welcome. Have a chair. Let's get comfortable." Serena returned to sit behind her large desk laden with dozens of photos and children's handcrafts. She took a deep, calming breath.

Fran settled as indicated and began, "My daughter Dhyan will be staying with the Chos this coming week ...."

"Yes, I heard. Angela's very happy with Dhyan."

Fran smiled. "They hit it right off on the phone, and it just keeps going. It's a bit of a surprise both ways, given their age difference, plus Angela's pretty quiet while my girl's a constant party ready to happen."

"Quiet, but far from shy. In fact, she's one of the most determined little girls I've ever met. I don't know what you've come to hear from me, but I really can only speak in generalities. We work in the strictest confidence, and there's a lot that even the Chos don't know."

"Well, that's the thing," Fran said. "I understand absolutely, and I respect the necessity and legalities of this, but Dhyan has heard some things—snippets of what's going on here—that made me think I'd better get a heads-up from the source."

Serena stiffened. "What kind of things?"

"Process more than anything. Tactics for getting Angela to reveal her dreams."

Serena tightened. "I work from a broad base of training and experience, with dream therapy as the cornerstone of my practice. Angela is, as I said, very determined, very resistant. I use a variety of strategies to overcome this."

"Word from Dhyan is that Angela doesn't like some of the interpretations you give her dreams."

Voice rising, Serena asked, "Such as?"

"Making them appear darker and more nefarious than they are."

"You realize the seriousness of what you're impugning?"

Fran smiled. "I don't realize anything at this point, except that I hope you can fill me in a bit, set the record straight."

Serena looked rattled, her eyes restless as she considered her options. After a couple of conscious breaths, she leaned forward and asked, "Can I trust you to not say a word beyond these walls? I mean, you're a reporter and all."

"If you recall, I'm the reporter who kept Angela from a media feeding frenzy after I found her, and I pleaded on my sign-off broadcast for the world to give her the privacy she needs to realize her sweetest dreams. Now we're talking about not-so-sweet dreams, and I'm worried about them—and not, absolutely not as a journalist, but as someone who cares a lot about this amazing little girl."

"So listen," Serena said conspiratorially. "I can tell you this much. She had troubles in her life well before the crash. Dark and nefarious behaviors, as you so nicely put it, within her family."

"What—some kind of abuse? Cult stuff? Satanic? How bad are we talking?"

Serena nodded and blinked anxiously. "This is very difficult. She recites her experiences as ... well, dreams basically, mixed in with the present as a means of ...." She searched for words. "... of keeping her balance as she lets go of her formative reality."

"Nightmares, you mean? Dhyan hasn't noticed anything like that, and they're sleeping in the same room together—with Joanne too, who'd make some fuss, I'm pretty sure. She's on to just about everything Angela does and says."

"Angela doesn't relate to them as nightmares."

"So maybe they're just dreams."

"Oh, please. They're very graphic, detailed, and immediate, nothing a child could make up—any adult either for that matter."

"Can you give me an example?"

"No," Serena said quickly, jumpily. "Strange things go on in them with elements of ... what can I say? Evil. In her innocence, she's positive about them and possessive too, which isn't entirely surprising, because they're her only connection to her lost grandmother, mother, and baby sister."

Fran said, "And her father and brother?—they died too."

"Well, yes, but Angela identifies almost exclusively with ... no, I'd better not get into that. Listen, as far as Dhyan is concerned, it's imperative that she not probe any of this, not make any kind of fuss or comments about it. It's far too dicey for any but a trained professional to deal with."

"And what do the Chos know about this?"

"Very little. They've been wonderfully cooperative about leaving these aspects of Angela's former life with me, so as not to color or taint their present normal and healing environment in which Angela can thrive. You mustn't tell them anything I've said to you, or ... well, the delicate balance we've forged could be upset with disastrous consequences. Angela's home life is working for her now, and I don't want anything to change that."

"I certainly agree there. As for what's working here or not, I don't have a clue, but I guess that's your business. Nothing goes beyond these doors, Scout's honor."

Serena eye's fluttered shut in relief. "Thank you. Now I really can't say anything more, and I'm sorry, but my next appointment is ...." Her voice trailed off as she glanced at her wrist watch.

Fran rose to go, extending her hand to shake. "I'm booked too, flying out in a few hours. Thanks again." Serena's palm was sweaty. *Poor woman,* Fran thought, *she's in quite a state over this. Poor Angela too, working with such a high-strung confidante.* But then, what did Fran know about counseling in general or this particular situation? Only enough to tell Dhyan to stay tuned and tread lightly.

"Goodbye then," Serena said, squaring her shoulders and forcing a smile as she saw Fran out her office door. *"Bon voyage."*

Ralph paced his office on heavy heels, nostrils flaring. One hand held a cordless phone to his ear, the other waved freely to punctuate his words. "So you dumped her in Oregon? I can't believe you sometimes. Give me a break, damn it! I'm worried sick, I don't like her so far away ...."

He listened for a moment, then conceded angrily, "Yeah, yeah, better to have a six-year-old puppy friend than an eighteen-year-old biker, but it's a long flight, and she's got to come home by herself. God knows what'll happen or how she could get waylaid."

He slumped into the chair behind his desk. "It's not a question of trusting her. I do trust her as best I can. It's you I don't trust. You're a flake, you're all over the board .... Okay, okay, have it your way. Haven't you all along? This better turn out one-hundred percent, let me tell you, or I'll ... well, just you wait and see."

Mrs. Ralph Roma sat primly on the edge of Fran's Algerian sofa piled with big soft pillows. She refused to let her eyes light on any item in the room. When they drifted to an unusual object, she quickly pulled them back to adjust her diamond engagement ring, centering the large stone on her finger. She studied her perfect white-tipped fingernails and picked pieces of imaginary lint from her three-piece polka dot ensemble.

Fran's living room was as cluttered and eclectic as her kitchen. In every direction, oddball items and clever details caught the eye and tickled the brain. Fran called it her open-storage museum, her live-in landfill site.

She could tell endless stories about the very real looking Amazon shrunken head, the eagle feather gift of Gitk'san friends, the original Picasso

"Bum" sketch, the sad donkey oil painting on a bracket fungus, the first edition of Captain James Cook's voyages—once proudly the only cook books in her house, except for Julia Child's signed copy slopped with oyster juice by the great chef herself when she and Fran .... But forget the stories; Cindy had never been interested and definitely was not now.

She'd called ahead to ask for this emergency meeting, thus giving Fran all of ten minutes to get ready for it. Fran put coffee-and-cookies preparation ahead of changing from workday khakis into a her own seldom-worn version of polka dot afternoon drop-in attire.

Looking like a plumber, she poured from a shining silver coffee service into fine china cups atop a rosewood tea wagon, the only part of the scene that suited Cindy's tastes.

"The casserole was great," Fran said warmly. "I froze half, so Dhyan had some too. Thank you so much."

"You're welcome. I put an extra prayer in every bite, and I know that made all the difference."

Fran took a cigarette from a package. "Do you mind?"

"I thought you'd quit."

"I did, and I will again. This is just while Dhyan's away."

"I should think it's hard enough to quit once. Not that I ever have."

Fran laughed. "You're so right. I'll quit once and for all—ten times and for all, I swear—but not today."

"I'd say no if Dhyan were here, but since she's away ...." Cindy shrugged her permission.

Fran turned on a small smoke absorber, lit the cigarette, and sat down in a rattan chair opposite Cindy.

Cindy said, "Ralph is so upset, I just had to see you. I can't pussyfoot around this, so I'll just say it straight out. How you could leave that beautiful girl in a strange city, especially after she just ... well, I'm afraid I don't understand."

"Exactly. Ralph's not getting it either. This is the best thing for her, believe me."

"This is hard for me, you know. I mean, I have to deal with Ralph, and he's taking a lot of tranquilizers, way too many."

"And I'm back to smoking, so sign us up for Junkies Anon', separate groups please. What can I say? He's your husband. I can't help you deal with him, I'm sorry."

"No, but you could help with the situation, which is in your own best interest as well. The thing is ... well, you won't like this, but ... well, he's talking about applying for sole custody."

"He's what?" Fran exclaimed.

"Sole custody, Fran."

"Legal, physical or both?"

"Well, physical for sure, and whatever else he can get, I guess. I don't know how it works, except he wants Dhyan living full time with us, and I'm not sure if that's what we need, especially if you're going to be in town more so Dhyan could be over here, if you'd just be more strict and reliable."

Fran sighed in frustration, "Oh God."

Cindy shot her a condemning look. "Swearing is another problem, Fran, and you might think it's minor, but taking the Lord's name in vain is ...."

"I'm sorry. I meant small 'g' god, as in 'zilla, Zeus, okay?"

Cindy straightened her diamond again. "In our house, we can watch what she says, and that's important, because we have two very impressionable little boys who are learning bad things from their big sister. We need to get control of the situation, that's what Ralph says. Complete control."

Fran said, "Two things you need to know and to tell Ralph: one, I'm doing all I can for Dhyan with her best interests totally in mind, and two, she's alright and she's going to turn out just fine. Keeping her from me, keeping her from staying here isn't the answer, believe me. Complete control will be complete disaster."

"But the thing is, she's not staying here, not right now, and she's not at home, and poor Ralph's in knots ...."

Fran interrupted, "At this moment, she's perfectly safe and fine. Ralph knows that, he talks to her every day. As for his knots, give him some more tranquilizers with a whisky kicker. He can detox when she's safely home—and she will be. Trust me, trust Dhyan. That's what it's all about."

"God is the only one I trust. God and Jesus. And Ralph's my third angel."

"High praise."

"I had a rebellious time in my life too, you know. I was older than Dhyan, but I was swearing and dressing like a tramp, looking for trouble. I was only half straightened out when Ralph noticed me and talked to me and saved me from slipping back to my old wicked ways. We both let Jesus Christ into our hearts one weekend when we went off to ... well, it's very personal, very private, hard to explain."

Adultery always is, Fran thought, but held her tongue.

Cindy continued, "Now that I'm saved, truly saved, it's my duty to God to try to help others. When Dhyan ran off both times, I just know God heard my prayers and brought her safely home, and now I'm praying every minute about this awful Oregon situation ...."

Fran interrupted, "It's not an awful situation. It's not even a situation. We know where she is, and we know she's fine. She's with a nice family. She's a smart, capable kid." Fran's voice softened. "You've done a lot of good things for her, and I really, really appreciate it. I know I do things different than you, Cindy, but we all have her very best interests at heart. Can you assure Ralph of that?"

Cindy forced a hopeful smile. "I'll try." She hesitated, then asked, "Fran, would you pray with me?" Fran's surprised silence was permission enough. "Dear Lord God Almighty, Father of my personal Savior and great Creator who made woman in her frailties, the weaker vessel into whom ...."

"Oh Cindy, I'm sorry," Fran said, reaching to touch Cindy's arm. "It's just not my style, not the way I ...."

Cindy deflated noticeably. "But it's prayer. It's not about this way or that, it's about God and His infinite mercy."

"I know, and you're so right. It's just that ... well, prayers are different for different people, but listen, I have an idea. Would you sing for me, maybe 'Amazing Grace'? I would be most honored if you would."

Cindy happily treated Fran to the best rendition of the old hymn since Joan Baez's voice had thrilled millions of the once-lost, now-found. "*Brava!*" Fran cheered after. "What an incredible gift. Thank you, thank you. I'll book Carnegie Hall for you next weekend, what do you think?"

Cindy primly replied, "No, I sing for God now, only God. And I'm a mom, that's work enough for any woman."

"Hm. Well, you're a lucky and talented one, and I'm glad you came to see me."

After another cup of coffee and proud talk of her boys, Cindy left Fran's restored to full inflation, not a speck of lint on any of her polka dots or in between.

When Fran stepped from noon sunlight into the midnight interior of the Old Vaudeville Theater, her eyes momentarily went blind. Her nose filled with a potent mix of old popcorn and people smells, new fabrics and paint. Gradually, gilded features spangled out from the darkness.

She stepped carefully down a sloping aisle toward the softly lit stage, finding her way toward it past tiers of black, empty seats. At center stage, a lanky, towheaded man held court with a half-dozen actors, showing the nuanced gestures he expected of one of them. He appeared almost albino, although his eyes were dark and simian-quick.

He saw Fran mid-way down the aisle and immediately announced with a slight Dutch accent, "Okay guys, now you're perfect. Practice for an hour and get even better." He held up a hand with fingers widespread to Fran, whom everyone now noticed, and said, "Give me five minutes, darling. Go to the bean shop next door and order me a shaking zombie latté. I'll be there in six."

At the Bean There Bar, Raoul and Fran perched on stools by a busy window, drinking giant mugs of coffees. "It's been crazy lately, Raoul, real tough. I don't know half of what's happening and that includes with Larry. I've been trying to talk with him, especially about his health, but ...."

"What do you know?"

"Nothing, that's the problem. Nora's worried enough to drop hints, but she's too loyal to spill it. I figured I'd talk with you before I ambush him and demand to see his medical chart."

"Good plan. He ... well, let's put it this way: I'm worried too."

"How worried?"

"Very. I'm supposed to pretend nothing's happening. He figures no one will notice until he drops."

"Drops from what?"

"I'm not supposed to tell but what the hell. We're talking trench warfare, uh? Chemo, radiation ...."

Fran whispered, "Cancer?"

"Oh, just don't say it. Don't ask what kind either. It's bad enough without names and numbers."

Fran's eyes filled with tears. "Damn." She collected herself, then asked, "Has he started treatment?"

"Hah! If oodles of wishful thinking and mental banishment count."

"Poor guy. What's the price of delay?"

"Big, I'm sure, but what do I know? I just love him, listen to him, try not to cry."

"Thank God he has you. What's his strategy other than denial?"

Raoul shrugged. "More denial."

"I want to talk to him, Raoul. Any idea how I broach the subject?"

"Tell him you ran into me. Tell him I'm a bad actor. Tell him I'm worried sick."

"You think I dare?"

"Someone's got to. Someone with brass and balls."

"I'll tape some on and do my best."

"Thank you." Raoul took a sip of coffee and winked at Fran over the rim. "Just change his mind, sweetheart, not his persuasion."

Larry spoke urgently into his office speaker phone. "Fran, listen to this, just in. That Nova Scotia fisherman's been murdered—the one who survived the whirlpool. He was tied up, beaten, and shot." Fran had been leaning back in her home office chair when she took the call. With each word, she sat further upright. Larry continued, "Nasty home invasion in a little outport where these things just don't happen. Only his kid's rock collection was rifled and a few taken. Any idea why?"

"Not a clue. I mean, Sandhu's Uncle Sid's got a pet rock, but ...."

"What do you mean 'pet rock'?"

"He's got this nondescript pebble, clutches it like a kid with his favorite marble, but you're talking murder, Larry. That's different entirely."

"Yeah, I guess. I'll fax it to you. For the file."

"Naw, don't bother."

"What?"

"Bring it over instead. Dhyan's still away, and I'm tired of eating lettuce over the sink. Come for supper tonight, tomorrow, you name it. Bring Raoul if you can. I ran into him, did he tell you?"

"Yeah, he mentioned it. He's got rehearsals and more rehearsals, forget him. I can come tomorrow, if that's alright, and maybe bring someone else, someone you've got to meet."

"Aw-w. I mean, I'd just kind of like to talk with you. And Raoul's okay, he tolerates us, but it'll get pretty boring for anyone else, us talking shop, personal stuff, you know."

"So I'll bring two, we'll be even. Battle of the bores. What do you say? Is that too pushy?"

"Way, Larry."

"Seven okay?"

"Seven what? O'clock, people, courses to the meal? Just come—whenever, whoever. See ya."

Candlelight danced over the new, lush greenery in Fran's sunroom and the foursome at her dining table. She presided over a delicious spread that came, every bit, from catered boxes.

Mae's earlobes hung heavy with amethyst earrings like tiny grape clusters, her padded shoulders wide in a sequin-swirled sweatshirt. A gilded butterfly caught its feet in her biggest black wig. Nikos wore his usual light gray shirt and dark gray pants, with a blue tie, bright as the Greek sky, to dress up his driver's 'uniform'. Larry, in jeans and jean shirt, relaxed now to the point that his dark-shadowed eyes looked ready to sleep. Mae and Fran watched him with concern.

Mae asked, "Larry, do you have the sachet Maya gave you?"

He pulled the little sack from under his shirt. "Of course. For luck." The scent had dissipated and was further lost in the smells of dinner. He took off the necklace and wiggled the small pebble inside with his fingers. "Complete with pet rock." He handed it to Fran.

She felt it. "Everyone's got one around their necks. What's this new craze? I'm feeling left out."

Mae reached to her gold purse hanging from the back of her chair and retrieved a larger rock like Sid's. She handed it to Fran. "This is mine, from the same place as Larry's. Nikos brought it to me." To Nikos, she said, "Why don't you tell Fran about it?"

"I should?" Nikos asked doubtfully.

"Yes. Where it's from, what happened, how you got it."

Nikos began reluctantly. "It is from Mount Parnassos. You know where that is?"

Fran nodded. "I've been there."

"I have just returned, from Chryson."

"Nikos's hometown," Mae added. "Near Delphi."

"The mountain shattered on Friday, February 12th, an hour and seven minutes past midnight. A large piece broke into thousands of small pieces."

"You recognize the date?" Mae asked Fran.

"Only too well. Little rocks, miraculous survivals. Help me, I'm not very good connecting this dot to dot."

"Me either," Nikos said, smiling shyly at Fran.

Mae said, "But you know what happened there. And to whom."

"I should give names?" he asked.

Mae nodded.

Nikos continued, "I drove Mrs. Solari and her daughter ...."

Larry eyes widened. "Maya Solari?"

"Yes," Mae said.

Larry asked, "How does she fit?"

"She died at Delphi, I told you that, dear. Nikos drove Maya and her daughter Alma there." She looked to Nikos to continue.

"They stayed at my place in Chryson two days, nobody saw them. Then Alma and I took her mother to Delphi before midnight of February 11th, becoming the 12th. We left Mrs. Solari alone there and drove back to my place. A little past one that morning, kaboom! Lightning filled the sky, the houses shook with thunder. The next day, they found a shadow of an old woman burnt into the ground. By the caves of the Oracles. Parnassos splintered into small pieces like this. Friends of mine, those who dared, collected some to ward off bad luck or maybe bring good, I do not know. Greeks are very superstitious. I brought one piece for Mrs. Singer-Jones."

Fran looked at the little rock in her hand. "I'm still not getting it. I mean, I get the possible connection, but who-o-o ... it's a stretch, and I'm not superstitious at all."

Mae said, "That's good. One should never jump to conclusions or build on received interpretations. Evidence is what you want and keeping on with the file is what you should do." She reached to retrieve the rock from Fran. As Mae returned it to her purse, she said, "Now, may I have a little more of that lovely salad."

Fran placed the half-full bowl of greens, honey-peppered pecans, and fresh raspberries in front of her. Mae took one leaf, one nut, and one berry. As she seasoned them with a dollop of thick raspberry dressing, she said, "Fran, I would like to tell you how Larry and I are related, because he's going to inherit my house, which has a few files in it that relate to the one you're working on."

Larry snorted. "A few files. And the Pacific Ocean has a bit of water." To Mae, he said, "I still have questions about Maya—how she died, how this ties in with her injuries and activism."

Mae spoke firmly. "My father and Larry's great-grandfather, bless them, were brothers." She smiled at Larry, who dared not protest. "This makes Larry and me first cousins twice removed, if you use the Scottish system, which I do. I will tell you later why it's superior. To clearly understand lineage requires that you begin from the ground up, which means in this case going back to 1836 when Josiah Singer arrived in New York City from Belarus, or White Russia. He was in his early twenties, trained as a tailor. He arrived alone, although he had set sail in a small fleet of ships, one of which carried his fiancée and her family. Propriety, or perhaps just chance, dictated that he take a separate vessel.

"His ship made New York, but hers got swept by a fierce storm to Brazil, where they landed and made lives for themselves there. He never saw her again, and it took several long years before he found out what happened to her ship—lonely, hopeful years as you might imagine.

"He devoted himself to his business, and not until his middle years did he consider another woman. He courted Alzina Elliot, a sympathetic *shikseh* woman who, at age thirty-three, was well past any hope of marriage. The Elliot name has a proud heritage dating back to the Pilgrim fathers. For the love of Josiah, our Alzina converted to Judaism, unlike Larry's mother .... no, that's later, we'll get to that."

Nikos checked his watch: ten twenty. Mae progressed slowly from the trials of patriarch Josiah to the adventures of his sons. At ten thirty, Nikos discreetly glanced at his watch again. Fran noticed and caught Nikos's eyes for an amused, intimate moment.

At nearly eleven, the genealogy lesson concluded. To Larry's relief, Mae left Solomon out of it. Abel was Larry's father, Bea was his Christian mother, and they lived happily ever after a surprise elopement. Mae concluded, "Another great family love story built on faith, not religion, with enough belief in each other to put all their troubles behind them. *Shalom* and Amen."

Nikos's warm, hangdog eyes met Fran's again the next day at her front door. She was nearly ready to head out, with jacket on and purse over her shoulder. "Hey, what a nice surprise," she said.

Nikos looked at his wristwatch. "Time to get Dhyan, *ne*?"

"Yeah, her flight arrives in an hour and a half."

"A gift for you," he said, his burly hand holding out a padded envelope addressed to her in his heavy printing. "To say thank you."

"How sweet! May I open it now?" she asked as she took it.

"If you have time."

"I do. I'm leaving early because I just can't wait." Fran opened the envelope, pulled out a wrap of tissue, and found in it a loop of square silver beads. Tassels of silver, turquoise, and black beads hung from it. "It's beautiful!"

"Worry beads," he said. "From Olymbos." He used the Greek pronunciation of Olympus.

Fran laughed. "I need them, do I?"

He shrugged, eyes smiling bright. "Sometimes. We all do. Now maybe I am being pushy, but I must go to the airport now too. I could take you."

"Really?"

"I am getting samples. I do imports, *ne*? I have a quick pickup, nothing to delay you."

"Then why not? Your car or mine? Hey, the wheeled ashtray is clean for my kid."

"I will drive, if you do not mind?"

"Mind? That'd be great. Is that your car?" She pointed to his expensive metallic-gray Fiat parked near her door. Nikos kept it beautifully polished, chrome glinting.

He nodded.

"Dhyan's going to love this. Squire away. Thank you so much." Fran shook the worry beads to include them in her thank you, then looped them on her wrist.

At the Arrivals parking lot, Nikos put Dhyan's big duffel bag and small carry-on in his trunk. As Fran made for the front seat, Dhyan complained, "Aw-w."

Fran said, "What? You want the front? Yeah, I suppose ...." She looked at Nikos, going for the driver's door. "She's a brat, what can I say? But she's my brat, class A, front-seat variety."

"No Mom, I want you in the back with me. I've got like, so much to tell you."

"Aw-w," Fran said softly. "My queen of hearts. You mind, Nikos?"

He shook his head, eyes merry. He drove, listening to Greek taverna music.

Dhyan bubbled to Fran, "Angela told me stuff, totally awesome stuff, you won't believe it."

"Such as?"

"She has these dreams, but kind of awake dreams like things are really happening, and ..."

Fran said, "You weren't supposed to get into any of that stuff with her."

"I didn't, Mom, not till last night. Man, that Serena quack, she's so out of it. I gotta tell you, but ...." She paused, looking at Nikos. "I don't know. Maybe I should like, wait and ...."

"No, I think it's okay. Unless Nikos minds. Nikos?" No response from him. She asked a little louder, "Nikos, do you mind our chatter?"

He glanced back. "Pardon? Is my music too loud?"

"Not at all. I like it."

"Good." He moved his shoulders sensuously to the music. "Spiro's taverna. We dance, *ne*?"

Fran laughed. "You bet." She held up her new beads for Dhyan. "See? No worries. He dances, we talk. So Angela told you about something she dreams ...."

"It's so amazing, Mom, she sees so-o-o much, and it's so cool, like when Angela was alone in the jungle, she just dreamed until you found her, and she was never afraid. She just knew she'd be okay."

"Wow."

"So she had this dream right in front of me, there was this lady doing things and talking, not doing anything to Angela at all, nothing. Angela just like, watches."

"Who's the lady?"

"No, no, first you gotta know how it happened, 'cause it's so hard for Angela to talk to me without Guard Dog Joanne always being right there."

Joanne commandeered the top bunk, Dhyan took the bottom bunk, and Angela slept on foam on the floor. The last night Dhyan stayed, she got up past midnight to go to the bathroom, catching a foot in Angela's bedding on the way. Angela roused enough to turn over.

Dhyan made it to the bathroom guided by a nightlight glowing from the razor outlet. She closed the bathroom door and, when done, opened it to Angela standing in the doorframe, her eyes wide and glittery bright as if still dreaming. Dhyan jumped.

Angela nudged her back into the bathroom and shut the door. She uncurled her hand to show Dhyan a small rock like Uncle Sid's.

Dhyan said to her mom, "She squeezed the rock and kept dreaming right in front of me, her eyes wide open, it was kind of freaky. She said strange things, talking about turkey eggs and aphids and parthe ... partheno ... oh man, she said it easy as pie. Weird for a six-year-old, huh? Something about a parting-kind-of-genetics anyway."

"Parthenogenetics?"

"Yeah, that's it. Someone in her dreams was using all kinds of big words and weird science stuff, and Angela was just saying them, telling me by talking along."

"No wonder the counselor's a little flipped out."

Back in the bathroom Angela's eyes grew more focused as she surfaced from her dream. She squeezed her eyes shut and held the rock hard, whispering through her lispy front teeth, "Don't go, don't go. She's going away."

"Who is?"

"The lady."

"What lady?"

"The one with the baby. But the baby's not there. She's with her grandma, and the lady's in her white coat where she works at science stuff."

"In a lab?"

Angela nodded.

"So you dream these people when you hold the rock? Always the same people?"

Angela nodded again.

"That's so cool! Can I hold it?"

"No," Angela said quickly, clutching the rock tightly. "It's a secret. You can't tell anyone."

"Who else knows?"

"Nobody. Auntie and Uncle saw my rock when I came here, and they tried to get it out of my hand, so I hid it in Teddy. Don't tell anyone. Alex and Joanne and Sarah are mean. They'd steal it."

"Does mean old Serena know?"

Angela shook her head solemnly, her lips tight.

"Do you tell her your dreams?"

"Sometimes. I can't go home till I say something."

"Then she freaks?"

"She keeps asking me about the lady and the grandma and baby, and where they are, and what they're wearing and doing, and ... and there's an old lady too, she died when I got the rock. She was really old."

"Who are these people? Are they like, scary sometimes?"

Angela quickly shook her head. "They're nice, like you. I wish you could stay here. Nobody else understands. You won't tell, will you?"

Dhyan said to Fran, "I promised on my life."

"So where did she get the rock?"

"I told you, when the old lady died. Angela had it in her hand when you found her."

Fran said, "Oo-o, goosebumps. You know, when I saw her in the hospital, she held one or the other hand closed tight all the time, and I couldn't get her to unclench it. I figured it was a trauma thing, and I guess everyone else did too. When I held her little fist, that's exactly when I knew I had to come home for good. Powerful rock, hey?—if that's what did it."

"So what do you think? Is this the most awesome thing to put in your file or what? I mean, first Uncle Sid, now Angela."

"It's totally awesome, sweetheart, but no file entry. It's a secret, right?"

Dhyan sighed, "Yeah, I guess so. I really want to find out more. Can I go back at spring break?"

"I don't think so. Your dad's talking Epcot or Bahamas or something."

"Aw-w. This summer then? Please, ple-e-ease."

"What's this go, go, go stuff? What's wrong with stupid old home?"

"Nothing you'd understand."

Fran burst into laughter. "You're hilarious, kid. I'm so glad the circus is back in town."

Dhyan suppressed a grin, smacked Fran playfully and said, "Shut up!"

"What?" Nikos asked quickly. "Too loud for you?" He quickly turned down his stereo.

"No, no, it's great," Fran said. He turned it back up. Fran asked, "Who's playing?"

"A little Greek rock band." He looked back and winked. He *had* been listening. She smiled at him, their eyes connecting with the same spark as the evening before.

Dhyan missed it. She wrinkled her nose at the music and said, "It's too weird."

Fran hesitated outside Larry's office door. She glanced at Nora, who crossed her fingers. Fran took a breath and ventured in.

Larry's desk was still piled high and heavy with Randy's droppings. Larry slumped in his chair, eyes closed. Fran whispered, "Lar?"

He opened his eyes but otherwise didn't move. "Fran. How nice."

"Nora tells me you have a little hole in your sched'. Can we talk?"

"Sure. Grab a chair. I've got more on the Nova Scotia fisherman." He checked through his phone notes to find the one he wanted.

As Fran sat down, she muttered, "Not about that."

Larry continued, "I called Cole Preston, the CBC guy who broke the story, but he won't disclose anything by phone, fax, e-mail, nothing transmitted, only face to face. I said you'd arrange a meeting."

"You're doing my job; the guilt meter's rising."

Larry smiled. "Good, you owe me. I'll fly him down here, okay? Save you going there. From the little he said, I'd guess there's drugs involved, a little smuggling business. Not much for fish boats to chase in February—any time of year these days—and there's big bucks in dope, hard to trace through remote outports. He wouldn't say anything about the kid's rock collection, why it was ransacked."

"Good place to hide hash, a little private reserve."

"Could be."

"I'll check it out. Now Larry, please listen. When I saw Raoul, we talked a bit about ...."

"Hey, he opens in three weeks. I need a date. Will you come with me?"

"Love to. Raoul tells me that you ...."

"He's always been good, but this time he's got some fairy godmother sprinkling fairydust everywhere, doing wonders, or so he says. Bring Dhyan too, she'll like the production, although it's definitely P.G."

"She'll like that better."

"How is she?"

"Great. We're in the afterglow of her sweetness with Angela."

"Hey, Dhyan's a sweet kid, a chocolate chip off the old spud."

"Two old spuds. She's way ahead of Ralph and me. I've never danced so fast in my life. Right now, however, I came to dance with you, and you're not cooperating. You look tired; I want to talk about it."

"Of course I'm tired. The big gorgonzola won't override Boy Wonder and his stupid ideas. He just keeps telling him to crap on my desk until some gems drop out. I'm trying to find a boulder in the basement to stuff him under, but even the low lifes down there don't want him. Two things scare me about him: one, when he's in my office, and two—far worse—when he isn't. Look at this slag heap. It's all superficial process, not a whiff of content worth selling for manure."

Fran added, "Yeah, these damned top-down experts, with or without doting uncles. Tellman doesn't know squat about what we do from the ground up, from the inside out. It's Ralph's kind of expertise, exactly what you're saying, all 'management' ...." She made quotation marks with her hands. "All process, no content. Hell, you can't separate the two like that."

"God, you're so right. I should do a piece, a huge feature on the history of this separation of knowing the ropes from running the ship. Man, the chaos and incompetence it's wreaked on industry and government. What do you think?"

"Great idea, but don't look at me. I'm out of the game, and I've got too many opinions, too much bias. Now, can we talk about how you're doing? You're making this difficult, Larry."

"Difficult Larry, that's me. The day I'm not, then you worry. You've cheered me up immensely, Fran, got me thinking about a dynamite new report, to hell with wading through this crap." Handing Fran the slip of paper, he said, "Here, take Preston's number, do what you can."

Fran took it, leaned forward, and said urgently, "Larry, I have to talk with you about your health."

Larry checked his watch. "Oh damn." He hit a button on his phone. "Nora? Get me Randy, please." To Fran, he continued, "Sorry, I'm late telling him he's an asshole today. And I'm going to tell him about this new feature, give him the starring role as Incompetent Supreme. He'll be all Twinkletoes about that."

"Larry-y-y. Five minutes, can you give me that much?"

"Not now, but a whole lunch hour when Cole's here. I want to meet him. And book the twenty-third, I'll be yours all evening, I promise."

Fran gave up and rose to go. At the door, she asked, "Mind if I bring Nikos to the play?"

Larry said into the phone, "Yeah, Larry here. Wait a sec'." He asked Fran, "You two a number? Wow, we gotta talk about this."

"We gotta talk, right. I ain't tellin' you nothin'."

As she closed the door, he said to her, "Hey, you owe me an introduction fee." Into the phone, he said, "Listen, I've got it solved. We've got to get you in front of the cameras, starring role. No, I'm not kidding."

As Fran emerged from Larry's office, Nora looked expectantly at her. Fran threw up her hands, saying, "Larry is Larry, what can I say?"

"Oh dear."

"Exactly."

"I like this room a lot," Nikos said, surveying Fran's living room. "Better in daylight, more to see."

Fran smiled. "More junk, you mean. So you want to watch a movie? Play cards? Make fudge brownies?"

"I would like to look a little here, if you do not mind."

"Sure."

Nikos pointed to a semi-circular painting, about a foot across, at the top of a bookshelf. "What is that?"

"A fungus, believe it or not. A seventy-year-old fungus from upstate Vermont." Fran tiptoed to get it and handed it to Nikos. Its face bore a primitive oil-painting of a sad donkey in a snowstorm looking through a window into a bright, warm house where a family was enjoying a jolly feast. "My great-aunt Ethel painted it when she was young."

Fran gently turned it upside down. A scritchy old lady's hand signed and dated the bottom. "I met her on her last legs, a frail old bird. I got her to sign it then. She'd given it to my mother on her eighth birthday. Some present for a kid, huh?"

"Your mother liked it?"

"Treasured it. Aunt Ethel made a career of feeling left out and sorry for herself."

"I can see that."

"Mom took to this painting like a fish to water. She'd almost roast herself in the oven with the holiday turkey, then felt left out as we were carving and eating her."

"Where is your mother now?"

"The big left out. She died years ago. I was fourteen, a year older than Dhyan is now. She drank a bit. Fell asleep in the garage with the car on. The insurance company didn't buy that it was an accident, but I don't know."

Nikos let her talk, his eyes tender. Amazed at how readily she took to a kind ear, Fran continued, "She left a letter for Dad—a sort of journal entry, a poetic letting go, I think, of her hopes for him separate from her. Since she wasn't given to poetry, I guess a sudden attack of it didn't fit the actuarial tables. She didn't leave a note for me, no special goodbye when I left for school that day, nothing. I turned fifteen a couple of weeks later too and ... I mean, what mother'd do that just before her only kid's birthday? I still think she had a little extra vodka that morning, passed out waiting for the car to warm up and just didn't make it to work that day."

"Oh Fran, I am so sorry. I ask too much."

"Actually Nikos, you're the first person who ever came into my house and asked at all. I'm really glad you did—if you're up to it."

Nikos said warmly, "I am. I like to know."

Fran impulsively bussed him on the cheek, then took the fungus and tiptoed it back to its shelf. Nikos helped her, taking her hand and holding it in his. He didn't try to pull her into a hug nor did she fall into him and take one. After a long sweet moment, she said, "Now what? You hit the dreary jackpot right off. Pick again, try for a laugh. Or how 'bout coffee and a kitchen tour?"

Nikos asked, "Do you have something here from your father?"

"Sucker for punishment, aren't you?" He nodded and smiled. Fran turned to a seashell-encrusted side table and, from the lower shelf, picked up a small, finely woven ball made from dried grass. The lid of the ball fit so perfectly in size and design that it was only discernible as Fran lifted it. From inside, she pulled curls of even more finely woven snakes—nine total, one with two heads—which she put on the table top. "They really do have basket-weaving classes in the loony bin. My dad was the best, even won a few prizes. In-house, of course, nothing that hit the news."

Nikos took the ball and studied it carefully.

Fran continued, "His family has a long history of dementia—males only, shows up at about age thirty, skips some generations. A lot of brilliance too. Mom fell for the brilliance, didn't know about the insanity, but then, she had her dark secrets too. So I ended up with a lush and a nut for parents, which, come to think of it, Dhyan does too, except her dad's the lush and I'm the nut. Someone's got to fill the roles."

Nikos chortled lightly. "You are funny. And this is beautiful."

"And full of snakes. Nine for the tripartite goddess, three times three. Nine for the devil's number upside down. Nine for the arms of the menorah. Nine for half a golf course and his favorite club, why not? And a mutant with two heads for magic and evil; they look two ways for the god Janus and his own 'di'—for two—'mentia' or split mind."

"Where is your father now?"

"Pennsylvania. On an Amish farm—Beachy Amish, they're less isolated than the strictest sects, although they keep to the old ways too. They welcomed Dad back to the fold since his grandparents came from there. They moved west when his mom was a kid. By grade eight, she refused to drop out of school—that's the rule for Amish children—which caused a big uproar, excommunication, she never talked about it. She became a nurse, married outside the church ... oh, it gets complicated, but what matters now is that Dad's got a great home with some great people. Do you know much about the Amish? I've got some books and articles." Fran started scanning a nearby bookshelf.

Nikos said slowly, "I would like to know, but first, how did you manage after your mother died?"

"An aunt came to live with us. I got into the school newspaper, then broadcasting, and didn't surface till ... well, now."

"You have made a good life from tragedy. And your father?"

"He kept slipping and sliding. It didn't seem to worsen his condition, but then, he was pretty deep in his own world by then." She smiled. "You should see him now. They've got horses and buggies and sleighs, and in winter, he rides hell bent for leather on snowy, misty roads, a picture right out of two centuries ago. I do a little time travel with him once in a while. He's quite a character when you meet him in his own zone.

"Always call a bluff, that's his thing, and he's been calling bluffs until the emperor's got no clothes, no shoes, no castle, no help, no nothing. Conspiracies everywhere, and damned if he isn't half-right, except he goes too far. Way too far." After a beat, she said, "Now, enough about me and my parents, and I mean it. I want you to tell me something about yours."

Nikos thought for a moment, then said, "*Tavli*. Backgammon. Do you have a board?"

"Of course. Two or three, maybe more. We can play, if you like." Fran pulled a foot-square box from a bookshelf, saying, "You know, I think I bought this one at Delphi. It's a replica of some ancient set."

"That is lucky, for both of us. My father, he was very good, very fast. I will show you."

Nikos sat on the edge of the Algerian sofa and set up the game on a small chest that served as a coffee table. Fran faced him from the sofa's matching hassock. He wowed her with fluid moves obviously slowed so she could be in the game. He told her a story from when he was too small to remember, his older brother Spiro's favorite tale.

Their young mother got angry at their father about his *tavli* playing, a foolish pastime that made him late for meals. He got worse as time went by. She tried everything she could think of to entice him home, to nag him out of his bad habit, to get his children to plead for their father's company, but Yorgos was a Greek man, he did as he pleased. And she was a Greek woman determined to be a good wife, too proud to ask family or friends for advice or help.

One day, she grew so angry that she dared walk into the local taverna full of smoking, coffee-drinking men. They stopped talking, almost stopped breathing, as she walked to a game his father had just begun, took over from his partner, and won so quickly he didn't know what happened.

Nikos took the brakes off his playing and cleared the board at lightning speed. Fran giggled her amazement.

His mother then asked his father if he wanted to play again. He said no, he lost because he was hungry. He would go to home to eat and win against her when they returned. Everyone clapped and cheered as they left.

"My mother," Nikos said, "she never again went into the taverna—except for the one night a year when only women go, that does not count. She never again touched the game, she never again mentioned it, and my father never again came home late for a meal." With twinkling eyes and solemn voice, he concluded, "In my family, we do not underestimate women."

Fran laughed until tears ran. "Or a lifetime *tavli* player. You're beyond lucky."

"Sometimes." He pulled his worn worry beads from his pocket and automatically flicked a few through his fingers. "Today I am."

She came around to sit with him on the sofa and look at his beads. For a long time, they studied the little amber balls, each with its own hue and crystalline flaws. They slipped into examining each other's hands—life and heart lines, traces of injuries, flexibility—falling ever deeper into each other's warmth. With hands palm-to-palm to compare size, Fran asked, "What's your place like?"

"Big and beautiful while my wife lived. She was generous, she liked a party. She liked many people to enjoy her home. Without her, I could not...." He took a breath. "I sold our house, gave everything to friends and charities. I have a room at the back of my warehouse. Very Spartan. I have a little place in Chryson much the same."

"No real home?"

"Yes." He touched his heart. "In here."

Fran put her ear to his chest. "Mm, a good solid home. I could dance to it." He laughed. She said, "This is nice, isn't it? I mean just sitting and talking and being here together. Of course, if Dhyan wasn't upstairs in her room ...."

"Sh-h-h. This is enough."

Fran burst into Larry's office, travel forms in hand. She set them in front of him and said, "Larry, we're talking Nova Scotia. I'm going."

"What?" Larry asked in surprise.

"A little get-away." She leaned closer and whispered, "With Nikos." In her normal voice, she said, "I'll interview Cole Preston, of course."

"What about your daughter, young lady?"

"She's at her dad's this weekend—Cindy's birthday, big whoop. Actually, I haven't told her about Nikos. No sense breaking the news to her if the trip's a bust and there's nothing to tell."

"I don't know. You're asking me to aid and abet some serious mid-life delinquency here."

"Yeah? So? Nikos has never been to the Maritimes, and a little outport snuggling could be very educational."

"Hm. I suppose there's only one way to test this snuggling hypothesis?"

"Only one way, boss."

Larry signed the forms and handed them back to Fran. He wouldn't let go as he said, "It'll cost you a complete report."

"Tit for tat," Fran replied, taking the papers. "I talk, you talk."

Larry still didn't let go. "And then there's the little question of my introduction fee. The interest is rising daily."

The Halifax harbor stretches several miles from east to west, spanned by two bridges connecting its populous south and north shores. Ships of all types dock along extensive piers. The city's waterfront is a tight collection of old warehouses and wharf buildings turned into a tourist haven. Brick and cobbled streets run between them with charming views around every corner. The air is rich with the smell of the sea and two-hundred-and-fifty years of recorded seafaring history, lively with heroics, horrors, and ghosts.

At Nikos's insistence, Fran had rented a modest hotel room—waste not, want not—a short walk to the waterfront and historic properties. They checked in, dropped their luggage in their room, then left to drive to Foggy Cove with Cole Preston.

Foggy Cove's fourteen-house outcrop sat picturesquely on wind-whipped rocks. Nikos got out to walk and nose around. Fran and Cole drove twenty minutes southwest to remote, barren Dreadnaught Beach.

An icy, stinging blow pasted their coats hard against them and carried their voices away. Cole led the way to the water's edge, then walked parallel to it. He continually looked warily around for spies. Fran shouted, "I don't understand your paranoia."

Cole shouted back, "This is dangerous ground, wide open like this. Better if we'd stayed in Halifax."

"Sorry. I wanted to see where Gerry surfaced, get some perspective from here."

Cole stopped to check up and down the beach before speaking, leaning close to Fran. "Okay, it's like this. Gerry McMann was close to cracking.

He hallucinated like crazy after his survival, and he made extensive notes on his computer. He told me some of his wacko thoughts. They were some weird. I figure the big guys got pissed off with his ramblings and wasted him."

"Who are these 'big guys'?"

"I don't know, and I want to keep it that way. I've got little kids, Fran. The less I know the better. He never said a word to me about the heavies or how he'd been making ends meet."

"But you know now, right? How'd you find out?"

"I got a CD. From Gerry's kid." Cole huddled closer to Fran. "The killers wiped his hard drive and floppies—one big magnetic swipe, eh?—and busted up all his CDs. Computer too, nothing to retrieve. Then I get this CD from Gerry's teenage son full of his dad's weird writings and a little file on the side that's different, scary different. It spells things out, way too clear."

"Why'd his kid have the CD?"

"He found the disk in his bedroom mixed up in a mess of clothes on the floor, one the murderers missed on their rampage. It had some pirated music on it, plus this stuff of Gerry's. The kid passed it on to me."

"So let's back up a bit. What was Gerry hallucinating about?"

"He was cracking up, like I said, on about some strange women and science research, energizing explosions, sacred sites, geology, all kinds of freaky stuff."

"Related to the rock?"

Cole narrowed his eyes. "What do you mean?"

"The little rock that precipitated his dreams."

Cole stopped in his tracks. "How do you know?"

"I don't know anything. I'm just taking ... oh, a New Age flyer on why the kid's rock collection was rifled and a few pebbles taken."

"So what is this—I mean Gerry's ramblings and dreams—some Internet chat-cult or something?"

"Yeah, something like that. It's out there, don't worry. What you're saying, though, is that Gerry's ramblings and the rocks—plural—weren't in any way connected, right?"

Cole closed his eyes in relief and said with forced certainty, "Yes."

"So what's with the rocks?"

His eyes opened and darted about as he struggled for words. "They were ... I figure they were looking for anything that crackled—pitchblende, uranium, hot slag. I mean, if they had a Geiger counter, I don't know ...."

"Hot slag?" Fran's voice rose in pitch. "Hot rocks?"

Cole nodded quickly and drew in close to Fran. "It's all on the CD, file name NWD for Nuclear Waste Disposal. Gerry and his fishing buddies dropped bundles of hot stuff way out at sea. Slag, pellets, canisters of plutonium, iridium ... the file's got numbers, dates, payoffs. Big money, all in secret offshore accounts."

Fran's eyes popped. "Holy shit! Who-o-o, hot story."

"No story, man. I'm no Deep Throat, no Woodward and Bernstein."

"So listen, I break it from the States—no connection to you, except as the reporter who covered Gerry's survival, and you're right out of the loop."

"Hah. Not to the murderers. They know I know more about Gerry's last trip in the *Black Swan* and his crazy babblings than anyone. I mean, talking to you right here, right now could be the end of me."

"I'm sorry, Cole. Really sorry. Most guys in your position would be dying to cover this."

"That's just it. I'm not dying for any of it. First and foremost, you've got to understand, I'm a family man. A black family man with deep roots here, hundreds of years, and yet my people are still just getting somewhere. I'm working for all of us, doing everything positive. You know how me being killed like Gerry McMann was would play here? None of this mess has anything to do with me, not where I come from or where I'm going."

Fran nodded her understanding, then asked, "So what do you want? You've thrown the ball to me, and I can run with it if you give me the CD or a copy."

"Oh man, you can have it. It's stashed at work. C'mon, let's go get it."

Fran checked her watch. "Can't. We've got to pick up Nikos, then my evening's all booked. First thing tomorrow morning though, is that okay?"

"Sure, come to my office. I start at seven." Cole turned and retraced his steps in high gear.

Evening in Halifax belonged to Fran and Nikos. When she opened the hotel room door with Nikos behind her, she saw a cart set with retsina on ice, two white wine glasses, Greek *hors d'oeuvres,* and a bouquet of daffodils.

Fran beamed. "Oh Nikos, this is so nice."

His eyes twinkled. "I think you might want a little food, a little drink."

She laughed. "Big presumptions. I might just be here to discuss the weather with you, you know."

He waved toward the window facing a moody northern sky. "I order that too. Lots of it."

She laughed again. "You are so sweet." In a low, intimate voice, she said, "And we're finally alone. No one with big ears upstairs supposedly doing her homework." She moved easily into his arms, which he wrapped around her, pulling her into his sensuous hips. Kisses came tentatively and tenderly; lovemaking took a slow, sweet hour.

"Maturity," she said after, clicking her full retsina glass with Nikos's in a toast. "The hunger is as deep, but the dining is so much finer."

From a harbor-front restaurant, Fran and Nikos sat by a wide window and watched night settle over the port's restless tides and trade. By fading view and brightening candlelight, they sipped and supped.

Fran asked, "Did you really knock on doors at Foggy Cove while I was out with Cole?"

Nikos nodded.

"To do what? Ask for directions, buy a coffee?"

"Exactly. You are very clever." He kissed her hand. "And beautiful."

"Did you score some coffee?"

"Good coffee. Good company."

"What did you talk about?"

"These people live by the sea, so I talk what they know. I say, I am Nikos from Greece. I come on a boat from Piraeus. We have a rough crossing, but we get our business done."

Fran played along, her eyes dancing. "What business?"

"What we sail to do. Important business, lots of money."

"Did you really come to North America as a sailor?"

"*Ne.*"

"What, on a cargo ship?"

Nikos nodded.

"Carrying what?"

He shrugged. "We transfer goods."

"No kidding. What kind of goods? Greek exports?"

"Ah, yes. You are very smart."

"Manufactured goods? Produce? The beginnings of your little import business?"

"More or less. We bring things; we leave a little between ports too."

"What do you mean, 'leave a little'? As in, dumping?"

Nikos nodded. "The ship gets lighter."

"Dumping what?"

He leaned forward and lowered his voice. "It pollutes."

"No way. You were on a ship dumping pollutants out in deep water?"

"You are surprised?"

"What were you dumping? Really dangerous stuff?"

"What does not belong in the ocean is dangerous. Can be deadly."

"But what?"

"It was illegal. I am sworn not to say."

"Ah, so maybe toxic garbage or stuff like old warheads?"

Nikos smiled, sphinx-like. "Could be. I see it go in the water."

"C'mon, tell me, tell me. You were dumping nasty stuff, right? Maybe even nuclear waste."

Nikos took Fran's hand. "My dear, if we replayed this conversation, you would discover I told you very little, I give only general information, and I say 'yes' every time you second-guess me. See how quickly I find out what is on your mind. Like most people, you ask questions with the answer in them. Even the best reporters do it, maybe especially them."

Fran pulled back, then laughed, "You are the slyest devil I've ever met. I can't believe it!"

"I sailed. We dumped our bilge on the way. The ship grew lighter. I saw it. You had me dumping nuclear waste at sea."

Chagrined, Fran said, "You're good. You're very good."

"I know everything about Foggy Cove. I know what they do for work and play; I know what they worry about. I could write their newspaper now, a thick one. Greeks have neighborhood broadsheets, you know that, *ne*? Nothing escapes them."

"So is it true, were they dumping hot stuff from Foggy Cove?"

Nikos smiled merrily. "Yes, my darling."

Fran groaned, "Oh no, you got me again!"

Nikos said quietly, "And you are right. Everyone is whispering and worried sick. None of them knew anything about the problem, this terrible business, until the boy found something on a computer disk. They are afraid to tell anyone, to call the police and make bigger trouble."

"I'm amazed they talked to you. You are amazing."

"*Ohi*, I just listen. I worry for them. Something must be done."

At seven the next morning, Fran entered the CBC building and reported to the front desk security clerk, who buzzed Cole Preston. He came out in a flash to greet her, wearing his coat and looking as tense as she'd left him.

"Morning," Fran said. "You got it?"

"Sh-h," he whispered, then spoke up for the clerk to overhear, "C'mon, I'll buy you a coffee."

"Sure. Hey, I've got some good news for you."

Fog swaddled downtown Halifax streets. Wispy, sea-level clouds muted views and dampened traffic noise. Fran and Cole walked together past historic buildings, grounds, and statues. He slipped her a small brown envelope containing the CD. "The letter's in it too."

She dropped it into her coat pocket. "What letter?"

"Came with the disk. I didn't talk with the kid. He dropped it off for me at work. After hours. It just turned up, and the letter makes clear he's not going to talk to me about it. Too scared and doesn't want to smear his dad. He wants it investigated but kept secret too. Tough spot, poor kid."

"Well, he's trying to do the right thing, good for him. I guess you didn't dare talk with anyone else at Foggy Cove—his mom maybe?"

"Not a chance."

"Well, let me tell you something. Nikos talked with half the town, and she knows."

Cole's eyebrows shot up.

Fran continued, "In fact, everyone there knows this dirty little secret. They're all worried and ashamed, none of them talking to the authorities, I'm pretty sure."

"Oh God," Cole groaned.

"No, it's good news—a good spin on bad news anyway, because there's safety in numbers. What'll the goons do now, kill them all? They won't be shocked either when the cops or CIA start showing up and snooping around, after we've done the right thing with this little bombshell."

"There's no 'we'. The only right thing for me is getting out. I've given my notice, two weeks now till I'm done, finished, walking totally away."

"So let's get this straight before you pack up and start over. Son finds CD, reads incriminating file, sneaks it to you, doesn't want to talk. Whole towns knows anyway, we—pardon me—I get it to the authorities, they investigate and blow it all open. Something's funny here, something I'm missing or confuses me, but I can't think, and I'm not the one to crack it anyway. Now, this letter, tell me about it, since I can't look at it here."

"Typed, ink-jet printer, nothing personal on it. I clipped my name off the top, and the envelope was addressed to me, personal and confidential, but it's long gone."

They walked a few paces without talking, then Fran said, "You don't want this story and, funny thing is, I'm not going to chase it either."

Cole looked surprised. "How come?"

"My hot-shot days are over; I've got other stuff happening now. I'll just give it to my boss, he'll pass it on to ... oh, probably the CIA as an anonymous dropoff at Media 8, which removes it from me and you, and this trip's right off the record."

"Good."

"The investigators are still going to want to talk with you. They might catch you on some details, realize you know more than you're saying."

"The only connection is the kid saying he gave me the CD. What CD? I didn't get any CD." He paused. "And so it turns up in the States—what's that got to do with me?"

"You know, down the road when it's all settled, safe, and hits the news, you could be a star. You want to take some credit then?"

"And admit I was lying? Not a chance."

"More like protecting yourself. I think the police and public will cut you a lot of slack. Cole, this takes courage, and there should be some rewards."

"Uh-uh. I've seen the guts of this business, and I don't need the glory."

The CBC building loomed back in view. By the entrance, Cole said, "I've got my eye on a shop across the harbor. Sporting goods. I can equip my kids and their teams wholesale. My five-year-old, he's going to be the next Gretzky—a total hockey nut. And I'm going be his proud ol' pop, no other heroics."

"Yay, Dad!" She tapped her coat pocket containing the envelope. "Thanks, Cole. You've done good work. Best of luck at the blue line."

Silvery morning light flowed into Fran's home office window. She waltzed in carrying her big coffee mug and singing, "What a day for a daydream, ta da da da ...." She looked fresh and beautiful in jeans, sweater, and silver worry bead bracelet.

She dialed the phone. "Hi Nora. Fran here.... Yeah, I had a great weekend, best time in ages. Big scoop too, hot as they come. Larry's going to love it. He there?"

She paused; her face dropped. "Oh God, no. What happened? ... Oh, damn." Tears welled up. She scribbled the address Nora gave her. "Thanks. Yeah, I'll let you know. Bye."

Fran hurried to the big city hospital's cancer wing. At the nursing station, a nurse pointed down a long corridor with gleaming floors. "Room 418 South," she told Fran, who turned on her heel for Larry's room. "Five minutes max'," the nurse called after her. "No exceptions."

Fran peeked into the private room where Larry sat half-up in bed, his head bandaged and arms hooked up to several drips. His eyes were closed, his cheeks hollow, his skin almost gray.

She tiptoed beside the bed. Larry smiled wanly, eyes still shut. "Fran?"

She tenderly took his hand. "Yeah, it's me. How'd you know?"

"Smells like trouble."

Fran laughed. "Timber zone, I hear."

Larry struggled to open his eyes. "So I fell. You dance on a cleared desktop, you take that chance."

"Good. The cleared part, that is."

"It's all your fault. We're doing things my way now, no content-process splits. You inspired me."

"Alright." She looked at the drips. "What are they putting into you?"

"Snips and snails and puppy-dog tails."

"Chemo?"

Larry nodded.

"How's it feel?"

"Goes in easy."

"Anything you want, you tell me. Work stuff too. I can sit at your newly cleared desk and fake your job if you like."

"Thanks. You can help for sure, but I've got Sandhu lined up."

"Sandhu! Fantastic. How'd you do that?"

"Asked him. He said yes. And call Mae, okay? It's important."

"Okay. Hang in there, big guy."

Larry struggled to smile as he shut his eyes. Fran kissed him tenderly on a fevered cheek, then quietly withdrew.

A telephone, only a telephone, claimed the top of Larry's desk, a barren field open to new possibilities. Sunlight poured in through the sky-high windows.

Sandhu filled Larry's chair, impeccably suited in shades of teal. Fran sat opposite him. She asked, "So what'd he do? Call you as he was keeling?"

"No, just before. He got me two minutes off the plane from China, deep in jet buzz and desperate for sleep. He said he couldn't hold off treatment much longer. It was either that or go home for a permanent nap. I thought I was dreaming, having a nightmare."

"So he told you? He said the cancer word?"

"No. He made it sound like a rash of warts or something and he was going for a swim in Compound W. He asked if I'd take over while he had a little adventure, then maybe wrote the great American novel about it. I said forget the novel, just do the drugs. It had to be serious for him to ask; my answer had to be yes, no questions asked."

"So what'd you tell the thieves who stole you from us?"

"I made up a dozen lies and excuses, then settled on the truth. They're not happy, but so what? An old friend needs me."

"Lucky us. You know, for a boss you're my number one second choice."

Sandhu smiled. "Thanks. Larry wants you to help steer me straight and, I quote, 'Keep a ten-foot pole out for Randy Tellman.'"

Fran laughed. "Gladly. Where is R.T?—the r.a.t."

"Larry put him in front of the cameras, the head mug for some pilot TV-Internet game thing with lightweight—no, fluff—celebrities. He's way down in Studio F, working overtime with a bunch of Gen-X-Y-Z freaks on an almost zero budget. Who knows? He might surprise us."

"Oh, he will surprise us. Studio F for fowl-up, you watch. He's trouble on two legs with a pointy tail."

"I'll keep an eye on him. You're still off for, what? another week on the rock 'n' roll file. How's it going?"

"Sandhu, bossman, hang onto your seat. This is big, really big. And dangerous. You won't believe it. It'll have to go to the CIA, no question, and it'll be out of our hands the minute they know."

Sandhu leaned forward. Fran continued, "The trick will be to get them to promise the exclusive when they've cracked it. It's all on a CD, one nasty little file plus an accompanying letter. There's other stuff—a red herring they don't need, it'll throw them off—but it fits my file, so I'm keeping it."

"So spill it!"

"Remember the Nova Scotia fisherman who survived the shipwreck, same day as your uncle? He was murdered recently."

"Yeah, Larry told me, said you went to check out something. You and some guy."

Fran laughed. "Yeah, some guy. Nikos was a big help. It looks like Gerry McMann and his fishing buddies were into a little one-way drop-off business ...."

Fran and Nikos lay naked on her rumpled bed, spent and satisfied. She'd decorated the room in early Americana, from a jelly cupboard night table to a small spinning wheel in one corner. The duvet cover was a handmade star pattern quilt. The pulled drapes had the same stars, from big to small, dancing up the bottom half. A bedside clock-radio said 2:49 p.m. Fran reached toward it for her cigarette pack. Nikos said softly, "You did not smoke inside in Halifax."

Fran took a cigarette out and looked at it. "Little bastards. You'd think making fantastic love would be enough, wouldn't you?"

"You want to quit?"

"Of course."

He took the cigarette. "I will help you."

"Nothing helps. What can you do?"

He smiled. "I will smoke them for you. Do you have a light?"

"You don't smoke! Or do you?"

"My first in eleven years."

"Oh for God's sake, give me that." Fran grabbed the cigarette and pitched it across the room. "Nobody smokes here. Sheesh, I thought you were smarter than that. I thought I was." She snuggled into Nikos, and they lay silently for a warm minute, two, more. She traced her fingers over his swarthy, black-haired chest. He closed his eyes.

After ten sweet drifting minutes, Nikos opened them and said, "Larry says, 'Call Mae, it is important.' Mae says, 'Go to Athens.' She will buy our tickets."

"No Athens, forget it," Fran said, checking the clock, now at 3:10 p.m. "Oh boy!" she exclaimed, jumping up to gather her clothes strewn on the floor. "I don't want Dhyan to even guess this. I mean, she knows I think you're okay, but ... I don't know, I've got to break it to her so it's cool and gets some kind of blessing from her."

Nikos jumped up too, pulling the bed together as he did. Fran straightened it from her side, then both quickly put arms and legs into underclothing, pants, and shirts. Nikos said, "Mae does not waste money or time. It must be important."

"And Larry wants me to go, I know, I know. Just one long, exhausting weekend, I guess."

"One night in Chryson maybe."

"Now that appeals. I don't know. Let me talk to Dhyan."

Dhyan perched on a stool at the kitchen counter watching Fran chop vegetables for a steaming pot. Fran said, "I don't want to go. I don't want to leave you—or Larry. I'm worried sick about him."

Dhyan grabbed a peeled carrot and crunched into it. "He's getting treatment. And he wanted you to call Mae, right? I mean, duh, I wonder what he wants you to do. And I've got to go to the nuthouse anyway."

"No, you don't. I don't know where your dad gets off, splitting your month here down to the last Saturday and Sunday."

"It's Cindy. She'll do anything to get me to church every Sunday till we run out of Sundays. God, she's so obsessed. But it's okay this weekend, 'cause you should do this Athens thing." She paused, crunching noisily. "With Nikos."

Fran's eyes jumped to Dhyan's. "What?"

"Listen, for Dad and Cindy's sake—and, well, to protect myself from too much shrieking and praying—I let on that Halifax was just you, but I know you went with him. I know it turned out great, you've been singing till like, where's the off switch? So why not Athens?"

"How'd you figure Halifax?"

"He drove you to the airport all, you know, slicked up and whoa, powerful aftershave, and that little play-doctor bag in the trunk. Then there's all this singing."

Fran laughed. "You are so smart, and I am so dumb. You don't disapprove?"

"No! I want you to go again. I want you to get out of here. I want to go to church with Cindy."

"Oh man," Fran sighed despondently.

"You just don't get it, do you? I'm trying to arrange it so you'll be home more often, and you just don't get it."

"Huh? Are we switching languages now or what? Pick one I know, okay?"

Dhyan smiled disdainfully. She explained with mock impatience, "Nikos goes with you, right? He works in town, he can't take off all the time. So you keep hanging with him, and he keeps you here. Except for weekends. You can disappear then, 'cause I'm stuck with Snow White and the Two Dwarfs anyway."

"You're matchmaking to keep me at home? Am I hearing you right?"

Dhyan said defensively, "I'm being practical."

"So you like Nikos?"

"I didn't say that."

"Oh. What are you saying?"

"He's got big nails."

Fran said slowly, "Nikos has big nails. Which ones? Thumb, toe, little finger?"

"No, dummy. Big enough to nail your shoes to the floor."

Fran burst into laughter. "And a big damned schemer helping him. There goes the whole feminist revolution. What are you two plotting?"

"He doesn't have a clue. Don't tell him either. Guys are like, weird. They take off when they think you've got plans for them, but I mean, why else keep them around?"

Fran belly-laughed, barely able to say, "Man, if I'd known what you do at thirteen ...."

At night, the Acropolis of Athens is a floodlit fantasy of ruins crowning a restless metropolis pushing hard into the high-tech future. On the mound's eastern embankment is an ancient amphitheater. That March, it shone with unusual brightness, drawing crowds to a special presentation heralded by huge banners announcing in Greek and English, "Tonight! World premiere of SINOLOS by Alkis Leimonos, 9 p.m."

Inside, Fran and Nikos sat on the original stone seats that arc around the small stage. They perched in a sea of many hundreds who filled the tiers to overflowing at the season's must-see and be-seen-at event. Many were coated or caped in velvets and furs. Starlight fought its way through the city haze, thick despite a cool spring breeze.

Bunting marked with the Olympics' five-ring symbol reserved the best seats in the house. Athens was fêting the executive of the International Olympics Committee, renewed and reconfigured to keep this new millennium of the games on track. The favored few sat on purple and gold-trimmed cushions, served by a swirl of attendants.

A small orchestra claimed the two left-front rows. The first violinist started plinking a Chinese tune.

From behind the stage's bright red satin draperies, a Chinese gong sounded. The curtain gathered up to reveal a backdrop of a classically painted Chinese mountainscape. Theatrical smoke billowed.

A woman wearing a long white toga and golden diadem walked—almost floated—to center stage and bade the orchestra stop. The audience stopped too, profoundly silent, all eyes on her. She was middle-aged, beautiful, and very Greek, in contrast to the Chinese theme. Nikos's jaw dropped. He dared not whisper to Fran that he knew her. If Alma was in danger of being shot on quiet, remote roads, then she was taking an unbelievable risk by appearing so boldly before such a high profile public gathering.

Muffled, confused sounds emanated from backstage. The mist dissipated as the backdrop parted in the middle and slid to each aside, revealing a landscape from Olympia, site of the original Olympics. A painted apple tree dominated the foreground, covered with red-gold fruit and one all-gold ball. A large snake wrapped itself on a branch, its head and split red tongue sticking out from the faux foliage.

A graying, rotund man strode onto the stage, shouting in Greek, "Stop! I won't have this. I don't care who you are!"

The audience gasped and muttered. Nikos translated for Fran.

The woman on stage signaled to the orchestra to play a Greek folk tune, then waved him backstage.

He shouted, "Do you know who I am?"

The woman swept her arm toward the man and announced in Greek, "Alkis Leimonos, premier playwright and theatrical innovator." She led the audience in hearty applause.

Ten women dressed in white togas and four men in athletic tunics of ancient design joined her from behind the apple tree. Alkis groaned, "You've hijacked my cast!"

The woman said, "We will take only minutes. Gaiea must speak."

Alkis swept his arm toward the woman as she had to him and said to the crowd, "My friends, first the cartoon, then the main feature."

Laughter erupted as he exited. Gaiea raised her arms and instantly quelled it by her regal bearing. In a deeply compelling voice, she said, "Ten priestesses to represent the fifty of old, the fifty required to be the classic one-hundred-eyed, one-hundred-handed servant of creation and peace."

The ten priestesses sang a lament in Greek, a classic strophic chorus. "Fifty mouths laugh, a hundred eyes cry, we serve eternally and never die."

Gaiea said, "In honor of Gaiea and her long line, unending through the millennia, I proclaim these Olympic Games open."

The chorus sang, "She passes, but is forever, living on, leaving never."

Gaiea bowed her head. "Let us pray."

The cast sank to its knees. For a moment, all sound and motion stopped.

Into this deep silence, Gaiea said, "Let us pray for the wisdom to open the games in the spirit of their inception. The ancients noted that the Earth comes into a particular cosmic alignment every eight years, which they called a great year. They held a contest then to select the ablest man to serve Gaiea and her nation, that he might show all his people how to engender families born of love and to live in harmony with each other and upon the Earth.

"Gaiea is this supreme Olympian's guide, his conduit to God, without whom he and lesser of his kind descend into greed, destruction, and war. The priestesses are her emissaries, bringing wisdom and peace into every home.

"But every eight years was too long between Olympics, for humankind is restless, their attentions fickle, so Gaiea halved the great year and held the contest every four years. We have revived the four-year Olympiad in the past century. In the centuries to come, we must revive the other, most sacred purposes of the games, or they are a mockery. They are not Olympics and must not be called such.

"The opening ceremonies of each Olympics must make clear the history and purpose of the games. The closing ceremony must allow the Creator, through the symbol and wisdom of eternal Gaiea, to honor the athlete chosen above all others to dedicate his proven strengths to the promotion of peace among peoples and the care of this planet."

The four men mimed archery, discus-throwing, the start of a foot race, and high jump. Three then deferred to one. He took the golden apple from the tree and stepped forward to present it to Gaiea. She took it, blessing him with her other hand.

The chorus chanted, "She lives forever, leaves us never." They retreated from the stage, their voices fading, "She is with us, she is with us, she is with us ...."

Gaiea circled both arms wide, then brought her hands together in prayer. She bowed, and the curtain came down.

The audience sat transfixed for a few silent, surreal seconds. Fran blinked herself to action, whispering urgently to Nikos, "Quick, before she gets away! This has to be why Mae sent me—us." She bounced up, pulling him in tow.

As they scrambled out of the building and along a noisy street toward a backstage entrance, the orchestra began its Chinese piece again. The gong sounded, the curtain rose, mist swirled. A dragon entered followed by the actors wearing ornate Chinese costumes. They spoke in Greek with sing-song Chinese accents, their plaints drifting up into the Athens night sky.

Backstage of the original theater was not for the claustrophobic or pampered, so small was the space and decrepit from centuries of wear. Modern additions had been tacked on, a hodge-podge of rooms, doors, and clutter. Nikos and Fran slipped into the chaos using Fran's press pass to clear a security guard who pointed her to the green room—more like a closet.

Quietly, they asked cast and crew where Gaiea was, receiving in reply vague shrugs and waves toward the exit door, although neither Fran nor Nikos had seen a hint of white robes fleeing as they approached backstage. He still had not told her that he recognized Alma.

Alkis appeared and hissed in Greek, "Who are you? What do you want?"

Nikos whispered back, "We are looking for Gaiea."

"She escaped before I could kill her. Are you with her?"

"No," Nikos said. "This is Fran Roma, Media 8 News Service." She showed her press pass.

"Oh no," Alkis groaned, then said in hushed English, "I don't need this."

Fran said, "It's the best publicity you could get. International coverage. I need to find out who Gaiea is, how and why she did this."

"She is a great phantom of the theater. No one knows where she comes from or goes to. Actors die to work with her. She is Alma Solari."

"Alma Solari? Are you sure?"

Alkis nodded.

Fran turned to Nikos, her hushed voice rising. "My God, Nikos, why didn't you tell me?"

Alkis said, "Sh-h-h! So you are friends, are you?"

Fran said, "No, I don't know her from anyone, and her trail's getting cold as we talk. I just need to know where she went."

Alkis reached into his pants' pocket and retrieved a business card. He handed it to Fran, saying, "Here, she gave me this when she ran by me and escaped. She said to pass it on but not to whom. You keep it."

Fran took the card, but the light was too dim to read it.

"It says Minnesota," Alkis growled. "This is Athens. This is my play, my world premier. Forget her and go watch it. Write about that!"

Nikos said quietly to Fran, "He is right. We must go."

Fran resisted. "But the cast knows. I've got to talk to ...."

Alkis insisted, "*Exo*! Out, before I have you thrown out."

Fran said, "So throw out the press. That's a good story too."

Alkis said, "Out! Out!"

Fran and Nikos made for the exit sign, where they read Alma's card: "Pavla Blanca, Ph.D., Life Sciences & Interdisciplinary Studies, University of Minnesota" with "Mae " handwritten on one corner.

Fran and Nikos skipped the rest of the play and walked down the busy east boulevard to the Plaka or 'crazy' district that clings to the north side of the Acropolis. On cobbled, single-lane streets, they raised their voices over the din of cars, music, and chatter from tavernas and souvenir stands.

Fran said, "You watched that whole little piece and you didn't tell me! I can't believe it."

Nikos said, "I was shocked. I did not know what to say or if I should say anything. I still do not know. She is always in danger, people want to kill her."

"She's not too shy about standing up in front a big crowd, a lot of important people. And who are these killers? Why do they want to waste her?"

He whispered, "I do not know. I do not know anything, except that tonight she had something to say. It must matter enough to take the risk."

"And it matters enough to Mae to send us here, but then we can't connect with the very person I assume we're supposed to see. I don't get it."

"Maybe seeing is enough."

"You drove her all the way to Chryson, she stayed at your place. You must have talked."

"We had polite words. I do not ask her anything. She does not tell."

Fran sighed in frustration. "So who's this Pavla Blanca?" She held up her business card.

"Alma's daughter, I believe, but I have not met her."

Fran flicked the card. "Well, that fits, I guess. What in God's name is Mae up to?"

"Something very important, I am sure. But what, who knows? I am just the driver."

By bright morning light, Nikos and Fran sped in a rented car toward Chryson, from broad freeway to mountain highway. At noon, the first ruins of Delphi appeared up the winding road, a scattering of temples and tumbled stones on green plateaus midst craggy peaks. Fran said, "Hard to believe—six years since I was here. In some ways, it's like yesterday, in other ways like a lifetime ago."

"How long did you stay?"

"Just a day, one long day. I was covering some government uproar in Athens and started getting sick from the heat, the pollution, the whole scene, so I stole a day off. I felt great up here. I walked every square inch, memorizing every structure, every story."

Nikos smiled. "Then you can tell me. I have forgotten so much."

"Uh-uh. You were born to this. You know it by heart, not by rote. Nothing equals that."

Nikos reached to her hand. "I am so glad we are here." He slowed down to pull into the main Delphi parking lot, which had room to spare in the off-season.

Fran said, "No, let's go right to Chryson. I don't need to see where the old lady evaporated."

"No, I want to see the Omphalos, for good luck. I want to be at the center of the Universe with you."

Fran smiled, then asked hesitantly, "Did you ... of course, you brought your wife here."

He shrugged and said slowly, "That was then. This is now."

At the Navel Stone, Nikos circled the chest-high rounded cone, gently touching its once-intricately carved surface, now worn from millennia of weathering and reverent human hands. He guided Fran's fingertips over it. As they held hands across it, he said, "I did not think I would love like this again. I am so thankful."

Fran smiled, beautiful in his eyes. She said, "It's corny, you know, but I guess this is what belongs at the center of the Universe. Love. I can't think of anything better. Now get me out of here before I turn to pure sap."

Fran and Nikos spent the evening at Apollo's Taverna reveling into the darkest hours. Local men, women, and children crowded in to see Nikos and his new woman. Feasts of food and waterfalls of wine flowed. Live music pulsed; singers soloed and chorused. In a line of Greek men, Nikos danced beautifully, daring to be sexy for his lady love.

With his eyes and a flick of the head, he invited Fran to dance with him. She laughed, hesitated. Another woman started his way, but he stopped her by insisting on Fran.

She joined him. The crowd raucously approved as Nikos led their dance. Spiro led the applause. Fran was radiant.

♦ ♦ ♦

Two days later, Fran schlepped in sweats back into her home office. "Love lagged," she had said to Nikos. "We didn't have time to get jet lagged." Through weary eyes, she called up file after file of Gerry's writings on her computer screen.

> The baby's a spitting image of the mother, exact same as her mother's baby pictures, I'd put money on that. And the mother's the perfect same as the grandmother. Anyone could tell, just looking at them. They're like identical twins, only 25, 30 years apart. Can't say as I like it, spooks up my back a bit, but these are the facts.
> When I was down for the count, drowning for sure, I saw the old lady too, the great-grandmother, and she's one of them too, the exact same, though white haired and wrinkled like all old folk so it's harder to tell ....

Dhyan quietly appeared at the open door. She'd clipped up her hair and sheened her cheeks and eyelids with fine glitter. She wore a short satin skirt, color-matched sweater, and tottery high-heels. She watched her mom for a moment, then said, "No rest for the wicked."

Fran started but kept her eyes on the screen.

"That's what Cindy says."

Fran said, "Believe me, I'd rather be doing nothing if it'd get me off the wicked hook." She looked up. "Oh wow. What's the occasion?"

A bit defiantly, Dhyan said, "I'm wearing this to Raoul's play."

"Hm. Turn around. Show me you can walk on those things. They're not your usual clunkers, you know."

Dhyan turned and took a few awkward steps.

"Nope. Won't do. Walking lessons will commence in two minutes. You get your driver's permit when you can cross the room with the big Webster on your head."

"So can I wear this?"

"Of course. I've got a spare gunny sack to cover you from head to toe."

"Mom!"

"It's fine. I'll go anywhere with you, with pride." Softly, she added, "You're beautiful. Now go get the two-ton dictionary, meet me in the hall."

Dhyan left. She walked lightly, eyes sparkling. She sang quietly to herself, "Beautiful. I am beautiful."

Dhyan and party milled in the foyer of the splendidly refurbished Old Vaudeville Theater. With satin hips, heels, makeup, and sassy hair, Dhyan looked years older. Fran, Nikos, Mae, and Larry kept her under close guard.

Larry wore a soft brown yarmulke on his completely bald head. It almost covered the red scar where he cracked his head on his desk when he fell in his office. He wore peach slacks and floral silk shirt on his thin frame, the color perking up his sallow complexion. He tied the outfit together with brown belt and shoes. "So I lost the bottom fringe," he joked. "Maybe I'll get a full head back as a bonus."

"Ask for pink cheeks," Mae said. "Hair is an option." Her wig on this night was a black beehive bejeweled with dozens of twist-in rhinestones. Her painted her face almost—but not quite—made her look like a tarted-up dried apple doll. She'd sheathed her old bones in a long indigo dress, then draped on large, irregularly shaped amber beads, the centerpiece of which held a Cretaceous mosquito. Her attire ended in her grandmother's gold leather, high-buttoned boots from the Gay 1890s.

Fran and Nikos wore tasteful togs, tailored blacks and grays, but nothing notable beside Lolita, Scarhead, and Ancient Doll.

Dhyan snapped a photograph of her party, then Fran recruited a nearby fellow to take a shot with all of them in it. Dhyan's smile outshone her four chaperones' bright faces.

Fran then discreetly showed Pavla Blanca's business card to Mae, pointing out her name handwritten on it. She said, "I have to know."

Mae whispered, "Later, dear."

"I can understand why you said that to me on the phone, if wiretaps worry you, but I don't see any spies here. Please, I'm dying of curiosity."

"It's not spies. It's timing. I'm glad you're motivated."

"And spinning my wheels. I've found out that Dr. Blanca's on sabbatical, no forwarding address."

"Of course. She wouldn't give out her card if she was there."

"But she didn't give it out. It's from Athens via Alma, as you know. Why this wild goose chase?"

"You must be patient." Mae turned and said, "Nikos, shouldn't we be getting to our seats? Here, take my arm. Larry, you escort our two young ladies."

Darkness and expectant silence fell over the sold-out theater crowd. The curtain rose. At the center of a black, otherwise empty stage stood a shadowy shape with a haloed face. A sudden harsh white spotlight manifested Maya. "Oh my God!" Larry gasped, leading the collective surprise of the crowd.

She wore her navy dress, hose, and shoes, blood bespattered. Her face was slashed from forehead to chin, continuing down her neck, a jagged red-yellow wound. Her white hair was dirty and matted.

"I appeared with my head uncovered in public," Maya said, struggling to overcome great pain. "I encouraged women to do the same as they voted for the right to this choice in a country where they must be veiled from head to foot. Where they must carry written permission to be outside of their homes. Where they are persecuted and even killed for showing an ankle or a lock of hair. For laughing in public. A zealot attacked me and others, abetted by the police. All record of this protest was destroyed, and all news was banned. This ...." She indicated her state. "... did not happen."

A bearded mullah approached her, shrouded in black. She closing her eyes to steel herself.. He unzipped the back of her dress and roughly pulled it off her shoulders down to her waist, revealing a dark slip underneath. He took a whip from his robes, turned her side-view to the audience, and proceeded to flog her.

A man stood up from his seat and shouted, "Stop it! Stop this insanity!" Other outraged audience members joined him. The flogging continued. At the count of one dozen, Maya collapsed, and the cleric disappeared into the shadows.

A woman wearing a white toga came on the stage, ethereal under a golden spotlight. She looked stunningly like Gaiea in Athens only twenty, thirty years younger. "Oh my God!" Fran exclaimed, as shocked as Larry had been.

The young woman held up both hands to quiet the crowd. To the hushed audience, she said, "Her name is legion, it does not matter. She survived the flogging but died days later. They killed her. You are the first to know. At intermission, in the lobby, there will be a petition to sign and a fundraiser to support, that we might gather forces to help women everywhere get free of such barbarity. To be full citizens under the United Nations Charter and Declaration of Rights and Freedoms. Thank you."

The curtain dropped; the lights dimmed to black. The audience, as had the one in Athens, sat stunned and murmuring until a spotlight tracked Raoul onto the stage. His pale hair shone brightly in contrast to his black suit and shirt. "Our play tonight is a dark comedy about persecution of another sort entirely, but in the eyes of justice, it's all the same. You have just witnessed the first and only record of the recent events leading to this old woman's recent demise. Thank you for your unexpected participation and supportive reaction."

Raoul led the crowd in self-congratulating applause, which started as a smattering until the man who'd shouted out before bellowed, "Freedom and justice for all!" The clapping went wild. Some people stood. Others joined them. Raoul's play started with a standing ovation.

Later, it finished with one too, as satisfying as the first.

After the play, Larry and his guests adjourned to his and Raoul's penthouse apartment. It was fabulously, whimsically appointed. Raoul, an interior decorator by avocation, filled the living room with stage props, *trompe l'oeil* painting, innovative trim, and oddball furnishings. Comfort wasn't a first, second, or third consideration, but there were seats enough for everyone.

Larry went immediately to lie on a wide divan, a winged art deco fantasy. Mae perched in the curl of his torso and hips. Nikos and Fran found oddball 1950s-style wingback chairs. Dhyan sank into a stack of Afgani pillows, whispering, "Wow! Oh, wow!" at every detail. Raoul, pumped from his success, served wine and juice from one-of-a-kind glassware, bent and bizarrely threaded with glass designs.

When all had drinks, Fran raised her glass high, "To Raoul! What a risk. What a payoff."

Mae said, "Yes, to Raoul. To triumph!"

Raoul grinned, wonderfully abashed, high as a spring kite. All agreed and cheered enthusiastically. Larry added, "What a guy. Even skips the cast party for me."

"This is the party," Raoul quickly replied.

The telephone rang. Raoul got it and said, "Yes! Fantastic! Come on up." He soon opened the door and welcomed in Alma Solari, enveloping her in a bear hug. She had scrubbed back to her own age but wore Maya's navy coat over clean navy dress, hose, and shoes.

Fran's jaw dropped. Larry's eyes popped. Dhyan blinked and shook her head. Nikos grinned. Mae pulled herself up, eyes happy with tears, and led the rest in a quick round of applause. Alma curtsied her pleasure.

Raoul bowed and, with great flourish, introduced her, "Alma Solari, director *extraordinaire*. This is Fran Roma and Fran's daughter, Dhyan."

Alma smiled broadly as she shook Fran's hand. She then took both of Dhyan's hands and looked admiringly at the whole of her, saying, "What a beautiful girl."

Dhyan beamed shyly.

"You have good presence. Power. Use it wisely."

Now Fran beamed proudly.

Raoul said, "You know Nikos, of course." She kissed his cheek, saying, "Thank you. For everything." He shrugged and blushed.

"And Alma, this is Larry."

Larry was instantly in tears, streaming freely, as he pulled himself up to greet her. "No, stay resting please," she insisted. "I'll get a chair."

Mae rose, saying, "I've warmed a spot for you." Larry patted where Mae had been sitting, welcoming Alma to it. She snugged in close. While she and Larry talked, Raoul kept Mae, Fran, Dhyan, and Nikos entertained with backstage stories.

Larry said quietly, "I met your mother the day before she went to Mashad. We only had ten minutes together, but she had an amazing impact on me, while I ... I did nothing for her. I'm so sorry. I could have helped. I could have investigated after and ...." He broke down.

"Sh-h," Alma said softly. "You inspired her more than you know. More than I can tell you at this juncture. As for her protest, there was nothing you could have done before or after. Any interference would have made things worse, believe me. There are ways you can help now though."

"Anything. Whatever you say."

Alma shook her head. "No, whatever you say, from your heart. What would you like to do for her now or make of the advice she gave you?"

Larry took shallow breaths, struggling to match words with feelings. Alma took his hand and waited. At last, he said, "Raoul said you videotaped your performance tonight. I'd like to run it, play it up, give the world half the jolt I got seeing you on stage tonight."

Alma smiled. "I'd like you to give them that too, but not through the video. It's not available to the public."

"But it was public performance, a publicity ... ?"

"Stunt, yes, you can say it. But the record of it is not to be replicated and distributed, I'm afraid. Maya remains a mystery—an untraceable, nameless woman like those she represents. And because, quite literally, I'm afraid. It would invite close scrutiny of her last days, which would seriously endanger me and my family. Soon enough, Maya's story will be told."

"Then why ... ?" Larry's voice trailed off in confusion.

Alma continued *sotto voce*, "There's so much that the world doesn't know and won't be ready to accept until the groundwork is laid. Improving the rights of women worldwide is one requisite, and this present effort is one small tool. Maya isn't the point of tonight's exercise. Effecting change is, through concerted engagement of all who know better. That's what she died for."

Larry closed his eyes, confused at his lack of understanding and pained at his continuing powerlessness to help Maya. He opened them and puzzled, "So the video of the re-enactment is for what purpose?"

"The record. For safekeeping with the rest of the much larger, longer story. To add to Mae's prodigious files ...." Alma slowed her words, to see if

Larry was curious about exploring that broad avenue, but the news-hound in him kept to the obvious.

"So it kicks off a petition and some fundraising, which I gather you want publicized?"

"Yes."

"Can I mention the re-enactment?"

"Oh yes. By broadcast and in print."

"How? By interviewing people who saw it, would that be fair game?"

"Certainly. You can cover the buzz I hope it creates. The story of the story, from person to person, could be very effective. What's missing, overlooked, or forgotten is the point, and most pointedly with regard to women's rights in so many parts of the world. There's a hole at the core of every powerful story, which is completed by dropping in the missing piece."

"Rosebud," Larry whispered, goosebumps rising.

Alma smiled. "Yes."

"I'll get a reporter right on it. We'll get interviews with everyone we can who saw you as Maya ...."

"No names mentioned, please," Alma interjected.

"No worry. It'll be interesting to see where this goes."

"Thank you." Alma grinned happily. "Now, Mother told me she gave you a piece of paper containing, essentially, a recipe. The idea for it is actually mine. She was my messenger, although I didn't know who she'd share it with. I just knew she'd choose well."

Larry winced. "I haven't done anything with it, I mean beyond the first point, looking for the broader context when telling news. That's what I put Fran up to before she found Angela. Talk about pay-off. Did she ... did your mother really work with Orson, the attentive Mr. Welles, as she called him?"

"He listened to her, yes, and look at what he achieved. So point one of my plan served you well. Are you interested in the other three, how they all fit together?"

"Yes!"

"Point two is that readers and listeners must have a vested interest in news and its telling, to keep them connected and caring. Subscribers must be shareholders, that is, much like a credit union where account holders are shareholders. Those on board then recruit more like-minded people to become subscriber-shareholders, and thus increase their collective strength and shared benefits.

"Subscriber-shareholders would sign onto the philosophy and direction of the publication and trust the publisher to work on their behalf, the same way owners of investment funds trust managers do, with the same sort of quarterly reports and direct say at annual general meetings.

"Point three covers advertisers, to be selected for their big picture and ethical views. This is a relative thing, of course, but for example, people are going to buy new vehicles anyway, so why not steer them to environmentally responsible models? When they buy clothing, why not quality, eco-smart garments, responsibly made? I'm sure you can come up with a long, varied, and lucrative list.

"And finally, point four, delivery. Every new subscriber-shareholder gets Internet delivery with a start-up ream of tree-free paper for printing out whatever parts and types of reports they choose. No more huge printing plants turning out thick newspapers made from trees that take a century and more to grow, producing pages that take minutes to read, if they're read at all. Readers would use their home and office printers to make paper copies of the reports they specify by on-line choice or by preprogramming.

"There, that's the rush tour, the quickest of overviews," Alma concluded, "Does it make sense to you?"

Larry blinked, dumbfounded. He muttered, "Good lord, it's ...." With rising enthusiasm, he said, "It's brilliant, it makes total sense. It's one heckuva huge idea though."

She laughed. "Could you do it?"

"Someone will. It's too good not to get done."

"I'm asking you."

Larry took a deep breath. "I suppose ... yeah, you know, I could. It'd take a million bucks to get started, a handful of good people, and a world network of experts. It would be fabulously exciting."

"If you're interested—and you're the only one who's seen or heard the plan—it's yours unless you don't act on it in, say, the next six months. As for financial backing, I can work that out, as much money as you want."

"Are you serious?" Larry asked disbelievingly.

Alma looked him hard in the eye. "Completely. Are you?"

Larry nodded slowly, solemnly.

Alma said, "It's got to be drawn up first, the whole organization and business plan, marketing strategies, time lines, etcetera. You could work from here, perhaps a good activity while you're recuperating."

Larry's pulse raced, his cheeks pinker than they'd been in months. "Yes, yes! It's so perfect. It's telling news exactly the way I'd like to see it told, and the delivery ... well, it's bound to fly. I'm in a morass at work, desperate to do something that makes a difference." His eyes brimmed with joyous tears as he said with conviction, "Alma, I can do it. I will do it."

Alma beamed. "So get to it, minding your health, of course. When it's all outlined and ready, you'll be surprised at how quickly it comes together and takes off."

Larry blinked in disbelief. Was he dreaming that he could kick off something—a real world something—with as much lasting impact as his movie hero? He reached for Alma's hand, holding it for long sweet seconds before she said, "I'm sorry, but I must go." She kissed his forehead. Larry kissed her hand before letting it go, smiling and flush with her blessing.

Alma stood up and said warmly, extending her arms to Raoul, "Thank you, Raoul. You are splendid. Your show is most compelling and worthwhile, sure to make a difference. Now I must vanish."

As they hugged, Dhyan said, "Wait! I want to get a picture of everyone!"

The party quickly gathered around Larry. Dhyan, Nikos, and Fran each took shots, midst quick shuffling and small talk to arrange and rearrange the party. Alma stood behind the high end of the divan.

Flashes and smiles done Alma said, "Now I really must go. I'm so happy to have met you, Larry, Fran, Dhyan." She beamed at each person in turn. "And Nikos again, I owe you for your brilliant driving."

"*Ohi,*" he said quickly, "I could drive you now."

"Thank you, but I'm safe for tonight, as safe as can be." To Mae, she said, "I'll see you soon," and blew her a kiss.

Fran followed Alma and Raoul to the door, then said quietly, urgently to Alma, "I have to talk with you." She showed her Pavla Blanca's card. "I got this from Athens, just as you planned, yes? Is she your daughter, playing Gaiea tonight?"

"Oh dear, I'm late as it is. Keep on with the file, Fran, the answers are in there. Our re-enactment tonight is important but in other ways, not this. Try parthenogenesis."

Fran looked at her quizzically. Alma smiled for all and waved goodbye. Poof, she was gone.

Nikos drove Fran and Dhyan home in his Fiat, Fran in the passenger seat, Dhyan in the back. Dhyan bubbled to her mom, "Did you hear what she said to me?"

"Yeah," Fran said. "She nailed you. 'Good presence. Power.' She's absolutely right."

"What did she mean exactly?"

"You shine, babe. You've got something special—smarts, I'd say, and a way with words. Gorgeous too, but that's a given. Smarts, you have to work on. If you do, you'll just get better and better, darlin'."

"Wow. I can't believe it. I mean, Raoul said she's some kind of genius and fairy godmother. Who is she?"

Fran asked, "Nikos, who is Alma Solari?"

Nikos shook his head. "I do not know. I do not even know for sure what I have seen, except things happen when she is around. She appears, she disappears. A fantastic woman."

Dhyan asked, "Mae could tell, I bet."

Nikos said, "She knows a lot, but you cannot push her. I take her as she is, that is why I work for her, why we stay friends. I do not press her, do not ask questions. Dhyan, some things you push hard for, like doing well at school. Other things, you let happen. Mrs. Singer-Jones is in your life now and maybe Alma Solari too. Wait and see. Your paths will cross if they are meant to."

Fran said, "Wise words from a man of few. Thank you, Nikos. Good advice for me too. I guess I should back off, but I'm just not trained that way. I smell a story and root for it like a pig crazy for truffles."

Nikos eased the car in front of Fran's place. She asked, "Care for coffee?"

He said, "No, it is very late, and the night ends perfectly here. Thank you."

Fran leaned to kiss him on the cheek, whispering, "You're wonderful."

"Thanks, Nikos," Dhyan said, bounding from the car. "It's been the best night of like, forever."

Nikos watched until his ladies were safely inside. Scampering to the front door, Dhyan said, "I love it here. Everything is just happening like I can't believe."

Fran couldn't be happier, couldn't smile wider. As she and Dhyan stepped into the house, she waved and flashed a happy grin back to Nikos.

In the house, Dhyan said seriously, "Mom, I'm going to really try. I'm going to stay here, okay?—as much as I can. I'm going to work at school. I'm going to aim for like, this wise thing."

Fran laughed and pulled her into a hug, "This wise thing, this wise old thirteen-year-old thing. If anyone can do it, it's you, babe."

Larry and Raoul had compromised on their oversize bedroom. Raoul envisioned the ultimate decorating experience, using his props in ever-changing scenarios from fairytales to dungeons, innocent romps to S-and-M adventures. Larry wanted to go to bed and wake up at home. The deal, therefore, was that Raoul had unrestricted fun with the rest of the apartment while Larry controlled the bedroom, a plain, unchanging room. His main decorating feature was a sound system so good that he could revisit the monks chanting in the highest monastery at Metéora in Greece or return to the mud at Woodstock where a few hundred thousand revelers heard Jimi Hendrix squeal the American anthem as an anti-war protest.

Acoustics demanded that sound waves and reflections take precedence over decor. All the furnishings were built-in, including a king-size Murphy bed so Larry could hike it into a wall when he wanted total sound quality. Since he'd been recuperating long hours at home in bed, however, the room was morphing to new needs and interests.

He had set up a meditation corner, a simple shrine with a minimalist floral arrangement fresh every few days. Before it he placed a wooden sculpture, a gnarled kneeling Bhudda split in half and hollowed out so Larry could fit into this nutshell, an empty, peaceful space for himself and his thoughts. He seldom did it. Looking at the sculpture from the bed was sufficient to imagine himself there. The perfect absence of sound in this new little realm appealed to Larry as much as achieving its perfect presence.

This night of Raoul's theatrical triumph had exhausted Larry. He gratefully climbed under the soft, cool covers to rest against the pillows Raoul had propped for him. Raoul brought a fresh glass of water and set out Larry's compartmentalized pillbox. He stepped into the ensuite bathroom, close and visible to Larry, to wash up.

Larry asked, "Who are these women? Maya, Alma—and the younger one, what's her name?"

"Pavla."

"They give me the willies. I mean, in the nicest way, but there's something ...."

Raoul laughed. "Yeah."

"So why'd you risk opening with that bit of shock theater? It could've been so bad, killed you from the start."

"I didn't know what they were going to do. I just gave Alma the stage and took the chance. She watched one rehearsal of the play and made a dozen little mind-blowing fixups. She's a helluva cheerleader too, had me walking on air for the things I'd done right. So I said sure, do what you want." He walked back to the bed, grinning from ear to ear. "First play since God-knows-when that opened with a standing ovation, uh? Finished with one too. Unbelievable."

"Lucky bastard."

Raoul air-kissed him. "My second name. I saw her making a little mind-blowing fixup of you too, if you were paying attention."

"Paying attention? My God, I'm still in shock. She damned near finished me, doing Maya like that. I haven't been so stunned since ... who-o, I don't know. She is the old lady somehow, it's weird as hell."

"So did you listen to her while she yattered at you on the divan?"

"Every word. I've got a new project, Raoul. A new *raison d'être*, delivered by her mother. I'll tell you tomorrow and probably too many days after that what an incredible gift this is."

"Good. And I'll make you do it too. Only an idiot ignores the pom-pom girl's advice." Raoul gave Larry a peck on the cheek and tucked the covers under his chin. He rounded the bed to his side and flipped off the light. Larry snuggled into his warm cocoon of sleep and dreams.

On Mae's sofa, Larry and Raoul sat hip to hip as tight as conjoined-twins, crowded in by her research. Mae wore pastels today, kindergarten kids' favorite Easter colors. She took her favorite chair. Around her black rubber boots, Lord Byron doted on his crone.

Mae said, "Maya stayed here fairly regularly, and Alma drops by now and then. Now that her mother's gone, I'm encouraging her to make more use of my place. It's very handy, so close to D.C. She needs safe havens in this neighborhood—everywhere, really. She's in continual danger."

"I gather," Larry said. "But from what? From whom?"

"There are people who would like to get rid of her, dear. They have through the ages. It's who she is."

"Get rid of her ... through the ages? That doesn't make sense."

"As you get to know her, you'll understand. All you need to know now is that she must have safe places to stay, and my house has been one of the safest. I hope, dearly hope, that it continues to be so for her, her daughter, and granddaughter. Pavla even came by for tea this time, I was so pleased. Brought you a new ball, didn't she?" She scratched Byron's ear. "Nice lady. Now Larry, because their visits and staying here affects your inheritance, we need to talk about it."

Larry shrugged. "I'm trying to get rid of stuff, simplify my life. Leave it all to Alma."

"Impossible," Mae quickly said. "We can't put her name in writing on any legal, traceable public document. She must have no address anywhere, no formal association with any place, including this one. She and her line have all kinds of names, I.D. passports, etcetera, but I doubt that Alma Solari is a legal entity, a verifiable person at all."

Larry said, "All these tantalizing hints. Why won't you tell us? I don't want to badger you, but ...."

Raoul said, "Oh, badger away. She loves it."

Mae smiled. "Sometimes I do, but not in this case. It's complicated, while the question of my house and Will is fairly straightforward, if we can come to an agreement."

Raoul said, "Why don't you leave it in trust? Larry can oversee it."

Larry said, "And Raoul after me, I'll pass it on to him."

Mae said, "None of that, Larry. You're going to live to be older than I am, much older. Let's stick to my Will. You have another fifty years to get yours in order. Creating a trust for Alma and her line is a good idea. Do you agree, Larry?"

He shrugged. "Sure, and I'll look after it—happily—until I'm old as Methuselah."

Mae grinned. "That's the spirit. The Singer spirit."

"What about all these papers?" Raoul asked. "How do we deal with them?"

"You don't. They'll be all finished and organized in five years. Nikos will help when I'm ready to put them away—too much cross-referencing still, I can't do without any of them. My present Will instructs you to ship them out before keeping or disposing of the house as you choose."

Raoul sighed in mock exasperation, "Oh, for Pete's sake, you two. It's so simple. Leave the papers here, and make the purpose of the trust to take care of them, in perpetuity, in this very house."

"That's an excellent solution," Mae said, looking pleased. She asked Larry, "What do you think?"

He smiled and sat back. "Perfect. You two work this out, put my name on anything you want."

Mae said, "Thank you, Raoul. You're a smart man."

Raoul smiled, then pointed to the papers around him. "What is all this anyway? Goddesses by the yard, I'm not blind, but to what end?"

"It's a very big picture. These are endless details that serve a simple common thread, but I'm not about to explain any of it until I've explained it all. Then it will explain itself. Please, let's not get sidetracked from the business at hand, if you don't mind. I'll put the house in trust to protect my work, and it will remain available to Alma and her family to use as they wish, as long as they wish. They can't be named in the trust, but I'll refer to them as research associates or something who require accommodation. I'll get my lawyer onto this immediately."

Ralph repeatedly checked his wrist watch as he paced his office. He looked out the window, then fiddled with the settings of a TV and VCR on a rolled-in cart. Cindy perched on the edge of an easy chair, impatiently adjusting the cuffs and collar of her pink and white candy-cane dress.

After long minutes, the young receptionist opened the office door for Fran to enter. Fran forced a smile. "Hello, Ralph. Good morning, Cindy."

Cindy said, "It's eight minutes past ten."

Ralph said, "Late as usual. No apology, of course."

Fran said, "Oh come on, I ran over some nails in your parkade, got a flat, my cell doesn't work there ...."

Ralph held up his hands. "Sorry, sorry. I'll get help for you after. Let's just get on with this." He hit 'play' on the TV-VCR. "This is the eleven o'clock news two nights ago."

Head shot of a suited, slick, middle-aged ANCHORMAN.

          ANCHORMAN
And now for tonight's arts report.

ZOOM OUT to a high-gloss woman REPORTER next to him.

         ANCHORMAN (continuing)
Hi, Sheila. How's our woman on the scene, our
eye on culture?

           REPORTER
Great, Bob, thanks. Big opening tonight at the
Old Vaudeville Theater, and what a splash it was.

                                    CUT TO:
Overview of the theater's foyer, then a pan of the crowd.

        REPORTER (voice over)
Look at that gorgeous place. Look at that glitzy
crowd.

ZOOM IN on Larry's party, closer still on DHYAN in her sexy get-up.

Ralph froze the shot. "This is how we saw our girl on statewide television, and let me tell you, we were shocked and sickened."

Fran said, "Why didn't you me call right away?"

Ralph said, "We had to get this footage from the station first, for you to see through sober eyes that ...."

Cindy jumped in. "She looks at least eighteen or twenty, all gussied up like a ... a ...."

"Streetwalker," Ralph said. "There she is for all to see and worse, attending some sick fag play and some other horrible thing about an old woman getting flogged. This is an outrage!"

Fran quickly said, "What you see and what you think are two entirely different things. For one thing, Dhyan chose her own clothing, most of which Cindy bought. For another, the 'horrible scene' was a complete surprise and deeply meaningful. And as for your slur on homosexuals ...."

Ralph said, "Enough! I knew you'd try to worm your way out of this, and I won't have it."

Cindy added, "I bought Dhyan those clothes for fun, for private parties, girls-only dress-up stuff. I just assumed you'd know that a little fun with girlfriends is different from procuring on the streets."

Ralph turned to his wife. "She's doesn't, Cindy. That's my point." His eyes bored into Fran. "And this kiddie-porn shot watched by half the state proves it. This evidence plus your years of absence, leaving everything up to Juanita until she left ...."

"Neither of us left 'everything up to Juanita'." Fran interjected angrily, "and she got married, she didn't ...."

"Missing Dhyan's birthday, so she ran off—that's why she ran off, you know, she was so mad at you for letting her down yet again. We've tried to protect you from this but ...."

"Oh jeez! Spare me the crap psychologizing."

"That was for two days, and she came home on her own. It took a police escort to drag her from a whole week with a dope-selling biker when she was supposedly in your care, and what do you do after? Drop her in Oregon, run off for dirty weekends, probably far worse at home, and God knows what else. You're finished, Fran."

Fran stood speechless.

Ralph continued, "You can give up the play-acting, no more pretending to be some kind of mother. Cindy is all that Dhyan needs in that regard and most especially in the teaching of Christian values."

Fran said darkly, eyes narrowed, "You've applied for sole custody. Physical or legal?"

Cindy said, "I tried to warn you, but you wouldn't listen to me."

Ralph said, "Physical custody with strictly monitored visiting rights. The wheels are in motion, Fran. No more warnings. No more accommodating. Go back to your high-flying life, chasing bad news all over the place. It suits you, and believe me, it suits me better than turning our girl into bad news."

Fran fought to contain herself. "There's no reasoning with you is there?"

Cindy said, "Only if you pray and take the Lord Jesus into your heart."

Ralph said, "Say good-bye to Dhyan after school today, at the school. We'll be there to pick her up. No funny stuff before, during or after, you hear? It can and will be used against you, if it comes to that."

♦ ♦ ♦

J.C. Junior High School released most of its students from the main front door. Fran spotted Dhyan sauntering and laughing with a girlfriend, both laden with homework-heavy backpacks. "Hey Ma," Dhyan said, "whatcha doing here?"

Fran pointed to Ralph's new sport utility vehicle parked at the closest curb. Ralph sat rigidly behind the wheel with Cindy beside him. "Oo-o-h," Dhyan shuddered. "The God squad. Come to exorcise." She spun her eyes in circles. "Help me, help me." Her friend giggled.

Fran said, "They're applying for sole physical custody, meaning you live full time with them and we get to visit with a church-approved chaperone. Until it's settled, I'm out of your life for a while."

"What? Those fucking jerks, I hate them! I'm going to kill them."

"Hey, I gotta go," the girl said, rushing off.

Fran continued, "You've got to play along. I've got a lawyer, and I'm working it out, but it'll get really ugly and expensive if we're not smart. Kicking up dust will only make it worse, believe me."

"They can't do this. No fucking way."

Ralph got out to open the back door for Dhyan.

She yelled, "You dirty bastard! You can't do this!" Student heads turned to look. Some stopped to watch.

Fran said quietly, "Go on, hon', get in quickly and quietly. Don't prove their point and make it easy for them, okay?" She gave Dhyan a big hug, then gently turned her toward the SUV.

Dhyan threw her backpack into the back seat and climbed in after it. Ralph returned to the driver's seat. Cindy kept her eyes looking forward. Dhyan hissed to her, "I hate you most, you warbling witch."

Cindy snapped her head around to Dhyan and took a deep breath. "Dear Lord God, for what she has just uttered, forgive this wayward child who will, with our help and Your unfailing grace ...."

"You fucking bitch, just shut the fuck up! I get some say about this." To her dad, she screamed, "I get some say!" He sat like a statue. "I GET SOME SAY!"

Ralph started the vehicle, then said, "You'll get your mouth washed out with soap. And grounded permanently."

"Child abuse! I'll call the hotline, damn you." Dhyan lowered her window. Ralph buzzed it up. Dhyan strained to hold it down with her hands. "Mom!"

Crying now, Fran said, "Dhyan, don't make it harder than it is. We'll work it out, I promise. Bye, Angel."

Ralph gunned the motor and drove off. Dhyan turned and watched her mom grow small in the distance and disappear around a corner.

In Cindy's pink and rosewood dream of a living room, Ralph brooded in front of a Saturday afternoon football game on TV, downing his third brandy-laced coffee. Cindy and the boys were out shopping.

Quietly, Dhyan put every little-girl thing from her room outside of her door, making a high, sprawling pile. Inside, she stripped every surface until only a few books and papers remained on one shelf. An old poster of her favorite pouting, defiant band hung above her bed by one tack. Shabby old rabbit half hid under her pillow. Dhyan had banished all other stuffed toys.

She pounded a large nail at eye level into her doorframe. As she pounded a second nail into the door in line with the first, Ralph appeared and demanded with a slur, "What in blazes are you doing?"

"Well, duh!" Dhyan slammed the door shut and held it with her foot as she wrapped a thick shoelace around both nails to make a crude safety chain. Ralph tried half-heartedly to push it open. She splayed the nails outward to help hold the tie.

Ralph pushed the door open an inch, far enough to see why he couldn't open it more. "You untie this right now! And clean up this mess before your mother gets home!"

"She's not my mother! She's a stupid fucking control freak!"

In the distance, they heard the garage door buzz open and the heavy door slide up. Cindy's car pulled in and parked.

Ralph pleaded through the open slit, "Dhyan, get a grip, okay? And be reasonable."

"You be reasonable, you old lush!" He backed off from the door, which she kicked shut, then fell on her bed and covered her head with a pillow.

Ralph met Cindy and sons toting in big plastic bags with expensive labels. "I'm late, I'm late," she said. "My soap's half over, traffic was so bad." When she spotted the great mound outside Dhyan's door, she shrieked to Ralph, "Lord help me, now what? What has this child done? Make her put it back, every bit of it!"

"Leave her alone," Ralph said, then warned the boys, "Completely alone. Go play in the rec room while Mom watches her show."

"Can we try our new computer game?"

"Yeah, new, old, whatever you want. Go on."

The boys scampered off.

Cindy sobbed to Ralph, "This won't do. This won't do at all! Dear God, look what happens when I go out for a few hours."

Ralph put his arm around her shoulder and walked with her to the living room sofa. She kicked off her shoes and rubbed her stocking feet. He flipped on the TV to the last minutes of her soap, then brought her a glass of sherry. She wiped under her eyes with the back of her forefingers, to avoid smudging her mascara, and locked into the show.

He sat close to her as she explained, "That's Jay, he's the illegitimate son who's been seducing Tara, and he doesn't know she's his aunt, because his mother flew off to Bolivia when she was pregnant, and now ..."

Ralph sighed and nuzzled her neck. She leaned close to him, saying, "Oh, oh, oh, I can't believe it! That's Jay's father. Oh my goo'ness, what have I missed?"

As soon as the show was done, Cindy checked the boys. Ralph put his ear to Dhyan's door. "All quiet," he whispered.

"Boys too," Cindy said. "We could ...." She snuggled up to him. "You know."

"It'd have to be quick."

"Race you."

"Ah, my cupcake," he said, grinning.

Dhyan blocked out the world with her disc player, listening through earbuds to the angriest music she owned. She eventually switched to sappy ballads her friends would scorn if they knew. Through tears, she took a photo envelope from an empty shelf and pulled prints from it. The first showed her at the theater, looking model-beautiful. She found a thumbtack on her dresser top to pin the photo to the wall beside her bed. She looked through the rest of the shots—her with friends, indoor and outdoor scenes—until she came to those taken at Larry's and Raoul's apartment. Alma wasn't in the first, second, or third one.

Dhyan stared at them for a long time, touching the spot where Alma should have been. She tacked the three shots on the wall. Puzzled and pained, she said to herself, "Mom, what's happening?" Anger rising again, she muttered, "Who can I talk to? Who knows fucking anything?"

Fran had dressed up for work in silk, earrings, and a touch of make-up, but she still looked ragged. Sandhu, in shades of burgundy to salmon, half-sat on Larry's desk top. The desk behind him bore a telephone, stacked in-out baskets, writing materials, and a photo of Sandhu and kin grinning by Uncle Sid's hospital bed.

Fran ran a hand through her hair. "I'm a mess, Sandhu, barely coping. I know it's all this custody bullshit, but this 'Coincidentals' file isn't helping." She threw it onto the desk, its edges curled and coffee cup rings puckering the cover. "I'm finished with it, at least until Larry's back."

"Hm." Sandhu paused. "If he's back."

"What you mean 'if'? Is he ... damn, is he just pretending to ... ?"

"No, I think he's fine, as fine as anyone after chemo. He's talking other plans, that's all, a whole new direction. Actually, he's trying to rope me in too. Gave me the overview the morning after the play, bubbling like a kid about it."

"Overview of what?"

"He's working up this plan to ... you know, maybe I'd better not tell you if he hasn't sprung it on you himself. He probably will when you've got things squared up again. Suffice it to say that the plan is brilliant, and he's dead serious but .... Listen, you were at the play, you saw the old lady on the stage, you saw him talking with Alma whoever-she-is. Was it really powerful enough to blow a whole new start into his brain?"

Fran nodded thoughtfully. "Yeah, it was. He almost fell off his seat in the theater. Me too. Alma had him crying buckets and pink as a newborn by the time she left his place. He was really up, totally inspired. What, is he finally going to run off and write the great American novel?"

Sandhu laughed. "That's the other half of the year. He's cut me in on his new enterprise so I can take the helm for six months while he writes his blockbuster, a tell-all about the business and bullshit of the news ...."

"Hey, if anyone can do it ...."

"Yeah, it'll be great, called TELLING NEWS."

"Wow. Perfect title. So c'mon, sharing the helm to do what? Give me a hint."

"A new publication, Fran, new ways of framing up and delivering news. Go see him, I'm sure he's got big plans for you too."

"I bet. Not right now though."

"What about now? What do you need—time off, stress leave?"

"God, no. I've got to keep busy, distracted, just nothing too crazy, no big ideas. I've got to keep my head clear for endless rounds with lawyers, counselors, Prozac pushers ...."

"How about an in-depth piece on the show-stopper at Raoul's play? Larry's real keen."

"And take on the world again? Naw, it's too big. I'm too worn out."

Sandhu pointed to the file. "What's the problem with this?"

"I can't pursue it, and it's too damned weird anyway."

"What do you mean, 'can't pursue it'?"

"Every lead I'd normally chase is a dead end. Lots of stuff overseas, I guess, if I wanted a world tour of miracles. I've got to talk with Alma and Pavla, whoever they are, but they're as elusive as ... oh hell, I don't know, rainbows. Normally I might enjoy this goose chase, but right now, it just pisses me off."

"Does any part of it interest you?"

"A tangent or two, I guess. A peripheral, as Larry would say. Alma's parting word to me was 'parthenogenesis'. I guess I could find out what's happening there."

"Wow. Could be really hot, all this genetics, cloning, ethics stuff."

"Just no more artsy-fartsy run-arounds. I could probably stir up a little fire in my belly for a science feature, something educational if not exactly news, lots of context and peripherals."

"So throw on some fuel, make it roar. Earn your next Scouting badge for it. Do a bang-up job, and I'll throw in a jamboree."

She laughed. "I'm having a jamboree, that's the problem. How 'bout I just do the story?"

"Sounds good to me." Sandhu picked up the file to give to Fran, who pretended horror and made a cross of her forefingers. He asked, "Where do I keep it?"

"Same question I've been asking. Tell you what, give it back to me, and I'll return it to Larry's cousin Mae—she started it. Now there's a story."

"So find an angle and do her."

"No way. Frying pan to fire. I'm sticking to simple things like virgin birth." She poked the file into a briefcase sitting by her chair. "Now what about you, pal? You haven't got a word in edgewise. How are you doing?"

"Me? I'm too busy to tell, a news-free zone. Good health, good help, good luck ...." He rapped the wooden desk top. "No personal life. Couldn't be better."

♦ ♦ ♦

FRAN stands before an image of the Acropolis in Athens, appearing to the viewer to be on the well-worn rocks leading up to the sun-bathed ruins. She's lit by a spotlight imitating a sunny day. Her hair blows slightly in the breeze from an unseen fan.

>   FRAN
> The Parthenon in Athens, everyone knows it. *Parthenos* means 'virgin' in Greek. This was the temple to the great virgin goddess Athena. She was a great warrior too, apparently born full-grown from Zeus's brow, no mother in sight.

The lighting switches to footlights. The background image changes to the Parthenon at night.

>   FRAN (continuing)
> This was quite a magical trick, an unequaled bit of conjuring by the old thunder god. Women have been explaining questionable pregnancies for eons and very creatively too, but this was a first for men. I'd give Zeus, oh, a D-minus. Good try, but nobody's going to buy it, certainly not today.

>   CUT TO:
Fran sitting comfortably in an arm chair in front of a wall of books.

>   FRAN
> Dr. Jonathan Foulkes is a classical scholar who's studied a long list of miraculous conceptions and virgin births through many religions, over many centuries. Could you give us an overview?

JONATHAN FOULKES, a distinguished elderly gentleman in tweeds, sits opposite Fran.

>   FOULKES
>   (smiling, plumy English accent)
> Well, it was obvious from the start that men would never give birth, however wishful Zeus's

                    FOULKES (continued)
mythic tale. But for a long time, it appears that
men weren't fully cognizant of their role as the
only beings capable of impregnating women.

There was, therefore, little pressure on women to
provide proof or justification for their state. They
could as easily be impregnated by a goat, bull,
toad, tree, what have you, as by a man. Quite
free times for women, I would imagine.

Men slowly clued into their role in conception,
and then the trouble started. If a man kept a
woman for himself and she bore a child unlike
any he could sire, he would know she'd been
unfaithful. A wife could no longer plead that
these things just happen, that she'd dreamt a
black sheep and out came a half-black child.

If a dutiful daughter slipped out on her parents
and got in the family way, so to speak, she
couldn't say that the north wind blew up her
skirt, or the stars were fatefully aligned, or she
ate beans and got the breath of life.

A clever woman might convince her inquisitors
that a god such as Zeus raped her, while a sweet,
virtuous daughter might insist that a divine spirit
sparked new life without touching her. The child
would be half a god and must be treated with
special care. There are innumerable instances of
such claims.

                              INTERCUT HEAD SHOTS:

         FRAN
Virgin births, in short.

                    FOULKES
Yes.

FRAN
Parthenogenetic origins. Virgin begetting.

FOULKES
Precisely.

FRAN
Very few have gotten away with this story, have they?

FOULKES
(smiling)
I'm too old and wise to wade into the Virgin Mary's claim. Buddha's mother, Maha Maya, apparently saw a godly elephant and conceived her special son, but that's not so crucial to his story, since he was never considered a god or spawn of capital 'G' God.

But yes, in general, the notion of virgin birth in humans was thoroughly disbelieved, if not disproved, since, oh, about the brutal ascendancy of Apollo over Hera as principal deity at Delphi, the religious center of the classical world.

CUT TO:

Aphids crawling on a succulent plant stem.

FRAN (voice over)
Virgin birth occurs in other species, some as a matter of course. Swiss naturalist Charles Bonnet discovered this in the 1700s, and Englishman Richard Owen coined the word 'parthenogenesis' for this process in the mid-1800s.

Some aphids, for example, reproduce themselves without males, and the offspring are always female. Some wasps, bees, and ants do this too, as well as the odd snake.

CUT TO:
A snake pit with one large snake and a writhing ball of babies.

>   FRAN (voice over)
> Lone female snakes kept in captivity and isolated from males all their lives have shocked their owners by producing a mass of babies seemingly out of the blue. Some researchers believe that they were impregnated years earlier and stored the sperm until something triggered conception.
>
> There are cases, however, like this female snake at the University of Colorado, that produced offspring without, absolutely without, ever being in the company of a male snake throughout her life. All her offspring were male, exactly as they had to be for a fatherless conception.
>
> Chickens and turkeys can be induced to reproduce parthenogenetically, and it's becoming increasingly easy and more common. Can are humans be far behind?

CUT TO:
Fran in a genetics laboratory with RACHELLE DUPONT, a stout, elderly woman in a white lab coat. Several ASSISTANTS in lab coats continue to work around them, pipetting, checking cell cultures, and looking in microscopes.

>   FRAN
> Dr. Rachelle DuPont has been studying parthenogenesis in turkeys for several decades. Dr. DuPont, why parthenogenesis? Why turkeys?
>
>   DUPONT
>   (husky voice)
> Personally, I'm curious. It's fascinating research, but industry efficiency is also a driving force. Create a perfect bird, then make her the mother, grandmother, and great-grandmother of a long

                    DUPONT (continued)
line of perfect birds. Each one is a clone of sorts
of the other, and from that control and consistency, the farmer can more or less count his
chicks before they hatch.

                    FRAN
A clone, you say. That's a hot word. What do
you mean, 'a clone of sorts'?

                    DUPONT
First, you have to understand the development of
a normal fertilized egg.

                                        CUT TO:
An ovum surrounded by sperm. In a sped-up sequence, a sperm
penetrates the cell membrane, enters the egg and fertilizes it. One,
two, and three cell divisions occur.

                    DUPONT (continuing)
There, the embryo now has eight cells, that's the
morula, Latin for mulberry. That's how we all
start—little mulberries for a crucial moment of
our lives.

Now, cloning involves taking a fertilized egg,
when it's still one cell, and removing its genetic
material. DNA from a mature cell is then injected
into it. With luck, it will divide and divide again,
through the morula stage to become an adult
organism.

In science fiction and maybe in the future, we
could take a single cell from your fingertip—like
God touching Adam's fingertip in
Michaelangelo's Sistine Chapel ....

                                        CUT TO:
Michaelangelo's God and Adam touching fingertips.

> DUPONT (continuing)
> ... extract its genetic material, inject it into an egg that's had its DNA removed, then grow another you. Not likely, for some time at least.

> FRAN
> What about the cloning of sheep, mice, etcetera?

CUT TO:
Dolly, the world's first cloned sheep. ZOOM IN on the ewe's udder and teats.

> DUPONT (voice over)
> We take genetic material from reproduction-related cells found, for example, in teats and udders. They clone more easily than finger or nose cells, far more easily. Parthenogenesis gets over the problem of needing specialized cells for viable results, because the ovum simply doubles its genetic material and carries on making ...

INTERCUT HEAD SHOTS:

> FRAN
> Wait! If the ovum simply doubles its genetic material, why can't we all do it?—all females, that is.

> DUPONT
> A trauma is needed, a mechanical or chemical disruption of the nuclear membrane without breaking it, or a shock of heat, cold, electrical current, vibration, etcetera. It's brutal and delicate on a tiny scale.
>
> By mysterious and complex means, the ovum's DNA replicates itself and produces, essentially, an identical twin. It's the mother's identical twin, always a girl, one generation removed.

> FRAN
> But the snake had all sons.

> DUPONT
> Hm-m. You'll need a diagram.

On a whiteboard, Dr. DuPont quickly sketches a circle.

> DUPONT (voice over)
> One turkey ovum. Or human, let's call it human.
> Inside, a nucleus.

DuPont draws another circle inside the first one, then scribbles in the center of it.

> DUPONT (continuing)
> A mess of DNA—genetic material, the blueprint
> for another, essentially identical being.

Outside of the ovum, she draws twenty-three short lines.

> DUPONT (continuing)
> Tease out the DNA, and you've got twenty-three
> chromosomes in humans. One is an 'X'.

She darkens one line.

> DUPONT (continuing)
> It's about as big as the others. There's only one
> of each chromosome in an ovum, and we need a
> pair to make a complete new person.

She draws a sperm.

> DUPONT (continuing)
> Enter the gladiators. They have the other half, the
> missing DNA.

She draws a mate for each of the twenty-three lines. The last one is shorter than the rest.

                    DUPONT (continuing)
This is the 'Y' chromosome, not much there.
Sperm can have either an 'X' or a 'Y'. In
humans, all the pairs get together, and if an 'X'
sperm fertilizes the egg it combines with the
egg's 'X' and voila!—a girl results. A 'Y'-
bearing sperm makes a boy, and the egg's 'X'
gets turned off. Simple.

                    FRAN
What about the snakes?

                    DUPONT
Their sex chromosomes are called 'W' and 'Z'.
A 'WZ' combination makes a female. Two 'W's
make a male. Two 'ZZ's are impossible. When a
female reproduces parthenogenetically, therefore, males must result, and there the line ends.

Turkeys, however, are like us, with X and Y
chromosomes. Two Xs make a female, so when
turkeys reproduce parthenogenetically, females
always result, without end. The same would be
true of humans.

                                        CUT TO:
Fran strolling through a university campus on a pleasant spring day. As she speaks, ZOOM IN to her face.

                    FRAN
The question is, how close are we to creating a
human mother's parthenogenetic twin? We
couldn't do it now, that's fairly certain, and not
ever according to federal U.S. legislation, which
prohibits the NIH—National Institute of
Health—from using appropriated funds to
support human embryo research, including
parthenogenesis.

But edicts only come out against something that's
possible and likely to happen. That means that

                    FRAN (continued)
behind closed doors and in locked labs, perhaps
here and certainly in other less concerned—some
might say less scrupulous—countries,
parthenogenetic research is inevitable.

The need to try and the need to know are hard-
wired into the human species. Someone, somewhere is pursuing this. What are the odds of
success? What difference will it make? Why
should we care?

The best 'clone' of a woman would come from
using her own eggs, stimulating them to double
their DNA, then double and double again to
produce a morula, a fetus, and eventually, a
whole new human being. Female, always female.
The process may not be as difficult or as distant
as we think.

Sperm don't have this capacity. Men can't
reproduce themselves to make more men; they'll
always need women as intermediaries. Men
would be out of the loop again, this time not
simply from being ignorant of their role in
procreation but because they would genuinely be
dispensable.

Fran sits on a pleasant bench under a blooming tree. She's joined by
JANET MCELROY, a thirty-something female scientist in a white
lab coat. She has cropped red hair, freckles on tawny skin, and
thick, lightly-tinted glasses.

                    MCELROY
Wait, wait! You're over-simplifying and danger-
ously.

                    FRAN
This is Dr. Janet McElroy, geneticist and
women's studies specialist. What do you mean,
Dr. McElroy?

> MCELROY
> Genetic diversity and hybrid vigor are cornerstones to the creation of healthy individuals and populations. Sexual reproduction gives far superior—that is, variable, adaptable, yet tending-to-the-mean—genetic products in an unpredictably changing world, whereas asexual or parthenogenetic reproduction requires conditions and prevailing cycles to stay fairly constant within predictable pockets or niches.
>
> Parthenogenesis as the sole means of reproduction could supply extremes of mutation, which sexual reproduction dampens, hence provide the quantum leap necessary for significant evolutionary advances over large populations and large geographic areas during times of great change.
>
> The price to any given population during times of upheaval would be catastrophic, with no guarantee that the species in its entirety would survive.
>
> FRAN
> (to the camera)
> Did you get that?
>
> (to McElroy)
> Dr. McElroy, could you possibly simplify that or is that as simple as it gets?
>
> MCELROY
> (smiling, voice soft)
> I'm saying that the mix is good. Men and women mixing it up is vital for genetic diversity and, ultimately, our survival. Parthenogenesis is not the way for humans in general to go, not now, not ever. It's too risky. Too marginal. Learning to live and love together is the key.

                              CUT TO:
Fran again standing alone in front of the Parthenon, this time as it shines golden at sunrise.

                    FRAN
          Athena, virgin goddess of this temple, had her
          moment of fame as a great warrior, then lost her
          following and crumbled to this. Perhaps that's
          what this abandoned shell stands for. Men
          fighting men, men and women divided—it never
          comes to a good end. Compare this ....

Fran sweeps her hand up across the Acropolis, then turns 180 degrees and points downward.

                    FRAN (continuing)
          ... to the thriving city below.

View from the Acropolis down to the busy streets of Athens, humming with traffic and life.

                    MCELROY (voice over)
          Learning to live and love together is the key.

Upon completion of filming under the tree, Janet McElroy lifted her glasses to smile at Fran. In the dappled sunlight, her irises glinted blue-green-gold, precious metal flecks sparkling in dark ores. Pavla Blanca, no doubt.

She and Fran walked toward the nearby Life Sciences building, a fortress-like structure. Fran said, "You've shocked the life out of me twice now—at the OVT last time."

"I'll have to work on my disguises, won't I?"

"No, it's perfect, not a freckle out of place. It's not the look, it's the feel. I just knew it was you."

"My apologies for the disruption."

Fran chuckled. "You only caused a half-dozen retakes while I found my tongue. How did you ... how did this connect?"

"I asked Rachelle to call me if you took Mother's advice and pursued the topic. We expected you'd seek her out, but how I might fit in was a last minute decision."

"Last minute incredible, thank you. What a great quote ... well, the one I understood."

Pavla laughed. "Sorry. I'm fairly immersed in this."

"No kidding. Care to tell why?" Fran and Pavla had reached the middle of a long gray corridor and the unmarked door to Dr. DuPont's lab. "Or is that too big a question?"

"For here and now, yes. Too public too." Pavla looked from one end of the corridor to the other. "I move about freely at times in my various alter-egos, but what happened today is rare. And dangerous. I take risks all the time, but they're calculated."

"Then I'm even more grateful."

Pavla extended her hand to Fran. As they shook, Pavla said, "Thank you, and good luck." She turned to enter the lab through an unlocked door.

"Thank you," Fran said. "May I contact you again? Through Dr. DuPont?"

Pavla looked back at Fran, shook her head slightly, and said quietly, urgently, "No. And please don't try." She closed the door between them.

Fran stood stunned for a moment, then started toward the door. The temptation to follow Pavla was great, but she decided better of it and left.

Dhyan's room stayed barren. Cindy sorted through the mound of childish items outside the door, making a large pile to give to charity, a small pile of keepsakes, and a tiny pile of garbage.

Ralph checked the piles cursorily, making no changes whatever. He put the give-away stuff in big garbage bags, the keepsakes pile in a storage box, and took the final one to the household's outdoor garbage cans.

After midnight, Cindy awoke to a faint, acrid odor. She sat up and sniffed. "Ralph," she said, poking him. "I smell something." Ralph didn't budge. "Ralph!"

"Wha ... what?"

"I think I smell smoke."

He muttered something incomprehensible and continued sleeping.

She lay on her back, eyes open. After several minutes, she threw the covers back and jumped up, "I do smell smoke. If you won't wake up and check, I'll go out in the dark all by myself." She rose from bed and stubbed her toe on her way to the closet for her housecoat. "Ow, ow, ow!"

Ralph sat up. "What're you doing? You okay?"

Cindy said angrily, "I smell smoke, Ralph."

He sniffed, leaping up instantly. "Why didn't you tell me? You stay here. I'll deal with it." He fumbled on his trousers, tucking his nightshirt into them as he rushed from the room.

Cindy said, "I'll check the boys."

In the middle of the backyard, flames from a small, smoky fire leapt and sparked into the moon-bright sky. A crouched, shadowy figure tended it.

Ralph got a gun from his locked cabinet and dared face the intruder, certain to be crazy if not dangerous. From the opened door, he cocked the rifle, took aim, and said ominously, "I've got a bead on you. Hands up, or I'll shoot."

"Da-ad," Dhyan said, staying crouched.

"For crying out loud, Dhyan, what are you trying to do? Give me a heart attack?" She stayed silent and still as he set the gun carefully by the door, then walked to her. Up close, the fire was clearly the remains of the keepsakes box.

Dhyan stirred it with a stick, pushing a once-frilly doll into the heart of the flames. "C'mon, burn, baby, burn. That's what you said when you were young and cool, didn't you, Dad? Burn, baby, burn." She laughed. "When you were cool." And laughed again.

Ralph put an arm firmly around her, saying, "That's quite enough." He sniffed her. "You've been into my whisky haven't you? We're marching in, little miss. We're talking with Cindy."

"God, you mean," Dhyan muttered. "God's biggest suck-up, like He's so insecure you gotta tell Him he's wonderful all the time or He'll smote and smite, forsake you all over the place, what a jerk."

"Shut up or I'll wash your mouth out with soap—pine tar soap, I swear," Ralph said, trying to push Dhyan toward the back door.

She stiffly held her ground, then ducked out from under his arm with a taunting laugh. "Capital J Jerk. You go report to God yourself, leave me out of it."

Ralph caught one of her arms firmly and said, "Dhyan, don't make me force you. And show a little dignity—that's got nothing to do with God and everything to do with you." In the half-light, Dhyan's face twitched as she fought between sticking out her tongue and hiding her deep contrition. Ralph's voice softened. "Please. Go on in. I'll be there in a minute."

Dhyan plodded into the house. Ralph turned on the garden hose to douse the fire, then found a large plastic bucket into which he shoveled the soggy, smelly cinders. He clapped on its lid and carried it to the trash. The boys didn't need to know about this.

He opened the door back into the kitchen to be greeted by a blast of fluorescent light and Cindy's shrieking and praying. Dhyan—a sloppy, sooty mess—held her hands over her ears and sang "La la la la la la la!" to drown out Cindy.

"Enough!" Ralph bellowed.

Cindy stopped mid-word. The oldest boy appeared sleepily in the kitchen doorway and asked, "What's going on?"

Ralph said, "Nothing. Go back to bed, son."

Cindy said, "Ralph, you can't just brush this under ...."

"Sh-h-h!" Pointing to the doorway he said, "Go to bed. All of you." Cindy and boy reluctantly vanished.

Dhyan didn't move. Ralph said, "You too. We'll talk sensibly in the morning, and if that's not possible, you're grounded in your room until it is."

"So ground Cindy too, she's half the ...."

"To bed! Scram." Dhyan looked at him defiantly, on the edge of tears. He smiled tightly and said, "Oh Dhyan, I'd tell you to grow up, but that's obviously what you're trying to do. Let's talk strategy tomorrow. Drinking and burning are ... well, just not that smart. Now give me a hug, then beat it."

Dhyan did, tucking her head into her dad's shoulder to hide her tears, then scooted out fast. Ralph went to the liquor cabinet, poured a generous snifter of whisky, and muttered before belting it back, "Just not that smart." He wiped his mouth with the back of his hand, considered the empty glass and, said, "But necessary sometimes."

After school the next day, Dhyan sat on her bed, alternately chewing the end of a ballpoint pen and using it to write on a pad of lined school paper.

> Dear Mom
> Dad and the Ditz killed the computer for me just their sucky boys get it so no e-mail and they said if I phone you they'll go wild and make things real bad at court.
> I can't write and I can't call and they think I'm so dumb I won't find a way to get to you. I hate her I hate her I hate her.
> Last nite I burned a pile of baby stuff in the back yard and she went balistic. Dad was sortof cool but he drinks which beats praying I'm so sick of her praying. I'm OK tho so don't worry they can't do anything with me.
> I'm writing cuz somethings bugging me and even makes me cry

(Cindyrella can't do that she just makes me mad) and it's kindof a little thing but it bugs me.

We took a picture of everyone at Larry's right? Alma was there right? She was in the pictures we took three but Mom I got the pictures back and she's not there I mean totally not there. What's going on? You've got to see her I mean if you can cuz I need to know. I wish I could see her again I wish I wish I wish.

The Retinol-A dragon is due to come steam at me so I'll get it ready to mail on the way to school. If she doesn't notice a missing stamp I'll have beaten her again. If she notices and goes weird I win too.

XO Dhyan

Dhyan's crude handmade envelope containing her letter plopped onto Fran's floor through the mail slot, along with a raft of bills and junk mail. Fran heard the delivery but didn't move from the sofa where she sat flipping through the newspaper. Minutes later, her cuckoo clock's parrot burst out and squawked once for half past the hour—10:30 a.m. She took a last swig of cold coffee from her pottery mug and pulled herself up to fetch the mail. The sight of Dhyan's schoolgirl hand brought a whoop of joy.

Fran read her letter hungrily standing by the door, then returned to the sofa to read it again. When tears came too close, she covered her eyes with both hands and said, "No, no, no. Think, Fran."

Out the front window, she saw a car pull up that she didn't recognize—a maroon, late-model four-door sedan—with Nikos behind the wheel. "Huh?" she wondered aloud. "New steed, same white knight, yes!" She bounced up to greet him, half-singing, "'Just when I needed you most.'"

He double-parked the car and raced around it to open the front passenger door. He took a baby from a child's safety seat and ran for Fran's door. She opened it for him and his tiny charge.

Breathlessly, he handed the child to Fran and looked back, saying, "No one following, good. In, in, lock the door. I will move the car two, three blocks away and come in your back door. You open it, *ne*?"

The baby, a dark-haired, tawny-skinned girl about nine months old, zapped Fran with an electric look from blue-green-gold flecked eyes. "Oh no," Fran said, goosebumps of recognition rising.

Nikos hurried off. The baby clutched Nikos's amber worry beads. Fran said, "Yeah, hang on tight, sweetheart. Looks like a really good day for those." She closed and locked the front door behind him, then pulled shut the vertical blinds on the front window.

"Now we gotta open the back door for Nikos." The baby struggled to get down. Fran stood her on tiny feet and chubby legs, then offered two fingers to be enwrapped by a tiny fist. "Oh sure, do it yourself, that's the stuff. C'mon, it's this way."

Fran helped the baby walk to the back door. Fran snapped the deadbolt open. The little girl reached up for it, so Fran picked her up and let her have a try. It was far too stiff for her small hand, but with Fran's help, they locked and unlocked it several times before Nikos slipped through the back gate by the old shed and ran through Fran's renewed garden toward the house. He carried a shoulder bag holding the baby's supplies.

Inside, puffing and distraught, he said, "They got Pavla. We were in traffic, Pavla and baby in the back seat ...." He gasped to catch his breath.

The baby grew alarmed at Nikos's sweating urgency and started to fuss. Fran kissed her on silky hair and rocked her gently.

"I give you beads," Nikos said, reaching to touch them. The baby turned away from him, holding them tight. He continued to Fran, "I give them to her when we meet, so she laughs for me. I pick up Pavla and baby near the university, in my Fiat. We are going to the airport, that is all I know. I stop at a light, we are first in line ...."

"Where?"

"Near the freeway, heading south. Long light, car crosses in front of us going west, pulls to a stop just past us. Two big guys get out, both in black. I don't recognize them. The driver, I know him from Greece, he has white hair. He stays in the car.

"Boom. First big guy blows out Pavla's door lock with a pistol, silencer, hardly a sound. He opens the door, the baby is right there. Other guy uses a knife to cut the belts from the baby's seat. Pavla grabs his wrist, twists it, the knife drops. Then she leaps—she is very fast—and he is on the ground. I hear a crack, something broke. He is dead maybe, I do not know.

"First guy grabs her, puts a cloth on her face, she passes out. I am out of the car to help, but the light changes, traffic is honking, some people saw, most did not. She is in the other car, they take off, leaving the hurt man on the street. I drive away. The back door swings open and shut, it cannot close, but the baby is scared, she stays okay in her seat. I drive a few blocks, carefully, no one follows me, then I see car rental place. I leave my car in a back alley parked very close to a big wall, it hides the open door and bullet hole. I rent another car and come right here."

"Did you get the license number?"

"No. No time."

"Did you phone for help?"

"I tried, on my cell. I dialed nine-one-one, then I think, how much should I tell? Maybe nothing. Maybe Pavla is in more danger if I tell. So I hang up, and I call Mae, but she does not answer. Rings and rings, twenty, thirty times. She is only out when I drive her. I do not know what is wrong. I am afraid to go to her house with the baby in the car. Men could be there too."

"So let's try her again," Fran said. "Maybe your cell's the problem." She handed Nikos her cordless phone, and he quickly punched in Mae's number. Again, it rang and rang at Mae's end. "Answer, please Mae," he pleaded. "Please."

As the telephone jangled on Mae's paper-stacked dining table, she lay in a bony heap on her kitchen floor. Her pink chenille housecoat and floppy slippers lie askew, her wig nowhere in sight. Lord Byron yapped at the phone and pulled at his lady love. Mae struggled with skinny arms to pull herself toward the phone but couldn't overcome the pain to move more than an inch at a time.

"Byron," she said, "go get it. Go get the phone. Go. Go on!" He ran away from her, then ran back. "Go. Get the phone."

He ran off again, farther this time. "Yes," she said. "Go! Go get it." He leapt up at the table and snapped at the phone, finally grabbing the cord and shaking his head angrily, pulling and growling until the whole thing crashed to the floor, the receiver flying free.

"Mae!" she could hear Nikos's voice say faintly from it.

"Nikos," she croaked as best she could, then passed out.

Nikos hung up and said to Fran, "She is there. In trouble." He rushed for Fran's door. "You stay here, *ne*? I will be back as quick as I can."

Nikos vanished out the back door. Fran said to the baby, "Hey, sweet girl, now what? My God, you're beautiful." With the help of tiny hands, Fran pulled shut the rest of the blinds and curtains. She got a banana for her company, and they returned to the living room with it.

She sat on the sofa and removed the girl's sweater, setting it to one side of them. Dhyan's letter lay open on the other. "You and me kid, we're between a rock and a hard place, aren't we? It's a crazy world, isn't it? Doesn't make any sense. Can't make any of the trick ponies do what we want. We gotta keep trying though."

She wiggled a finger on the baby's chin, eliciting a slight twinkle from those uncanny eyes. "What a sweetie. Yeah, we gotta keep smiling. And keep trying. Sit tight and keep trying. Hurry up and wait. Are you getting mixed messages here too?" The baby grabbed for her lower lip, and they laughed together.

Fran peeled the banana and offered her a bite. She dropped the worry beads to take it. She mucked the banana playfully into her mouth past eight little teeth, four top and bottom. Fran asked, "What's your name, Sunshine? You got a name? You got a thousand names?"

"Mom, Mom," the baby said, offering Fran some of her mushy bite.

"Yeah, Mom-Mom Pavla," Fran said. "And you're baby ...?"

"Lu-na," the baby said.

"Lu-na. Or is that baby talk? La-la."

"Luna," the baby said again, this time pasting Fran's mouth with mash.

"Yum. Well, it sure sounds like Luna. Hm-m, Luna, Luna. It'll do for now. I suppose you know that a Lunarian is an inhabitant of the moon, as distinguished from Lunatic, one whom the moon inhabits, with thanks to Ambrose Bierce for that. I think you're the Lunarian, if not from far beyond, while I'm the Lunatic, what do you think?"

Luna patted her two gooey hands together, sending banana bits flying, which made her laugh more.

Fran carried her to the bathroom, where she used a clean, wet cloth to wipe up the mess. The baby took the cloth and continued wiping on her own. Fran looked at their reflections in the mirror and said, "Luna Blanca, I presume. Fran Roma—Francine Gypsy, if you please, my little White Moon. You know, it fits. I like it." She looked back at Luna, tickled her tummy, and said, "And I like you."

Fran toddled Luna back to the kitchen, Luna chanting happily, "Mom, Mom, Pavla Mom."

"Oh, sweet babe." Fran breathed deeply to contain her tears. "She's gone, but where? Another orphan—God, I hope not—lands in Fran's arms. Say it ain't so. Don't even think one bad thought, okay? Don't think anything but good, hey Sunshine?—Moonbeam, I mean." Fran talked herself back into a smile.

Luna let go of Fran's fingers and tottered ahead, pleased as Punch with her brave walking alone.

Nikos unlocked Mae's front door, his hands trembling in fear of what lay inside. All was quiet. All was untouched. There had been no struggle, no evidence of invaders.

Nikos quickly found Mae in the kitchen, barely conscious, but muttering, "I'm fine, I'm fine."

"Don't speak," he said. "Don't move." He ran to the living room to fetch an old pillow to slip under her head and a ratty afghan to cover her chilly limbs. He called an ambulance, which arrived within minutes.

A paramedic checked her thoroughly. An attendant brought in a gurney.

"What happened?" the paramedic asked.

Mae whispered woozily, "I twisted. I fell."

"What medications do you take?"

Nikos said, "Here." He pointed to two small vials above the kitchen sink.

The attendant asked, "And your dentures?"

Nikos said, "I will get them." When he came back with Mae's teeth from the piano top, the ambulance workers had her on the gurney and were tucking blankets around her. Nikos said to them, "It was the dog, I am sure. He knocks her over. My fears come true."

Mae croaked, "Byron got the phone. He saved me." The paramedic injected her with morphine.

Nikos said, "He is a good dog, dear Mrs. Singer-Jones, but you need live-in help, I tell you that for years. When you come home, we arrange it. Then you will have Byron and someone else to look after you."

"I don't want anyone snooping ...."

"Someone special, Mrs. Singer-Jones. Someone who understands."

"Impossible," Mae said, closing her eyes, relaxing with the painkiller. Nikos stayed by her side as the attendants carried her to the ambulance. At its open back doors, he said, "I cannot come with you. Something else, very important, has come up. Can you tell me where Alma is, how I contact her?"

"Why? You never ask. What's wrong?"

"Nothing. Fran wants to see her."

"I don't know." Mae's voice trailed off. She closed her eyes and mumbled, "Look after Byron."

"Of course," Nikos said, squeezing her old hand, then the attendants slid her into the ambulance and closed the doors. It pulled into traffic, siren wailing.

Fran walked and rocked Luna until her long eyelashes closed over rosy cheeks. She carried the sleeping cherub to her bedroom, where she nudged her bed against the wall, lay Luna down, and built a surrounding fortress of pillows.

"Hurry, please hurry," Fran muttered as she paced between kitchen and bedroom, one ear tuned for Luna's waking, the other for Nikos's return. Finally, the phone rang. Fran snatched it up before it could warble again and wake Luna. "Nikos?" she guessed.

"No, it's Alma Solari."

"Oh thank goodness. Nikos got hold of you then, through Mae?"

"No, Luna's got a tracking device on her. I know she's there."

"So her name is Luna? She told me, she's so amazing."

"I can read her location, but I've lost Pavla at an intersection some miles from you."

"That's right. She was with Nikos on the way to the airport. Alma, I'm so sorry. She's been abducted by some white-haired guy you saw in Greece and two beasts in black."

Alma groaned.

"Pavla put up a good fight, maybe even did serious damage to one of her attackers. Nikos couldn't save her—it happened so fast—and he was worried about Luna, making sure he got her out safely."

"Bless him. He's a brilliant man."

"You can't read Pavla's tracking device?"

"No, there's an interference problem. Her abductors must know something about our communication system."

"Meaning that they can still pinpoint Luna?"

"No, the signal's scrambled and rescrambled continually; penetration's highly unlikely. They must have traced Pavla some other way, but they know enough about the system to block it once they have her, using something as low-tech as a magnetic field. Luna's signal is clear, but I'd like you to destroy her transmitter anyway. It's on an ankle bracelet. Could you remove it right now? The barrel clasp takes a lot of twists, then smash the bead with a hammer. I'll call back in exactly five minutes."

Fran delicately removed Luna's socks and found the bracelet with a little metal canister bead. Luna fussed in her sleep as Fran fiddled with the clasp, but upon its opening, the baby sank back into deep slumber.

In the kitchen, Fran pounded the tiny ball with the first tool she could find in a junk drawer, a heavy wrench. The bead flattened but didn't break open. After dozens of smashes, its guts of chips and circuits were certain to be destroyed. Alma called precisely when promised.

"It's defunct, I'm sure," Fran said. "Now what?"

"Nothing else as far as Luna goes. Can you keep her at your place for a while?"

"For as long as you like. Any special instructions? She's clearly a very special little sweetheart."

A smile warmed Alma's words. "Yes, she is. And a completely normal baby too. You've raised a lovely daughter; I'm sure you know the baby basics."

"A little rusty, but if rapport matters, we're good buddies already. God, she's wonderful."

Alma laughed lightly. "Thank you ... so much. I'm on my way there now, flying in, in about fifteen hours. Could you have Nikos fetch me?"

"Of course."

"I'll call an hour before we land and give you instructions."

"You know, maybe I should pick you up, using my car. They don't know me or it—whoever 'they' are. Nikos can stay with Luna."

"Yes. Yes, that's smart. Now I have another favor to ask."

"Anything."

"The white-haired man is Dr. Dino Trigliani." Alma spelled his last name. "Could you call Dr. Rachelle DuPont and ask her to compile everything she's got on him? Pavla's been searching, but I don't think she's found much that isn't publicly accessible and research related. Any bit of new information could provide a vital clue, so whatever Rachelle finds might help."

Fran said, "Maybe I could help too."

"It's a kind offer, but I think Luna's too close to you, too traceable if someone notices and gets suspicious. In fact, I'd ask most specifically that you don't pursue this. Rachelle and Trigliani are colleagues, competitors. She can search almost with impunity. She may find something on Pavla's lab computer too. She'll need the latest password, which is ...." Alma spoke slowly. "The date of the first manned moon landing in S.I. notation—year, month, day—converted from numbers to the alphabet, starting at L for Luna."

Fran said, "Let's see, one nine six nine ... hm, zero eight, then zero is L? One is M?"

"Exactly. It'll be like looking for a needle in haystack, but tell Rachelle I'd appreciate her trying. And when you call her, use a land line, will you? No cell phones—too open to eavesdropping. Now I'm boarding any minute, so I'll see you tomorrow. Thank you, dear, more than I can say."

Fran burst with her news to Nikos when he was barely in the back door. She concluded her report with, "Alma doesn't know about Mae. I couldn't tell her, I don't know anything either. What happened?"

"The good news is no bad guys got her. The bad news is stupid dog knocked her down, broke her hip."

Fran groaned, "Oh no."

"Then smart dog pulled down the phone so I hear her. I found her on the kitchen floor, barely conscious. I called an ambulance, they took her to hospital. I left food and water for Byron."

"Poor dog. Maybe he should come here." She laughed. "First a kid, next a dog. Maybe Barnum and Bailey is going through and has some spare elephants."

Nikos smiled and shrugged. "Maybe Larry could take him."

"Oh my God, Larry. Did you call him?"

Nikos shook his head. "Not yet."

Luna's voice, a faint waking fuss, came from the bedroom. Fran headed immediately for her new little charge, waving Nikos to follow. "Come on, let's play a bit first. She's incredible."

Fran picked Luna up, saying, "Did you hear that? Did you know that I'm crazy about you?"

Luna beamed at her, then looked warily at Nikos.

Wisely keeping his distance, he said softly, "Of course, you worry. I drive while Mama is taken. Then we switch cars, we rush here, big bad man."

Fran pointed to Nikos, saying, "Nikos. Can you say Nikos? He's my hero, you should know. Everyone adores him."

Luna glanced at Nikos, then looked intently at Fran's face. She gently touched Fran's mouth with tiny fingertips. Fran went, "Skn-n-ow-w!" as if to eat Luna's hand, which made her giggle. She tentatively reached for Nikos's mouth, and in the air, he did a quieter, gentler version of the game. She giggled louder. They played again and again until she was nearly as comfortable with Nikos as with Fran.

"This is the worst day of my life," Cindy said to Ralph on the phone, "and it's barely half over." She'd called him at his office, catching him as he walked in from a late lunch.

"Oh no," Ralph groaned. "What happened?"

"You've betrayed me. I can't believe it, and I'm so ... so ...."

"Betrayed you? What do you mean, betrayed you?"

"And you thought you'd never get caught, but your daughter's too smart by half for you, Ralph Roma." Her tongue dripped acid as she repeated, "Ralph *Roma*."

"Oh boy. I'm coming home. Give me half an hour."

"You'd better have name-change papers with you when you do."

"This is really old news, this is ridiculous."

"Brand new news to me, dear."

"Just hang on. Let me get home, and we'll talk this out sensibly."

"Sensibly! There is no 'sensibly' and no sense talking either. You just do the right thing, starting this minute."

"Yes, dear. Hang tight, sweetheart. I'm leaving as quick as I can."

Dhyan's smirk reflected in Cindy's rosewood dining table, polished to lemon-wax perfection. She looked like the cat who'd just eaten the mine's only canary. Cindy held a small rolled-up newspaper and gasped for air.

The instant Ralph walked in, Cindy stabbed the paper at him and said, "It's all in here. The whole world knows. I am so ashamed."

Dhyan sat perfectly still, continuing to smirk. Her dad unfolded the paper—the J.C. Junior High "Students Ink"—and read the headline: "Are you man enough to take a woman's name?" Under Dhyan's byline, the column started, "Ralph Roma, WonderDad, did ...."

Ralph smiled, struggling to hold in a laugh. "WonderDad!" he choked out. Cindy's blood pressure went sky high; her barometer read 'Tornado'. "I'm sorry," he said, "but this is the funniest, best thing I've ever read. WonderDad ... open-minded ... sensitive .... Thanks, kid."

The eye of Cindy's storm descended. In measured words, she said, "I will not have it." To Dhyan, she said, "You have humiliated me." To Ralph, she continued, "And you shock me. I will be Mrs. Ralph Rommel, or I will not be your wife."

Dhyan said, "Why not Mrs. Erwin Rommel? Go for broke, the full effect."

"Shut up!" Cindy said. "We've had quite enough from you, Miss Smarty Pants."

Ralph said to Dhyan, "It's not an Erwin Rommel thing, I told you that. He was a very distant relative, and as the Desert Rat, he was actually fairly respected. I didn't care about that either way."

Dhyan said, "Yeah, but you still traded a Nazi name for 'Gypsy', that's so cool, from the oppressors to the oppressed."

"That's not the point. Rommel wasn't a Nazi , and I was just trying to be, I don't know ... liberated. Forget any historical connections; I just wanted to be a man of my times. I mean, women have been changing their names forever, by the millions ... billions. It's not a big deal. I liked it for business too: Roma and Schultz."

Dhyan said, "Hah! You didn't want two Kraut names, one of them a buddy of Hitler's, admit it."

Ralph slapped the paper on the table. "Stop pushing it, Dhyan. It was just something I did when I was young and idealistic. There's nothing to explain, and there's nothing wrong with any part of it."

"Nothing wrong!" Cindy wailed. "Nothing wrong with me being Mrs. Roma? Fran's been laughing at me for years over this, it's so cruel, you're all laughing like hyenas." Cindy broke into tears, heaving for breath.

"I can't change it back, sweetheart. I mean, it's my legal name and the boys' name and ... and it's on all my business cards, forms, the 'Net, advertising. We're talking big hassles, hon', and big bucks, it's not worth it. And what if my birth name was Roma and Fran took it, then kept it? Divorced women do that all the time."

"You just don't get it, do you?" She sobbed louder.

"So why not change it to another name entirely? Your maiden name, if you want."

Dhyan said, "Mr. Cindy Lakowski. That is so cute."

Cindy's mascara ran like black grease on a clown. "Don't you dare make fun of me. And what kind of man are you anyway, who doesn't want to give his wife his real name?"

Dhyan retorted, "He's the best kind of man, you blond! Can't you see that's the point of my whole article? He's sensitive and egalitarian and secure enough to ...."

Ralph stopped her mid-sentence with a hard look. "Go to your room, go! Leave us to talk." Dhyan snatched the newspaper from the table, punched the air with it in clenched fist, and left with, "Gypsies rule! Forever!"

Ralph pulled a chair up to Cindy's and said quietly, "Roma *is* my real name."

Cindy snuffled and thrust out her bottom lip.

Ralph held her chin gently in his hand. "C'mon, smile my beautiful girl, my sweetest cupcake. Let's pick a new name we both like. How 'bout Mr. and Mrs. Cupcake?"

She suppressed a tiny smile. "You're making fun of me. I want Rommel. It's honest, and it's yours. And I'm your woman, all yours."

He sighed. "And I'm all yours, so why not your name? Or a whole new name, let the boys have a say too. And can we keep Roma for the business, does it really matter?"

She pouted.

"We've got to do it your way, don't we? The whole nine yards."

She smiled—finally. "We do." She thought for a moment, then said, "When we got married, we each said 'I do.' Now it's 'We do.' Isn't that romantic?" Excitedly, she said, "Ralphy, let's get married again, let's say 'We do' together, in front of everyone—and God. The whole thing: church, reception, everything, okay? Let's do it totally right this time, right down to the right name. Oh, this will be so fun."

Ralph sighed as he headed for the liquor cabinet. "This calls for a toast to the bride." He poured himself a generous drink and a light splosh for Cindy. Handing her the drink, he said, "To you."

She raised it and clinked his glass. "To me. Mrs.—ta da! and proud of it—Ralph Rommel."

♦ ♦ ♦

Larry sat on his bed surrounded by the paperwork of his new venture. He filled file folders with detailed plans when inspiration hit and his energy flowed. He dropped to sleep when he needed recharging.

The phone on his night table rang only once before the message machine cut in with his greeting: "Hi, Larry here—or maybe not. Do the usual, thanks. Be-e-ep."

"Larry," Fran said, "if you're there, please, please, you've got to call back."

Larry could hear a baby giggling in the background. He hit the speaker phone button. "Babies, Fran?" he said. "What's up?"

"I've got Luna, Pavla's daughter. She was abducted, Nikos was driving. He saved Luna, brought her here."

"Pavla was abducted?"

"Yeah, and there's more. Mae fell and broke her hip."

"Oh no," he groaned. "Where is she? What happened?"

"Byron probably knocked her down. Nikos got her an ambulance about half an hour ago. She's at the hospital. Nikos left Byron at the house, we've got to deal with that. You interested in dog-sitting?"

"Can't. No dogs allowed here. I can find him a nice kennel though."

"No, forget it. I'll take him. Could you do me a big favor and bring him here? Then we can talk more. It's nuts, Larry, totally spinning out."

"Sure, give me an hour. You're a doll, Fran. Hang in."

At Mae's house, Raoul stood at the door to the bedroom Maya slept in. He shut his eyes, dreading what paper mess and dust might greet him. He opened them to ... pleasant contrast, tidy and clean quarters. The decor was 1920s/30s with vintage furnishings, a lovely little museum-quality room. He sighed in relief and returned to Larry on the sofa, saying, "Well, thank God, she's got one sane corner. It could be her only redemption."

Larry continued teasing Byron with the ball from Pavla. Larry laughed. "This," he said, waving a hand over Mae's midden of paperwork, "is her redemption. Cleaning is her curse; chasing dust means neglecting what really matters."

"If dust is the measure, she's saved many times over." From a stack of file folders, Raoul picked up one marked "Holl". "What is all this anyway, uh? I mean, other than the obvious."

"She's tracing us all back to Adam and Eve and their pet dog, right Byron?" Byron playfully growled as Larry pulled the spit-slippery ball from his mouth. "Except scratch Adam."

Raoul flipped through the folder. "So 'Holl' is for Holland, yes, I knew that. Let's see what she says about my *alma mater*, my own Alma Solari." He sing-songed her name.

"Don't make fun, Raoul. She *is* my fostering mother, picking up where Maya left off."

"I know, I know," Raoul said, putting the file down. "Sorry, darling. I guess we just clean up this place blind, no reading, no levity. And you've got to think about that, because this whole mess could fall on us any day now."

"Uh-uh. Mae's going to be fine, you watch. She just needs live-in help, like Nikos said. We'll put a nurse-*cum*-research assistant in an upstairs room, and they'll have it organized and tidy by Christmas. Then she can just hang out and have fun for her last ten, fifteen years."

"Well, I've had my fill of paper and pandemonium for now. Let's get this filthy mop to Fran's, poor girl. Dogs, babies ...." He shuddered.

Larry found Byron's leash on a peg by the front door. "I got her into this mess, now she's buried. What do you think the going rate is for babysitting, dog-minding, kidnap-busting?"

"Lots of zeros. A modest little one or two in front."

"Hm. No scale? No blue book value?"

"It's off the charts. Forget the check. She's trapped and will have to do it for love. Precluded by insanity."

Mae sat propped in her hospital bed looking as fragile as a ceramic doll, not a wig in sight, her own hair a white mist. Her pale green hospital gown matched pale green hospital sheets. She shared a room with three others: a moaner behind curtains, a pacer between bed and bathroom, and a giggler with a loud-voiced female visitor.

At 7:30 p.m., a soft-spoken nurse arrived with a sleeping pill and glass of water. Mae clamped her lips shut. "Please," the nurse coaxed.

"Not until my young cousin Larry has come. Perhaps you've heard of him, Larry Singer, he's news director at Media 8—my second cousin twice removed, on my father's side."

The nurse shook her head and said, quietly exasperated, "Mrs. Singer-Jones, this is ordered for seven-thirty, and you really must take it." She put the pill and water to Mae's lips.

Mae turned her head aside. "Not until Larry has come and gone."

"But I have to mark on your chart that you took it now."

"What does it matter, another few minutes? I don't want it anyway. Give him time, for heaven's sake. He's been sick—he was in the cancer ward recently, perhaps you saw him there, handsome fellow, a bit bald."

"No, I didn't see him, I'm sorry. This is a very big hospital."

"You come back at eight o'clock, not a minute before. He'll be here, you'll see."

The nurse heaved a sigh and continued her rounds. At 7:45 p.m., a burly nurse charged in with the first nurse following meekly. Without a word, the big nurse put the pill in Mae's mouth, tipped the water into her mouth, and down went the pill. Mae was too surprised to protest. "There," the nurse said to her. "The chart says seven-thirty. We run a tight ship, ma'am, and entirely for your benefit. It's either the pill or a shot, and refusal next time will get you the shot." To the other nurse, she said, "See? Be definitive."

She bustled out. The smaller nurse started to wind down Mae's bed for the night, but Mae told her, "Don't you dare! I will sit up until eight o'clock. I will not lie down one minute before."

"But you'll be asleep ...." She stopped winding.

"No, I won't. Not until eight o'clock. Is winding down my bed on my chart?"

"No."

"Then leave me for now."

The nurse gave up and left the room.

Mae's eyes were woozy when Larry and Raoul arrived minutes later. Raoul carried a vase of freesias and mums. "Sorry we're late," Larry said, kissing her cheek. "We took Byron to Fran's, then stayed a bit while he settled."

"Oh, that's good. Poor wee Byron."

"He'll be fine, Mae. He's got a baby to play with and Nikos is there too."

"A baby?" she asked groggily.

"Luna, Pavla's daughter. She's got them babysitting—nothing to concern yourself about."

"Well, that's very good. Byron's a good lad, he saved me."

Raoul gave her a light kiss on the forehead, then proffered the flowers. "They're tacky and cloying, I've never understood freesias. I tried to stop him, but you don't argue with a Singer. Where shall I put them?"

Mae smiled wanly, contentedly. "Thank you. Put them here." She vaguely pointed to the bedside table as her voice trailed off and heavy eyelids fell shut.

Larry pulled a chair close to the bed, took her hand, and lovingly watched her sleep. Raoul wandered to the window and peered through Venetian blinds to the busy parking lot below.

At 8:00 p.m., all lights automatically dimmed, and the senior nurse with lumberjack arms bustled in to wind down the bed. "That's it, visiting hours are over," she said.

Larry snugged Mae's covers around her tiny shoulders and kissed a parchment-thin temple. "Sweet dreams, sweet Mae."

He and Raoul left her in the shadows, looking like an alabaster angel next to her bedside bouquet.

At 8:00 p.m. in the Roma/Rommel household, Ralph sank into the living room sofa, hiding deep in the newspaper. Cindy pored over a stack of bridal magazines, sharing the odd thrilling detail with her husband, who replied, "Yes, dear," and "No, dear." The two boys pounded at a "Frustration" game on the floor, occasionally pounding each other in response to winning and losing streaks. Dhyan stayed banished in her phone-less, music-less bedroom to do homework.

The living room telephone, a modern 'antique' in white and gold, rang. The oldest boy scampered to it, kicking at his brother on the way, who rolled over and feigned massive injury. Cindy saw that the kick hadn't connected, that the noise was unwarranted. She shushed him without effect while cocking an ear to the phone call. Big brother listened briefly, then shouted loud enough for Dhyan to hear, "It's long distance for Dhyan. Will we accept the charges?"

"Give me that," Cindy said, jumping to get it. Into the receiver, she demanded, "Who is this?"

Dhyan popped her head out her room and leapt for the receiver, which Cindy held tight to her ear. "Operator, ma'am," the calling party said. "Angela Cho wishes to place a person-to-person collect call for Dhyan Roma."

With Dhyan jumping around her, Cindy said, "Dhyan does not receive phone calls, local or long distance, and certainly not collect," then she hung up the phone.

"Da-a-ad!" Dhyan cried. At Cindy, she shouted, "How could you, damn it? Who was it?"

"No swearing! How many times do I have to tell you?"

"Angela Cho," the older boy said. "Leetle Angela, she's so cu-u-ute."

"Angela! You hung up on Angela? Man, how could you? You people make me sick, like totally sick. Dad, I gotta call her back."

"Your mother's decided otherwise, Dhyan, no calls ...."

"She's not my freakin' mother!"

"Ralph!" Cindy shrieked. "You stop her right there. I surely am not her mother, but by all that's holy, I am mistress of this household, and I will not, repeat, will not put up with this nonsense for another ...."

Ralph said quietly to Dhyan, "Go make the call." To Cindy, he said, "I'm sorry, dear, but a little girl making a person-to-person collect call sounds important to me."

Cindy screamed, "How dare you! How dare you override ... How could you ... agukh-h-h!" She cried, sputtered, choked.

The youngest boy grabbed his heart and toppled over backward shouting, "Eeagh-ag-ak!" Big brother fell on his tummy, winding him, and the punching and hairpulling began.

Cindy ran from the room, shouting, "See what you've done, you're creating monsters. You deal with them. I don't have any say in this madhouse anymore, as if I ever did." She stormed all the way to her bedroom, "I'm so tired of the disrespect I get for all my work trying to teach values and responsibility. All I get is ...." Wham! The slamming door cut off her lament.

Ralph picked up both boys in a knot and carried their wildly flailing arms and legs to their bedrooms. He deposited one to each room, then returned to his newspaper, reading peacefully at last.

From the kitchen, Dhyan grabbed the cordless phone and ran with it to her bedroom. She called Angela, who answered it before Dhyan heard a ring.

Angela said, "She's gone, Dhyan!" Her front teeth had grown in; she no longer lisped. "The lady in my dreams, the mom, she's gone! She just disappeared, I can't dream her, I can't see ...."

Dhyan said, "Where are you?"

"In a closet, I fell asleep."

"What do you mean, 'in a closet'? What's going on?"

"Joanne and her mean friend locked me in. They're babysitting, so they said I had to be a baby. They made me wear a diaper and say 'goo goo'. They're so stupid, I hate their stupid games. I took Teddy and the phone and I hid in here. They looked and looked for me, even in here, but they didn't see me. Then I moved and made a bang, so they found me, and they locked me in."

"But you've got a phone. Why didn't you call your aunt or uncle?"

"I can't. It's about the lady and my dreams. I can't tell them, only you."

"I mean when you were first locked in."

"I'm going to stay in here until they come home, then they'll see how bad Joanne is and her stupid bad friend."

"Do they know you have the phone? Doesn't it ring? Can't they hear us talking?"

"No, they turned on their stupid music so loud they can't hear anything. I screamed and screamed and cried and cried, and I fell sleep, that's when I saw the lady ...."

"You saw her? I thought you said she's gone."

"No, she was in a big house, and there were some men. They were eating, but she didn't eat and then the white-haired man, he took her to a door, and that's when she went black. She went through the door and disappeared like a TV turning off. The grandma's flying in an airplane, and the baby's like ... it's like she's with your mom, but she's okay. But it's the mom who's ...."

"Wait, wait. It's like the baby's with my mom?"

"And a man and a dog, and she's okay, but the other mom, I can't see her, she's gone!"

"Oh man, this is so weird. I'll call my mom and find out if she's got a baby, but ...."

"Uh-oh, they turned off the music," Angela whispered. "They're coming." Click. Angela vanished.

Dhyan stared into the dial-toning receiver. She quickly punched in her mom's number.

Fran answered the phone in the kitchen, leaving Nikos on the sofa reading a baby book to Luna. Byron snugged up to his feet.

"Dhyan!" Fran said, delighted. "Is this allowed?"

"No, but listen, I got permission to call Angela in Portland, she called me collect, then I just called her back. She said ... oh man, she said some weird stuff, like she just had a dream about you with the baby from her dreams and the mom lady disappearing, she went black like a TV turning off."

"Wait, wait, slow down. The mom lady disappearing, what do you mean?"

"I don't know. I just called to see if you've got the baby."

Fran got goosebumps. "Well, I have a baby."

"And a dog? And Nikos is there?"

"Yeah."

"Oh man, what's going on?"

Fran wasn't sure what she should disclose and to whom, even her own daughter. Any slip from anyone could jeopardize Luna's safety, maybe Dhyan's too. She asked, "What else did Angela say? How did the mom lady disappear?"

"She was in a big house with some men, and they were eating, but she didn't eat, and then this white-haired guy walked her to a door and poof! she went through it and that was it, she went black. And the grandma's on an airplane ...."

"Whoa boy, that's wild."

"So who's the baby? How come you got a baby?"

"Nikos ...." Fran thought fast. "Nikos knows this lady who needs help with her baby while she ... while she gets over a problem so we said sure, we'd help for a while."

"I wonder how Angela picked up on that?"

"Coincidence, I guess."

"It's too freaky, Mom. It's like ... it's like Alma disappearing from my pictures. I told you that in my letter. Did you get it?"

"Yes, I did. Thank you, sweetheart."

"She's magic or something. I gotta know. If you see her or maybe Mae— I bet she knows—you gotta ask, okay?"

"You bet. Are you doing okay?"

"Oh man, I'm like, so grounded that I barely get out of my room, and after I wrote about Dad in the school rag about him taking your name, I'm like, grounded forever."

"You wrote about Dad taking my name? And published it? Oh boy."

"And now Cindy's making him go back to Rommel, and they're getting married again, big white church thing—God, gag me. It's gonna be hell, I'm gonna make it hell. Mom, you gotta ...."

From outside her door, Dhyan heard her dad shout, "Dhyan, that's long enough!"

Dhyan said, "I gotta go. I gotta know too. How are we going to keep in touch?"

"I don't know, but we can't push it or we're both sunk. No more stamp stealing, you hear? I'll think of something. I'll talk to your dad, okay? Not now, at his office tomorrow."

"Yeah, good ol' Dad."

"That's right. That's the stuff. Night-night, my darling."

That night, Fran slept in her big bed within arm's reach of Luna. Byron guarded them from his basket at the foot of the bed. Nikos stretched out on the sofa.

Luna woke bright-eyed and cheery, the morning still dark and cool. Byron waggled-tailed around the house until all were roused. Luna and playmates giggled, played hide-and-go-seek, and romped until the sun at last rose. Fran and Nikos could start their own day now, as played-out Luna rubbed her eyes and slipped into a two-hour nap.

While coffee perked, smelling rich and necessary, Fran called Ralph's office. The cream-tart receptionist cooed, "Mr. Roma's not available."

"But is he in?"

"Yes, but he's not here."

"Are you expecting him in the office this morning?"

"Yes."

"Listen, this is urgent. The second you see him, tell him to call Fran. First thing, call Fran, you got that?"

The girl wrote on a pink message slip, "Second. Call Fran, first thing."

Ralph's receptionist greeted him breathlessly with, "Your ex called, and there's two things. First ... no, second, you've got to call her."

"What's the first thing?"

"I don't know." She handed him the pink note. "She's in a rush. She didn't make sense."

Ralph shook his head, making for the sanctuary of his office. While dialing, he muttered, "Ditzy broads." When he got an answer, he said sternly, "Fran."

Fran sat on a kitchen stool with a fresh cup of coffee. "Thank you, Ralph. Listen, Dhyan called me, and ...."

"She called you? She knows she's not allowed ...."

"So she's a mite contrary, I'm sorry. And sneaky too. She tells me you're renewing your marriage vows, going back to Rommel. Congrat's and best wishes."

Ralph mumbled, "Yeah, sure."

"When's the big day?"

"Did you phone just to talk about this wedding thing? I'm sorry, but ...."

"Dhyan's going to make it hell, that's what I've phoned to say. She's in a ... let's say, mood about it. I have a suggestion that could make it a lot easier with me right out of the loop, nothing to do with her coming back to my place."

Ralph said nothing.

Fran waited a beat, then said, "Prep school. It's still a great idea."

Ralph stayed silent, his face flushing with thoughts and emotions.

"Well? You said you'd think about it. How do you think Cindy would take it?"

Ralph said slowly, "I think she could get used to it. Real fast probably."

"When's the wedding?"

"December 20th. Same as before."

"That's a lot of lead time for Dhyan to upset every apple cart. She'll love prep school, you know it, and you'll want her at the wedding, but believe me, not all the weeks and months before."

Ralph conceded heavily, "Yeah."

"Will you do me the huge favor of asking Dhyan about prep school? I haven't said anything to her yet, nothing, not a hint. It's late to apply, but we can still do it."

"Give me a day or two."

"Good. But time's tight, okay? You know, Ralph ...." Fran paused for a long moment. "This could cut our lawyers' bills down to nothing. Save a lot of trouble and heartache. Money, too. I'll cover all the prep school costs, and you'll have some spare nickels for the honeymoon."

He groaned, "Honeymoon? Oh no. Cindy hasn't mentioned that yet. I guess it's my department."

"I guess. Would you rather do the safari or send your lawyer on one?"

"You make this sound easy."

"Better than hard."

"Jeez, Africa, I'd love a safari. Enough to get married again."

"So just do it. And make your daughter happy while you're at it. Prep school could save the day and the piggy bank."

"Yeah, it could. Things are a little rough on the Dhyan-Cindy front."

"I gather."

"So I'll let you know. Real soon."

"Thanks. 'Good ol' Dad'—those were Dhyan's parting words last night."

As Fran hung up, Nikos appeared from the bedroom carrying the baby. She said to him, "Bingo. I think Ralph bit."

"Good," Nikos said, handing Luna to her. "She needs changing I think. Food too, if this is any sign." He indicated his chewed and wet collar.

"Mom, Mom, Pavla Mom," Luna sang.

Fran blinked back tears as she kissed Luna's sweet-smelling, satiny hair. Nikos hid his tears by turning to fill the kettle.

Mid-morning, Alma called Fran to say she would be arriving and cleared from the Industrial Airport, Hangar G, in an hour.

The small jet taxied directly into the hangar. Her flight had been wearing, her worries more wearing yet. She perfectly felt her disguise of frizzy gray wig, old woman clothes, cane, and arthritic gait. She climbed into Fran's car, which Nikos had tidied as best he could, although years of neglect and cigarettes were beyond elbow grease and cleaning products.

"To Mae's?" Fran asked.

"Yes, please."

"I've got the key, but I have to tell you ... brace yourself. Mae fell yesterday and broke her hip. She's in hospital."

"Oh no. I'm so sorry. How bad is it?"

"Serious, of course, but it could be worse. Larry said she's on morphine and seems comfortable. They expect a good recovery, no pins, not too many needles."

"I hope so. I'm afraid I can't go to see her. I can't spare a minute while Pavla's trail is still warm. Did you tell Mae I'm coming?"

"No, but she knows I'm babysitting Luna, not why though. She's happy Byron's got a playmate."

"Well, tell her I know she's in hospital and send her my prayers. I would also love to run to Luna, but it's too risky. I never know who has a bead on me, particularly at this time. How is she?"

"She is incredible, the new owner of my heart. She's beyond special, right up there with my own kid."

Alma sank back into her seat, smiling. "That's wonderful to hear on a terrible day. She may need foster care for ... well, who knows how long if you're able to keep her? Otherwise I can ...."

"No otherwise. I would love to, provided you think she's safe, for as long as she needs me. Us. Nikos is crazy about her too."

"Thank you," Alma said, tears welling up. She closed her eyes and whispered, "How will I get through these days?" She struggled to hold in tears but could not. Softly, she cried, "How will I manage without my beautiful girl? How will I find her? This is our worst crisis in centuries."

Fran kept her eyes on the road, blinking hard to contain her own tears. "I got hold of Rachelle DuPont, she's digging up everything she can about Trigliani, but she says he's all academia, very little to trace personally."

Alma nodded, wiping her eyes with an old-lady handkerchief. "Yes, I expected he's covered his tracks quite well."

"What do you think he wants with Pavla? Why does anyone want to kill you—the whole string of yous?"

Composed again, Alma said, "We present a problem to the fundamentalists of every major religion, and we have for a long, long time. Trigliani is an interesting variation in the history of our would-be destroyers. He's a scientist, as is Pavla, plus he's connected in some way to the Roman Catholic Church. It's not all that unusual for a scientist to be devout, but Trigliani seems torn between his instructions from superiors to kill Pavla, no questions asked, and his desire to share their scientific pursuits. Practically speaking, he should kill her immediately, and he doubtless knows it. Her body will be invaluable to his research, dead or alive. I'm hoping, however, that his desire to talk with her, perhaps even collaborate with her, gives her the time she needs to escape."

Fran's mind boggled with questions. She negotiated a busy intersection and wove in and out of hectic traffic before saying, "While playing Scheherazade, enchanting him for a-thousand-and-one nights."

Alma smiled faintly. "Let's hope."

Fran asked, "How do you think he zeroed in on her? Through their research connections, or something else entirely?"

"His research is important, I'm sure, that's why his superiors find him so useful. He's got access they couldn't possibly have. It could be as simple as someone in Dr. DuPont's lab spying on Pavla, maybe slipping a tracking device onto her, then bingo! he's got her. We may never know exactly, even when she's back safely, and she tells us everything she's been through."

"Alma, I don't know how much stock you put in dreams, but yesterday, my daughter Dhyan got an urgent phone call from Angela Cho, the little girl who survived the airplane crash at the same time as your mother died. Apparently, she dreams you people ...."

Alma straightened, her eyes keen. "Yes! A dreamer! I haven't been able to talk to any yet, not that we know or talk to many ever. What did she say?"

"Angela was terribly upset because—and I quote what Dhyan told me—the mom lady in her dreams was in a big house, went through a door, then zap, she went black like a TV going off."

"When was this?"

"About seven-thirty, eight last night. Our time."

"Where is Angela?"

"Portland, Oregon—three hours time difference, probably getting ready for school right now."

"I'd like to call her from Mae's. This could be crucial."

Hesitantly, Fran said, "But Pavla went black."

"There are places that can happen. Safe places usually. She was fine at eight o'clock last night." Alma closed her eyes and sighed. "This could be very good news."

Fran picked up some stray advertising flyers at Mae's front door, then used Nikos's key to open it. Alma entered first. "Oh my God!" Fran exclaimed as she followed, stunned by the industry, clutter, and dust.

"Oh dear," Alma said. "I should have warned you." She took off her wig and shook out her hair.

Fran wandered through paper alleyways to the dining room, eyes wide, reading every label in sight. "Good heavens! And I thought the file she gave me was bizarre and complicated." The telephone sat on a stack of files where Nikos had hastily returned it before the ambulance arrived. Fran asked, "Should I call Angela for you? She knows me."

"Please."

Fran got a recorded message. She held up the phone for Alma to hear the usual "... and we'll get back to you as soon as possible." She asked, "Should I leave a message?"

Alma nodded.

Fran said, "Hello, dear Chos all. Fran Roma here. I would really like to speak with Angela. If you could have her call me the instant she can, that would be great. Collect please. I'm at ...." She gave Mae's number.

Fran hung up and said to Alma, "I might know another survivor, an old gentleman with a rock who clings to it with his life. He's had a stroke and can't speak, so I don't know if he dreams or not."

"If he clings, of course he dreams. You know, if he can draw even a crude picture, he might be able to confirm Angela's descriptions."

"He lives fairly close by. He's the uncle of a friend and colleague. His name's Siddhartan Singh, Uncle Sid to family. I'll make some calls. The phone's useless with him; we'll have to visit or get him to you somehow."

To keep Mae's phone line open, Fran called Sandhu from her cell.

Sandhu recognized Fran's number on his call display. He was in Studio F in the bowels of Media 8, with half a dozen film crew members milling and cursing around him. "Fran, help!" he said. "The pilot's live at noon, right? and Randy forgot—get this—to book the featured guest. The only thing he had to do. Now he's vanished, out wandering the streets looking for some reasonable or unreasonable substitute, God help us."

"Oh man, I'm sorry. Listen, something's come up with the 'Coincidentals' file, something serious. I need to see your Uncle Sid a.s.a.p."

"Oh boy. How 'bout this afternoon, when we've pulled this out of the fire?"

"Can't wait, unless we really have to. Any chance you could you arrange for us to visit him on our own?"

"Yeah, why not? I'll call his nursing home and tell the staff you're coming, what, in an hour or two?"

"I can't say exactly. We're waiting for a phone call on a land line. Probably in an hour, maybe later. There'll be two of us."

"No matter, he's got all day. He's at ...." Sandhu gave Fran Uncle Sid's address, then gasped, "Oh no, Randy just walked in, he's got some dolled-up guy ... drunk, stoned, something's really wrong."

Fran laughed. "No kidding. Hang in, hey? And hang Randy while you're at it, that'll get you ratings. I'll call you later. Thanks, Sandhu. Thanks so much."

In Mae's kitchen, Alma put a fragrant sachet into Mae's Brown Betty pot and poured in boiling water. Fran said, "It's like Larry's sack with the pebble."

"Exactly," Alma said. "Herbs from Mount Olympus. My mother lived there as a girl."

"It smells heavenly."

"I'll give you some for Luna—steep it in milk."

"Any other special foods I can get or things I should know?"

"Not really, in terms of her daily care. Like all babies, she needs consistency of routine and lively, loving minds to interact with. From what you've said and I intuit, she'll thrive with you and Nikos."

"And we with her. She's a joy."

"I do have some requests in terms of daily habits, things like wise resource use and counting one's blessings. It's important that she see careful economy, generous sharing, consistent recycling, giving thanks for every good fortune big and small. It means always making that extra effort I know, but ...."

"No problem. I'm no saint these ways, but I'm all for trying. I mean, if our kids aren't worth it, who is?"

"Like all little ones, she's keen on nature and outdoors. I hope you won't be shy about taking her out and getting a little grubby, with due respect for whatever creatures and habitat she might disturb, of course."

"My pleasure, rain or shine, if that's okay. I've got a perfect backyard, full of more nature than I know what to do with. It's pretty private too."

"Good. You'll find she picks up the names of things quickly. She's good at words, languages."

"No kidding. She told me she's 'Lu-na'. That's genius at her age."

Alma smiled. "The more you expose her to different languages, the better—your own, of course, TV, radio, recordings, songs, trusted visitors."

"What fun. Nikos can speak Greek to her. I have working Spanish, college French, a bit of Russian. Larry's got a some Yiddish and Mandarin, Raoul has Dutch and half a dozen other languages, Sandhu speaks Urdu."

"If each sticks to a separate language with her, she'll catch on quickly."

"Is this a family ability, or has she invented this one herself?"

"It's a gift. She'll be fully fluent in about fifty unrelated languages, that's average for us. We get by in hundreds total."

Fran blinked her amazement. "That's scary. I've got a million questions for you and no idea where to start."

"So just start. Ask me anything while we have time."

Over tea and biscuits in the living room. Fran said, "Pavla went black in Angela's dream, and you said she could be safe, but what are the odds that ... that she's ... ?"

"Dead?" Alma filled in. "She disappeared going into a room—that's good. What happened in the room I can't guess, but with luck, it's a steel or lead-lined holding cell, bank vault, something like that, where they're keeping her incommunicado. Our lives aren't complete open books to dreamers. Lead is one barrier. Caves are another."

"How does it work?—I mean, scientifically."

"It's something simple like blocking gamma radiation in conjunction with ... oh, I don't know. Science is Pavla's forte."

"Does it bother you being dreamed? I mean, Angela saw me and Nikos with Luna, I'm not sure I like that."

Alma smiled and shook her head. "No, I'm not bothered in the least, and not because I'm used to it, but because of the nature of dreams. Dreams lack the word 'no'. They're a world without need of permission or guidance by shame. There's nothing you can do in another's dream that's outside of their acceptance, and if it's outside of their experience or readiness for it, it simply doesn't compute, isn't experienced, is beyond memory and remembering. We're very safe in other's dreams, whatever they make of our reality in their most private hours. It is without doubt the most privileged place to be in the Universe. It's our common thread, our deepest humanity, our eternity."

Fran let her words sink in before saying softly, "That's beautiful. Thank you. Do you dream the dreamers? Is it reciprocal?"

"Oh no, thank goodness." Alma laughed. "It would short-circuit our brains, too many at once. It's not possible anyway, because dreamers' sensitivity comes from plugging into Mother's energy field when she died, which includes us. They're sensitized to us but not vice versa."

"How many survivors-*cum*-dreamers are there? Dozens? Thousands?"

"We don't know. It all happened in the split second when Mother's death coincided with their own heightened state of certain demise. It's a matter of statistics, of course, but the file you're keeping is the first such global record as far as I know. Mae knows better than anyone."

Fran said, "And they all get a rock?"

"Yes, at the moment of survival, but many drop it right away or shortly after. Many more discard or lose it in the days and months following. Others quickly discount the associated dreams, and if they sleep without it, there are no dreams, of course. Dedicated dreamers are few in number and very secretive or risk the label of madness."

"How does the rock get there? How do little pieces of Parnassos show up all over the world?"

"It's complicated, but in essence, the connection—the force path—is so profound that matter transfers through energy to matter, and the rocks remake themselves in the survivors' hands."

"Which saves them?"

"Not the rock, but the energy field that connects and charges them, suspending life forces and thus stalling death for the critical moments. Frozen in time, in a way."

"And do you all end the way your mom died? Will Pavla ... will she explode—is that the right word—if she ...?"

"If she's killed? Not necessarily. Much depends on trauma and location. Mother had suffered for days, that increases the charge, plus she died where she was born, and Delphi is one of the great sacred sites of the world. Mother was the first in millennia to be born there, since the ascendancy of Apollo. Her death was the most stunning of ages, the herald of a new era, we dared hope. Now Pavla has disappeared, and we are more vulnerable than we've been in many years, since the late 1700s really."

"What happened then?"

"Another stunning death followed by the American Revolution, the French Revolution, the expansion of the British and Russian empires, the unraveling of the Spanish empire, the opening of trade with the Orient, the completion of the world map, the beginning of the Industrial Revolution. What didn't happen then? Some dreamers paid attention; it makes quite a difference—not all for good, alas, but overall, a few steps closer to enlightenment."

Fran blinked, speechless for a moment. "So this could be a real turning point, the start of a new era"

Alma shrugged. "It depends on who's paying attention, on what people make of it. If we lose Pavla, if those dreams vanish ... I don't know. I can't predict."

Fran looked around at Mae's files, scanning hundreds of names of goddesses and women of myth, legend, and lore. "And these, this research ...?"

"The most comprehensive study of our line to date."

"Oh my." Fran's jaw dropped, then the telephone rang, startling her. She leapt to get it.

"Hello? Angela, my angel, I'm so glad you've called. Are you going to school soon? ... No? You've got a sore throat? Well, I hope you're better real soon. Listen, Sunshine, I've got someone very special to talk with you."

Fran handed the receiver to Alma, then returned to the living room. She flipped through a thick file marked "Demeter", Persephone's daughter, who spent half her life underground. On the topmost page, Mae listed Ceres, Core, Proserpene, Hecate, Daffodil, Asphodel, and Asteria, noting that they were two generations at most, between the 130th and 140th, followed by Artemis, also known as Selene and Diana. Fran marveled at Mae's exhaustive research and kept her ears cocked for Alma's conversation.

"Hello, Angela. I'm Alma Solari."

Angela said breathlessly, "You sound like .... Are you the lady ... ?"

"I am, dear. If you dream about a mom and a grandma and a baby, then you know I'm the grandma."

"You're real?"

"Very real, dear, as real as this telephone call. If you were dreaming with your rock right now, you'd see us talking together."

"O-o-oh."

"Thank you for calling back, Angela. This is very, very important. You told Dhyan that the mom lady went black, right?"

"I was so scared."

"Bless you, sweetheart."

Brightly, Angela said, "I dreamed her again before I got up. I did, I saw her this morning."

Alma's face softened with relief. "You did? Oh, that's so wonderful."

"She's in the big house still. She disappeared yesterday when she went in a room, but I saw her again when she came out. Then she went to another room, a science room, different from the other one."

"Was she with anyone?"

"A man. Then two more, they had white coats like she wears sometimes. They talked about parthenogenesis and other big words and stuff. Then the lady wrote on a big board like at school."

"She was explaining things to the men?"

"Yes. She's not happy."

"That's true. Was she okay though? Did she look hurt or scared or anything like that?"

"No."

"That's good, isn't it? Do you know the mom's name?"

"She has lots of names."

Alma smiled. "Me too. Did you know my name before I told you?"

"Mm-m. Maybe."

"Could you draw me a picture of the house where the mom is? Or what the science stuff looks like? Or the men—what color their hair is and maybe eyes? And if they're fat or thin or tall or wear glasses?"

"One has white hair, he likes the lady."

"Oh, that's good. You know, he and the mom lady are sort of lost. If you could draw me pictures, maybe we could find them."

"I'm a good drawer. I'm the bestest at school."

"I bet you are. If you draw me some pictures of the lady and where she is and who she's with, I would love that. I know you'll do beautiful work."

"'kay."

"Thank you so much. You're wonderful, Angela—but you know that."

"Serena says I'm bad, really bad."

"Who's Serena?"

"Stupid counselor." Angela's voice dropped. "She hit me. And she told me not to tell."

"She hit you? Why?"

Angela started to cry. "I'm not supposed to tell, and she hit me again, so I promised."

The aunt took the phone. "Hello, I'm Angela's aunt. What's going on?"

"Did you hear what Angela said?"

"I think so. Who are you? How do you know Angela?"

"I'm Alma Solari, a friend of Fran and Dhyan Roma's. Angela knows me from ...." Alma thought fast. "... just after the crash. We met then, and she says she sees me in her dreams, which is very sweet. Could you tell me, who is this counselor?"

"Serena Allan-Sanchez."

"How did you choose her?"

"She called us as soon as Angela came to live with us. She specializes in trauma recovery and really wanted to see her. We checked her out, and she seemed just right. Good training, lots of clients, kids especially. We know Angela doesn't like her much, but this is the first I've heard of any hitting, anything like that."

"Why doesn't Angela like her much?"

"It's very difficult, what she's getting Angela to remember and work through, these dream things like she was just telling you. She lets a bit slip to us, but we're not supposed to ask questions of Serena or interfere in any way. It'll ruin the therapy."

"Does this not seem suspicious to you?"

"A little, but ...."

"Please listen carefully. I've been counseling for ages, it's my primary profession, and there's something very wrong with this Serena woman. Now she's hit Angela not once, but twice. Do not—repeat—do not take Angela back to her. But enough for now. You need to tend to Angela and, please, give her a hug for me. I'd like to talk to her again, maybe tomorrow morning, would that be okay? About this time?"

Mrs. Cho agreed.

"Thank you. This is very, very important. Goodbye—and goodbye to Angela."

Alma wore her old lady disguise and walked, arthritic again, from Mae's house to Fran's car. Fran slid behind the wheel and, while backing out of Mae's driveway, said, "It's about fifteen, twenty minutes to Uncle Sid's. Do you mind if I ask more questions?"

"No. Go ahead."

As they spun along busy streets through in-filled suburbia and ethnic neighborhoods, Fran said, "Well, first, it's just a detail, but Dhyan has photographs of us at Larry's after the play, and she says you're not in any of them."

Alma laughed lightly. "I ducked. I'm fairly fast."

"Hm. Good trick, but when I took my shot I know I saw you, except for the split-second the shutter clicked. That's beyond fast."

"It's a high stimulus moment. We miss all kinds of things. Magicians count on it."

"Ah, so you're a magician then? Not some kind of magic?"

"I wish. The truth is, photographs can be dangerous, not only for me, but for everyone seen with me. We'd had two abduction attempts to that point and a survivor in Nova Scotia—a fisherman—murdered. I didn't want to put anyone at risk if our pursuers did some follow-up work on my whereabouts. Photos are too tangible."

"So why'd you agree to have your photo taken?"

"To not make a fuss. To pique your curiosity. To keep you interested in Mae's file. I said 'parthenogenesis', which you nicely followed up on."

Fran smiled. "I still don't get it. Three times, three split-seconds, you vanish like that." Fran snapped her fingers.

"We all have martial arts training. The first lesson is also the final one: to avoid trouble, just don't be there."

"Man, you're good. You sure you're not magic?"

Alma laughed. "Well, if you need a fancier explanation for Dhyan, tell her ... oh, I don't know, tell her it's a transcendental ability, an energy-absorbing process that blocks the oxidation of photographic emulsions. No magic, all physics—very advanced, of course."

"Now that I believe."

Alma got serious. "Fran, do you know anything about Serena Allan-Sanchez?"

"Angela's counselor? Yeah, I visited her, and she told me a bit about Angela and her spin on Angela's dreams. We parted as allies in protecting Angela's privacy, but we'd never be any kind of friends. She's too ... oh, I don't know, she looks for deep dark stuff, and I just don't function there. I mean, I know it exists, but when you're chasing the news, what you see and get is trouble enough without digging in people's souls for more. I was distracted, too, with a few bigger concerns—more selfish, anyway—like Dhyan going wild and Larry sick but not telling anyone."

"Serena hit Angela recently. Twice. Made her promise not to tell."

"Really? Wow. Angela kept telling Dhyan she was mean."

"In what way?"

"Pumping hard for her dreams, then interpreting them as the worse sorts of abuse—sexual, satanic, you name it. But what do I know? Trauma counseling's not my game at all."

Alma's eyes widened. She muttered almost to herself, "That must be how Trigliani got to Pavla this time."

"Pardon?" Fran asked.

"Serena must have passed on Angela's dreams to him. I have to go to Portland to see Serena. While I visit Mr. Singh, could you get me on the next flight out?—any airline, any seat, direct nonstop."

"Of course."

"I'm Mrs. Pina Giuseppe ...." From her handbag, she pulled out a leather folder with a passport and credit cards. "I'll write down the name and numbers you need to book the ticket."

"Should I do it from the nursing home while I wait for you?"

"Would you?"

"Then I'll drive you to the airport, if you think it's safe enough."

"Thank you, dear."

Fran pulled up to a modest, bungalow-style care home facing a strip mall. Seniors shuffled to shops and services with canes and walkers; some zipped on motorized carts.

In the entryway of the home, a craft nook sold the handiwork of residents still productive with Phentex, popsicle sticks, tumbled rocks, and glitter paints. A round and pleasant senior lady manning the counter directed Fran and Alma to Mr. Singh's room at the end of the men's wing. They found their own way there, unquestioned by staff too busy to be curious.

"Siddhartan Singh" labeled his door, penned by an old hand in shaky calligraphy. Alma rapped lightly, then peeked inside. A hint of sandalwood incense greeted her.

Uncle Sid sat in his wheelchair, turbaned and tidy, facing a window that looked out on nondescript shrubbery. The window ledge held a colorful procession of school photos of his grandchildren and other grand-kin. The wall above his bed held many framed photographs of him as a young athlete, of his bride, and of his growing family.

"Siddhartan?" Alma said gently. He turned his wheelchair quickly using his left arm. The sight of Alma so shocked him that his eyes rolled up as if he'd faint. She took his trembling left hand and said, "Hello, my friend. I thought you'd know me."

Fran entered and said, "Hello, Mr. Singh. I'm so glad you showed me your rock at lunch. Thank you." His eyes filled with tears. "Now I'll leave you two alone." To Alma, she said, "I'll wait for you in the foyer."

As Fran departed, Sid reached with his left hand into the neck of his shirt for his leather pouch and fumbled the rock from it. He held out the stone to Alma, letting her take it.

She squeezed it tight, saying, "I need your help."

Sid nodded eagerly and smiled his lopsided best. She gently tucked the rock back into Sid's hand. He shakily returned it to his pouch. "Can you draw?" she asked.

Sid nodded as he pointed to paper and pen on his night table. The top page had a shaky picture of a mushroom on it, crossed out.

Alma said, "Either you don't like mushrooms or are you allergic to them."

Sid made a small face.

Alma smiled. "Fair enough. You'll be a big help, I know."

Sid beamed, eyes glistening.

At noon, Ralph drove up to Dhyan's school, parked, and walked to the main office. To a secretary, he said, "I'm Ralph Roma, Dhyan Roma's father. I have an appointment with her counselor."

"Ah," the secretary said with a smile, "WonderDad."

Ralph blushed.

"You've caused quite a controversy here. We need more guys like you." She ran her finger down the entries in a large day book, got him to sign on the appropriate line, then pointed him to the counselor's office.

Dhyan sat in one of several chairs in a small waiting area next to the counselor's door. She stood up in surprise. "Dad! What are you doing here?"

Telling Maya 199

"I made the appointment, had you hauled in here."

"So I'm in like, deep doo-doo? Bummer." She sat down heavily.

"Hey, it's going to be okay."

"So what's the deal?"

"Just wait."

Dhyan dropped her head. "Oh man, big trouble. What, are you going to make me homeschool with Cindy so I'm her prisoner and she can talk God till I crack?"

Ralph took her hand. "Dhyan, sweetheart, this isn't about trouble. It's about getting out of it."

"Oh shit." Dhyan withdrew her hand.

The counselor appeared, shook Ralph's hand, and introduced himself. "Pleased to meet you, Mr. Roma. You're quite a hero among our progressive thinkers."

Ralph tried not to squirm.

Dhyan said, "Yup, take a stand, do the right thing, that's what Roma's do."

Ralph dropped his eyes. His cheeks flushed red.

The counselor led them into his small office overstuffed with file cabinets, shelves, books, and brochures. Inspirational and thank you notes from students covered every wall. As he settled behind his desk, Ralph and Dhyan took chairs in front of it. He leaned forward and asked, "Now how can I help?"

"Prep school," Ralph said. "I want to talk with Dhyan about prep school this fall."

Her eyes popped. "No way! Are you serious?"

The counselor looked puzzled. "You haven't discussed this with her?"

Ralph said, "No, this is news to her. Things are, uh ... well, emotions are running a little high at home, and we need a quiet, rational discussion about the whole plan. We need to find out what's possible too, what's still available ...."

The counselor nodded. "I see. Well, it's late for this coming school year, as you know. But first things first: do you want to go, Dhyan?"

Dhyan said, "Wow! Do I want to go? It's so ... I mean, I never even thought it, 'cause it's ... I mean, it costs a lot, and Dad, he wants me totally close, so close I'm like, grounded forever." Her face was sunnier than it had been in weeks.

"I take it that means yes," the counselor said. Dhyan grinned wider. "And Dhyan's mother? She's in favor?"

Ralph nodded, "It's her idea."

"I knew it!" Dhyan said. "She's so cool."

Ralph looked down.

"Aw Dad, you're cool too. I mean, you're here, and we're gonna do this, right? Oh man, I can't believe it! Where can I go? I don't want Garrison Forest or Oldfields—that's way too close—or Phillips Academy or Dana Hall. No snoot stuff. I want something real different, real ... oh, I don't know, real like trees and mountains and wild stuff."

Ralph smiled. "Wild stuff. That's my girl."

The counselor said, "Good. Small, out-of-the-way schools are still possible at this time of year. Big name ones are out of the question unless you have some big connections or big bucks." He got up and looked through a file cabinet, pulling out half a dozen files. "Enough to buy a new library, endow a new arts program."

Ralph laughed. "I can donate my firstborn, that'll liven up any place."

"Da-a-ad."

The counselor dropped the files on his desk and sat down again. "These are all good schools. Definitely small, though, and out-of-the-way. How does New Hampshire sound?"

"Oh yeah!" Dhyan said.

"Let's start there, discuss the pros and cons of each, work out the details."

"Thanks, Dad," Dhyan said quietly, warmly. To the counselor, she said, "I want one with a really good newspaper, maybe their own radio station. Gypsy hits the waves."

"Oh boy," Ralph said.

Larry walked—almost bounced—to his dark blue Jaguar coupe parked in the bowels of his luxury highrise. His white cell blood count was high enough now to get on with his changed life. First, he'd cheer up Mae, then on to tell big Al his news.

He wheeled into traffic and wove his way through congested streets, singing along with easy-listening songs on the radio. Despite the "Full" sign over the hospital parking lot, he zipped in and got lucky as a car backed out of a spot near the main entrance. He parked and bee-lined to Mae's ward.

With a big smile, he entered the room to greet her. A large woman lay snoring loudly in her place. His smile vanished.

At the nursing station, a long-faced aide scanned a list and said, "Mrs. Singer-Jones isn't listed here, that's all I know. You'll have to go back to general admissions to find out where she is." She turned to deal with other matters.

At general admissions in the main foyer, a smiling woman hired for her patience and honey voice said to Larry, "She's in intensive care. You'll need clearance to see her there. Down that hallway, follow the blue line."

Through the bureaucracy and maze, Larry finally found Mae behind curtain-walls lying on a pre-op' cot. An octopus of tubes wound its way around and into thin veins and nostrils. She was awake and breathing with difficulty.

Larry slipped his hand into hers and bent to speak directly into an unaided ear. "Mae, my beautiful Mae, what are they doing to you?"

"They're going to ...." She coughed.

"Don't talk," he said. "I'll find out."

"Aspirate," she managed. "Pneumonia. Lungs full."

"This came on awfully fast."

She nodded. "Larry, my papers ...." She coughed lightly, painfully. "Look after them."

He took her hand. "Of course. They're safe, you know that."

She shook her head. "No. They have to be ...." She wheezed. "... continued. Finished."

"Don't talk like this, Mae. You're going to finish them and have an extra decade to do nothing but sing and play with Byron. And me."

She smiled with difficulty, closing her eyes. A nurse appeared with a needle in hand and spoke loudly, "A sedative, Mrs. Jones. You'll be in and out in half an hour. You'll feel one-hundred percent better after, believe me, just a little sore where the needle went in. Let's hope we don't have to repeat the procedure."

Mae whispered, "One way ... or the other."

"I'll see you later," Larry said, kissing her on a soft, sallow cheek. "I'll be back for supper with you. Then we'll go dancing."

Alan Tellman's office covered a few thousand square feet with a 360-degree view of the waterfront and city. He had work and lounge areas for viewings, meetings and the occasional soirée. New electronic media devices dotted the space, portly Al's techno-toy heaven.

He sat stripped to his undershirt with his face resting in a donut pillow, melting into his massage chair as a blond Barbie worked over his neck and back. He moaned in sweet relief from the endless stress of empire-building.

Al's receptionist escorted Larry into the room. He had his new business plan in hand, a folio containing a tight overview to pitch to financial backers, starting with big Al and Media 8, if they could reach an arm's length deal.

He hadn't shown Alma yet; he preferred to give Al first dibs before asking his elusive fairy godmother for funding. As of now, the director's job was free and clear for Randy.

Al half-lifted a hand to Larry and said, "Give me five, ten minutes. Oh-h, oh that's the spot, God I need that. Get a drink, hey? Bourbon for me."

"This isn't a social call, Al," Larry said, holding up his paperwork. "I've got the perfect job for Randy, and it's coming open ... well, as we speak."

"Yeah, yeah, we'll get to it. Ah-h-h, you hit it, babe."

"I'm quitting, Al. He can have my job."

Al sat up slowly and drilled Larry with small, puffy eyes. "Say that again."

"You heard."

Al motioned for the woman to hand him his shirt from a nearby chair. As he put it on, he dismissed her with a wave. She was gone in seconds. "You can't," he said to Larry. "I mean, you're back in good health, fighting trim ...."

"That's why I'm here. I've got something else ...."

"But Randy's not ready, you can't ...." He grabbed his neck. "Damn, the knot's back. He needs you, you hear. What do you want? Give me some numbers."

"No raise, Al, I'm sorry. No perks. It's time to move on and ...."

"Move on, nothing. We need you right here, where things are moving ... I mean, media's changing so fast, you blink your eyes, and it's a new game. You're at the top of it, you're going to take us to the next step and then, sure, Randy can take over, that's the plan."

"I'm not doing anything to help him take over, I'm sorry, except vacate my chair. He hasn't got the right stuff, Al, and he never will. He doesn't get it."

"You've paved his way already, you've proven that someone with your, ah ... orientation can do it and be accepted, respected, and very successful."

Larry narrowed his eyes. "With my what?"

"Listen, anything to keep you, and here's the truth. One of the big draws of this merger—and don't get me wrong, there were plenty—was the trailblazing you did on the lifestyles front. First gay news director of a major broadcast studio, that's not anything Randy could do on his own. He's too much an idea man, a boat-rocker, I know, that's why he needs you to forge the way and temper him down a bit. Damn, I thought you knew he was one of yours."

Larry was instantly white-hot and too stunned to speak.

"C'mon," Al said jocularly, going to get a bourbon from a nearby bar. "I'm outing the truth, and it's about the time we all faced it. Not quite like your outing, but hey, it's all progress."

Larry said, word by slow, furious word, "The penny finally drops. You are so low, and I am so gone."

"Oh for God's sake, get real. We're just talking, being honest, working out a deal. And if you get snitty, it's just your word against mine, and what I'm saying is totally positive: having a gay director on staff tipped the whole takeover, what more could you people want? And I'm opening up the business for more, that's better yet."

Larry's jaw dropped as Al pressed on, saying, "We've got Sandhu back, and we're going to keep him, he's going to do the same for us on the ethnic front, although his color's not the same kind of secret as your ...."

"You despicable sonuvabitch!" Larry interjected. "Sandhu and I have earned everything we've achieved, no tokenism required, wanted, or tolerated. Moreover ...." Larry pulled a small tape-recorder from the inside pocket of his jacket. "I'm still enough of a reporter to get back-ups on important interviews. My quotes are always rock solid."

"Give me that!" Al made a weak lunge for the tape deck, knowing he was bested. Larry stepped neatly aside.

Al said, "Oh shit. Listen, this can't get out, and you know it. Randy's having trouble enough with his ... well, you don't like the word, but orientation. We asked him not to tell you, not to play that card with you, and he obviously hasn't. Good for him." Al took a large gulp of bourbon and wheedled, "We need you here, and we'll do what it takes to keep you, you name it. You're Randy's best hope. Have a heart about this. The family's going through hell with him, okay?"

"You're going through hell because he's an utter complete asshole with the savvy of a three-year-old on a permanent sugar high, and you're just serving it, his Sugar Daddy supreme, mainlining the poor jerk till he's spinning himself crazy and everyone around him. He needs discipline. He needs someone to read him the riot act ...."

"And that's you. Stay on and I promise, no more letting the boy loose in your office, no more stoned impersonators." Al chortled. "You gotta admit, that was funny."

"Yeah, drag is a real laugh. And funnier still that he screwed up so badly. Do you know what Sandhu went through to pull that one out of the fire and save Randy's butt?"

"Oh c'mon, that's why we pay you guys the big bucks. And I'm offering you more, lots more. I think you and Randy have just got to open up, you know ... I mean, he won't talk about it with us, we're all the lustiest bunch of heteros you ever saw, we just don't get it. In theory, sure, that's one thing, but when the problem comes home to roost ... well, we're trying, and I'm doing my best to shape up the goddamn world for the boy so he can succeed without going through some of the shit you did."

"I didn't go through any shit. I hit the war zones the same as everyone out there. We dodged the same bullets and not one of them gave a damn — if they knew—about who I was missing back home. What he's lacking, which I had in spades, is the complete, unassailable advantage of being competent." Larry waved his tape recorder to make his point. Then he waved his business plan. "See this? I came in here to talk about a new position for myself here masterminding the biggest, best innovation in smart news-telling you've ever seen, but you jumped to the conclusion that I'm walking entirely, and you blew it. Damn, you blew it so big, I can't tell you."

Al went limp. He looked at Larry's folder and said, "What've you got? I'll give you whatever you're asking for it, sight unseen, and whatever budget you want to develop it, get it running, totally your baby, hands off, market you to the sky."

Larry shook his head and said quietly, "You know, we worry about corporate concentration in the news business, and you, Sir, are exactly the sort of fat-ass toad we fear is behind it. Kiss a prince at the top of this overbloated media funhouse, and this is what we get. I'll have my lawyer draw up terms for my departure."

With a mock tip of his hat, Larry slipped from his former boss's luxury penthouse office.

Larry joined Sandhu and Fran at a coffee bar across from the Media 8 tower, where time and decor stopped at 1955. Elvis sang "Love Me Tender" from a monaural sound system. They sat in a corner booth of worn naugahyde, arborite, and chrome. A small, four-tunes-for-a-quarter juke box hung on the wall.

A gum-chewing waitress in gingham apron and matching caplet took their order: coffee for a dime and cinnamon buns for top dollar.

Larry put his business plan on the table top. "Damn, it's a good day. One step closer to this." He tapped his binder. "I showed it to Al and got myself a golden parachute, unless he wants to go public and duke it out for more, which I doubt."

"Huh?" Fran asked. "He didn't jump at your proposal?"

Larry smiled. "Oh no, we didn't get that far. We started and ended with Al telling me that I was a deciding factor in the takeover because ... ta da! I'm gay, and as a gay pioneer in the business, I am to pave the way for young Randall, who is, surprise, gay. Sandhu will be bribed with big bucks to stay on too, because he's ... ta da! ethnic, and as an ethnic pioneer ...."

"Oh no," Sandhu moaned.

"Oh yeah," Larry said. He reached into his jacket pocket and pulled out his small tape deck. "All on here. Your bargaining chip too, Sandhu, if you want to sever your ties with these nice people. And join my team. I will have nothing but fringe elements, questionable minorities, and total misfits, no tokenism whatever, not one fat-ass toad or nitwit nephew on the payroll to save our souls. Are you in?"

Sandhu laughed and shook his head, "In what—sane? I'd be crazy not to join you after the hell Randy's put me through, and now this little slap in the face."

Fran pointed to Larry's binder and asked, "So what is it?"

"Your salvation, darling, if you'll hop on board. Of course, you will. It's a gift from Alma and Maya, and it's pure genius. So here's the whole story, from 'Once upon a time ....' Maya came into my office, hit me in the gut about the mess on my desk, my failing health, my fading dreams, and more, then left a little piece of paper with an idea written on it—Alma's idea. It's changed my life, and it's going to change the big world of news and its telling."

Larry opened the binder to Maya's "recipe", her precious handwriting protected in an archival acetate sheet, and brought Fran up to the minute.

"Prep school?" Cindy shrieked over dinner in the dining room to Ralph, Dhyan, and the boys. "That's ridiculous. I can't do the wedding without Dhyan. There are a thousand and one details, and she's promised to babysit while I do ...." She counted on long magenta fingernails. "... invitations, wedding party ensembles, my trousseau, flowers, photos, catering arrangements, music ...."

Dhyan said, "Promised to babysit, yeah right, so I can come out of my room sometimes."

Ralph shot her a look. To Cindy, he said, "We'll hire a babysitter. And someone to help you too."

Dhyan made a banner in the air with her hands. "Wanted: help doing big white thing for world's oldest virgin."

"Dhyan!" Ralph thundered, hitting the table with his open palm.

Dhyan continued, rapid-fire. "I suppose you'll need help getting that stitched up. I was reading about Arab women ...."

"Enough!" Ralph stood up.

"Oh!" Cindy said, boo-hooing into her napkin. "That is so ... so unspeakably, oh-h ...." She heaved a deep sigh and rolled her wet eyes upward. "Dear God, whatever are we going to do with this child?"

Ralph sat down, took a deep breath and said loudly, "Prep school."

The youngest boy laughed so hard that he choked on his mouthful of food and spewed it over the table. His older brother, laughing harder, rose to smack him on the back and fake a Heimlich maneuver.

Dhyan kept a straight face and asked, "Dad, could you please pass the buns?"

As Ralph handed her the basket, he said, "That's not funny, young lady."

"Bun passing never is," she agreed, proper as a queen.

Alma's flight taxied into the Portland International Airport late at night. At Arrivals, an ordinary-looking man—her Nikos in Portland—greeted Mrs. Pina Giuseppe. She was a well-dressed Italian widow this time, with black hair in a bun, black coat, and black-rimmed glasses. She had only a carry-on bag, which her host toted to his beige station wagon.

In a middle-class suburb, she disappeared into a split-level house. Her bedroom had the trappings of its owner, a teenage girl keen on soccer, now away at college.

Alma's first phone call from this room was to Serena Allan-Sanchez's office. The recorded message said office hours were from 11a.m. to 6 p.m. weekdays, weekend appointments by request.

Alma's second phone call was to Angela at 8:00 the next morning, as promised. "Hello Mrs. Cho, Alma Solari here." She didn't tell her she was in Portland—too sudden an appearance of an already disruptive stranger.

"Yes, hello. Angela's in bed. She drew some pictures for you yesterday and got all feverish about it. I'm keeping her home from school again today."

"Oh dear, I'm sorry. If she's awake, could I dare ask to speak with her?"

Mrs. Cho hesitated. "I guess so. Just a minute." She took a cordless phone past the bathroom, where Joanne was washing her face, to the darkened bedroom where Angela lay in rumpled bedding on the lower bunk. "Angie," she whispered.

"Do I have to go to school? Joanne says ...."

"No, you're too sick. Alma is on the phone and wants to talk with you."

Angela sat up smartly and reached for the phone. Her aunt left to hurry Joanne off to school. Angela said to Alma, "She's in a van. She's driving, driving, she can't see outside."

"Is anyone with her?"

"The white-haired man. He's talking about stuff, about finding her, she wants to know how he did it, but he won't tell. She asked if he used satellites and computer stuff and other things, but he still won't tell."

"No talk about dreams, about using dreams to find her?"

"No."

"Do you think the white-haired man knows about people who dream her and me and the baby?"

"I don't know." Angela said quickly, then got confused and worried as she remembered more of her night's dreams. "Maybe, I don't know. He talked about Gerry McMann, he's a fisherman, and he had dreams just like mine, then he died."

"How do you know about him?"

"Serena told me. She was scared of the bad guys who hurt him."

"I see. What did the white-haired man say about Gerry McMann and why he died?"

"He said he got hurt and died 'cause ... 'cause it was a mistake, a stupid mistake and other stuff, I don't remember. The lady cried and got mad at him, but he said no fair, 'cause Gerry McMann shouldn't have died. Serena said he was bad about his dreams, that's why he died, and I had to tell mine."

Alma said, "Oh dear. Did that scare you?"

"Sometimes. She got so mean after he died."

"Well, I'm going to help her stop being mean and hitting kids."

"Good."

"Can you tell me where the white-haired man and the lady are going? Did he say where?"

"She asks and asks, 'Where are we going? Where are you taking me?' but he won't tell."

"Could you see anything like hills or trees or houses?"

"Uh-uh. They drove and drove inside a van, it's got no windows. When I went to sleep, they were in an airplane, they were flying, it was crowded and made a lot of noise."

"Crowded with people?"

"No, just them. It was dark with little crowded seats." Angela paused. "You were flying too, in a big airplane."

"Yes, I was. You remember your dreams very well, Angela. Did the man and the lady fly for a long time?"

"Yes, all night. Now they're driving. He said it's a long, long way, and she said, well maybe they were going in circles, that's why it took so long. He thought that was funny."

Alma asked, "Is she okay now?"

"She's not scared, she's not crying now. He told her the baby's safe, she cried then, and I wished I could tell her too that the baby's happy with the dog and Dhyan's mom and the old Nickels guy. Why can't she see her baby like I can?"

"She doesn't have a rock, poor lady, so she can't."

"I could give her mine."

"Angela, that is so sweet. It only works for you though. You're very, very special. I'm so glad he told her that the baby's safe."

"He said nothing bad would happen if she didn't cry and if she always cooperated. She said that's okay, she'll try, and she'll be his kinda friend. He likes her, he says he's going to keep her safe, but other people want to kill her. He won't let them do that if she cooperates."

"Angela, what you've told me is so important. Thank you so much. Your aunt says that drew pictures for me too."

"The big house with all the rooms and the science room and the men, they're hard to draw, except the one with the mustache."

"I'll bet you've done a great job. I can't wait to see them. Now I'd like to talk with your aunt again so she can arrange to send your drawings to me. Could you give the phone back to her?"

"'kay."

"Thank you and good-bye, sweetheart .... Hello, Mrs. Cho? Could you do me the favor of couriering Angela's drawings to me?" Alma gave a downtown address. "Make it C.O.D. Thank you so much. Now I have to talk with Serena Allan-Sanchez. Do you have her home phone number?"

"It's unlisted, I don't think I should ...."

"Mrs. Cho, Serena needs help, which I can provide. Hitting children in our profession is very, very serious. I don't want another child to be at risk, not for one more day."

"Well ...," Mrs. Cho hesitated, then relented.

Alma said her grateful good-byes and got on with phone call number three.

Serena's phone rang just as she was leaving her apartment to take her Doberman for a walk. "Oh darn," she muttered. She hurried to get the phone, commanding the dog to "Sit. Stay!" It sat stoically guarding the open door.

"Good morning," Alma said. "I'm Delrina North, with Dr. Dino Trigliani. I'm in town to wrap up your involvement with Angela and to reward you for your services."

"Oh God." Serena blanched, her heart racing.

"I'd like to meet you this morning, if possible. At the Arboretum in, say, half an hour. Can you make it for a walk and talk before work?"

"Do I have a choice?"
"Of course. Why so worried?"
"Gerry McMann comes to mind."
"It will be brief and sweet, I promise."
Serena licked her dry lips. "May I bring my dog?"
"Certainly. Meet me at the entry to the main parking lot. I have blond hair, and I'll be in a blue coat carrying a large canvas handbag. I'll know you, of course."

Alma drove her host's car and parked near the entrance to the famous Hoyt Arboretum. She met Serena and her leashed dog, and they were soon on a meandering path amid 800 prime specimens of trees from around the world. Serena peered anxiously ahead and behind in this sea of sun-dappled green. "No one's with you? No one's following?"
"What makes you think you'll suffer Gerry McMann's fate?"
"I know what he knows, same as Angela, what she dreams about. He tried to tell the killers again and again that they're just dreams, just some women and a baby ... I mean, they're weird and freaky and up to some crazy stuff, but ...."
"How do you know what he tried to tell the killers?"
"The video. I watched it all like I was told. God, it's so vile." She almost wretched.
"Ah. I recommended that they spare you, but apparently, it was necessary."
"I was doing my best, I swear, I didn't need that to ...."
"You weren't brilliant with Fran Roma."
"What, is she with you guys? Oh no," Serena groaned.
"No, she's not with us. That was our concern."
"So how do you know? Have you bugged my office?"
Alma said nothing.
Serena continued, "She just landed on me and threw me for a loop, so I made up a story about Angela and her dreams, dream therapy, stuff I know. I thought I did okay. I mean, I put her off, but then Gerry got killed, and I got the video. They're connected right?"
"No, nothing you did caused him to be killed, but his death certainly kept you on track—right up until you hit Angela."
Serena looked as if she'd crumple. "It got really hard with McMann gone, without his dreams to get Angela to spill hers."
"You managed well enough. Did you keep copies of all her dreams?"
"No paper copies, all notes shredded as instructed. I archived my computer files, e-mails, everything Gerry sent me and I sent you guys. All

files are on my hard drive and some backup disks, totally secure with passwords and code names. Was that a mistake too?"

"No, that's good. Now tell me why you hit Angela."

"After Gerry was snuffed, Angela got more and more stubborn until she refused to tell me anything. I got so stressed, so afraid I'd be next that, well ... bang!, my own years of abuse ...." She broke down. "I'm sorry. It's unforgivable. I always thought I'd rather die than hit a child."

"Angela is like Gerry was, so protective of the women in her dreams and the baby ... well, who can blame a baby, but the women give me the creeps—all these strange forces, bizarre research, and weird simultaneous dream stuff. It got McMann tortured and killed. I hate it. It's got to be evil."

Alma said, "Well, whatever you think it is, you're finished now."

Serena's face dropped, gaunt with fear.

"As in, free to go. Off the case."

Serena stopped and looked at Alma. She blinked several times. "Just like that?"

Alma smiled. "Yes. It's obvious you need a break, and I would suggest you get some intensive counseling. I'm here to help you get away and get healthy." Alma checked her watch. "Let's head back." She turned and started retracing their steps. "How soon can you pack up and leave town? And I don't mean a short holiday, I mean an extended retreat or even permanent relocation."

Serena looked confused. "I don't know, I uh ... I mean ...."

Alma repeated slowly, "How soon can you move from town?"

"A day, couple of days, I don't know. I don't have much money. I could get a loan and ... well, my colleagues could take my clients, we've got a holiday arrangement. Long holiday. Oh God, this is crazy."

Alma opened her large handbag and withdrew an accordion folder. She opened the flap to reveal a neat, thick stacks of new bills. "Fifty-thousand, all unmarked and untraceable. It's yours."

Serena was too dazed to talk for a few steps. Finally, she whispered, "How do I know it's not a trap?"

"You're beyond paranoid, poor girl. You've done good work, you made a couple of mistakes, nothing unforgivable, and now it's time to start over. This is your reward. Your freedom. There are a few catches: first, you must use it to go away and look after yourself. Second, you must leave immediately—and I do mean immediately. Third, don't leave any forwarding address if you want to vanish completely from our organization. And finally, we want every bit of material you've got on this case. The video too. I assume you still have it."

Serena nodded. "I hid it. I almost destroyed it, but I didn't even have the courage to do that."

"Go right from here to gather everything associated with this case—and I do mean everything, no copies, no duplicates of any sort, nothing left on hard drives or disks, nothing. Put it all on CDs, then into a reinforced envelope, well-sealed and marked with my name: Delrina North." She spelled it out. "I'll have a courier pick it up at your office at noon. Can you do it?"

"Oh yes. Gladly." Alma gave Serena the folder. She was still too wary and overwhelmed to say more than a breathless "Thank you." She hurried her dog to her car, and they zipped away as fast as she dared.

In the bright sunlight, Larry's sleek Jaguar shone like deep ocean water. Raoul drove; Larry sat beside him. Raoul let him off at the hospital, saying, "Don't take a bite of Mae's food, promise on your life. They had their chance to kill you."

"I'll bring you a pudding!" Larry teased as he got out and closed the door. "Blood pudding!" Raoul revved the motor and took off into traffic.

Larry went directly to Mae's room in intensive care where he had visited her the previous evening. Again, someone else was in her bed.

At the nursing station, a staff member turned to another and blurted, "Mrs. Singer-Jones—the morgue, right?"

Larry blanched. "The morgue? What are you talking about?"

"I believe she died early this morning. I wasn't on shift. I'll check." She reviewed a sheet on a clipboard. "Yes, she died before the seven-thirty shift change. Let's see ... pneumonia plus heart failure. She was, what? Ninety-five."

"I saw her last night after they cleared her lungs. She was sleeping peacefully."

"Did you talk to her?"

"No, but she was fine, breathing easily."

"Well, our seniors often just slip away on us. I'm sorry. You're welcome to go to the morgue. Here, I'll give you a map." She got one from a xeroxed stack and used a pink feltmarker to trace a path for Larry to follow.

Larry took it, then loudly addressed the nursing station in general. "How did this happen? Why did no one call me? I'm available anytime, twenty-four hours a day. I'm on her chart, I'm her next of kin."

A senior nurse rushed over and said, "Sh-h, please. We're very, very sorry."

"You don't phone anybody? Just another useless old crone gone? Is that it?"

"I don't know why you weren't contacted. I'll look into it. It doesn't change the fact of the matter, which is that she's gone. To help you deal with it, we have grief counseling, a resident pastor, a formal complaints procedure, and I can certainly go with you to the morgue if you like."

"No. Just give me her little pack of possessions and let me out of here. I've had it with hospitals. God help me, you'll never see me in another one again."

The senior nurse said, "She'll be cremated with whatever she brought in here, and her remains ...."

"Cremated?"

"It's routine procedure unless noted otherwise. It's all rather well spelled out in our admission ...."

"Well, I'm Mr. Otherwise," Larry said, "and to hell with your procedures. I've seen enough of them. She's Jewish ...."

"It's not on our records."

"Well, I'm telling you now. Or have you been shaking and baking her already? Damn this place!"

"She'll be held for twelve hours. You really must go to the morgue. You have a map—good. Good-bye." She returned to more pressing business. He looked momentarily abandoned, then pushed himself into gear and numbly followed the pink line to Mae's tiny, cold corpse.

Two days later, Fran and Larry communed in Mae's living room, surveying the Herculean task of getting her home and estate in order. "I can't do it," Larry said. "Arranging the funeral service is my limit. You don't know how much I hate this dying stuff, and now the whole messy estate. I mean, I'm getting my business off the ground and everything else down to the essentials, not an ounce of energy left over to deal with this."

"I think it's fascinating," Fran said. "It's like ... like a wild treasure trove, like stumbling into the cave of the Dead Sea Scrolls or something. Look at it; it'll take forever to go through and organize."

"Fifty years so far for Mae, although she's been independent for the last twenty—retired, widowed, and financially secure."

"Well, that would be an incentive—not the widowed part, the retired and money thing."

Larry looked at Fran, suddenly inspired. "Fran, tell me I'm nuts. If the estate matched your current income, would you be willing to work on this, get it tidied up at least, then come work with me after—after everything's settled with Dhyan?"

"I was talking academically, not realis ...."

"So get real on me. What do you think?"

Fran looked with new eyes at the decades of past work and years yet to do. She blinked, thinking hard. Slowly, she said, "I may regret this, and I'm nuttier than you are for sure, but ... yes."

Larry's whoop was punctuated by a knock from the brass snake on the front door. He leapt up and welcomed Alma disguised in a cropped auburn wig, wire-framed glasses, and the same coat and large handbag as she wore to meet Serena. They hugged warmly, with Fran next in line.

Alma stuffed her wig into a coat pocket. Larry took her coat and, as he hung it by the door, said, "Alma, you won't believe it." He grinned. "Fran's agreed to carry on Mae's work, get it into some kind of order. I'll pay her from the estate, there's enough to keep her going for a few months at least."

"Wonderful!" Alma looked around and took a deep, wistful breath. "Hard to believe she's gone. She had so much life. Did such important work. I miss her—Mother *and* Mae, both gone so suddenly. Bless you, Fran, for stepping in exactly when we need you most—with Luna, of course, and now here."

In the living room, all three found seats. Alma continued, "I have access to funds as well—large sums for helping with things like Larry's new venture and for getting Serena's files and helping her vanish."

"From where, dare I ask?" Fran said. "Are you free to tell?"

Alma shrugged. "Wealthy benefactors. Trust funds. Other endowments. Money is never a stumbling block, although I have none of my own. We can't afford the profile and risks that personal income, taxes and such things bring. We contributed to Mae's upkeep and her employment of Nikos. For continuing her work, there's plenty to keep you going indefinitely."

Fran said, "Indefinitely? Oh boy. I'm full-time for Luna as long as it takes, that's a given, but with luck, she'll be back with her mom real soon then ...."

Larry jumped in. "We'll keep Nikos on to help you here, speed things up. He's been itching for years to do some cleaning and painting—major refurbishing now. He'll love it. In fact, Fran ...." Larry looked inspired again.

"Uh-oh."

"Instead of tending this place and yours while paying to live there, why don't you move in here?—I mean, when it's cleaned up. You, Nikos, and Luna." To Alma, he said, "What do you think? Would it be safe enough?"

"Hm. Mae's accident obviously had nothing to do with Pavla's abduction, or the house would have been ransacked and torched by now. And Mae would have told, of course, if she'd been threatened in any way."

Larry groaned. "What a horrid thought. Who are these God-awful people?"

"God-awful, yes. Working in rigid, predictable ways for God as they see Him. Fran, if you'd like to live here with Luna, I'd say fine. It's as safe a place for her as any. The backyard is especially nice—private, with lots of potential. If she's here long enough to start learning from Mae's work, that would be a great plus."

"Uh-uh," Fran said quickly. "She'll be back with Pavla long before then, please, please. And Nikos might not want to ... ?"

Larry smiled. "Yes, he will. He's our ringer. You're in, sweetheart."

Fran laughed. "Got any more plans for the odd five, ten minutes I might have left over of my life?"

Alma said, "Actually, I do. This is nasty business though, I'm sorry. Serena gave me a video of Gerry McMann's execution." She pulled an unmarked white envelope containing the video from her bag. "I'd like both of you to view it, then treat it as you would any anonymous package and pass it on to the appropriate authorities. You'll see that it's a vendetta and a botch-up—wicked stuff, the worst.

"In one of Angela's most recent dreams, Trigliani apologized to Pavla for the fisherman's death and called it a mistake, but his team still found the recording handy for terrorizing Serena and thus, I suspect, getting the dreams they needed to zero in on Pavla. I'd like you to make a copy of it to store here—a gruesome part of our reality—and pass this one on to whatever authorities you choose."

Alma handed the video cassette to Larry. He winced as he took it. "Sure."

Relieved, Alma said, "Thank you. I've brought everything Serena gave me about Angela and her dreams, and Gerry McMann's writings too, to leave here. Now the good news, or at least as good as it gets: according to Angela and corroborated by Siddhartan, Pavla and Trigliani are flying and driving together, driving and flying, a long trip in closed transport with unidentifiable transfer points. They could even be going in circles, ending up very close to here, or they could be half a world away.

"As long as Pavla cooperates, Trigliani says she'll be safe and so will her family and friends. She'll do her utmost, I know, and I have to believe him. I have nothing else to go on. The bad news, however, is that early this morning, she disappeared from Angela's and Sid's dreams, gone black again, and I suspect for a long spell. I'm not thinking the worst, however. I'll keep looking for her for as long as it takes, as best I can."

Pained, Fran asked, "What can we do?"

Larry said, "I can put out feelers for you, tap every source I've got in every country."

Alma smiled. "Thanks. I'll remember that, but it's an inside job at this point, very inside. You're helping plenty already by keeping and loving Luna, arranging Mae's estate, forwarding her work. I am deeply grateful. The only way to Pavla now is through Trigliani. I've recruited Rachelle DuPont to get as close as she can to him."

♦ ♦ ♦

To: trigliani@homeport.com
From: rdupont@.umgen.edu
Date: Thurs, March 30, 15:33:36 -0600
Subject: new spin
Dear Dr. Trigliani - Major breakthrough imminent on mitochondrial factors. Broad ramifications.
Contact me asap - Dr. Rachelle DuPont

♦ ♦ ♦

"A rare pleasure," Trigliani said to Dr. DuPont as she got into his Lamborghini in front of her research building, near the tree and bench where Fran had interviewed Dr. McElroy.

"A necessary pleasure," DuPont said in her throaty voice. "Let's not gush too conspicuously and ruin our reputation as the best of enemies."

Trigliani laughed. "This could be like two porcupines mating ...."

"No. A hedgehog and a porcupine trying."

"The trick is to proceed carefully."

"Very."

Beyond the city limits, Trigliani drove well over the speed limit without his radar detector beeping once. He said, "You are not famous for sharing. Why now?"

"I am when I'm certain, then I share with the world. My publication list is scanty compared to yours, but it's rock solid."

"You are saying mine is not?"

DuPont smiled. "Definitely prickly. Have you seen the latest citations index?"

"Of course. I have fewer papers, more hits—on balance, no better or worse than your score. Besides, you are on enough editorial boards to cut me off cold, and you do not, so clearly I fulfill your minimal requirements."

DuPont conceded, "You do adequate research, occasionally very good. We might do some notable work together, who knows?"

"But why now? Why this?"

DuPont shrugged. "Funding. Facilities. Personnel."

Trigliani smiled, "So you are admitting that I have a few talents in those regards, if not as a scientist."

"You're a genius at it. If you were any smarter, there wouldn't be a nickel for the rest of us. I'm at my grant limit, nothing left over to explore these mitochondrial tangents, which could have immense ramifications."

"All the more reason not to share," Trigliani said.

Annoyed, DuPont said, "You frustrate me at every turn. I'm not in it entirely for myself, as you are. This is too big and too important to play tight-assed games, okay? Do we talk mitochondrial factors and try to work together, or do we not?"

"Okay, okay."

Trigliani slowed to pull onto a paved secondary road. DuPont had noted the time they'd traveled from the last city bridge and their approximate mileage. She could return to within a few miles of the small, mud-spattered, twisted sign where they turned off. The distant buildings and the lay of the land were too nondescript to provide reliable clues. She'd likely not find the road again on her own.

As the green, rural landscape zipped by, Trigliani continued, "It might surprise you, but I recently stumbled on the possibility of the mitochondrial connection myself."

"No wonder you jumped at this meeting despite playing coy and difficult. And no wonder you've got a secret lab out in the country. It all fits. How did you stumble on this connection? It's a quantum leap."

"Luigi Boreli and Henry Krebs."

"No! They're not that good. I don't believe it."

"So don't. The thing is, I am on to it, and I am going to make something of it. What is your source?"

"Hm-m. This is the difficult part. I've done something ... unusual for me. It's justifiable, but ... well, you'll like this. I'm doing an end run, getting even."

"Really? This is interesting. Do tell."

DuPont sighed, then reluctantly said, "Our dear Janet McElroy ripped me off in her last publication, after I'd been so good to her. Rather than take her publicly to task, we talked it out and she appeased me with tidbits of her latest research. I can still do her in any time I want—all these editorial board positions—so she's pretty much where I want her. Her work is mindblowing. I don't know how she made this big jump, but she's got some edge on us that makes me think she's not playing straight."

Trigliani smiled slyly. "She is not. She has done the impossible. I will tell you later."

After several miles on the single-lane highway, Trigliani turned onto a gravel stretch that wound through thick scrub alder. The car bumped; the gravel crunched.

DuPont asked, "What do you mean, 'the impossible'?"

"Later. If this works out. She is in deep with her research." He smiled. "Very deep, just a breath away from trouble."

"I knew it, with her secretive work, unpredictable appearances, then this latest dirty trick, well ... enough is enough. I'm either going to nail down her research, or I'm just going to nail her."

Trigliani smiled and shook his head. "I cannot believe it. You are turning human on me."

She said, "Coming from you, I could worry. It's just that as I get older, with less time to waste, I get more practical, less tolerant of bullshit."

Trigliani said, "I, too, like to cut to the quick. We might make a great team." He took a hard right turn onto a narrow rutted lane, which rolled and curved through pleasant woods, then opened suddenly to an impressive estate. A pseudo-old manor of fieldstone, timbers, diamond-paned windows, and functional shutters—all closed on the ground floor—rose from a wide meadow with graceful trees and a pond.

One of six garage doors opened and swallowed up the Lamborghini.

Trigliani led DuPont down a beige corridor with several unmarked doors on each side of it, leading to a roomy white-and-steel laboratory. It had high ceilings, no windows, and bright, full-spectrum lighting.

"Well, well," DuPont said. "Life in the country."

Trigliani smiled as she quickly assessed every part of it. Her eyes lit on a large whiteboard filled with writing and diagrams. Shocked, she said, "That's Janet's writing! She's been here! You should have told me."

"Why? Showing you is better."

"She's working with you then? I can't believe it. You and she are underhanded beyond ... well, I'm stunned."

"Practical, as you said. We are all practical. We need her on side and perfectly contained. It is a matter of control. And I have it."

"So tell her I'm here. I'd like a few words with her."

Trigliani shook his head. "But she is not here, not anywhere near here."

"So where is she?"

"Privileged information. In fact, I am the only one in the world who knows her whereabouts by name, rank, and serial number. She may publish as Janet McElroy or Pavla Blanca or any number of other names ...."

"She has other ... ? Wow. Sneakier than I thought."

"Many aliases." Trigliani reached into the inside breast pocket of his suit jacket and pulled out Pavla's University of Minnesota business card, the same as the one Fran picked up in Athens. "I work with her as Pavla Blanca." He held the card up for Rachelle to read. She reached to take it.

"No," Trigliani said quickly, putting the card back in his pocket. "We will call her Pavla, but I warn you, do not bother trying to trace her by this or any name. I am telling you this to save you a wild goose chase. She is doing highly illicit research—even by our standards—with unbelievable success. We need that research, and she needs cover, so we have made a deal. I keep her in perfect secrecy and safety. She continues her work. We share the results and, I hope, the substantial fruits of it."

"'We' meaning Boreli and Krebs as well?"

"Yes."

"Where have you got them hidden?"

"No need. They work here, and they also work at their usual facilities. They are free to come and go but not to write—or even think—a word about this without running it past me and Pavla. There could be room for you; it depends on what you bring."

DuPont laughed. "I guarantee that I know more at a glance about what's written on this board than you three put together. I've got a key missing piece, one our dear friend very cleverly left out of this overview. I can save you so much time that the question is, is there room for Boreli and Krebs?"

"There has to be. They are in already."

"Too bad. Oh well, they're harmless, and I presume I can talk to them without these clandestine, low-level flights to the boonies."

Trigliani laughed. "Yes. Discretion is advised. I can show you a video recording of what happened to an associate who was indiscreet and uncooperative. My funding source plays hardball."

"Forget the threats. Who is this funding source?"

"A large corporation with deep roots and deep pockets. A world force and highly respected. I am not at liberty to disclose. We would not want to bring disgrace upon it should we fall afoul of the law."

DuPont snorted. "Hah! They make nasty videos doing God-knows-what to whom, and we worry about disgracing them? They're lucky to have you; you're as slick as a greased fish. I should find that alarming, but it's comforting actually."

Trigliani grinned. He knew and DuPont guessed that their conversation was being taped. This last comment would play well to the bosses. She continued, "So how do I communicate with Pavla Whoever-she-is?"

"You communicate through me, only through me. You may use e-mail, fax, regular mail, and courier. Whatever you choose, I will get your correspondence to her. No phone calls or real-time connections of any sort. And no trying to outsmart me in this regard. The price could be ...."

"Stop it. I have no interest in this cat and mouse crap. I'm here to work, not play games. Just tell me, what's this impossible thing she's done?"

"Top secret."

Exasperatedly, she said, "I am really tiring of this, quite ready to leave with my ...."

"Sh-h-h." Trigliani lowered his voice dramatically. "I'm taking a chance telling you this, a chance to get you on side. She ... she has reproduced herself parthenogenetically. The baby is nine months old now, no anomalies whatever. None."

DuPont's eyes popped. "No! Are you sure?"

"Absolutely."

"Oh boy. If this gets out ... well, the publicity will be deadly for us, by association, who cares that we work with turkeys and mice? We'll be hounded by the news, dogged by the ethical uproar. No wonder she slips around like a fugitive. A criminal. No wonder she's happy in your sweatshop, wherever you've got her."

"No, no, she is in a beautiful place. An excellent laboratory."

"Where's the baby?"

"Safe and thriving. Please, no more questions about this. Just tell me what you have got."

DuPont walked to the whiteboard and pointed to the mitochondria. "I know how to get you from here to the nucleus like that." She snapped her fingers. "Save you years."

Trigliani said, "Give me a hint."

"Pavla's got the nuclear part figured, making it a fairly quick jaunt for us to get back to the mitochondrial application, assuming we cooperate perfectly, employ impeccable techniques, and Lady Luck smiles. Without me, you're stalled at square one."

"I know that. Just give me an appetizer."

"It's transcriptional. An element you'd never expect."

"Literally, an element?"

"An enzymatic process at the core of which, yes, is a key element."

"Trace, I assume?"

"It bridges a fascinating gap. It can be both the needle and the haystack, depending on your perspective and purpose. Whatever else Dr. Pavla is, she's brilliant for having figured this out."

"You are not going to tell me as we stand here, are you?"

"Of course not. I'm in and we shake, or I'm out and I'm gone. You can have the preliminary data when you drop me off at my office."

Trigliani extended his hand and they shook. He lowered his voice. "You had better not let me down."

DuPont smiled. "Sounds like a threat, if I didn't know you better."

Trigliani smiled in return. "You know me well enough."

♦ ♦ ♦

Sandhu lived in an apartment high above the downtown core. When he worked at Media 8, he walked three blocks to work. Now his commute took two-minutes by elevator ride to the third floor of his building, where he and Larry had rented office space for their new headquarters, the bare beginnings of their innovative new reporting service called—with thanks to Clark Kent—The Daily Planet, or TDP on the Internet.

They would work together until winter to get underway, then they'd split their time at the helm. From winter to spring, Sandhu would run the show while Larry retreated to the Bahamas to start writing his blockbuster, tell-all novel. Sandhu didn't have plans yet for his summer and fall off, but he was in high demand; something exciting would come up.

"The arrangement is an experiment," a business magazine article quoted Larry about his new venture, "with cancer to thank for forcing all sorts of creativity. It'll be news-telling like you never knew you wanted until you got involved."

TDP offices were still a few thousand square feet of empty, bland walls and carpet. A carpenter and a painter stood in the center of it, conferring over plans to create a bright-colored maze of modular work spaces, complete with light pipes to keep plants green and employees cheery.

A telephone-and-cable employee worked at the edges, measuring and calculating myriad connections. By a luncheon nook with sink and fridge, a graphic artist/webmaster sat at a computer on the lone table in the place. Mellow blues and jazz pulsed from her speakers as she designed TDP's website and got the bare bones of it up and running.

Larry's new desk took a full-windowed corner. He crouched on one knee to assemble cabinets and shelves. Sandhu carried in boxes of files and books to put in them. Money was too tight during these start-up days to hire any but basic help and besides, both were enjoying these blue jean days and the nuts and bolts, literally, of setting up. They bantered a bit and hummed to tunes from the webmaster's computer.

Fran arrived before noon carrying two bunches of mixed spring flowers and Pina Giuseppe's big canvas bag slung over her shoulder.

"Hey Fran, nice surprise!" Sandhu said.

"One for each new desk," Fran said of the bouquets. From the bag, she retrieved two clear glass vases wrapped in tissue. She took them to the sink to fill them with water, then quickly returned to arrange the blooms.

"Nice touch," Larry said. "Sixteen tons to follow."

Sandhu looked puzzled.

Fran pulled a white unmarked envelope from her bag and extracted a video cassette. "You're invited to watch."

"In the editing room," Larry said. He raised his voice and said to the others, "Hey guys, lunch time! Break till one, okay?" To Sandhu, he said quietly, "No questions until we're inside. C'mon."

The editing room held half a dozen chairs in front of a TV-VCR. It would soon be crowded with audio and visual editing equipment. The space needed soundproofing yet, but no matter, since any overhearing ears had gladly scattered for a long hour.

"It's Gerry McMann, the Nova Scotia fisherman, getting wasted," Larry said, hitting the power button. Fran took the cassette from the envelope.

"You're kidding," Sandhu said with a wince.

"Sorry to spring this on you," Fran said, "but forewarning wouldn't make it any easier. You certainly don't have to watch if you don't want to."

"No, it's okay," Sandhu said. "Where'd you get it?"

"Anonymous drop-off," Larry said. "At least, that's the official story when we give it to the CIA." He dropped his voice. "In truth, it's from Alma, Uncle Sid's new friend."

"How's she connected?"

"Long story. Gerry McMann was a survivor like your uncle. He had a rock too."

Sandhu's eyes widened. "Uncle Sid could be murdered?"

"No, McMann talked. He wrote down his dreams, shared them."

"Well, no problem there, and not much nuclear waste dumping in my family."

"Actually, we don't think that's what got McMann killed. The hot rocks story might be completely bogus. The CIA may be chasing a lie, and we've got to tell them."

Sandhu said, "Then why was he killed?"

"Don't know. That's what this should tell us. There, ready to roll. Fran, could you hit the lights?"

Fran asked, "You ready, Sandhu?"

"No, but let's do it."

Complete blackness enveloped them. Larry hit 'Play'.

In a small den/computer room, GERRY MCMANN sits duct-taped to a chair. Violent rap music blasts in the background. A hand-held, home video camera ZOOMS IN on him, then ZOOMS OUT again.

A slightly-built MAN wearing a black sweatsuit, thin black gloves, and black Halloween eye mask works on a computer in a corner. He's burning CDs from other CDs and floppies. He throws the cases onto the floor beside him, then adds the disks he's finished copying to the heap. He puts the new CDs he's made into a metal box.

Two muscular, masked men, also in black sweats, masks, and gloves, work over McMann. THUG #1 has a neck brace and left arm in a sling. He holds a pistol in his right hand. THUG #2 is taller and beefier. The edge of a dark birthmark or tattoo rises up the right side of his neck.

> THUG #1
> Where is she? Where the fuck is she?

McMann refuses to answer. Thug #2 clobbers his face, distorting it and snapping his neck.

> THUG #1
> Where does she live?

> MCMANN
> I don't know, I don't know.

Thug #2 uppercuts McMann's chin. Blood runs from the corners of his mouth. They continue working him over, breaking face and finger bones as they interrogate. Teeth crack and hang crooked.

> THUG #1
> Bullshit!

> MCMANN
> She moves around.

> THUG #1
> Where?

> MCMANN
> (voice thick, words slurred)
> All over. They're just dreams. I don't know.

> THUG #1
> Dreams my ass. She broke my arm, you see this?
> Some dream, you lying bastard.

Thug #2 guffaws as he eagle-claws McMann's thumb, then cracks the joint back. McMann opens his broken mouth to scream, but he gags on blood bubbling out.

> THUG #1
> That feel like a dream, hey dickhead? You tell me something useful, or you'll be feeling a lot more. Where's your rock?

> MCMANN
> What rock?

McMann gets a hammer-fist to an ear for this. He throws up.

> THUG #1
> You fucking pig!

> MCMANN
> (whimpering)
> She's just a woman ... with a baby. Protecting her baby.

> THUG #1
> So why you protecting her?

> MCMANN
> I'm not. She's nothin'. I don't know her.

McMann slumps. Thug #2 lifts his head by the hair.

> MCMANN
> (croaking)
> By jeez, you're sick.

> COMPUTER THUG
> All done but the plant, boss.

                    COMPUTER THUG (continued)
                (to McMann)
Why don't you tell them where she is? If they kill
you, I'm planting a story on a CD ...

                (holds up a CD)
... about you dropping off nuclear waste at sea, a
scuzzy racket you and your buddies were in, you
understand? You'll look like shit, all of you, and
nobody will know the real reason you're pulp. I
mean, covering for some whore who beat up my
friend, what's the matter with you?

                    THUG #1
So where is she?

McMann MOANS, shakes his head slightly. His eyes stream tears and blood.

                    THUG #1
Where's the fucking rock?

McMann's voice is a death rattle. He CROAKS something unintelligible.

                    THUG #1
Oh for fuck's sake, just finish up.

Thug #2 swings a hammer broadside at McMann's mouth. It caves in. McMann passes out. Thug #1 puts the pistol to McMann's head and blows his brains onto nearby walls.

The computer thug snaps shut the lid to the metal box containing the CDs he's copied. He plugs in an electric wand that creates a powerful magnetic field, which he uses to wipe the hard drive and the mess of floppies on the floor. He uses the hammer to smash the computer and disks.

Thug #1 and #2 roam the house, searching every shelf and drawer as they go.

> THUG #1 (voice over)
> In here!

The camera catches up to him in the teenage son's room. They paw through a rock collection dumped from a box onto the floor, taking a few pebble-sized ones. The computer thug enters and holds up a CD.

> COMPUTER THUG
> The kid's disk of stolen downloads. Perfect, eh?
> A little red herring for the bloody red fishermen.
>
> (laughs)
> Dumb fuck.

The computer thug throws the CD onto a pile of dirty clothing, then kicks it underneath.

The three thugs meet back at the blood splattered room. Thug #1 pumps another shot into McMann, who bounces for the last time.

The video turns to electric lines and noisy static.

Fran jumped up to stop the VCR, then stood rooted beside it, too stunned to sit down again. Larry and Sandhu sat paralyzed. Finally, Fran said, "Now what?"

They sat longer, working on breathing and blinking. Zombie-like, Sandhu said, "I need air. Sunlight."

In the 1950s coffee shop, Fran, Larry, and Sandhu took the corner booth they'd last occupied. Pat Boone sang "Love Letters in the Sand", still yearning after all those years. The three huddled in shock, speaking quietly. Sandhu said, "The rocks ... the rock they wanted, you think it's like Uncle Sid's?"

Fran nodded. "Pretty much."

"You sure he's not at risk of ... ?"

Fran quickly shook her head. "No, I wouldn't worry. The situation's very different now, plus your uncle doesn't speak or write either, not like Gerry, who kept extensive notes. That's what they were copying from the computer. There was no percentage in what they did to Gerry, which was really a vengeance crime, the price he paid for the woman injuring a couple of nasty beasts."

"Who is she?"

Fran said, "Alma's daughter."

Sandhu's eyebrows shot up.

Fran continued, "Another set of goons got her last week, abducted her. That's why Alma's talking to your Uncle Sid, to see if he can help locate her. His rock gives him ... well, it gives him kind of a psychic edge. He's been drawing pictures for her, corroborating other reports. He's safe, don't worry. The whole exercise is a long shot, but it's the best Alma's got right now."

Sandhu said, "Wow. Uncle Sid's always been brave and a bit mystical. This probably doesn't faze him at all."

"I wouldn't spread it around the family though."

"No kidding."

"He's just visiting with a nice lady, a counselor friend."

Sandhu nodded. "He's crazy about her, the liveliest he's been since his stroke. Has he been able to help her?"

"A bit. We know her daughter's with a colleague, some guy who wants to work with her."

"Is that all? Why the abduction, all the intrigues, not to mention murder, just to work with someone? I don't get it."

Fran said, "Me either, not totally. It's really complicated, really arcane. What matters right now is that Pavla's probably okay, nothing newsworthy, that's for sure. Nothing the cops need to know."

Sandhu said, "But McMann got killed protecting this woman. That's not exactly a detail."

"True, but what can we tell the authorities about her? I know more than you two, and it's still mostly nothing. And I won't direct them to Alma because she doesn't want that, really doesn't want that. It would jeopardize the situation and distract the cops from chasing the tangible clues, which are all in the video."

Larry said, "It's easy then. We pass it on, same as the CD. Hello Feds, package for you, we don't know nothing."

Sandhu nodded. "Suits me fine. I'm too confused to help them out of a paper bag right now. I just want to get rid of this piece of hell, the sooner the better."

Fran nodded. "The sooner the better for Foggy Cove too, get them off the hook over this hot rocks b.s., on top of a murder, on top of the shipwreck. God, what a wringer they've been through. I sure bought the scam, only had a passing twinge that something was funny about it. Best damned red herring going, and now it's back to square one."

Larry said, "Square zero. Just a fisherman's dream woman—read 'affair'—and some rock or other she gave him. Or maybe a diamond ring-type rock he gave her, and a jealous, pissed off killer who wants it or his woman back. Looks like a nasty domestic to me. Or maybe an internet romance turned ugly."

Fran shook her head. "Poor McMann. The town's off the hook, and he's back to being crazy. And still dead, very dead. At least, the killers have bodies and masked faces and voices now. Who cares why they catch the bastards, as long as justice is done."

"Amen," Larry concluded.

"All Season Sports" splashed in big blue letters over the yellow awnings of Cole Preston's Dartmouth, Nova Scotia, main street shop. Red and white banners shouted "SALE!" across the wide front windows.

Inside, multi-color "Special Offer" starbursts dotted the walls and racks. He'd filled his seven-hundred square feet with summer goods from beach balls to roller blades, from breezy clothing to high-tech water bottles. Hockey equipment permanently filled a back corner.

Cole stood behind the sales counter near the front door. He could see bits of the Halifax harbor through the treed waterfront park across the street. Wind tussled the sea into whitecaps shimmering in the high, late spring sun. He tended paperwork and inventory when not serving the occasional customer. Summer business had been slow but was picking up.

An overweight mother and her gawky teenaged boy walked in. "Hi," he said, grinning broadly. "Anything special for you?"

"Just browsing, thanks," she replied.

The phone rang. "All Season Sports," he said brightly.

"Cole," Fran said. "Fran Roma." She sat in her home office in front of her computer screen, eyes tracking the snaking colored lines of a screensaver.

Cole's face instantly sobered.

"I'm calling about the video—of Gerry McMann. You know it, right?"

Cole blanched and twitched. He pressed his lips together, his mouth suddenly dry. He swallowed hard, then croaked, "No, I, uh ..." He tried to clear his throat. "I wouldn't know about that."

"Yeah, I thought you'd seen it. Why else would a young reporter run so fast from the story of a lifetime. It's a powerful persuader. Were you sent a copy, or did you get a personal showing from the killers?"

Cole's hands trembled. He couldn't control them or gather his thoughts. Fran waited. After long, painful seconds, he said, "The line's bad, I'm sorry, I can't ...."

Fran sighed. "I'm sorry you can't too. I assume you watched the whole thing so you know that the hot rocks were a scam, a plant."

"No, I didn't. I don't .... Oh God." Cole struggled to keep his composure.

The woman in the shop turned to ask him a question, but stopped when she saw his agitation. She mouthed, "Are you okay?"

He quickly nodded his head and turned away from her.

Fran said, "I got a copy of the video recently, and it's clear that the CD was a plant, the hot rocks are red herrings. We've let the CIA know—same way as before; Media 8 turns it over, we don't know who sent it—so they can get on the right scent and catch the killers. Cole, this is good news."

He pulled himself together as best he could. "Well, thank you for calling. I'm sorry, I, uh ... don't carry videos, nothing like that."

"Wait, there's more. The goons got the woman, the one Gerry was protecting. She's alive and probably okay. They got what they want, you hear? You're not in danger as long as she cooperates, and she is, believe me. You can stop trembling in your boots."

"Boots, yeah. Sure, I got hiking boots, wet suit ...."

"Cole, for God's sake, I'm trying to tell you not to worry if the CIA or cops come back to you for more information. You don't have to play completely dumb anymore, okay? If they press you about the rock, you can tell them Gerry picked it up when he survived the shipwreck, a good luck charm from the beach, something like that, just an ordinary rock. The killers were way, way off base."

"I don't know that, I'm sorry."

"No, I guess you don't, and I can't convince you this way. We need to talk, really talk. Let's set a time, and I'll tell you things about Gerry and his ramblings that'll put your mind at rest."

"No, I can't. I'm not in that business."

"Okay, okay, I give up. I *will* let you know when they get the killers though."

"If."

"Either way you can stop sweating it. You're out of the loop."

"Yeah, I've made sure of it." He swallowed, his mouth still dry. "As sure as I can."

"I guess you have. Good luck, Cole."

"Sorry, ma'am." He hung up.

Fran walked downstairs to the kitchen to find Nikos and Luna sharing arrowroot cookies. Luna's cheeks had rosy patches the size of quarters, and her bib was wet with drool. Lord Byron looked up hopefully from Nikos's feet, waiting for a cookie of his own or at least a crumb to fall.

"He's seen it," Fran said. "He's still in total denial. Maybe he'll get over it when the killers are caught. If they're caught, as he just said. The CIA probably likes the nuclear waste idea, even though it's clearly a plant. It's simple and has a macho appeal compared to the real story, which I sure as heck don't understand. I mean, why does some cabal of fundamentalists want to waste these women, this bright little spark. What's she done?"

Fran took Luna in her arms and gave her a kiss on each red teething patch. "Oo-o, you're warm! And wonderful," she said, evoking a twinkly grin. "And I am so lost. What do you know that I don't know? And Nikos," she asked him slowly, "what in the name of all that's holy are we doing?"

"The right thing," he said, putting his arm around Fran's shoulder. He held up his big worn hand to Luna, who wrapped her tiny, plump grip around his fingertips.

Under the hot morning sun, Fran packed an unwieldy cardboard box containing her home computer from her car into Mae's house. She made several increasingly sweaty trips from car to house fetching her monitor, scanner, printer, and manuals.

She cleared the dining table by stacking files yet higher on the surrounding floor. Soon, she had the machine and its peripherals wired and working in their new home.

She scanned a sheet of Mae's bold schoolteacher hand, identified it as a form of "quillscript", then ran it through an OCR, or optical character recognition program. The output wasn't acceptable—too many letters misidentified.

She narrowed Mae's hand to make it a more condensed font. She ran the program again. Better, but not much. She tried another font. Worse luck. She manipulated it. Marginally better. She read the on-screen help. She flipped through the manual and pored over some sections several times.

By noon, with face and underarms dripping from heat and frustration, she still didn't have anything adequate enough to proceed. She was beaten, but like a dog with a bone, wouldn't let it go. "It's got to work, damn it. Customize." She again searched the manual's 'customize' section. "Customizing characters. I need to create an average, a new Mae average."

She leaned back in her chair and exclaimed to the ceiling, "I can't do that! I can't do s.f.a. with this. Help!"

The front door knocker thunked. "Oh damn," she muttered on the way to answering it, "I don't want any, and if you can't help, go away." She opened the door to an arthritic, frizzy gray-haired old lady in a silky floral dress. She rested one hand on a wooden cane and clutched a manila envelope in the other. "Yes!" Fran said with delight, ushering her in quickly.

Inside and safe, Alma stood up straight and took off her wig. She shook out her hot hair, saying, "I've just come from seeing Luna. Nikos said you were here."

"Oh great! One thrilled baby, hey?"

"Yes. And one thrilled grandma. I'm going to visit her now and then, when I'm in town and on route to or from the Capitol."

"Will you stay with us? Or maybe here?"

"I'm tempted, but ... no, I've got other accommodations. When things have settled more, I will, if you'll take me at a moment's notice."

"Of course."

"Now what am I interrupting?"

"Nothing, except keeping me from pulling out my hair. It's break time. Would you like some lemonade?"

Alma nodded.

Fran led Alma through the dining room, past her humming computer, to the kitchen to get a big, full pitcher from the old fridge. "I'm trying to scan Mae's notes and convert them to text. It'll be a lot easier to read them that way, and then we'll have duplicates, all tidily stored on disk. It's not working yet, and I've tried everything. I'll have to become an OCR programmer, I guess, and make my own reading of Mae's hand. This could set me back years—I'm no computer whiz."

"I'm not either, I'm afraid. You know, you needn't read everything as you go. Just putting it away in categories would be a good start."

"That's Plan B, but this scanning will be relatively quick when I get it working, then the reading will be easy. If we're going to move into here by winter though, I'll have to take the easy route at some point, won't I?"

They adjourned to the living room and wilted into the furniture. Alma still had the manila envelope, which she held up. "I've got more work for you. Good news too, I guess—as good as it gets." She took a dozen printed pages from the envelope and put them on a stack of Mae's files. "Rachelle DuPont's report."

"Great. What's she found?"

"Rachelle connected with Trigliani and promptly got onto his research team with two others, Dr. Luigi Boreli and Dr. Henry Krebs. Boreli's key to this report, bless him. And Rachelle too, she's brilliant. Luckily, Pavla shared just enough of her findings to let Rachelle squeak in. She'll have very filtered contact with Pavla, strictly about their research. My daughter is apparently alive and well in a beautiful place, but unreachable. Unrescuable." Alma sighed heavily. "And no end in sight to her disappearance."

"A beautiful place where?"

Alma shook her head. "Only Trigliani knows, and he's adamantly secretive about it. I suspect he might not even have told his superiors, to keep them and their henchmen away from her. And perhaps to keep his bosses from killing him too, as long as they have to go through him to get to her. It's a dicey game. Gerry had more than one killer, more than one person willing to murder to get to her, and since she injured a second man—much more seriously than a broken arm—she's in great danger if they ever locate her."

"Where do you think Trigliani would hide her?"

"Where dreams are blocked, that's all I know. In a lead-lined structure or cave. I won't continue to actively search for her for fear that I might inadvertently lead assassins to her. Rachelle will stay tuned to Trigliani and keep us posted, but finding out where my girl is could be far more dangerous than not knowing."

Fran said, "Tough job, sitting tight, doing nothing. I had a little taste of it with Dhyan lately, and it nearly killed me."

Alma nodded with a sad, appreciative smile. "He might drop a clue now and then. Rachelle can push him a bit, but a little too far, a little misunderstanding and snap! she's first in the line of fire."

"She's one brave lady."

"And very clever, thank goodness. We have such dedicated supporters, so many working behind the scenes at great risk for us. Rachelle knows that Pavla's research is invaluable and will have immense, positive repercussions, so her help is for altruistic reasons, as well as for personal."

"Do you think Pavla knows Rachelle's on board?"

"Oh, I'm sure. It'll help her be contented and focus on the task at hand, biding her time while working out possibilities of escape. Rachelle confirmed what Angela said, that Trigliani is enamored of Pavla, which may be her trump card, if she plays it right. We'll see."

"How did Rachelle get this report to you? You can't be seen with her, can you?"

"No. It came through an assistant or two and ordinary post, which is surprisingly efficient and anonymous. It's the only copy. It's too dangerous to leave files on her computer, even her private one that's unconnected to any others. You'll find a dresser drawer of material about Pavla in Mother's old room here. One drawer each for Mother, me, Pavla, and Luna. Could you add this to Pavla's records?"

Fran took the envelope. "Gladly. May I read it? And the other material in these drawers?"

"Of course. It's all yours."

"Should I start there? I really don't know what to do with any of this—where to start, how to make sense of it. I'm just a trained puppy, you know, a news-hound. I don't have a clue what I'm after until I'm given the scent. Wanting to figure this out isn't anything like knowing how to go about it. And don't say 'peripherals'. I'm so deep in peripherals here, I'm lost."

Alma laughed. "I'd suggest you start your reading, if not your scanning, with all the material in Mother's drawer. She wanted her story told in book form, a concise biography written ...."

Fran's eyes widened. "Oh no, not me."

Alma smiled. "No, it should be someone who met her, even briefly, to have sensed her immense vitality, her charisma. If you could scan all of her notes and Mae's onto a single CD ... well, that would allow for safety in transport and help a biographer immensely."

"That I can do. Thank you. Now what about the rest of this?" Fran threw her hands wide to indicate Mae's vast handiwork.

"It's quite simple really. Think of these—every file in this house—as beads on a string. The string is a unifying theory ... no, more like a unifying reality. Get to know some of the beads, and they'll all fall into line. Actually, I've got a little task to do here that might help. Mother made films in the early 1920s, and they're stored in the basement. Mae and I watched one recently, and it appeared to be well preserved, but I'd like to get them stabilized, then digitized. Perhaps you could help with that."

"Sounds interesting."

"Would you like to watch one with me? It might be worth a thousand words of explanation."

"I'd love to. No blood and guts though. I'm not up to it, even play acted."

"Oh Fran, that was an awful thing to do to you. I'm sorry, but you have to know what some people will do to get to us and what hatred drives them, far more than a few broken bones merit."

"It's crazy and horrifying. I don't understand at all."

"So let's get on with filling you in." She finished her iced tea. "I think you'll like Mother's old films. They're about new life and love, I promise."

As Alma set up the projector as Mae had done, she said, "Maya experimented in twinning sound with images, as you'll see. This is from a series of talkies made in 1921, '22 ...."

"Really? That early?"

"She inspired Dr. Lee De Forest—the dream connection—whose first talkie played publicly in 1923. All Mother's productions were made behind the scenes and put immediately into storage. This is the only copy."

"What a terrible risk if anything happened to it."

"It would be a bigger risk to have copies scattered about here and there. Luckily, they've been safe here, and Mother's experiments with film chemistry and its storage have paid off remarkably well, as you'll see. All her films are in excellent condition. We have the scripts for backup—no identifying images in those—and they're stored several other safe places. They're adequate for the record, for the day when the world will be ready for this. Now, could you draw the drapes?"

Fran pulled the heavy old fabric tightly shut. Alma flipped the toggle switch for the projector's motor and advanced the film to the opening bull's eye. In Mae's hot, dark living room, the title "Mary" flickered on the silver screen. An original symphonic score composed by Mae's first husband Davide came sweetly to life again, and young Maya's ghost rose once more.

MARY is very pregnant under loose robes and head shawl. She's played by Maya Solari in her 20s.

Mary's mother ANNE, wearing similar clothing, stands near her. She's played by Sunoqua.

JOSEPH, bearded and berobed, helps Mary sit side-saddle on an donkey outside a peasant's adobe home. He's played by Davide. He exits, leaving the two women alone.

> ANNE
> They're brutes these census-takers, forcing this journey for their convenience.

> MARY
> Please, Mother, it's torment to keep hoping and wishing that you might come to help with the birth. I'll be fine. You've instructed Joseph well. He'll keep me safe and everything clean.

> ANNE
> (sighs)
> I hope so. The risk will be worth it if you make Bethlehem's caves, a most propitious place for our birth. Still, I'll worry until I see the three of you safely back here.

Joseph enters and overhears her last words.

> JOSEPH
> (hand on Anne's shoulder)
> Mother Anne, I can't tell you not to worry, but I will protect them with my life and every shred of my wits.

Anne hugs Joseph. He leads Mary away on the donkey. Anne walks a short distance with them holding Mary's hand, then lets go and waves goodbye.

CUT TO:

Joseph and Mary meeting a SHEPHERD on rolling hills. The sun is setting, burnishing Mary to ethereal beauty.

> SHEPHERD
> My God! An angel.

> JOSEPH
> (laughs)
> No, just a man and his wife ... and child to be. We've come for the census and require shelter.

> SHEPHERD
> Hah! You've come too late. There's nothing available, unless you're filthy rich.

> JOSEPH
> We understand there are caverns ...

> SHEPHERD
> Where we keep our sheep, and even they are crowded these days.

> JOSEPH
> Might we use them nonetheless?

> SHEPHERD
> Madness for such a pregnant woman, but suit yourself.

> SHEPHERD (continued)
> (pointing to the distance)
> In the hills behind town. They're crude and dirty, hardly suitable if she gives birth ... and adds that mess to the mud and dung.

> JOSEPH
> We'll give you no grief, I swear to you, as God is the Father. and the birth ...

The donkey BRAYS, obscuring his words.

> JOSEPH (continuing)
> ... wherever it takes place, will be clean.

Sound is clear again.

> JOSEPH (continuing)
> Immaculate.

CUT TO:

Joseph and Mary creeping by lantern light into a small half-cave on the eastern edge of Bethlehem. They share it with sheep, cows, and other livestock that drink from rough-hewn troughs. In a nook, Joseph and Mary make a bed of blankets over straw.

CUT TO:

Clouds over the shepherd's field shifting to reveal a startlingly bright 'star' rising on the eastern horizon. The shepherd looks in awe.

> SHEPHERD
> (mutters to himself)
> God is the Father ... the birth immaculate ....
>
> (eyes widen, starts running)
> The Christ! It must be!

CUT TO:

Mary's face contorting in labor. The contractions are intense and close together.

Joseph enters the cave with a pitcher of water and sits beside her. Her face relaxes between grimaces.

> **JOSEPH**
> Mary, I'm worried. The woman who sold me this water—for the price of wine—is shaking from the news, from the rumor, that the Christ has come to be born here. A shepherd from the Field of Ruth said he saw an angel, an angel bearing the news. From descriptions, I think he's the shepherd who directed us here, and now he's run off to tell the world and distant kings.
>
> Worse, Mary, an amazingly bright star has risen in the sky—a powerful portent.

> **MARY**
> (groans)
> Oh no. Luckily the hills are riddled with caves. It will be difficult for anyone to locate us in this one. Does the woman know why you wanted water? Did anyone see you return here?

> **JOSEPH**
> (shakes his head)
> No, and no. We are one of many couples in need of water and food. I saw numerous pregnant women.

> **MARY**
> (wincing as a contraction grips her)
> It's too late to go anywhere else, and it's safer in here than out there.

> **JOSEPH**
> If they find us here and discover the truth, is that so bad? Perhaps it's time for the truth to be known.

Mary pants, fighting for breath, sweating anew. As the contraction eases, she's able to speak.

MARY
(touching his cheek)
You are so sweet. No wonder I love you so. Joseph, dear Joseph, the truth will shock and anger them, for they expect the Christ to be a boy, and my divine child can only be a girl. What they cannot accept, they will kill.

JOSEPH
Then I will give them their boy, if and when they find us.

SQUALLING announces the birth of Mary's baby, which is clearly a girl. Joseph washes the babe with a clean rag, swaddles her in white linen, and lays her by his exhausted wife's side. He leaves Mary to sleep.

Joseph returns to the cave carrying a BABY BOY similarly wrapped. He approaches Mary, bending on his knee to whisper in her ear.

Mary's eyes flicker open; she rouses herself. Her faces shows renewed worry about their predicament.

JOSEPH
I have a boy child, an orphan. His mother has died, his father is long missing. His siblings cannot keep him. He needs to nurse and he needs a home. We need a boy. It's so simple. He's healthy enough and only a few months old.

MARY
A few months? They'll be looking for a newborn.

JOSEPH
They are looking for the Christ, searching every cave. Let the shepherd find us and identify us now. Look at him. He's small and hungry, but beautiful. He will satisfy them.

Joseph makes a cradle from a feed trough. Mary kneels to tend the baby boy in it. Joseph stands close by. The girl baby sleeps to the side in the blankets on straw.

THREE KINGS in opulent robes and jewels fall to their knees in awe, offering their gifts to the infant in the manger.

> FIRST KING
> My Lord, the Christ child.

Mary's baby starts FUSSING, clearly newborn cries. Mary turns and looks anxiously at her. Joseph puts his arm around her shoulder.

> FIRST KING
> Another child? What ....

> JOSEPH
> (quickly)
> A girl baby. We are crowded in here, no rooms in town. Her mother is nearby and hears her, I'm sure.

Mary smiles. The kings ignore the cries of a mere girl and return their attention to the divine boy.

> SECOND KING
> What is our Lord's name?

> MARY
> Jésus Emanuel.

> THIRD KING
> Ah, the Lord is come! We are saved.

> MARY
> (smiling at Joseph)
> Yes. We are saved.

♦ ♦ ♦

As Alma reopened the drapes, Fran sat motionless, unable to catch her spinning thoughts to form even a simple sentence. Alma said, "I was in Nepal preparing to make a sequel to Mother's film about Buddha's purported mother, Maha Maya, when Pavla was abducted. We were going to make a sequel to this one in Bethlehem later this year, then others elsewhere. Without Pavla, however ...." Alma's voice faded as tears welled up.

Fran whispered, "What will you do?"

Alma gathered herself. "No more re-enactments, that's certain. I don't have the energy to do any theatrical work now, even as a consultant for plays such as Raoul's or the other storytelling work I do. I'll get back to it, I'm sure, but for now, I'll just keep up some of my usual rounds. And stay tuned to how I might help Pavla, of course."

"What are your usual rounds?"

"I travel the world seeing all sorts of people, acting as an advisor, a counselor—an encourager, really. I'm in Washington a lot for obvious reasons, influencing where I can. Very few know my true identity. To most, I'm a lobbyist, consultant, whatever position works. It's the family business, more or less."

"What do you counsel?"

"Whatever people need to hear to realize their potential and make a better world. Larry, for example, needed the courage to shake up his life and get on with making his dreams come true—either that or risk losing his health to a killing job. He's done his homework over the years and, with the right nudge, has shown that he was ready to begin his real life's work."

"More than a nudge," Fran said. "Your idea is brilliant."

Alma smiled. "Thank you. I hope it will be, at any rate. We have to change how we view and tell the news, for the collective good on this overburdened planet. Larry, bless him, seems to be the perfect choice—Mother's choice—for forwarding my idea. I knew she'd place it just right.

"Another case in point is Siddhartan. We share a passion for yoga, and he's interested in developing a program for others in wheelchairs. I'll help him publish it eventually. He's a genius, with more to share now, in ways, than when he was able-bodied."

Fran laughed lightly. "He can dream you doing yoga, what a handy shortcut."

"And a handy inspiration for me, keeping me doing it at times like this when discouragement could immobilize me. I can't dream him though, so I'll visit as often as I can. He has so much to teach me and the world."

"I suppose you'll stay in touch with Angela too, in case Pavla returns to her dreams."

Alma nodded. "Yes, I'm going to meet her soon, and I so look forward to it, quite separate from our dream connection. She's immensely capable, a truth-seer and -sayer of the first order. I've assured her aunt that she'll suffer no ill effects from Serena's disastrous counseling, because Angela's so certain of herself from the deepest inner core. To back it up, I've suggested that they rely on her school counselor for practical advice—she's a spunky and astute woman, just what Angela needs."

"You contacted this counselor?"

"Yes, by phone, with Mrs. Cho's permission. We shared some thoughts and I made a suggestion or two. We agreed that Angela's bound to succeed with or without professional help, as long as she has good health and a supportive home base, which she has in spades. How she'll express her strengths, who knows? It won't matter. Even in a most private role, even as 'just' a mom and homemaker, she's sure to make an important difference. Good parenting always has enormously positive ripple effects."

Fran laughed. "She's certainly rearranged my life from the minute I found her, turning me into 'just a mom and homemaker'. Who else is on your rounds?"

"We know all sorts of prominent people, leaders in many fields. We're always at various stages of meeting and courting them, gaining their confidence. But you see, I'm still thinking as 'we'—Mother, Pavla, and me. I can't cover half the ground we used to because I'm alone now and because much of our work is taxing and risky. I'm too distracted to be as aware and cautious as I should be, so I'll only see established connections and selected new ones for the time being."

"It seems so unfair," Fran said. "You work tirelessly so that everyone you know, me included, ends up better off for knowing you, yet here you are, with life is being unbelievably cruel to you and Pavla."

Alma closed her eyes briefly. "So it seems, but two thoughts come to mind. First, we're also better off for each person we know and trust. It's entirely a two-way street. Most who dream or listen to us go on to greater success, which is why it weighs terribly on me that Gerry McMann suffered so unspeakably, the worst by far in recent times. I grieve more that his suffering was used to intimidate others, and it may yet be used in that way for years to come."

"What a horrid thought," Fran said. "Of course, they'll use it to shut up anyone who's seen Pavla lately or knows where she is. What beasts."

"And that's my second thought: that our enemies don't know us, that's the problem, and there's no hope of either camp being better off until they do. They've rejected the very idea of our existence."

"But why? What have you done?"

"Mary's story is particularly illustrative. It's one of hundreds on a long line of 'beads', as I've said, strung on the thread of parthenogenesis, which you've probably deduced by now. We go back to the beginning of recorded history to Inanna, Nin-Khursag, Nin-tu, Lilith, Eve ... which one was the first in name has become jumbled over time. That's what Mae was sorting out, to make a definitive lineage of begats from our first mother, a line that continues to this day, to Luna."

"Begats begun how?"

"A divine spark, but we make no attribution, for it would be just a name. We're fully human without knowledge of our pre-births, and we're of special creation too, with unique gifts and particular work to do. Since the beginning of written language, for many hundreds of generations, we have been active and to varying degrees successful. We're a long, thin line, and we continue.

"Pavla is the first to figure out the science of our reproduction and trigger her replication using *in vitro* techniques. I thought this ability would strengthen our line by removing that difficult, uncertain process."

"How, in particular?"

"First, by removing the sort of trauma required to force parthenogenesis. It can be brutal, nothing any mother wants for her girl."

"What sort of trauma?"

"It involves great love and great loss, an emotional, psychic, and physical reaction to the point of near-death."

"Such as?"

Alma shook her head. "It's too soon to tell you such details now. The second reason for cheering Pavla's *in vitro* success is the possibility of our having a second daughter should the first be killed. It's getting ever harder to hide and flee in this shrinking world, with recording devices everywhere."

"Why not have two living daughters? Three?"

Alma shook her head. "We must accept the wisdom of our history. There's always only been one. It's obviously part of the plan. Luckily, our one newborn is immensely healthy, and each of us has made it to date, haven't we? To Luna.

"There are rumored tales of the youngest of the line dying and a second being engendered from that horror, although Mae's research hasn't added much to this knowledge. The process is not easily triggered or endured twice.

Pavla's work may uncover and overcome the reasons why, but that won't make it practicable or desirable, unless it's absolutely necessary.

"Even if we dared to have ten children, one is best, since we travel endlessly for our work and to avoid danger. Imagine trying to pack up, dodge, and run with two or more children together, or worse, apart. It's a constant war zone out there for us."

Fran sighed. "Unthinkable. I don't know how you do it."

Alma smiled. "We're blessed with great health and self-healing, but we do get tired. Pavla's achievement has eased one aspect of our lives, yet her success has exposed us to the priesthood of high science, which now controls our fate to a large extent. At least science wants Pavla alive to exploit our physiology. The traditional priesthood requires our removal entirely."

Eyes wide, Fran said, "Everything you say generates a thousand more questions until I could burst. I don't know which to ask first." She took a breath. "The story goes back to 'In the beginning was the word', doesn't it?—the written word. Why then?"

"Perfect question. We appeared when man began smelting metals. There was great good in this, as well as untold powers of destruction. Our first mother gave humankind the gift of written language, for only in transmitting knowledge and wisdom in this way could the deadly effects of metal truck and trade be mitigated, could civility continue and civilization grow.

"It's a double-edged sword. The same alphabet, in all its myriad forms, that educates and saves us from our basest nature also perpetuates recipes for destruction. Fortunately, the benefits outweigh the dangers, and humanity has flourished—in recent times too well. As ever, language and education must be employed in new ways to save us from our rapidly-reproducing, over-consuming selves.

"Advising and enlightening our elite, whose power is global and growing, has never been so important. I do that, as I've told you, and I use the power of storytelling too, on the stage as you've seen, to press some issues. This is my primary passion, while Pavla's is scientific research. Mother was a martial arts, body-mind master. We all must be physically adept, but she was supreme. She expressed herself in many disciplines over her life, all rooted in the strength of Dhyana Zen."

"Dhyana, as in my daughter Dhyana?—that's her full name."

"Yes. Meaning meditation, as I'm sure you know. The penultimate step to enlightenment."

"So why didn't she aim for the top?"

Alma smiled. "That could be a conceit ensuring it's never attained. The view from the penultimate is of the ultimate, and the vision suffices."

Fran laughed. "I invited that, didn't I? Stupid question to ask the walking fount of hundreds of generations of wisdom. I have never felt so small."

"Oh, my dear, we're no different than you in most ways. We're fully flesh and blood, and we learn as you see Luna learning, from the ground up. We have some gifts to be sure: an enlarged language area in our brains, as I've told you, and other physical gifts, one of which is an enhanced immune system, which Rachelle's report touches on—the topic of interest to Pavla's captors that's keeping her alive."

Fran looked puzzled. "What do you mean, 'an enhanced immune system'?"

Alma smiled. "We're very resistant to disease and toxins. We heal quickly. The physical basis for this, I couldn't begin to tell you. Rachelle's report will fill you in a bit, and I believe Pavla sent Mae a private paper or two about her understanding of it, which should be in her drawer here."

"How is it saving her?"

"It's the card she's playing with Trigliani, but don't ask me for details. Pavla's and Mae's researches boggle me as thoroughly as they do you. I needn't burden myself with remembering even a fraction of it—unless that were my bent, which it isn't—because the operative truth remains simple: through our calling and accumulated wisdom, we've had the ear and hearts of many great leaders who have led the world and tried to teach loving, civilized ways of living together. Moses, Buddha, Confucius, Jesus, Mohammed—these are a few and among the most outstanding of all time. Every continent and time has its charismatic wise men who have listened, taught well, and risen to the heights of inspired leadership."

"And you and your ancestors have been with them all along?"

"Everywhere and with every prophet, guru, and holy man who mattered. If we weren't there, unfortunately, they came to naught. Even when we were, measurable success was rare, though spectacular when achieved."

Fran dared say, "This sounds ... I'm sorry, it sounds almost mad. Counter to everything I've ever learned about the march of history, at a fundamental level. At the causal level. You're saying that all the great men, all their great words and deeds, were all inspired by the seven muses—the many-hundred muses, I should say."

Alma nodded.

"But why? Why always underground?"

"You've seen what danger we're in when we surface, when we can be located even for five minutes. We have to work with the nature of the animal. Humanity insists, with rare exceptions, on following dominant males, and we have had little influence changing that. We must operate through the established order of things, at least until society is ready for other patterns. At no time throughout recorded history has the world been ready to accept that divine women or divinely-inspired women can be independently revered leaders, although the great revolution of our time, where women have risen beyond their animal functions and serving daily needs, gives me hope that in this new millennium, my descendents will be able to live and work freely and openly. And advise independent women to the topmost positions."

"But why would anyone want to kill you? You engendered Buddha's wisdom, for example, so he's no less wise for having learned it through you. He didn't mind crediting the paupers and wise men he met in his travels, although I guess it would rock the foundations of a few hundred million followers to give a woman her due."

"Those who can't accept us feel compelled to destroy us. We've been unfailing supporters of the preferred male hierarchy—preferred by many women too—from our beginnings, in every culture that insists on it. Much of our work is to advise men to be thoughtful and wise, as you heard me say as Gaiea on the Athens stage, but we're seen as usurpers, as ones whose very existence undoes the legitimacy of every bastion of male-dominated power, particularly of the major world religions."

"So Mary gives birth to a parthenogenetic daughter, and she and her daughter raise the son and brother Jesus to be the great Christ?"

"They tried and mostly succeeded. He grew to be a truly great man, but he failed in his choice of supporters. Judas did him in, and Paul carried on but tainted his ministry with a deep misogyny. They had their own agendas and notions of what God intended. Jesus, alas, put loyalty to them over his own true understandings, and he paid with this life. He refused to fully follow the advice he was given."

"By his mother? His sister?"

Alma nodded. "And grandmother Anne."

"Who did they listen to? Who do you ... ? I mean, do you hear God?"

Alma smiled. "A certain wisdom seems innate, an inner voice that guides with irresistible force and power. It's deeper than hearing or any of the senses. It's a profound knowing, with this earthly body as its conduit. It's sufficient work—and pleasure—to keep the instrument tuned in every way, so that we might resonate fully with our gifts. We're all conduits really; the trick is to honor the temple and to mind what we pass on.

"Still, our best efforts spin out of control without constant correction. Mohammed, husband of Khadija—one of our line—is a good example. He listened to her, but his understanding was imperfect, his transcription worse still, and his teachings among countless millions are now horribly skewed by power-mad clerics. Mother risked her life trying to right some of this vast misinterpretation and misrule."

Alma stood up to stretch her legs. "We've covered a lot of ground. Let it filter and settle in. You've got the core truth of it now. All the rest is details."

Fran sat immobile, her eyes surveying Mae's massive piles of work. Slowly, she rose and, in awe, read aloud the names on the spines of files within view. "Anath, Cybele, Zikum, Dictynna, Chokmah, Fo-Hi, Tiamat, Isis, Pessinuatica, Neith, Persephone, Mater Matuta, Pele, Miriam, Gaiea, Leda, Sophia, Varimate-Takara, Callileach, Khadija, Teleia ... and these are just a few of the thousands of names that make up hundreds of generations."

Alma nodded her head. "Every continent. Every society. We're on the move continually and have lived everywhere. We are maiden, mother, and crone. We're all here, as many as Mae could gather over a lifetime. Some of us have achieved splendidly; many could do no more than survive, but that's an achievement too. We live; we breathe; we work as best we can."

Agape, Fran said, "Luna ... my God, she scares the wits out of me. The latest of the line. It could be snapped like that. Luna should be raised in a fortress, on an island, in a place where she's guaranteed to be safe."

Alma laughed. "Oh no, experience makes clear the folly of that. Safety is in the most ordinary of healthy beginnings, living among millions, hundreds of millions. She's a normal, everyday baby in nearly every way, and the more normal and everyday her upbringing, the better she'll be equipped to apply her talents and stay close to the pulse. You live next door to the greatest power center of our time, and she needs to know this region well because she'll likely work a lot from here when she's ready. There's comfort and security in such familiarity.

"She has Nikos now, who showed me his colors when we traveled in Greece. For her, as for all children, good male influence is irreplaceable.

"And you ...." Alma smiled. "You have many positive traits by which Luna will thrive. Your ability to make decisions quickly, to assess situations, then get into or out of them without hesitating, could be vital to her safety. I know through your work and talking to Larry that your instincts this way are spot on, and when you're committed to something, it's total, no doubts.

"You're worldly. You've found your way in many diverse societies and, with admirable determination and grace, have gotten to the essentials needed for in-depth, quality reports. You've survived and thrive in arduous working conditions, undaunted by challenge. You're globally very aware and nicely rooted here now.

"I'm well aware that you weren't a full-time mother, but you're ready to take on that role that now—with gusto, I'm sure. Dhyan's is very much your girl, a strong, bright spirit who'll make a fine big sister.

"And you can teach Luna from Mae's work as you learn yourself. In total, this life can't match Pavla raising her daughter, but it's as safe as can be and full of good, dedicated, informed hearts."

Flushed with this assessment Fran said, "Thank you, but ... I mean, you've got all kinds of other contacts. Why not someone you know better?"

"I've considered this thoroughly. I trust you, Fran. You and Nikos. On my list of worries ... well, you're not on it."

Fighting to contain her emotions, Fran said, "I'm glad, and I'm ... Alma, I'm feeling very overwhelmed, very lightheaded and daunted."

"Don't. Let's call it a day."

"Is that all it is? You change the world for me and call it a day?"

Alma nodded. "And tomorrow's another. One at a time."

After Alma left Mae's house, Fran sat dazed on the paper-stacked sofa. She stared at Rachelle's report, unable to focus her thoughts sufficiently to reach for it. Uncounted minutes later, she forced herself to plunge into Rachelle's account of life at the sticky center of Trigliani's web.

◆ ◆ ◆

Dear Alma:

I was going to be coy and use encoded names throughout this but so much else is telling, why bother? This is a straight-up report, therefore, of what I know and have gathered so far.

First is a transcription of my interchange with Trigliani, with descriptive notes. I had a mike on me and I'm sure he was taping too, for his nasty bosses. What a game.

I met Boreli and Krebs at Boreli's lab. [Alma wrote 'Luigi, w/mustache' above Boreli, 'Henry' above Krebs.] We had a tight meeting, not very productive. Krebs remains suspicious of me—no, professionally cautious is more accurate—but Boreli was surprisingly forthcoming after Krebs left. He's glad I'm on the team and he's grateful as I am that Trigliani has some caring for Pavla. He was alarmed enough after his first meetings with her that he scribbled pages of notes. He gave me copies and I've worked them up into section 2 of this report.

Section 3 is a copy from Trigliani of the origins of Pavla's name, which he apparently read aloud when first introducing her to Boreli and Krebs. B put me on to it; T gladly shared it with me. Just to let you know what they know.

Finally, three postscripts, for what they're worth.

Regards, Rachelle

Section 1: DuPont's trip with Trigliani to the country mansion and lab. [Rachel's report as per pages 215-219]

Section 2: Boreli and Krebs meet Pavla

Boreli and Krebs first saw Pavla in the dining room of the country mansion just after 7 p.m. on the evening of the abduction. They had no idea then that she was there against her will. They were seated already, waiting for Trigliani to arrive. Big, deluxe room. Gourmet meal in the offing. Krebs at the foot of the table, Boreli to one side.

Trigliani escorted Pavla into the dining room. Boreli said they looked like a couple arriving at a French restaurant, she in a black sheath, pearls and hair up, T all dapper as usual. He seated her across from Boreli then took the head of the table.

Trigliani introduced Pavla by reading some notes about the origin of her name (Section 3) then introduced Boreli and Krebs. No background needed for them; she knows their publications and recognized them from published photos. T doesn't put his mugshot anywhere.

The new cult of the science stardom, she said—not too wise when you're up to no good. Boreli liked that about her, her sharp eye and tongue. Krebs was sour but that's Krebs.

Trigliani started the meal with a prayer, thanking the Almighty Father for this fateful day and meal then something about being honored by this opportunity to keep the sanctity of God's trinity—the inviolate perfection of Father, Son and Holy Spirit—pure and forevermore. And thanks for the food, good health, etc., amen.

Boreli is a practicing Roman Catholic, Krebs is almost—high Anglican—but a holiday church-goer now. They both closed their eyes and bowed their heads during grace but B peeked. Pavla sat with her head up, eyes on Trigliani.

Fancy meal ensued, lots of courses. Discreet waiters, good wine. Pavla scarcely ate. Trig invited B and K to query Pavla as they pleased. She was very cool. T said she was tired after a long day but would do her best to cooperate.

Boreli thought this odd but ignored it. He was concerned about getting to the point, not to tire her further. He told her that they were attempting parthenogenesis on human subjects and had been working in the lab at this location for several months with the understanding that she'd join them in early February. That didn't happen, apparently because she was not yet convinced to come on board so Boreli wanted to say up front that he was glad she was finally on the team.

She sat like a stone. Krebs spilled what they knew—that she'd reproduced herself parthenogenetically, based on hair samples from her and her baby. She looked surprised and asked Trigliani, What hair samples?

He said the ones she provided when they flew together to Rome. From her hairbrush, remember? Pavla clenched her jaw hard with that while Krebs launched into their need to discuss her work on maternal centrosomes, meiotic spindles and the polar body. He went on about skewed brain growth and premature death in parthenogenetically created mice, then how, in the second meiotic division using human ova, they'd reactivated the polar body but something's wrong in form or perhaps in energetics .... (Sorry. Shop talk. I'll try to limit it but I think that some of what's happening technically should be on the record.)

At this point Trigliani urged Pavla to eat, drink and enjoy the meal. Krebs boldly said that, while she might be tired and even unwell, it was obvious that she was resisting, which he found odd because her work is as proscribed as theirs and far more dangerous and illicit because she's done what they're only trying to do.

That got her talking—angrily. The hair samples, she said, could be genetically identical because they came from one source: her. Trigliani said that analysis of composition and telomeres made it certain that one is from an infant, one from an adult and that denying what she's achieved was not quite the cooperation he'd hoped for.

Since it wasn't working with them questioning her Trigliani reversed tactics and invited her to question them. They ate in near silence—just small talk while Pavla picked at her food—right up to dessert then Pavla asked to be excused.

Trigliani laughed at that—a question, at last—and bluntly said No.

Boreli was really squirming by then but couldn't cut the veneer of nice-nice to ask what really was going on. There was more awkward silence then Pavla demanded that Trigliani tell how he'd tracked her.

Trigliani said that their paths had crossed while traveling and the root of the word 'travel' means 'to err', and he was her 'knight errant'. Then he got vague and said a tip-off here, airline info' there, a little bug tied to GPS, that's how he homed in on her.

She asked who planted the bug. At last Boreli found his brain and tongue and demanded an explanation. Pavla said she was attacked, knocked out and dragged there although she was immensely grateful for being taken alive. That got Boreli screaming, What the hell is going on?

Trigliani said that their supporters wanted her and her baby killed on sight. He made sure she wasn't harmed although she was not so considerate in return. Apparently she made some quick neck-breaking move on one of her captors, the son of a big cheese, and rendered him quadriplegic. Now this overlord's demanding she be reduced to tissue samples. Trigliani's the only one between her continuing to breathe or becoming frozen meat.

He insisted that the baby be unharmed too and this soft touch resulted in the child getting away. That ticked the bosses and Trigliani said they could be vengeful. Even Krebs was getting perturbed over this.

If the injured man died T said he had orders to kill Pavla immediately and the guy wasn't listed as stable at that point. Until he was certain to live his father would be singing the same Kill Her tune. Protecting Pavla from the boss's bad temper is one of the reasons Trigliani keeps her hidden so well now.

Both K and B agreed that the whole setup was an outrage and preposterous, heinous and unscrupulous. Trigliani reminded them that their clandestine work in human parthenogenetic research didn't have them up for sainthood and if they wanted to continue there would be risk. Danger. It comes with the territory.

Boreli threw in the towel then—his napkin on the table at any rate and said he wanted out. Trigliani laughed and pulled a handgun from inside his lapel. He pointed it at Boreli and told him to sit down, which B did. Trigliani warned them that they could work the situation to their advantage and live long lives achieving fame and fortune or they could exit at a moment's notice with an obituary in the daily news. Accidents happen all the time.

Boreli has been very cooperative since then. Little wonder too that he's so keen that I know everything he and Krebs do. It puts me in the same danger they're in although I'm deep enough on my own. B and I agreed by wink and nod to tell the truth somewhere, thus this report. He trusts my discretion at least as much as I trust his. We'll hang separately, as the saying goes, if we don't hang together.

Pavla's got a little more to bargain with than Boreli, Krebs and I do. A lot really. After this gun incident at the table she refused to tell anything of her parthenogenetic work, reasoning that she'll be killed whether she divulges or not so why bother? She struck a deal, however, offering to share some other research she's doing—spin-off stuff—with world recognition guaranteed for the team, kudos for their patrons. Plus it might help them find the fountain of youth and live to be 120.

She didn't fill them in about this other possibility at the dining table, begging off with a headache—a humdinger no doubt after what she'd been through. She promised to tell them the next morning.

Trigliani had B and K escorted by gun-toting goons to their quarters, which was a first. They'd been free to come and go before then but they needed this little reminder that bolting would be a very bad idea. T hasn't been this heavy-handed since. Pavla's research and their own ambitions and fears are enough to keep them behaving themselves.

Boreli guesses that Trigliani saw Pavla to her room—such a wonderfully solicitous and opportunistic host. Poor sod. He's the one with Stockholm Syndrome. Boreli heard a vault-like door close shortly after he got to his own room, probably Pavla being slammed in for the night. [Note in Alma's hand: Timing matches Angela's report of P going black.]

At eight the next morning Trigliani and Pavla appeared in the laboratory. Boreli and Krebs were there already, eating a light breakfast set out for their arrival. They were in their lab coats ready to go. She wore a black keikogi pant suit, probably what she was abducted in, not the gussied up dress the Trig had arranged for her the night before. He was his usual debonair self, no lab coats for the prince and his lady.

Boreli offered her a muffin and coffee. She ate that morning to his relief—Trigliani's too. Then he announced that the bishop's son, so to speak, was stable and fairly certain to live. Further he'd thought it over during the night and realized that such bright minds would settle in and work better if any and all their questions could be answered so he invited them to ask him whatever they wished of any part of their arrangements.

Krebs right off wanted to know what sort of *mafiosos* Trigliani's patrons were. T mumble-mouthed something similar to what he told me—nice big corporation, lots of money, don't bite the hand that feeds you.

Boreli asked what Pavla had done to earn their enmity, their wish to destroy her without trace. Trigliani neatly answered that it was nothing personal rather the role she plays, what she represents. He said she destabilizes the present and desired world order.

He then said something Boreli found fascinating. Trigliani quoted Princess Diana in her famous TV interview, saying that her enemies were 'the gray men of the palace'. He said that there are gray men in far more powerful organizations than mere monarchy and they order the world as we know it. Just as Diana dared not identify her gray persecutors—the names she knew or could guess—Pavla Blanca is at the mercy of her own gray men.

Boreli liked the imagery but confessed that he still didn't get it. Trigliani told him he never would so stop wasting his time thinking about it. They were there to do science and this glimmer of the inner workings of the bigger world is tangential and inconsequential. They have a golden opportunity to further their own goals, maybe even win a Nobel Prize for it if Pavla's research panned out. Better than pointless death, Trigliani said. Such a way with words.

Boreli was still fighting, wondering how they could work under such constraints when he'd thought they were going to be a willing congress of like minds, meeting freely.

Trigliani assured him that there's no such thing, not at that level. Not if it matters. And their work would matter, focus on that.

Pavla got practical and suggested that since they had a lot of ground to cover they should get down to work. Trigliani embraced that, just his no-nonsense kind of woman.

She led the men to the lab's whiteboard and told them that she would share with them her research on her immune system, which has far superior resistance than that of the average human. Her studies are preliminary but indicate that the mitochondrial elements that we all share from a common matrilineal source can be made to mimic a nuclear DNA-RNA process that is requisite for human parthenogenetic reproduction—a process that leading researchers are far from discovering yet.

(Here comes the jargon. Bear with me or skip.) She's discovered that this nuclear process serves to correct, for example, the skewed brain growth of parthenogenetically produced mice and it also confers, as an apparent by-product, an *a priori* immunity to nearly every disease and condition induced by foreign agents including the ability to chelate or otherwise denature and excrete a wide spectrum of oxidants and toxins. It plays a role in healing as well—tissue regeneration, which holds hope for curing all sorts of injuries including severed spinal cords. For example, a spin-off benefit might be something that gets the quad' goon walking again. Smart move on her part. The p.o.'d dad had better keep her alive. She's his best hope to get his boy on his feet again.

She told them that the work would be hard and it would take years, even going all out as a team. And she warned them that it might not work at all—that's how real scientific exploration goes. Getting the more basic, immutable and singularly dedicated mitochondrial DNA to take on a subtle and complex function of a mutant nuclear DNA-RNA process conferred during parthenogenetic meiosis could prove insurmountable although she says she's worked out several possible means and mechanisms, which by close study, experimentation and refinement might reveal step-by-step how to make this giant leap.

Pavla's ace is that she's miles ahead of them in this research and she promised she'll keep a healthy lead. B's and K's position would be to help solve problems with the bits and pieces of her research while she'll mind the tie-in mechanisms and big picture, which they wouldn't likely know or guess without her inside knowledge. Luckily she shared enough with me so I could bargain my way in although she's a long way ahead of my inklings.

Krebs asked how they'd win the Nobel when she held and withheld the winning cards as she pleased. Boreli thought this was a dumb question and he loved the way Pavla nailed him. She said that they'd negotiate. That things would change, they always do. They'd publish jointly with her as Janet McElroy and everyone listed alphabetically so they'd get credit along the way. Then she asked if they should start at the kindergarten level of her studies and work toward graduation or should they argue about the color of caps and gowns right off?

She scored more points with Trigliani for that. B too. T chose the suggested kindergarten starting point and she went into detail. Forgive the jargon again. Important stuff to replication nuts.

We'll spend the first year or two reviewing normal meiotic functions and the replication of mitochondria because they're so imperfectly understood at key junctures that even this preliminary work will be groundbreaking. After we've solved these little riddles we'll fine-tune our understanding of parthenogenetic meiosis in naturally occurring and induced models across a wide variety of species.

This is the springboard from which we can launch our understanding of Pavla's mutated expression with its attendant immuno-superiority, leading to the next step: how Pavla's normal nuclear division differs sufficiently to confer life-long protection.

Typical specimens don't have this but mitochondrial replication from the pure maternal line holds promise. The quantum leap to inducing and controlling this ability in typical mitochondrial specimens up to and including human—well, it's possible, it's probable and it can be done. She concluded kindergarten lesson one by saying that this journey of a thousand miles begins like all others, with the first step.

Then she asked to be familiarized with the laboratory, equipment and provision possibilities in case they had to order or make some unique supplies. That's when Trigliani said B and K would continue working both at that lab and their own facilities but Pavla wouldn't be working there. This surprised her.

He said she'd direct them from a remote location—not on any map, incommunicado with anyone but him. No unusual means of communicating would be allowed either so don't even dream it. T emphasized 'dream' and Boreli caught Pavla's wince but then, why wouldn't a captive dream of every way possible to communicate and escape? Trigliani assured her that she'd be comfortable, safe and as productive as she wished to be.

She didn't question or protest the arrangements. She just picked up some markers and started filling the whiteboard with diagrams and equations to illustrate preliminary aspects of her DNA-RNA studies—the writing I saw when I visited the lab.

Section 3: Trigliani's notes re: Pavla's birthplace

Pavla Blanca's name was bequeathed for her birthplace at White Sands in New Mexico. An Apache creation myth tells us that the Giver of Life warned the Apache people of a great deluge, directing White Painted Woman to safety in an abalone shell. She survived the flood and the shell beached at White Sands. She gave birth to two children, Son of the Sun and Child of the Water. [Alma's note in the margin: Sons often added/substituted. Ref. Buddha, Jesus, et al.]

This woman was the Apache's greatest figure of power. They also called her Changing Woman. She knew how to rid the world of evil and she never aged but was endlessly recreated just as the sands are endlessly renewed.

Spaniard Hernando de Luna marched to White Sands with Conquistador Coronado in the mid-1500s. He brought his fiancée Manuela. Apache warriors killed the entire party. Manuela's ghost can still be seen at sunset, her white wedding gown blowing like sand in the wind. She is known as Pavla Blanca. To see her once is good luck, twice is bad luck, three times brings death.

Section 4: Three postscripts

P.S.1: Boreli told me that Trigliani concluded by asking, Is this not the source of your name? Pavla didn't answer but rather asked, Death to whom? And who's counting? This was Boreli's first intimation at the start of the meal that they were playing a deadly game but didn't get it at the time.

P.S.2: Boreli learned from Trigliani that Pavla's mother was born in Nepal at Lumbini—Buddha's birthplace. Her grandmother was born at Delphi and her great-grandmother was born on Haida Gwaii (native name for the Queen Charlotte Islands) in a sacred spot. Her daughter Luna was born at Pipestone National Monument in Minnesota.

P.S.3: Gave a copy of the following to Boreli:

"[A story] of Lakota origin, says that the first pipe was brought to the ancestors by White Buffalo Calf Woman, a messenger from the Great Spirit, thus forming a link between those on Earth and the spirit world. She taught them that the pipe—the bowl engraved with a buffalo calf—joins land and sky, and its smoke carries messages to the Great Spirit. She

showed them how to pray with the pipe, how to decorate themselves when praying to Mother Earth, and above all else, to use it as a peace pipe to be smoked before all ceremonies. She taught them the seven sacred rites, including the Inipi (the cleansing sweat lodge), the Wiwanyaq Wachipi (the sundance of thanksgiving) and the Ishuatua Awicalowan (the ceremony to prepare a girl for womanhood). In this last ritual, the girl is honoured like a towering tree; she is the source of strength, and like the Mother Earth, will bear children, raising them in a spiritual way."
"Pipestone National Monument: Quarry of Peace"
Spirit of the Land: Sacred Places of North America
by Courtney Milne

"Oh Luna," Fran sighed heavily as she finished reading Rachelle's report and rose to file it in Pavla's dresser drawer in Maya's old room. "Sweet babe, White Buffalo Calf Woman. Tall order."

Fran found Maya's bottom drawer solidly full of notes and photographs. She took a cursory look through the neat stacks of paper, much of it bearing Maya's handwriting. She had worked very small, to fit a long and spectacular lifetime into a single drawer. The order was clear: latest material on the right, the beginning on the bottom left. Fran took out the left-most pile, about a foot deep, and placed it beside her. She would start reading and scanning from Maya's birth.

Alma's second-up drawer was three-quarters full. Fran quickly flipped through a few pages. Alma's notes, too, were nicely compact.

Pavla's drawer was half full, with the same Spartan use of paper. Fran realized she'd have to scan and condense Rachelle's report so it would take as little room as possible. Putting it on CD was one answer. Being able to read CDs, however, would always require high-tech equipment, and without the right working machines over the next centuries and millennia, the information would be lost. Microfilms might be better because they could always be read with low-tech magnifying power.

"Yes," Fran muttered with relief. She'd start by putting everything on microfilm, then down the road might OCR scan them to make CDs. Solving this pressing technology problem cleared her mind for the huge task ahead.

Fran looked through Luna's nearly empty top drawer, which had photos of her at Pipestone, including some similar to the one Pavla had shown Maya in Tehran. "Luna Blanca" was explained as the obvious White Moon, linked to Evr-Opé, meaning true, open or full face—the goddess Europe, one of many names used for iconic woman in her fertile, fruitful phase. One of their line was doubtless the first Europe but that file wasn't in the drawer. Fran made a mental note to keep an eye out for it in Mae's vast work. "So far to go, little one," Fran said. "So much depending on me and Nikos and all the luck in the world."

Fran backtracked to look through Pavla's accomplishments and photos, but her eyes were swimming and her head was too full to take in another scintilla of information. She put Rachelle's report in the drawer for now, shut it tight, and left the bedroom, closing the door behind her.

As she locked the front door, leaving Mae's house of muses and mysteries, she muttered, "Tomorrow. Just another day."

Shadows stretched long on another hot, late-spring morning. A new gold Buick drove up to Fran's house and parked at the curb. Dhyan hopped out of the front passenger seat while Cindy turned off the car, the radio, the fan, put on the brake, dropped the keys in her purse, checked the back seat, and looked for something in the glove box.

Dhyan rolled her eyes in frustration, muttering, "Oh c'mon."

With pinched face, Cindy slowly got out and pressed the remote to lock all the doors and trunk. She checked a door to make sure all were locked.

"For Pete's sake!" Dhyan sputtered.

Cindy shot her a look, then warned her, "It's easier to drive home than drive here, you know."

"I thought brides are supposed to glow, not glower."

"That's it! That's it, we're heading home."

"That's what I'm doing," Dhyan said, bounding to the front door. "It's where the heart is." She pushed the buzzer and knocked. "Open up! Open up, or I'll huff and I'll puff and I'll ...."

Fran opened the door. With surprise and delight, she said, "Well, blow me down! Cindy too. This is wonderful. What's the occasion?"

Dhyan leapt and twirled into the living room. Cindy minced in, forcing a thin smile. She said, "Ralph requested that I bring Dhyan by to announce her prep school plans in person. The boys are at their music lessons. We have half an hour."

Nikos appeared from the kitchen carrying Luna dressed in pink T-shirt and pink-striped overalls. Lord Byron danced at their feet. Dhyan said, "Hey, a baby! Wow, I mean, you still have her. And a puppy! Boy, you sure fill up the holes fast when I'm gone. Who are these guys anyway?"

Fran laughed with more joy than she'd felt in weeks. Luna's eyes stuck on Dhyan. Her face lit up, and she clapped her hands happily. Nikos said, "Pat-a-cake, pat-a-cake ...."

Dhyan joined in, "Baker's man, bake me a cake as fast as you can. Roll it and poll it and mark it with a 'B' and thro-o-ow-w-w it in the oven for baby and me." She rolled her arms, then threw them wide. Luna squealed and giggled and started the game again.

Dhyan asked Fran, "What's her name? She's so cute."

"Luna. And the dog is Mae's." Quietly, she said, "You know Mae died?"

Dhyan's smile faded; she shook her head.

"A couple of weeks ago."

"Aw. What happened?"

"She fell, got pneumonia. Died two weeks ago."

Byron leapt up Dhyan's legs. Fran said, "Dhyan, meet Lord Byron; Lord Byron, this is the one, the only, the very best Dhyana Roma in the whole world."

Dhyan squatted to scratch his ears and fight off wet kisses. She laughed, "This is a madhouse. You've all gone nuts."

Cindy snorted slightly.

Nikos passed Luna to Fran. "I will get coffee or tea." He asked Cindy, "Which would you prefer? I have made rhubarb pie, fresh from the garden. Would you like some?"

"Coffee," Cindy said. "No pie, thank you. My wedding dress, you know. Size eight, the exact same as I wore before."

Nikos disappeared into the kitchen.

Dhyan said exaggeratedly, "Same old dress, same old bride, not an ounce of pudge to spoil the perfect day." Cindy looked wounded and petulant.

Fran said, "Best wishes, Cindy, I really mean it. It's always exciting to start over. Any way I can help?"

"Thank you. With Dhyan going away to school, I might just need a hand, although an ex-wife helping the next, well ...."

Dhyan said, "Prep school, Mom, picture it—me in the New Hampshire woods, howling at the moon."

Fran laughed. "Have you warned them you're coming?"

"Oh yeah. New Hampton, New Hampshire." She quoted their motto: "'In a world that expects you to fit in, we teach you to stand out.'"

Fran grinned. "I'm so glad they're going to draw out my little shrinking violet."

Dhyan laughed, "They won't know what hit them."

"You do me proud, kid. I expect big mouths to get big grades."

"You bet. I can't wait!" She looked at Luna, made a surprise face, and said, "O-o-oh yeah!" at her, which got a twinkly smile in return. "I can't believe it. Mom and Nikos with a baby. Luna what? Don't say 'Tic'."

"Luna Blanca. Moon white, moonbeam, moonshine."

"Weird. I mean it's cool, but it's ... different."

"So's Luna. She's as bright and wonderful and fun as you were."

"Will you have her when I'm home for Christmas holidays? I can stay here while Cindy and Dad do the honeymoon thing."

Fran looked surprised at Cindy. "Really? That's great!"

"Well, one has to be practical, and since you've set up house with a baby and ...."

"Shacked up with a foster kid," Fran couldn't resist saying. "The American dream."

Nikos brought out a lovely tray of coffee, everything matching with low-cal biscuits on the side. This and his quiet charm won Cindy's approval. "How nice," she said. "Dhyan will be fine here for a few weeks."

"She will, indeed," Fran said.

Dhyan asked, "So will the baby be here?"

Fran said, "I don't know. If all goes well, no, but then again, maybe yes. And we'll probably be moving into Mae's old house as soon as we get it cleaned up a bit."

"No way! What's it like? Mae was so awesome, the most totally awesome old lady."

Fran smiled. "Yeah. It's funky and junky, as awesome as Mae was. I'm going to work on her estate, with Larry still as my boss. I'm out of the news business for a year, maybe longer."

Dhyan exclaimed, "Really? Man, I can't believe it. I mean, if there's gonna be a roving Gypsy reporter, it's gotta be me, right?"

"The Roma by-line's all yours, darling."

Cindy tightened.

Dhyan clenched a victory fist. "Yes!"

"Angela's doing just fine," the school counselor told Mr. and Mrs. Cho in her small, bright office, which suited her small frame and bright eyes. "She doesn't pay full attention, granted, but she says she has things to think about instead of doing exactly as told. She's not willful for its own sake, so I wouldn't worry about it. Her marks are good enough—not brilliant, but she's imaginative and creative—and she's got lots of friends. She can be an imp at times, but we don't want to repress that in a child."

Mrs. Cho smiled. "No, but she's still a bit disruptive at home, secretive with our other kids. We're wondering if we should try regular counseling again, from someone she likes, like you."

The counselor smiled. "Well, I'm flattered. I like her too. I could see her on a set schedule if you want me to, but I've had two chats with her, and I don't think it's necessary. She seems happy and well adjusted. What's the biggest contention at home?"

"It sounds strange, but she had this recurring dream about some women and a baby. That's what we've figured out anyway from some of the oddball things she's told us and lets slip sometimes. When our other kids tease her about this, she goes wild. Or sullen and withdrawn—all over some sleeping, dreaming nonsense."

"Hm. What kind of 'oddball things' does she say?"

"Just stuff maybe a little too smart for her age. Good advice sometimes. She likes to try foreign languages too, not from any source we know of, although it really doesn't sound like she's babbling."

The counselor said, "Well, if she's got a gift for languages, why not get her some help? We've got a Spanish club here; they meet at lunch hour. I can introduce her."

The Chos agreed.

"Now, back to the sleeping, dreaming thing. Does she have her own bedroom?"

"No, she's in with Joanne, our oldest girl."

"Any chance she could have her own room?"

The Chos looked at each other. Mr. Cho said, "Only if we gave up the den."

Mrs. Cho said, "We'd have to move everything. I don't know, I guess we could do it."

"I'd really recommend you give it a try. And I'll talk with her further as I've said, but ..... ." She leaned forward. "May I tell you something about her that I think is remarkable? Something that doubtless helped her survive the whole crash ordeal."

Chos listened attentively.

"As you know, some people have a more powerful sense of themselves and their perceptions than others do. They trust their experiences and reactions—the ones who can't be duped into saying that the emperor has clothes when clearly he doesn't. No amount of coercion or counseling will dissuade them, at least without breaking their spirits a little, sometimes a lot. They're a five to ten percent minority, and I'd put Angela in this lucky group. It's a tremendous strength, and it's always a lot easier to work with than against."

Mr. Cho laughed. "Well, you've got that right. She's totally sure of herself, even when she's unsure, if you know what I mean."

The counselor smiled. "So why not try solving the sleeping, dreaming problem by accommodating it?"

Mr. Cho shook his head. "We don't want to spoil her."

The counselor asked, "Did Joanne have her own room before Angela moved in? Did Angela have her own bedroom in her parents' home?"

The Chos nodded.

"So this is returning to the status quo, and from both girls' perspectives, it's fair."

Mrs. Cho asked, "You think it's that simple?"

"For this one problem, it could be. It's certainly worth a try." The counselor stood up. "Other problems will require other solutions, of course—like getting her into the Spanish club. In general, I wouldn't be worried if I were you. Your caring is very obvious, and from talking with Angela, I'd say you've got a lucky, happy household."

"Thank you," the Chos chorused, rising to go.

"My pleasure," the counselor said, then shook each of their hands. "Call me any time."

Mr. and Mrs. Cho returned home to Angela and Joanne playing "Monopoly" in the living room. Both girls sat on cushions on the floor in the thick of play money, deeds, houses, hotels, Community Chest, and Chance cards. Angela kept neat stacks of bills; Joanne bunched hers in a messy pile.

Mr. Cho said a quick hello and disappeared. Mrs. Cho sat on the sofa and said warmly, "This is nice. Thank you for babysitting, Joanne."

"*Baby*sitting," Joanne said. "Wa-wa."

Angela stuck out the tip of her tongue.

"Stop it, you two," Mrs. Cho said. "You were getting along just fine before I came in. Don't put on a show for me." She took a breath, then said, "The school counselor says maybe we should give you each a bedroom, what do you say? One stays put, one gets the den."

"Wo-o ho-o!" Angela cheered as she picked up the dice. "My own room!"

"You mean out of my room!" Joanne said. "You get the stinky little den."

"Sh-h," Mrs. Cho said. "Is that okay with you, Angela?"

Angela nodded enthusiastically.

Mrs. Cho continued, "We'll paint it and fix it up, any color you want. We can start this weekend; you'll be an independent woman by next."

"Purple," Angela said enthusiastically. "With yellow glow stars."

"Oh yuk," Joanne said.

"Purple's fine," Mrs. Cho said, getting up to leave the room. "Light purple. Now you two keep playing nicely, and I'll bring you some cookies."

Angela closed her eyes and shook the dice. "Park Place, Park Place," she wished as she threw. A four and two came up. "Yes!" Angela exclaimed and "vroomed" her little roadster from Pacific Place six squares to Park Place. She held out her hand to Joanne and said, "I will buy two houses. No, four. Then next time, I'll buy a hotel." She counted out the required money from her tidy stash and handed it to Joanne.

"You're just lucky," Joanne said, sticking out her tongue.

"Yeah, yeah, yeah," Angela agreed, arms dancing in the air, then used her tongue to push her upper lip to her nose. Both girls giggled. Joanne flared her nostrils; Angela crossed her eyes. They made more faces and laughed until their sides seized up, and they rolled on the floor in shared delight.

◆ ◆ ◆

To: rdegros@.umgen.edu
From: trigliani@homeport.com
Date: Fri, Dec 15, 10:51:22 -0500
Subject: equipment request
Rachelle: I need a top-quality photograph of the moon for grad student's work on cyclic linkage phenomena. Would like to borrow your lab's camera. Please call my office after 22:00. DT.

◆ ◆ ◆

Rachelle worked at her lab until the last of her graduate students left before midnight. She telephoned Trigliani from her office, a glassed-in corner that held wall-to-wall books, journals, and reprinted scientific papers, which doubled as a library for her students and technicians.

"DuPont here. Didn't I tell you I don't lend my camera?"

Trigliani spoke from an austere office in the beige corridor of the country mansion. A blue, white, and gold portrait of the Virgin Mary watched over him. One shelf held books about the life, theology, and manifestations of the Madonna. "Perhaps you did. I am sorry. Perhaps you would you kindly take the photograph for me? I want a high-resolution shot of the moon, full to three-quarter face."

"What for?"

"An assistant has suggested working on luteal hormones tied to lunar phase."

"Assuming they're in synch'. Why such good quality?"

"If you must know, it is for a gift. A Christmas gift for a young assistant who has had this good idea. To encourage this aspect of our study."

"Cute. So you get the luteal and lunar cycles in synch' and look for what exactly?"

"We have them in synch'. Get me the shot, and I will tell you."

Rachelle sighed exasperatedly. "Why is everything a cat and mouse game with you?"

"Why do you keep forgetting who is the mouse?"

"The mouse with the camera."

Trigliani clipped, "I am sorry, this is too big an imposition. I will find some other means to get this *lunar* shot."

Suddenly, Rachelle understood. "Ah-h-h, I see." Carefully, she said, "Of course, the moon affects every aspect within our research, mine too. Very clever. You think you're running circles around me, Trig, but I'm way ahead of you. I'll not only get you the shot, I'll print it for you and deliver it right to your clever little helper too. Framed and wrapped. Just tell me what size print and where to take it."

Trigliani laughed. "That is kind of you, but no thank you. I will arrange pickup. Just get it done—and soon. Mark the envelope 'Luteal Tie-In'."

"Pushy, pushy. I could start to like that about you."

"High praise. We may yet become a close and trusting team."

Rachelle snorted. "Dream on."

"I shall. Good night."

♦ ♦ ♦

"Fran," Alma said on the phone, "Rachelle called. Trigliani wants a recent photograph of Luna."

Fran took the call in her office. Her eyes widened. "Oh my God. You trust him?"

"I don't know, but I trust Rachelle. She thinks it's okay."

"What does he want it for?"

"A gift, he says, a Christmas gift for an associate."

"Wow. Lucky Pavla if he's on the level. Follow the moon shot and get right to your girl."

"Oh no, I wouldn't dare."

"Or to Trigliani's evil bosses."

"Exactly. Either way could be a trap. On the chance the photo's for Pavla, I think we should provide it. Trigliani wants a single shot, full to three-quarter face, no unnecessary details—meaning traceable clues, of course. Can you take the picture in the next day or two, using a good quality camera? Digital preferably, then print a copy from your computer—no commercial development and no e-mailing."

"Of course."

"I'll pick up the print and get it to Rachelle, she'll take it from there."

"Alma, this is scary."

"Yes, but it could be wonderful too. Focus on that. And have fun doing it."

"You bet. The big fun will be with Byron. He and Luna are inseparable, and he'll be insufferable. He'll wiggle into every shot, and if we hold him back or shut him away, he'll howl and she'll cry."

"Fran, that's brilliant. Put him in, please. That's all Pavla needs to know."

"Assuming she gets it. Assuming it's a kindness, not a trap or a test or torture. Oh man, this is a big act of trust."

Alma paused, then said, "More like faith."

"O-o-oh, look at the giant Simba!" Cindy said, one of a dozen passengers in a van driving through the groomed hills and vales of Safari World. She'd wrapped herself in red, white, and blue stars and stripes from pop top, shorts, and sandals down to star-spangled toenails. Ralph wore a safari shirt, shorts, and hiking boots. They sat in the front right seat with the best view on board.

Just yards beyond the van, a prime male lion yawned and stretched. "Isn't he beautiful, just like the movie."

Ralph smiled. "Did you know that lions mate dozens of times a day?"

"Oh, you naughty boy!" she said, taking a playful swat at him, then looking around to see if the strangers nearby appreciated their banter. A few glanced at them. She snuggled in close, hugging his arm. She raised her voice to say, "Isn't this just the best holiday and the best honeymoon ever?"

The driver-guide looked back and asked, "You're honeymooners? Alright!"

Cindy giggled.

Over the P.A. system the driver said, "Folks, we got newlyweds aboard. They'll want to know all about the antics of our leos. There are children here, so let me just tell you that they're nature's best lovers, no doubt."

Cindy scrunched Ralph's arm again and said in a little girl voice, "No, they're not. You are."

He smiled and kissed her cheek.

Cindy sang out, "This wonderful man wanted to go to Africa for our honeymoon, but it's just so ... you know, far and unsafe, so we came here. It's just the best, just like the real thing." As the van rounded a corner and drove within a few feet of half a dozen huge, lazy beasts, she said "Oh, look, a whole big pride of lovers."

The driver laughed. "That's right. They sleep, they mate; they mate, they sleep. A honeymoon everyday. Life is hard here, very hard."

Cindy whispered close to Ralph's ear, "Let's skip the next tour, okay? We can watch the video of our wedding again while we ...." She giggled and whispered closer, "You know."

"Mm hm-m," Ralph agreed warmly, grinning contentedly.

Alma's hotel room overlooked Manger Square in Bethlehem. Franciscans prepared for their annual Christmas Eve processional to the Grotto of the Nativity. The afternoon had been hot; now the dropping sun began magically gilding the spiraled, ancient town and its surrounding fields. A welcome breeze wafted soft and warm into her open window, three stories up.

She breathed deep the air of Rachel, Naomi, and Ruth, who had each given birth and died nearby. Rachel, mother of Benjamin, died in childbirth. Naomi was mother-in-law of Ruth and great-grandmother of King David, also known as a savior and the Christ. Mary, of course, rode to this place and found a cave in which to bring forth her holy child. Queen Helena, mother of King Constantinople, built a church for Mary over the sacred site.

Alma thought of what a miracle it would be if one of her line could give birth again in the Grotto, now plastered over with two millennia of buildings and modifications, fueled by ideas about what had happened so long ago and by ever-changing ideals of beauty and tribute. She sighed. Not in her lifetime, that was certain, and perhaps not in Luna's either. Humankind has so very far to go.

The hubbub below her window grew louder, more insistent. Crowds now lined the processional route, with a wide central path held clear for the Patriarchal Fathers of the Primitive Church.

She sat at a small desk and set out letterhead reading "Holy Grotto Inn, Manger Street, Bethlehem." Its logo was the fourteen-pointed Star of Bethlehem that marks the spot where the holy babe was born, encircled by *"Hic Maria Virgine Jesus Christus Natus Est"*—"Here Jesus Christ was born of Mary."

December 25th

Dear Fran:

I've come to pay homage to Anne, Mary, and Magdalen. To Rachel, Naomi, and Ruth. To Miriam, who lives yet in two sentences of the Bible, for all the help she gave to Moses and Aaron. So many stories, so much untold. How easily the mind slips back through countless years and tales, but cannot guess tomorrow.

We should have been filming here. Will Pavla and I ever be able to update Mother's pioneering movies? Or will this fall to Luna, when technology will allow her to play all roles from young woman to crone? Perhaps she'll do it virtually, no actors required whatever. She'll have Mother's scripts, of course, but she may wish to tell other tales of our ancestors.

I'd begun a script in Nepal as I waited for Pavla to join me, the story of the first Karmapala Lama, who made a hat from the hair of several of our line. This black hat remains sacred to successive such lamas; they cannot claim full wisdom or authority without it. I'll leave my telling of this story with you when I visit next.

I meet an enlightened ear tomorrow near Jerusalem, a new, apparently trustworthy contact—a risk, but one I have to take if there's ever to be peace in this region. To achieve peace worldwide, Mother died believing that we must surface and our truth be known, beginning with the publication of her biography. Your work putting all notes pertaining to her life onto microfilm will be invaluable. I will deliver them soon to a potential biographer, a talented writer I hope will agree to the task.

My prayers for Pavla's release are tempered by knowing that her captors are inadvertently keeping her safe. This may be especially vital when Mother's biography is published in a year or two. However long Pavla is lost to us is immaterial in many ways, as long as Luna is thriving, with great thanks to you. We are a thin line, one so nearly lost so many times, yet we continue.

Alma put down her pen and rose to look out again at the procession now wending its way toward Mary's ancient cave. "Yet we continue," she repeated. She lifted her eyes to the vast dome of the sunset sky and prayed, "Please."

♦ ♦ ♦

Gray marked the limits of Pavla's new world, light, sparkly gray of native salt crystals in an abandoned mine. In enormous caverns, high-tech buildings comfortably housed a subterranean village of a thousand souls. Greenery grew lush, providing habitat for carefully chosen amphibians, reptiles, birds, and small mammals. Myriad shafts, like airport corridors and shopping mall links, connected the 'cells' of the site. The entire biosphere was complex and pleasing enough to keep bright people stimulated and happy without end. Pavla had no complaints.

She worked in a perfectly equipped twenty-by-twenty-foot laboratory. Three graduate students worked for her, each professional and idealistic. They had no inkling of her captivity or relationship to outside collaborators. They had signed on as eager volunteers in a long-term experiment in creating a self-sustaining colony that might survive global disaster or be replicated in a space station.

Pavla's research into enhanced immunity through mitochondrial factors fit well with the high-minded goals of the project. Funding and direction came from international government agencies and multi-national corporate interests. Top secrecy was necessary to maintain isolation and security.

Occasionally, above-ground research associates or sponsors came to confer with below-ground colleagues. They wore discreet visitor tags. They caused no stir, no second looks.

No one talked about their previous lives, except superficially and in passing. None probed others' pasts, as the rules dictated and common sense supported. The overall project precluded many degrees of freedom, but working as pioneer survivors and chosen, ideal specimens from an increasingly unlivable Earth was the much-voiced, vaunted goal, worth many short- and long-term sacrifices.

Pavla lived in a small suite several levels up from her lab, accessible by elevators and an attractive web of walkways. She decorated her private space with comfortable furniture and a few plants. It was relaxing but not homey— no pictures or mementos to remind her of other possibilities. She kept contact with Trigliani via a notebook computer on a small desk, her messages encrypted and received by a circuitous route only he knew. Her bathroom had a jacuzzi to swirl away the tensions of long hours of work and report-writing, filling a schedule she alone planned and kept.

Her biosphere companions communicated mostly in English, although most spoke other languages. She quietly exercised some of her linguistic gifts, which explained as much as any needed to know about why she was chosen from many possible contenders to join this gifted society.

Holidays of all sorts sparked the passing of work-intensive days and weeks. They were deftly managed by the Psychology Department's recreation team, to corral any religious intolerance or fervor and to keep work and play in healthy balance.

Diurnal lighting mimicked forty-five degrees North latitude. The increasing darkness of November and December had the expected sobering effect on the colony. At winter solstice, the need for light, fun, and celebration became palpable. It was Christmas and Hanukah for some, Santa and gift time for all. Presents had to be simple and handmade: a bouquet of flowers from communal gardens, mugs from the pottery studio, various sorts of friendship bracelets, fudge made in shared kitchens, clever cards galore. Rec' directors made sure everyone took part equally and fairly. As anticipated, psychological well-being of the biosphere project was as vital to maintain as its biological and technological systems.

Pavla had arrived just months after its opening. At the first winter solstice festival, the community proved happily established, with fewer wrinkles to iron out than expected. All sorts of contingency measures to catch social disturbances would stay in place, although it would take inordinate disruption by a majority of colonists to upset the many checks and balances in place. Forecasts predicted more of the same indefinitely.

On the first New Year's Eve day, Pavla worked in her lab until late afternoon. She then returned to her bedroom and changed from lab coat into a simple satin sheath and pearl choker. She clipped up her hair and slipped her feet into stylish heels.

The evening's gala filled the central assembly hall, glowing with hundreds of candles and festive with shiny streamers. It promised to be a night of rare elegance, a banquet of gourmet pleasures. She sat at a round table set for eight, with six others already seated. A waiter poured tinkling iced water; a wine steward served champagne.

As she took her first sip of bubbles, Dr. Dino Trigliani slipped into the empty seat beside her. She nearly choked. "May I?" he asked. "You look lovely."

She caught her breath. "Why not?"

"Things are going well," he said—a statement, not a hint of a question.

"It's easy to make progress without distractions."

"Being brilliant helps," he smiled. "And an optimist. Your attitude is perfect."

"There's no other to have."

Trigliani looked at her, his eyes intent on hers. "You are ... most remarkable." His voice was intimate. "I have had to defend my position regarding your fate—with some difficulty, which may or may not be of interest to you—but there is no doubt that I am making the right choice. Those who think otherwise do not know you."

"Thank you," she said with a touch of warmth.

He leaned toward her and said quietly, "Is there a chance you could ever forgive me?"

Equally quietly, she returned, "For saving my life after taking complete control of it? Those who study this sort of phenomena say yes, absolutely." Conspiratorially she added, "I could, and probably should, fall in love with you."

He laughed. "You frame it so nicely." He reached for his champagne. "May I drink to your success?"

"Of course," she said, raising her glass to his. "There is no alternative."

"Quite," he quickly concurred. "To success. And more." They clinked and sipped.

After the meal, Pavla danced several formal waltzes with Trigliani and joined other livelier dances with men and women from around the world. She moved with eye-catching skill and grace. Trigliani watched discreetly, his heart tightly under wraps but on his sleeve nonetheless.

She allowed him the last dance—a slow waltz at proper arms' length, though they were each aware of the other's warmth and scent. As it ended, he dared ask, "May I ... see where you live?"

"What? Are surveillance tapes not enough?"

"There are no cameras in private quarters, no bugs."

"Then the experiment is seriously flawed. You must have them installed at once."

He laughed softly, then importuned, "Please. It is important."

She stiffly conceded. They walked silently to her living quarters through a series of passageways filled with bright floral paintings and thriving plants. Others in small groups talked and laughed as they returned home.

At Pavla's door, he said, "I would like to come in." Leaning close, he muttered, "Just thirty seconds, I promise."

She hesitated, then opened the door for him. He slipped in; she followed. She left the door ajar and stood by it, ready to let him out as quickly as he had entered. From an inside jacket pocket, he retrieved a large card-size envelope and handed it to Pavla. Rachelle had written "Luteal Tie-In" on it.

"More work?" Pavla said. "Charming." She dropped her voice. "And smuggled. I'm impressed."

"Sh-h. Open it."

Pavla did. She retrieved a five-by-seven inch photograph of Luna sitting with Lord Byron, her small hand clutching a string of amber worry beads. Tears welled up immediately. She blinked them back, held the photo to her heart, then looked at it again.

Trigliani said, "You may keep it, but you should hide it. I cannot guess what could go wrong if even cleaning staff find it. Better safe ...."

Pavla nodded. She sniffed, wiped her tears, then said happily, "She's obviously well. Thank you." she asked, "Do you know who's looking after her?" while thinking, *That dog, those beads—I could find her in a minute.*

He quickly shook his head. "No, and I do not want to know. I cannot be forced to say what I really do not know. Our sponsors will not press as long as we make progress. I have bought us about five years, and if we do well, maybe five and five and five years more."

Pavla sighed heavily, discouraged by this promise.

"I am not such a beast, you know. How can I prove it?"

"You know the answer."

"Only too well, but there are two ways of doing it, and I am working on both, believe me. The longer term has many advantages. The immediate is possible but very risky. That is why I am here. I must leave ...." He glanced at his watch. "Well, I am late already. You may leave with me, if you like."

Pavla's eyes widened.

"I will take you to the nearest town and set you free, with money to go wherever you wish. I am not clever enough to convince them for long that we are progressing without you, and they will be very angry when I say that our collaboration has ended. If I say you have escaped, they will look for you. Everywhere. They will look for Luna and your mother too, which I now keep them from doing. If I say you have died, they will double their efforts to find Luna and your mother, I cannot stop them. Dreamers will dream you again, unless you and Luna hide forever in a cave or a lead-lined box—no life for a child. And no hope for dreamers, if that's important to you."

"Of course," Pavla said. "How do you know about dreamers? That's how you tracked me, isn't it?"

Trigliani leaned close. "I can tell you in here, no tapes or bugs. Yes. A great aunt of mine was a dreamer, from Sunoqua's death. A nun too, who spent much of her life in an insane asylum. She dared to tell me things. I rescued her notes before she died. My mother was a very strict Catholic. She despised the devil that got into her mother's sister and feared it in herself. In me. I have been very devout. I am still, in my own way. I cannot explain further because we must leave immediately if you wish to go."

Pavla swallowed hard, stunned by the instant choice before her.

Trigliani continued, "Of course, I will be at risk of interrogation too, should you leave before our research bears fruit and, I hope, wins us our freedom. Yes, *our* freedom. I am under close scrutiny with very little freedom, believe me. If you slip from us, I will be tortured to tell all I know of you and your line, which is considerable. I have some control now. Without you, I have none. They will use every trick until I break and talk. They are rather sophisticated. And brutal, as required. I could not hold out against them. So, do we make a run for it? Or do you concede that our present arrangement is safe and functional."

Pavla struggled to answer, staring at the photo of Luna through eyes swimming with tears. Finally, she said, "There is no 'we', not as you might wish, and ...." Her voice cracked. "I cannot go. The risk is too great. Luna must live as freely as possible and thrive. She is everything."

Trigliani's eyes looked pained. "Is it terrible of me to give you this choice?"

She quickly shook her head. "No. I understand much better." She looked at Luna and smiled as best she could. "You've brought me this, a wonderful gift. Thank you. I must settle better, putting all thoughts of freedom—and certainly premature freedom—behind me. We have many years of work to do, and it satisfies me to serve the greater good. I'm prepared to finish my days here."

"You are immensely wise for a young woman." He sighed despairingly. "I am sorry, deeply sorry, that you must think this way, however necessary it is. When it is safe for me to come for you, I will do it but ...."

"The world has never been safe for my family, nor will I count on your rescue. In fact, I'm not counting anything—days, months, years—at all, only scientific progress."

Trigliani smiled broadly, ruefully. "We will do great things together. This non-'we', not together. Now I must go."

Pavla nodded. She kissed her fingertips and placed them on Trigliani's cheek.

He closed his eyes gratefully and held her hand to his face.

"When," she ventured to ask, "will you return?"

He looking into her remarkable eyes and said quietly, firmly, "Never is a safe assumption. Good night."

She opened the door for him. "Thank you," she whispered, then shut him out.

She listened to his footsteps fade to nothing, thinking, *You could be a great man ... one day, maybe. I have hope for you, if not for me, and that's something.*"

He watched his feet, pushing one expensive shoe after the other down the labyrinthine walkways, thinking, *One step at a time leaving; one step at a time getting back. How? How will I return? God help me find a way.*

He pulled a rosary from his trousers pocket and mouthed as he flicked the beads, "Hail Mary, full of grace, the Lord is with thee; blessed art thou among women, and blessed is the fruit of thy womb ...."

♦ ♦ ♦

From: "sandhu singh" <ssingh@tdp.com>
To: "larry singer" <larsinger@yahoo.com
Date: Sat, 30 December 21:51:29 -0500
Subject: **wheelchair bound, ungagged**

Larry:
Hey Bahamas boy, how's the great American first draft? On tap and running free I hope.

Some news just in, not festive but a relief. Young thug injured in an abduction attempt—says a woman broke his neck protecting her baby—is babbling revenge. Mentioned McMann's name, one of his nurses reported it. Tattoos match the video but he's shut up totally, no leads on the other guys. Is the woman the one they kept asking about in the video? No matter. He's in custody and the net's out for his buddies. Helps me sleep better. Hope it does you too.

Merry and cheers, etc. Sandhu

The bottom right menu bar of Larry's computer monitor read "December 31, 15:48 PM." The big flat screen showed a word-processing program containing the words:

TELLING NEWS
by Larry Singer

They sat centered in a sea of white space. Larry hunched before the machine, silhouetted against a wide window with a tropical ocean view. His chin rested on one hand, the other tapped the desk top. Beside it sat the DVD labeled "Rewind: One Life."

Nearby, all seventy-two of his personal notebooks, standing upright in two neat rows, filled a small bookshelf. Nothing else cluttered the scene. Nothing intruded between man, means, and intended masterpiece.

His eyes wandered from monitor to mouse to DVD, then drifted out the window. He gazed past the fringe of a thatched-roof verandah to nearby hibiscus shrubs with blood red flowers. A grassy slope lay beyond. A meandering path led to a silver strip of beach. Farther still, aqua surf rolled in tirelessly from the hard line where the dark blue sea met the pale blue sky.

Raoul appeared from the kitchen through a Dutch door. He carried a frosted tumbler—an off-kilter cylinder with beaded lines of multi-colored, hand-spun glass—containing fresh tropical juices. He read the monitor. "Fabulous, darling. Just a hundred-thousand words to go."

Larry took the proffered drink without looking up. He took a sip. "Mm, thank you. Maybe a million. I've got every possible story and angle input now. Look at this." He scrolled down the screen to the next page and the next, which contained a long list of headings and chapter ideas. "Enough for ten books, can you believe it?" He held up the DVD. "The key is in here. My Rosebud's in here."

"So hit Mr. Thatcher in the gut with it and get on with the show."

Larry nodded. "Exactly. I'm going to swack 'em all—every Sol and Randy and Al of my life and the business, every one of them who ... oh God, there are so many. But not get too personal, right? I mean, it's a novel, so I have to cut through the details and bullshit to get right to the truth, draw it up tight, concentrate the punch. The problem's narrowing it all down, hanging it on the right central character, the exact right hook."

Raoul said, "The hook you need right now, I'd say, is called a sentence. You'll need a few of those. Noun, verb, you know how they go."

"Uh-uh. I just need one noun. One Rosebud, where the hell's my Rosebud? What matters is what's missing but what ... exactly ... is it?"

"The whole freaking thing is missing!" Raoul guffawed. "And supper will be too if I don't get on with it. Any suggestions, or should I just fry the oatmeal lumps from breakfast?"

Larry muttered intently, "It's in the peripherals. It's in the context that defines the core, which is deep in the core character, of course."

"Ah, I'll look for the oatmeal there," Raoul muttered.

"My God, Maya's words exactly!" Larry started typing quickly. "Missing—the truth vs. reality, Sol vs. Abel, ostensible vs. surmised vs. known, solidify, iconize ...."

"Supper, darling," Raoul said. "If it's fish again I've got to check with Pedro."

Deep in thought, Larry said, "Yes, do that. It came in the mail, I think."

Raoul threw up his arms. "You poor lost loon. Excuse me while I go deep-fry some dingbats and have our New Year's turkey flown in from the funny farm."

Raoul returned to the kitchen via the swinging doors that blocked the sounds of his life from the silence of Larry's. Light jazz bounced from a CD player, filling this modern addition to an old cottage.

Bright sun poured in through the open entryway door, backlighting a woman wearing a broad straw hat and calf-length cotton dress. Raoul squinted to recognize her. Alma! He grabbed his heart to keep from fainting.

"My god, my goddess!" Raoul fell to his knees and kissed her hand profusely, making her laugh.

"I'm sorry I didn't warn you," she said. "I hope you don't mind."

"Mind? I have no mind. I'm living with a madman. This is heaven."

"How is Larry?"

"Healthy. Insane. Working like crazy, getting nowhere. And he won't invite you to help him until he's found his blessed Rosebud among a list of story ideas a mile long."

"Oh dear. I shouldn't have come without warning him, I guess, but I have a favor to ask, and I'm glad in a way that he's stalled. I hope I can kick-start him either on his own writing or something else entirely."

"Kick away, darling. But listen I've got a plan. Let him struggle and suffer until I drag him to the *lanai* for dinner, and there you'll be—gorgeous as a dream, and I'll have the nitro' ready for his heart attack—if you don't mind waiting a couple hours before seeing him."

"Do you think we should?" Alma's eyes twinkled.

Raoul laughed with glee.

"Splendid meal," Alma said to Raoul as he cleared the dining table of all but red grapes, Brie, and three tulip-whimsies of wine glasses.

"My pleasure," he said with a grin. "A dash of this, a twist of that. And the best of company."

"Indeed," she said. "Now Larry ...." She fixed her eyes on his. "You've been sketchy about your progress, and I've been vague about my purpose. It's time to tell you exactly why I'm here. I understand how important it is that you write your book, and you know that I'll help you with it any way I can. Nonetheless, I'm going to dare to ask if you would consider writing a different book for me first while your own ideas percolate."

"Too many ideas. A million and not the exact right one, the core peripheral, the exact heart of it, the missing piece."

Alma smiled. "And I've got a missing piece, all the peripherals, but not the exact right author. Yet. I'm hoping it will be you."

Larry cocked his head.

"Before Mother died, she asked that her biography be written and published. I think you're the one to do it."

Larry looked stunned.

"You're kidding?" Raoul asked. "Aren't you in enough danger without telling the world?"

Alma shrugged. "Given the state of this old world, Mother felt that the danger of not telling may be greater. Human impact on the planet has reached critical levels. We have zealously and most successfully husbanded every resource while failing to wife them in equal measure. Mother and the rest of us have worked behind the scenes for eons to keep this balance, but technology is swamping us. We must come out and work overtly—or die, along with life as we know it. On the positive side, we've never had such communication abilities and a global village ready for us, I hope.

"As for personal danger to our line, a lovely spin-off benefit of Pavla's captivity is that she's relatively safe. She also has the *in vitro* means to have another child should Luna ...." Alma shook her head. "No, let's focus on the positive. I promised Mother I'd oversee the writing of her biography for publication, and that has brought me to your door. Would you do us that honor, Larry?"

Larry blinked, slow to find his tongue. "Why me?"

"Brilliant journalist, straight-goods reporter, great with words. Worldly view. Finger on the pulse. Time and means. Met Mother and loved her—I assume."

"God, yes," he sputtered.

"So?"

"Who else have you asked?"

"No one. You're it, if I can tag you."

"Alma," Larry said, breathing deep for courage. "I will do it. I will try."

Alma grinned. "Wonderful! I've got everything you'll need with me. Fran has put all the notes about Mother's life from birth to death onto microfilm. I brought a scanner to run the pages through your computer. I hope you can read them that way; I'd rather they weren't printed out."

"No problem."

"The manuscript should be no more than three or four-hundred pages—no photos of Mother, although some of her well-known contacts, certainly. She wanted a standard biography, a chronological overview of her life. Nothing fancy, nothing overstated."

"Just scary as hell and inspiring beyond ...." As he searched for words, he realized in a bright flash, "Alma, she is Rosebud! You all are, my God! Forget 'Telling News', I'll be telling Maya, won't I? Telling the world her tale. Telling her, at last, that I hear her, that I'm paying attention and praying to her for wisdom and strength. Telling her ... I love her. May I call it that— *Telling Maya*?"

Alma thought for a moment, then smiled. "It's perfect."

Mae Singer-Jones's house sat empty, half a year since she left it and nearly a century since her father built it. The yard had been cursorily tidied while inside had undergone an eye-popping renewal.

Fran had moved Mae's papers into carefully labeled boxes, and Nikos had organized them in the attic, basement, and every available nook. They cleaned her brass ornaments of their dusty, webbed sediments and sold them to happy antique dealers.

They changed Mae's time-heavy draperies to light, bright vertical blinds and replaced Mae's living room furniture with Fran's. Only the upright piano remained with "Best Love, Mae" left sitting in her prime atop it, overseeing the transformation.

Painters brightened every room with undercoats of off-white primer. The walls would stay that way until Nikos and Fran worked out the full color scheme. Their only decor was a large oil painting Nikos had chosen and hung on one living room wall, an abstraction of Mount Parnassos and the goddesses and soldiers that haunt the Delphi Museum. Most of Fran's exotic, eclectic collections stayed packed in boxes yet. There had been no time for such details when cleaning, refurbishing, and organizing took every minute. She welcomed the monastic look and feel, in contrast to her and Mae's former lives.

In the kitchen, a calendar from Larry in the Bahamas hung from a bulletin board, its December photograph similar to his lush and turquoise view. Outside the nearest window, a winter wind made skeletal shrubs scritch their long fingers against the glass.

Maya's guest room had become the nursery. A crib snugged by the foot of Maya's old bed, kept ready for Alma. Baby paraphernalia dotted every room and filled the house with sweet scent and purpose. All was still, however, eerily quiet.

Apollo's Taverna in Chryson throbbed with music and motion, color, and feasting. Noisy cheer and rich cooking smells wafted from open windows to the heavens, which swirled with countless stars. Orion presided; the Big Dipper endlessly poured.

On a small patch of open floor in front of the musicians, Nikos took the microphone and sang a love song, his pitch true and voice rich with feeling. As the tempo hastened, he switched to dancing. He flicked his head for Fran to join him. Fran skipped to him with Luna in her arms, and the three sashayed and kicked. Luna giggled with glee, her heart clearly as big as her whole tiny being.

Dhyan clapped her hands wildly from her seat in the crowd, while a flashy young waiter hovered to serve her every guessed-at need.

Spiro worked the bar, where retsina flowed freely for his dozens of guests. He watched like a godfather and grinned like a new millionaire. Dhyan's waiter approached Spiro for another round of drinks on his tray, daring to shout for something special for the girl of his dreams.

The lad won a rollicking laugh for his sentiments. "She's too smart for you!" Dhyan's new 'uncle' shouted back. "Here, take her Coca-Cola and beg to be her slave."

"She needs retsina," the boy pressed.

"She needs a good talking to and the world to contain her." Spiro took the waiter's tray and leaned into his ear. "She needs to dance. Go! Go!"

Dhyan soon joined the crowded floor with her suitor, whose customers could fend for themselves.

At midnight, Elena clanged old pots together, signaling an eruption of loud cheers for the New Year. Luna jumped and cried with fright. Fran held her close, and Nikos encircled the two of them. Her wails turned to cranky fussing as she rubbed her eyes and whimpered, "Need bunny."

Dhyan hurried over to see what was wrong and offered, "I'll take her to bed. I'll babysit if you want to come back."

"Really? That would be great," Fran said. "You sure?"

"Yeah," Dhyan said, then flicked her head in her suitor's direction. "Romeo's a bit much."

Fran laughed. "C'mon, let's get her settled."

The nippy outside air revived Luna, who giggled to Nikos, "*Anypsotiras!*" or elevator. He slowly lifted her over his head, making a machine sound. With a ding at the top, he set her on his shoulders. She patted his head in delight. The four of them walked over cobbled, narrow streets, winding up the hill to Nikos's little apartment.

Baby things burgeoned throughout his small place, including a travel cot for Luna in the bedroom. Eschewing that, Fran settled her into the double bed where her great-grandma had spent her last two days.

Dhyan brought her shabby stuffed rabbit to Luna. The happy babe hugged it close, holding an old ear to her cheek as 'big sister' had done. Dhyan quickly got into her pajamas and slipped in beside Luna. "This is fun," she said to Fran, "but where will you sleep?"

"In your bed at Spiro's, don't worry."

Dhyan laughed. "Good luck! It's half this size."

Fran kissed both her girls. "Goodnight, my angels."

Dhyan stroked Luna's hair with her fingertips. She sang softly, "Lullaby and goodnight, close your little eyes tight ...."

Fran smiled as she turned out the light and pulled the bedroom door almost shut. In the bright kitchen, Nikos whispered to her, "Is it safe, do you think? I could stay ...."

"They'll be fine," Fran whispered back. "I trust Dhyan, and ... well, we're getting by on faith every day, aren't we? And doing rather well."

She tapped a small bulletin board tacked with their flight itinerary, crude alphabet figures by Luna, a newspaper clipping, and a color snapshot. The clipping bore "The NEW New Hampton Rag" masthead, editor Dhyan Roma, and a bold heading that read "Virgin bride redux" by Gypsy Rules. Fran chortled quietly, "She's a pit bull. Luna's in good hands."

Nikos shook his head, eyes amused. "Poor Cindy, if she ever ...."

"Sh-h. Don't even say it." Fran put forefinger to lips.

In the snapshot, Luna stood alone by the Omphalos, a vibrant toddler against great Parnassos and the dark patch that shattered when her ancient twin died.

Fran flipped off the kitchen light, leaving only a night light's glow from the tiny bathroom. She and Nikos left the apartment and locked the door securely behind them. Arm in arm, they navigated back to the taverna by the infinite wonder of the stars.

ABOUT THE AUTHOR

Brenda Guiled grew up in the Rocky Mountains, a lucky childhood among mythic peaks. She has an B.Sc. in honours zoology and an M.Sc. in environmental education, which she taught as part of curriculum research, development, and evaluation projects.

She has numerous publications as Brenda Guild (said "Guiled") and Brenda Guild Gillespie, most significantly:

> Weekly editorial-page columns in community newspapers, beginning in 1994, reaching ~80,000 doorsteps;
> *On Stormy Seas: The Triumphs and Torments of Captain George Vancouver*, Horsdal & Schubart, Victoria, BC, 1992;
> *The Riverview Lands: Western Canada's First Botanical Garden*, co-edited with Val Adolph, Riverview Horticultural Centre Society, 1994;
> *ENCORE: A Program of Environmental Studies*, co-authored with Patricia Keays, BC Parks and Recreation, 1st-prize winner in North America-wide curriculum contest, 1975.

She has worked as a graphic artist, preparing many written and illustrated works for publication, and as a technical illustrator, principally of fishes and shellfishes. These images are widely published and disseminated.

She has raised a daughter and a son and now teaches (with a 3rd degree black belt) "The Karate Kid" form of karate at her own *dojo*.

See samples of her work at www.bguiled.com.